A
PERFECT
TIME TO
MURDER

A
PERFECT
TIME TO
MURDER

A KEMBER & HAYES MYSTERY

N.R. DAWS

THOMAS & MERCER

Text copyright © 2023 by N. R. Daws
All rights reserved.

Published by Thomas & Mercer, Seattle

www.apub.com

Amazon, the Amazon logo, and Thomas & Mercer are trademarks of Amazon.com, Inc., or its affiliates.

ISBN-13: 9781542030090
eISBN: 9781542030083

Cover design by Ghost Design
Cover image: © oleshko andrey © javarman © DavidSamperio
© Burdun Iliya © 32 pixels © Nicholas Rjabow © Lanova Daria / Shutterstock;
© Raylipscombe / Getty Images; © AWL-Tom Mackie / Plainpicture

Printed in the United States of America

For Steven,
my brother and stalwart research companion.

PROLOGUE

Christopher Morris grimaced in pain as his stomach and bowels clenched, causing a wave of nausea that left him gasping for air and frightened for his life.

His breath came short and shallow, his chest felt like someone had taken to sitting on top of him to stop it expanding. His head throbbed as though his brain was trying to get out by hitting it from the inside, but fatigue prevented him moving enough to ease the knots of tension in his neck or to look across at his workmate in the next bed. Paul Ramsey hadn't moved for over an hour but that wasn't unusual for a tired mine worker. Paul always snored without fail, not disturbingly loud like an engine but more akin to an insistent purring. He tried to call out to his colleague but his mouth and throat were too dry to form any words.

He guessed the time to be about two or half-two in the morning and the dormitory felt unusually warm for this time in the small hours. He tried to move his arm to pull off his blanket but his stomach cramped again and he waited for the nausea to pass. It only faded a little this time, refusing to let him sleep. Tiredness fogged his mind as it had earlier. That morning, he'd become disorientated and confused while inspecting the underground mine works and had stumbled, although the floor in that section was even with nothing there to trip over. He knew he should have reported it and gone to see the doctor, but he'd put the tiredness and shortness of breath he'd suffered for over two weeks down to fatigue and the need for a few days off. He knew Paul had been feeling the same because they'd talked about whether it could be the flu or food poisoning. After all, the conditions here were not the best and the food could never be described as home cooking, but no one else had said they were ill and they'd all eaten the same food and breathed the same air.

The nausea surged again and the room spun as if he'd drunk ten pints and a bottle of whisky. He waited for it to subside and tried to recall his thoughts from a few seconds earlier, wondering whether he might have been thinking about the mine or food, possibly the war or weather. They were the only things around here anyway, but the gist escaped him and he promised himself he'd visit the doctor first thing. His forgetfulness had increased over the last two weeks as well and he was scared he was going doolally. He tried concentrating on something else, such as the five other men who slept in the hut, but as soon as the thought entered his head, he couldn't for the life of him remember who they were, where he was or why they were all here.

More pain shot through him as all the muscles in his legs and arms spasmed at once and something clutched his heart. Was this what it was like to have a fit or a heart attack and die? Lying on his back, he should have been able to see the roof of the hut beyond the open rafters but his eyes appeared to have stopped working and all he could see was black. In any case, it had become too painful to move them, so he squeezed his eyelids closed to ward off the fear.

It was the last movement he ever made.

Ten hours later and less than sixty miles to the west as the crow flies, the cloud base hovered a few hundred feet above the runway of RAF Redhill. Lizzie Hayes opened the throttle of the de Havilland Puss Moth and powered the three-seater along the airstrip, feeling the effect of rain-sodden grass dragging at the rubber tyres. With trees on the perimeter seeming to grow larger by the second, the little aircraft reached the speed committing it to take-off and Lizzie pulled back on the control column. The engine laboured as it hauled the Puss Moth into the air and began climbing above the Surrey countryside into the full drizzle of the depressing grey day.

Having delivered a Miles Magister training aircraft to Redhill a little over two hours ago, a glimmer of hope for better weather had come in the form of a weather report suggesting a slight improvement over the next hour. *That suits me*, Lizzie had thought. The chit in her pocket stated RAF West Malling as the delivery destination for the Puss Moth and she wanted to spend the night in her own bed at the end of a tiring day. Her last delivery three days ago had culminated in an enforced overnight stay in a draughty dispersal hut followed by an arduous journey back to RAF Scotney involving two trains, a taxi and a lorry. For this reason, she had judged the forecast window of better weather as sufficient to get her home, despite the meteorologist warning her about worsening conditions to follow pretty rapidly.

The flight east to the Surrey border was bleak and uneventful, but the deeper she flew into Kent, the lower the clouds seemed to force her. Seeing radio masts, telegraph poles, power lines and trees flashing past, she realised with a jolt that her mind had wandered. She glanced at the altimeter; it showed 150 feet, an altitude fraught with danger. A wall of cloud rose up in front of her and sheets of rain lashed the aircraft from one side. Reacting instinctively, Lizzie pushed the throttle wide open and pulled the control column back.

The Puss Moth lurched, banked and climbed steeply into black cloud that swirled around the cockpit canopy as if trying to find a way in. Lizzie shivered as the temperature dropped. The cloud layer was thicker than she'd expected and she had to dredge up every part of her instrument training to keep the aircraft steady and climbing in the zero visibility. With the compass showing south and the altimeter needle passing 5,800 feet, wintry sunlight blinded her as the Puss Moth shot above the clouds. She levelled off and turned eastwards away from its glare, candy-floss clouds stretching away beneath her as far as her eyes could see.

The anxiety and panic attacks that sometimes blighted her on the ground had never afflicted her whilst flying, but her heart raced with the realisation that she'd probably been heading into the ridge of chalk hills forming the North Downs. Fear and loneliness engulfed her: feelings she'd rarely experienced in all the hours spent alone in a cockpit.

As she kept to a line along where she thought the North Downs should be, searching for any gap in the clouds that would show the way down, she feared overshooting and becoming caught in the barrage balloons and other anti-aircraft defences around the naval dockyard at Chatham. But another danger lurked as the petrol gauge fell alarmingly. *I have to get down while I can*, Lizzie thought. As she eased the throttle back and pushed the column forward, the Puss Moth responded by dropping its nose into the clouds. The white, fluffy cotton wool soon gave way to dark, moisture-filled sponges as the altimeter tracked their descent and cold air buffeted the little aircraft. If she was right, the Kent county town of Maidstone would be visible below, with West Malling RAF station nearby. If she was wrong . . .

The Puss Moth broke through the clouds and a patchwork of fields appeared beneath. Her heart thudded as she recognised the amphitheatre shape of a chalk pit cut into Bluebell Hill directly

4

ahead. And above her! She yanked back on the column and tried to regain altitude, pulling the aircraft towards a field on her starboard side. She was a mile short of RAF Rochester with Maidstone behind her. The engine yelled in complaint but she was too late. The slope of the North Downs rushed to meet her. The fixed undercarriage skimmed the field and caught in the scrub, flinging the whole aircraft like skimming a stone. The Puss Moth slammed into the earth and pirouetted on its nose, coming to a standstill with one wing hanging by a wire, and the tail broken and askew.

CHAPTER ONE

Kember sat in Chief Inspector Hartson's office at the headquarters of the Kent County Constabulary, Tonbridge Division, waiting to receive his latest assignment or dressing down. It was always a toss-up which one it would be. He'd been taken off leading an investigation into black-marketeering that morning so he assumed he was about to be thrown in at the deep end again. But first, the ritual niceties.

'How is your . . . um . . . ?' Hartson said.

Kember knew the chief inspector didn't really understand marriages and relationships, even his own, and preferred to bluster along oblivious. Ever since Kember's wife had thrown him out to install her lover, Hartson had found it difficult to broach the subject of the failed marriage. This latest faltering attempt was the best anyone could expect by way of concern.

'I haven't heard from her, sir,' Kember admitted, unable to contain a sigh.

'Good, good.'

Not listening as usual, Kember thought.

'And what about . . . ?'

'She's all right, sir. Just a little shaken up.'

Lizzie's crash a week ago had shaken him too. All the Air Transport Auxiliary women were such competent pilots, equal to most men and better than many, that he'd never even contemplated pilot error as a possible cause for concern.

'Well, if Churchill will let women fly aeroplanes . . .' Hartson raised his eyebrows as if that said it all.

Kember ignored the comment. Amy Johnson, one of the best pilots in the world and famous for breaking flying records all around the globe, had taken off from Blackpool a week ago. On the same day, Jackie Sorour had departed from South Wales and Lizzie had left Redhill but the weather conditions had defeated them all. Of the three ATA pilots, Jackie had been fortunate to find a way down through the clouds to an airfield and Lizzie had survived her crash landing, but Amy had baled out by parachute and drowned in the freezing, storm-lashed waters of the Thames estuary north of Herne Bay. Amy had been the darling of British aviation between the wars and her loss, deeply felt, still filled many column inches in the newspapers.

Kember stared over Hartson's shoulder at the accumulated memorabilia of previous incumbents fixed to the wall. At the centre hung two photographs of Hartson receiving commendations from Chief Constable Davison for his leadership during the Scotney Ripper and Handyman investigations. In fact, Kember had led both investigations and solved several other crimes in the process, so the photographs irked him more than usual. It also amazed Kember that Hartson failed to see the irony of calling the memorabilia *a showy display of unnecessary ornament*, while adding to it himself.

Hartson cleared his throat.

'I've been speaking to my contemporary down in Canterbury; Chief Inspector Steven Brignull. It appears they have a suspicious death to contend with, one that occurred at Bekesbourne Colliery. Not the usual mining accident, mind you: he had a heart attack in his sleep, by the local doctor's reckoning. Curious situation, though.

7

Neither the doctor nor the pathologist could give a definitive reason for the cause of the heart attack, especially in such a healthy man, and the investigating officer, Detective Inspector Andrew Watson, is adamant that there's more to this than meets the eye.'

'How so, sir?' Kember asked.

'I have no idea how many healthy men die of heart attacks but the inspector was suspicious about similarities in the medical reports, which he thinks exceeds the bounds of coincidence. He was also highly dissatisfied with the answers the coal miners gave to his team, even though you and I know the common man is reticent about speaking the truth to us police.'

Kember was about to say *Not only the common man* but managed to bite his tongue.

'Apparently,' Hartson continued, 'Inspector Watson found two torn playing cards secreted among the dead man's belongings. A peculiarity which he feels was incongruous with the victim's other possessions, and seems to be right up your street, judging by your recent exploits.'

'Did he say why he thought them particularly significant, sir?' Kember said, ignoring Hartson's grimace of disapproval.

'It's all in here.' Hartson tapped the paper file in front of him. 'He wanted to stay on the case but Chief Inspector Brignull, who hasn't the resources to keep a man on the job full time, heard about your recent exploits and asked me "whether your Scotland Yard detective" is free.'

'And am I?' Kember raised an eyebrow. 'Free, that is?'

'You are now.' Hartson's petulant pout pushed his moustache out like a scrubbing brush. 'I dislike the insinuation that we are less important than Canterbury, or that I have boxes of spare coppers languishing in a cupboard, but I think your talents lie away from Tonbridge at the moment, don't you?'

Kember gave him a wry smile. *Out of sight, out of mind*, he supposed.

'I want you on the ten 0'clock train to Canterbury. Inspector Watson will meet you there with a car to take you to Bekesbourne Colliery. You won't be working with him on the case because, as I said, manpower shortage and all that. He'll merely brief you on his own investigation into the death and then leave you to it.' By way of dismissal, Hartson closed the buff file in front of him and slid it across the desk towards Kember.

Great, Kember thought, taking the file. When he'd left his lodgings at the Castle pub in Scotney village that morning, he hadn't expected to be given someone else's case, never mind meet the man whose investigation was being called into question. No matter that it was the higher-ups making these decisions, Inspector Watson would take it as a personal affront.

◆　◆　◆

Lizzie was sitting bolt upright on a hard wooden chair in a non-descript meeting room at the heart of the Air Ministry. The reek of cigars permeated the air and smoke clung to the ceiling like the clouds that had caused Lizzie's downfall. Three middle-aged men from the Accidents Investigation Branch sitting on the other side of the table were deep in conversation about her fate, having listened to her account of the air crash. The air commodore acting as chairman seemed to be on her side, but the group captain sporting a handlebar moustache, and a civilian in a loose-fitting suit appeared to want her hanged, drawn and quartered. She feared for her career and felt her anxiety levels rising as her cheeks burned and her breathing quickened, imagining her pounding heart trying to force its way out of her chest.

She thought of pinging the rubber bands on her wrists or sniffing the tiny cobalt-blue jar of Vicks VapoRub in her jacket pocket, two of the usual countermeasures she employed against a panic attack, but knew she couldn't do so discreetly. The civilian had already questioned her mental capacity and ability to handle an aeroplane. Worryingly, he'd hinted at a rumour that had filtered through to him about her afflictions but had declined to elaborate. She had always managed to keep her anxiety and mild Obsessive Compulsive Neurosis hidden from strangers. Even some of her family had no idea, but her close colleagues in the ATA knew and tolerated her because there were far more important things to worry about. And they knew she was a bloody good pilot. That these stuffy old fogeys had the power to take away her pilot's licence irked her. The ATA had short-sighted, one-eyed, one-armed and one-legged men in their ranks, for Christ's sake! They even nicknamed them Ancient and Tattered Airmen as a joke but still let them ferry RAF warplanes far more powerful than any the women were allowed to fly.

She picked at the skin around her fingernails and tried counting the coloured stripes on the array of medal ribbons on each uniformed chest, but their rising voices drew her attention.

'You heard her admission,' the group captain said. 'She deliberately took off in foul weather.'

'Not foul, exactly,' the chairman replied. 'And the forecast did suggest an improvement to come.'

'You can't act on what might be. That's absurd.'

'Don't we strategise all the time, based on forecasts and intelligence?'

'Poppycock,' said the group captain. 'We theorise and rationalise, something women are patently incapable of doing.' He placed his hand on the papers of an open file in front of him. 'This report tells us exactly what the problem is, or who, I should say.'

'Well, I'm not surprised in the least,' said the civilian, sitting back with an *I told you so* expression. 'I counselled against letting women fly in the first place because I knew they'd break our aeroplanes. Thank God it was only a Puss Moth and not a precious Spitfire.'

'Gentlemen.' The chairman held up his hands for quiet. 'Despite your obvious reservations about letting Officer Hayes continue flying, at least two other ATA pilots that we know of took to the air that day, with vastly different outcomes. The insufficiency of information about the events of that day inevitably casts doubt on whether she was entirely to blame. I feel the actions of all ATA pilots who took to the air that day should be examined in more detail than we have time for at this hearing. Therefore, I propose to extend the order grounding Officer Hayes, pending further deliberation. Can we at least agree on that?'

The two men grumbled but nodded their assent and the chairman asked Lizzie to stand.

'Officer Hayes,' the chairman said. 'We are acutely aware of the value of experienced pilots and the important service performed by the Air Transport Auxiliary, but you have heard our discussion and the conclusion to which we have come. A brief investigation will be held next week to consider the facts and provide clarity from which a final judgement can be made. You may return to Number Thirteen Ferry Pool at RAF Scotney but you will refrain from flying activities until the result of the investigation is known. Is that clear?'

'Yes, sir,' Lizzie said.

Soon after, having been dismissed from the hearing, Lizzie stood outside in the corridor with the door closed, trembling with anger. What else could she have said? *Would it have been clearer to you if you hadn't had whisky for breakfast? Why are you three men sitting in judgement over me when the bombers over London are the closest you've been to an aircraft since the war began?* She realised her fingernails were digging into her palms and forced herself to relax. She conceded her situation wasn't entirely their fault, old fogeys that they were. If she hadn't wanted to get home. If she hadn't risked flying in bad weather. If . . . if . . .

As her entire job comprised of flying, she had nothing to rush back to Scotney for, which suited her fine. That meant she could wander along the Strand and enjoy a cup of tea and a slice of cake at the Lyons Corner House before catching the Charing Cross train to Tonbridge.

Her one concern, though, was how to break the news to Flight Captain Geraldine Ellenden-Pitt, the head of Number Thirteen Ferry Pool.

CHAPTER TWO

Kember alighted from the train at Canterbury West station and looked for signs of a man with the appearance of a policeman. He wasn't sure what those signs might be but they certainly weren't present in the engaged and purposeful throng around him.

'Thanks for the help,' said a gruff voice from behind.

Dr Michael Headley, a Home Office-approved pathologist from Pembury Hospital and someone with whom Kember had a long association, placed a carpet bag and a large wooden box on the platform.

'I didn't think you wanted anyone touching your box of forensic instruments,' Kember said.

'I don't, generally, but a little assistance now and then wouldn't go amiss.'

Kember continued to scan the crowd as Headley cleaned the thick lenses of his round spectacles. He'd been led to expect some kind of welcome, even if it was only a constable with instructions about where to go, and was mildly irritated.

'We'd better go in search of our contact,' Kember said, picking up his small brown suitcase and feeling like some kind of evacuee.

He waited for Headley to hoist the strap of the box over his shoulder and grab the carpet bag with his free hand before they made their way out of the station. Being the last of the stragglers to emerge, it was easy to spot the black Austin with a bored-looking man leaning against it. He had a trilby jammed on his head and the collar of his raincoat pulled up for warmth. His breath and the smoke from a cigarette swirled around him before being whipped away by the cold January wind. Kember was not impressed. He expected a modicum of professionalism from fellow officers, even if his enforced presence was resented.

He walked over with Headley and the man looked their way.

'Sorry we're late,' Kember said, with more cheer than he felt. 'Our connection at Ashford was delayed by an unexploded bomb near the line.' He stuck out a hand in greeting. 'Detective Inspector Andrew Watson, I presume?'

The man took a long final drag on the cigarette, flicked the butt into the wind and slowly took Kember's hand. More of a passing touch than a shake.

'Andy. And you must be Inspector Kember. Of the Yard.'

The words had been said brightly enough, but the separate mention of Scotland Yard spoke volumes about the man's true feelings. Kember's suspicions about how his presence might be received had been spot on.

◆ ◆ ◆

Moments later, Watson drove from the station, turned left towards the centre of Canterbury and passed the police headquarters at Pound Lane.

'Are we not stopping?' Kember asked, a little surprised.

'Not at the nick,' Watson replied. 'I've instructions to take the good doctor straight to the mortuary so he can do the necessary, and to drive you on to the colliery.'

Headley had got in the back of the Austin with all the bags, while Kember had elected to sit next to Watson, all the better to discuss the case and size up the man who'd had it taken from him.

'I apologise if our arrival has caused any upset,' Kember said. 'We've as little choice in the matter as I suppose you have.' He hoped playing the downtrodden detective would chime with Watson and strike a friendly note.

'It's no problem at all,' Watson said. 'Canterbury's a crime-free city so I have all the time in the world to be your chauffeur, and it's not often we get the benefit of a visit from the famous Scotland Yard.' His false grin conveyed no warmth to balance the ice in his voice.

Kember understood the bitterness but hoped it wouldn't detract from the professional handover he expected.

'If it's any consolation, I had no idea about all this and was pulled from my own investigation.'

'I know.' Watson nodded. 'Chief Inspector Brignull wanted to close the case but I argued to stay on it because I knew something wasn't right. Healthy men don't drop dead of heart attacks without some kind of warning but that isn't all. I wasn't satisfied with the answers I got from the miners and I found two torn playing cards in the dead man's belongings. Brignull said he didn't have time to waste on a wild goose chase when I didn't have any concrete cause for suspicion. I reasoned with him and he said the best he could do was bring in a fresh pair of eyes. I went out on a limb to keep this case alive so if I'm wrong, it'll still be my neck on the block.'

Kember glanced sideways at Watson. 'What was it about the playing cards that piqued your interest?'

Watson dipped a hand inside his jacket, took out two cellophane evidence envelopes and handed them to Kember. 'Brignull took some convincing that they held any significance at all,' Watson said. 'It was only when I explained that both were the six of spades and both had been torn part-way down from the top that he conceded that it was unusual.'

'Couldn't they be bookmarks or a reminder to buy a new pack?' Kember asked.

Watson smiled. 'Some of these men can barely sign their own names, and Christopher Morris wasn't reputed to be a bookish man. As for new cards, he had a decent pack among his belongings that didn't look like it needed replacing. And why would you have two cards the same?'

'Any idea what it means?'

Watson shrugged. 'Military men have their strange signs and rituals, as do Romanies, navvies, the Masons, every gentlemen's club throughout the empire, and even tramps. The fact that no one seemed to know why he had them or what they might mean just made me more suspicious.'

He held the cards up but Watson declined to take them.

'You keep them. It's your case now.'

Kember slipped them inside his own jacket. Had Lizzie been with them, she'd have attached some great significance to the cards right there, but he was a detective. A copper's nose for trouble, danger and villainy was something he had respected from his first days in police training, and had experienced himself. If Watson thought something was odd, he was inclined to believe him.

A loud snore rattled from the back seat of the car and Kember looked over his shoulder to find Headley slumped to one side, head back and mouth open.

'Sorry about Dr Headley,' he said. 'It seems he has a busier life than we do.'

Watson chuckled; the first sign of the real man behind the detective. 'I think they must all be cut from the same cloth. The doctor who certified the deaths – Dr Paine, would you believe? – always looks as though he's about to doze off.'

'Must be all the house calls,' Kember said.

'Or the aperitifs.'

Watson chuckled again and was still smiling as he turned the car in through the four white pillars at the entrance to the Kent and Canterbury Hospital. Kember found the gleaming white walls and clocktower of the Art Deco building quite imposing as they approached along the peaceful tree-lined drive. It looked modern and gave the impression of being both efficient and a good place to recover and recuperate. Watson pulled up at the main entrance and got out to open the door for Headley.

'Wotsit?' Headley said, bleary-eyed and wiping drool from the corner of his mouth.

'We're at the hospital, Doctor,' Watson said.

'Ah. Thank you.' Headley took a few deep breaths, and heaved himself out of the car.

'If you announce yourself at the reception desk, someone will get you a cup of tea and take you to the mortuary.' Watson reached in for the carpet bag and forensic box and handed them to Headley. 'I'll collect you in a couple of hours, Doctor. Once I've taken Inspector Kember to see Bekesbourne Colliery.'

Kember watched with amusement as Headley nodded his thanks and staggered in through the main entrance, his bag and box banging against his knee and hip.

◆ ◆ ◆

Lizzie stepped from the carriage and pulled up the collar of her greatcoat against the thin but icy rain that had started almost as soon as the train had left London for Tonbridge. It had followed her to Paddock Wood and now Scotney, matching her bleak mood. By the time the steam locomotive tooted in answer to the whistle blast from the stationmaster, Lizzie had already left the station behind and was walking beneath the trees that formed a green tunnel in summer. Now bare of leaves, they offered no respite from the weather as she strode in to the southern end of the village. Passing the disused garage with its one pump standing guard at the crossroads, she continued on to the war memorial and telephone box.

She reached the police station next door, hoping the friendly figure of the village bobby would be waiting to offer her hot tea. Even having treated herself to that cake in the Lyons tea room, she was back earlier than anticipated but with no wish to return to the air station just yet. She tried the door and found it locked. *Botheration*, she thought. *He must be out on his rounds.*

The doors of the village hall swung open as Brian Greenway emerged, dressed in his ARP warden greatcoat and cap. He walked towards her, head lowered against the sleet, and almost bumped into her before she stopped him dead in his tracks with, 'Hello.'

Greenway looked up, eyes wide. 'Good grief. You'll catch your death out here.'

'I'd hoped Sergeant Wright would be in the police station,' Lizzie replied.

'He's in the hall but I'd be wary of going in, if I were you. Ethel and her cronies have enrolled in the Women's Voluntary Service and are holding a knitting session.' He laughed. 'WVS, I ask you. It's just another ruse for her gossip circle to stay in the know.'

'I'll take my chances,' Lizzie said, knowing her fate at the hands of the Air Ministry in London had been a hot topic of speculation in the village. 'At least it will be warm and dry.'

She turned at the squeak of bicycle brakes, moving her whole body to avoid sleet going down her neck. The face of James

Corcoran smiled back as water dripped from his post office cap and ran in rivulets down his cape.

'I'll bet we're not the welcome you were expecting,' Corcoran said.

'Better than the one I got in London,' she replied.

'Ah, yes.' Corcoran's smile disappeared. 'I wondered about that. How did it go?'

'It could have been worse,' Lizzie said. 'They're resting me for a few more days.'

It wasn't an outright lie because the outcome hadn't been decided, but if the stuffy men she'd sat in front of had their way, like a trio of headmasters handing out punishment to a naughty schoolgirl, a few days could turn into months, or forever.

'If it was me, after a shock like yours, I'd be grateful for any leave they gave me,' Corcoran said. A gust of wind lashed slushy ice against his cape. 'Anyway, best get in out of this. Looks like it's settling in for the duration.' He nodded and said, 'Miss Hayes,' before cycling towards the grocer's shop containing the sub-post office, his tuneless whistle incongruous with the weather.

'He's right.' Greenway looked skywards and squinted. 'It's getting worse.' He looked back at Lizzie. 'Get yourself inside, Miss Hayes,' he said, and touched his cap in salute before crossing the road towards his house opposite the police station.

The painted sign of the Castle pub swung from its wrought-iron bracket with each gust of wind, and water streamed from the awning left out over the grocer's shop next door as Corcoran disappeared inside. Lizzie reached the door of the village hall just as the sleet cranked up another notch.

Grateful to be out of the cold and wet, she found the group of four middle-aged women arranged in a square right in the centre of the hall. Ethel Garner was sitting opposite Mavis Ware, with Hilda

Tate to her left and Gladys Finch, the youngest of the four and Sergeant Dennis Wright's sweetheart, to her right. Resplendent in their dark-green WVS dresses, pinafore aprons and berets, Gladys Finch was the only one not wearing a maroon cardigan, a colour that matched the WVS lettering and crown on their grey badges. The women were working so feverishly on their woollen production line and chatting so intently that only Ethel paid Lizzie any attention, eyeing her with suspicion as she headed for the far end of the hall.

The whistling of a boiling kettle led Lizzie to Sergeant Wright, whom she found in the tiny kitchen behind the stage, just as he poured hot water into a teapot.

'Hello there,' Wright said, giving the teapot a stir before putting the lid on. 'You must have smelled the pot.' He covered the whole thing with a knitted tea cosy which left the handle and spout sticking out.

'Is that one of Mrs Garner's creations?' Lizzie asked.

Wright laughed. 'Yes, it is. Most of her output is going to the navy lads but she likes to keep me in her good books because she thinks she can wheedle snippets of gossip out of me.'

'Can she?'

Wright laughed again, and whispered, 'Only what I want her to know.'

His face became solemn and Lizzie knew the dreaded question was coming again.

'What brings you here? Did it go well in London?'

Lizzie sighed and repeated nothing more than she'd said to Corcoran, not wishing to elaborate. She noticed the funny look he gave her but appreciated his nod of encouragement and the lack of any probing questions. Having not long been discharged from hospital and endured the AIB grilling, there would be time for discussions after she'd come to terms with the possibility that her career as a pilot might be over.

'Any word from DI Kember today?' she asked. She'd hoped he might be in the village and free for a chat so she could get the frustration off her chest, but seeing Wright on his own had dashed any thoughts of that.

'He telephoned earlier to say he'd been sent to Canterbury,' Wright replied. 'Something about having another look over a recent murder case. He might be a few days.'

Lizzie sighed again. Even though he worked out of Tonbridge police HQ she'd been clinging to the possibility he'd be around later at least, but now her heart sank further. Just when she needed his support and understanding, he'd disappeared on another hunt for a murderer.

'Do you mind if I use your telephone to ring the air station for someone to pick me up? Although, I haven't yet decided what I'm going to say to my flight captain.'

'Don't worry about that, I'll give you a lift,' Wright said. 'But you're welcome to a cuppa first.'

Lizzie thanked him and offered to be his waitress in return. She waited for six cups of tea to be poured, put them on a tray with a small jug of milk and took everything through to the main hall. As she set the tray down on a low table, she marvelled at the speed with which the women worked, chatting to each other without even looking at the needles in their hands as they flashed in a blur, knitting row after colourful row. It was only after Ethel's needles stopped clacking that the others also downed tools and turned their attention to the tea, and Lizzie.

'Thank you, dear,' Mavis said. 'I suppose a cup of tea is just what the doctor ordered, after your ordeal at the Air Ministry.'

Gladys raised her eyebrows questioningly. 'Don't suppose they'll let you fly again, not after crashing one of their aeroplanes.'

21

'I said it was only a matter of time, didn't I Mavis?' Hilda said.

'Actually—' Lizzie began.

Ethel took the cup Lizzie offered. 'I was saying to Hilda – your toe's no better, is it love? – I'd not be surprised if they've sent you away with a flea in your ear. You mark my words, if you stopped hanging around with that detective – he keeps turning up like a bad penny – and got yourself a proper job, you'd be as right as ninepence.'

'I—'

'There's plenty of work to be done on the ground without the likes of you getting in the way of the men up there. They're crying out for more women in the factories and they can't get nurses for love nor money. My Albert says, if God had wanted women to fly, he would've given us all broomsticks.'

Everyone laughed except Lizzie, and she felt her cheeks colouring with equal measures of embarrassment and irritation. The tell-tale clutch of anxiety across her chest brought fears of a full panic attack, and she was relieved by the distraction of Wright bringing a plate of honey biscuits for the women.

'About time,' Ethel said. 'I thought you were out there baking them yourself.'

'I've only got one pair of hands, Ethel, and I really should be out there keeping the village safe, rather than waiting on you hand, foot and finger.'

'Don't make me laugh, Dennis Wright. You know you're only here because Gladys has joined us. And as for safe, the only safe you know is in Martin's Bank in Tonbridge.' She nodded at Lizzie. 'Now this young one's returned, there's no telling what else will happen.' She took a bite from a biscuit and began munching.

Lizzie could feel her cheeks burning and she beckoned Wright to one side.

'I'm sorry, I know you've just made tea but do you mind if I take you up on that offer of a lift now?' she said, placing her hand on Wright's arm for emphasis. 'I should be getting back.'

Lizzie had hoped for a quiet cuppa in the police station and time to think, not a confrontation with the Scotney gossip circle, and now seemed a good time to get away. It would mean bearing the attention of the air station's commanding officer and her own flight captain, but right at that moment, that seemed the lesser of two evils.

CHAPTER THREE

The Austin droned its way along the lanes of east Kent, the grey clouds and wintry light making the countryside appear washed out, like a faded photograph. Watson had said they'd be at the colliery in another ten minutes and Kember wanted to pick his brain before they arrived.

'My chief inspector gave me what he believes passes for a briefing,' Kember said. 'And I've read a summary of the case, of course, but I'd like to hear your version. Straight from the horse's mouth, as it were.'

Watson nodded. 'Happy to help but I'm not sure there's anything else I can add to my report. There aren't enough billets in the area to accommodate all the miners brought in from up north so the colliery built dormitory blocks. Eight days ago, six men went to sleep in one of the dormitories but only five woke up, including one who'd also been ill overnight. There were no signs of a fight, no injuries to the dead man, and none of the others saw or heard anyone go in or out. It was bitterly cold that night but the stove had been lit, the windows aren't the opening kind and the room was perfectly warm. Dr Paine is a local doctor used by the colliery. He has experience of unexpected deaths among mine workers and it was he who examined the body and declared the man dead from a heart attack. When I pressed him for a cause he said he couldn't rightly say, but suggested it may have been brought on by exhaustion and physical stress. My sergeant and I interviewed the five men and others at the colliery, but even though there seemed nothing untoward and we could find no conclusive evidence to confirm foul play, I still had a feeling we weren't being told the whole truth.'

Kember stared through the windscreen at the leafless trees and hedgerows passing by outside and rubbed the end of his nose in thought. No intruder and no wounds. Could this be a simple tragedy? After all, people died of all sorts of injuries and ailments every day, many of which lay beneath the surface, hidden from view.

'You seem like a good copper so what's your gut instinct? Exhaustion, accident or murder?'

Watson took a moment to think.

'The doctors say it was a heart attack and we found no signs of an intruder.'

'But?'

'I think he was murdered,' Watson said, bluntly. 'I have no more idea how or why than I do what or who, but this is one of those cases where you just know something's awry.'

'The copper's nose,' Kember said.

Watson glanced at him. 'There's too much going on and too little being said. I'm pretty certain it's being hushed up.'

'Hushed up?' Kember raised his eyebrows.

'There's a war on and coal keeps the country going. The mine owner prides himself on being a staunch supporter of the government, outwardly at least, and the last thing Churchill needs is for a scandal about essential workers killing each other getting back to Hitler. Lord Haw-Haw's radio broadcasts undermine morale enough as it is. And it's bad for business.' Watson flicked another glance in Kember's direction. 'The pit's had its troubles in the last few years so you won't get much real help from the owner, and I wouldn't be surprised if the miners have been paid off or frightened into keeping quiet.'

Oh, God, Kember thought. He hated conspiracies and cover-ups.

'Paine wasn't the only doctor to take a look,' Watson continued. 'A local pathologist called Dr Gunstone performed the post-mortem and came to the same conclusion, word for word. The thing is, he's a known associate of Clifford Burnley, the mine owner. They attend the same civic functions and various local events and have been seen having dinner together on occasion.'

'You think Paine and Gunstone have been paid off by Burnley?' Kember asked.

'I do, but it must have been in cash or favours because apart from Dr Paine's employment as the colliery doctor, we couldn't find any other evidence that linked them financially.'

'Did you tell this to Brignull?'

'Of course,' Watson said. 'That's partly why you're here.'

Kember frowned. 'I don't understand.'

'As I said, Brignull knew I wasn't getting anywhere but he believed me eventually when I explained why I thought there was something fishy going on here. On one hand, he's desperate for a positive result to clear up the case before the newspapers get wind of the story. On the other, he can't risk a dent to his repu-tation if his own men draw a blank.' Watson looked at Kember. 'It's all about local fiefdoms,' he explained. 'Brignull could bring in the Yard from London but he doesn't want his patch sullied by a full team descending on us. Your two big cases last year made headlines so he went for the obvious next best thing. It's the perfect solution for him. If it is a murder and you solve it, he'll get a pat on the back for bringing you in. I've gone out on a limb about this so if you make a hash of it, I'll be pensioned off and it'll be you, Chief Inspector Hartson and Scotland Yard who'll look foolish.'

Now Kember understood. It was the same reason Hartson had assigned him to the previous murder cases in Scotney village. Not that he was against the strategy. After all, he got to exercise the skills that had made him a respected Yard officer in the first place, he'd met the remarkable Elizabeth Hayes, and had enjoyed plaudits from his peers and the newspapers, even if it was Hartson who got the official commendations.

Twin towers with giant winding wheels marking the pithead of Bekesbourne Colliery appeared over the hedge tops. A spoil-heap of black, grey and brown formed a backdrop to more buildings, grey and unwelcoming, as they approached the entrance. Watson turned the wheel of the Austin and the car bounced and splashed its way down a rutted, puddle-dotted track past two large bulldozers. They stopped outside an office building and Kember noted the very nice Humber saloon car parked along the side, the unmistakable figure of a snipe bird in flight adorning the bonnet. *Must be the manager's office*, Kember thought. Watson turned off the engine.

'Well, this is it,' Watson said. 'Lovely, isn't it?'

Kember grimaced as wind lashed spots of rain against the windscreen. A group of men in miners' helmets with head-torches scurried from behind one building, their heads down and the collars of their coats turned up against the wind and rain, and disappeared through a door into another.

'You've got me for the next couple of hours before we go back to collect Dr Headley,' Watson continued. 'Then you're on your own. Brignull doesn't want me influencing your investigation. I thought you'd bring a constable, if I'm honest.'

'No one available at Tonbridge,' Kember explained. 'And the sergeant who helped me on the murder cases is a village bobby and can't be spared.'

Watson smiled wryly. 'Just you and me then.' He opened his door and the wind whipped icy raindrops into the car. 'Come on, I'll introduce you.'

Kember had to hold the door as he stepped out of the Austin and forced it to close against the cold wind. He'd left his short-brimmed fedora on the back seat with Watson's trilby; they wouldn't stand a chance of staying on in this weather. He followed Watson along the short path of concrete slabs, up some steps and through the outer door of the manager's office. The buffeting stopped and the warmth increased as soon as they were inside, the sweet smell of furniture polish hanging in the air, but the wind outside could still be heard whistling through gaps and humming past taut cables and stanchions.

A timid-looking secretary in a beige twinset, her mousy hair in tight curls, was running a duster around a typewriter sitting on a desk in front of a door with *Clifford Burnley Esq.* inscribed on a brass plate. She looked up and peered at them through spectacles that Kember suspected were little stronger than plain glass, and tilted her head.

'Can I help you, gentlemen?' she said, with a firm voice that belied her appearance.

The detectives introduced themselves and showed their warrant cards, Kember noting a wooden nameplate with *Mrs Rosemary Wall* painted in white, as the secretary sat on the chair behind the desk and put her cleaning things in a drawer. She seemed reluctant to let them in without an appointment or prior warning, but she relented and used the telephone on her desk to announce their arrival. The inner door opened and the barrel-like body of a man in a tight-fitting brown suit, and shoes that must have been at least size 12, blocked the way. Kember guessed the man must be an inch or two taller than his own six feet.

'You again,' the man said to Watson, through the overhang of a large and impressive walrus moustache. 'More questions, is it?'

'Scotland Yard are on the case now, sir,' Watson said, pushing forward until the man gave way and retreated to his paperladen desk. He indicated the man with his open hand. 'This is Mr Clifford Burnley, owner and manager of Bekesbourne Colliery. Mr Burnley, meet Detective Inspector Kember of the Yard.'

Kember winced at the introduction but shook Burnley's hand.

'Scotland Yard?' Burnley frowned. 'Whatever do we need them for?'

Watson ignored the question and motioned for Kember to sit on the chair in front of the desk while he sat on another to one side. Kember had taken in most of the relevant details as soon as they'd entered the office. The walls were covered in cork boards, to which charts, notices, air raid precautions and a map of the colliery site had been pinned; a draught blew across his ankles from an airvent at floor level but a coal-burning stove radiated welcome heat into the room; ceiling-high cupboards with open doors contained shelves of ledgers and box-files; a metal cabinet, also with its door open, contained a large assortment of keys on labelled hooks; and the desk supported piles of paperwork, more ledgers and a photograph frame that Kember supposed must contain a picture of Burnley's family. All this was to be expected in a workplace, but the rest was not. Numerous framed photographs of Burnley laughing with mayors sporting gold chains of office hung beside those showing him with his arms around other dignitaries. In even more photographs, he shook hands while receiving awards and stood behind lecterns on podiums in what looked like the full flow of giving speeches. The ornately carved mahogany seat in which Burnley now sat, high-backed and upholstered in squeaky red leather, very much resembled a throne rather than any regular office chair, and Kember was conscious of how low his own chair seemed in comparison. All pointed to a man who was proud of his many achievements and wasn't afraid to let others know of them or his own importance. As displays went, it was far more impressive than the one on the wall of Hartson's office, and equal to that of Group Captain Dallington's.

'I'm afraid the powers that be decided they wanted a fresh pair of eyes run over the case to tie up any loose ends,' Kember said. 'If there are any loose ends, I'm your man.'

'It's tragic and all that but I'm not sure what good will come of raking over old coals.' Burnley eyed him suspiciously. 'Watson looked into it and found nothing untoward, and the doctors confirmed as much. I'm doing a magnificent job here, Kember. In difficult circumstances. It's important work and I need to get on with it unhindered.'

Kember noted the omission of his professional title, and Watson's, as if they were colliery underlings. Arrogance? Deliberate discourtesy?

'Accidents happen quite frequently in the coal mining industry,' Burnley said. 'It's an occupational hazard.'

'I can't imagine many miners expect to die in their beds, though,' Kember said.

Burnley gave a dismissive shrug. 'Heart attack caused by exhaustion and physical stress, the doctor said. Could have happened to any one of them.'

'Really?' Kember raised his eyebrows in mock surprise. 'Are all your workers exhausted and stressed?'

Burnley's eyes narrowed at the challenge. 'It's a hard and dangerous occupation. Even I feel the pressure in here, trying to keep the place open and productive.'

'Very commendable. All for the war effort, of course?'

'That goes without saying.'

'Does it?'

'Now look here, Kember. The government ordered me to close down at night because we show too many lights too close to the coast. Normally, I don't stand for anything that affects production and losing a shift means harder graft for the rest of us. I could get dozens from the cream of society to vouch for how well I've done here.'

Kember saw Watson out of the corner of his eye, fidgeting in his chair. Not a statement the policeman agreed with, then.

'You?' Kember asked. 'Not the men?'

'A figure of speech. I meant us, although I am the one putting the most effort into this place.'

Kember gave Burnley a cold stare. The constant barrage of self-praise from the mine owner was already beginning to grate. The man was just another bombastic businessman trying to do as little as possible and driving his workers as hard as he could, while squeezing as much profit out of the product of their labours. In Burnley's case, you could add wringing cheap labour and high subsidies out of an already beleaguered government at war.

'You've had a wasted journey if you want to speak to the men from Hut Six,' Burnley said. 'I restarted the mining operation a couple of days ago because we were losing money hand over fist. Those men will be on shift for several hours.'

'What about Victor Young?' Watson interjected, looking at his watch. 'He works in the fan house and should be due his lunch break about now. And Terry Armstrong, the winding engineman.'

Burnley gave Watson a hard stare before looking back to Kember.

'I'll take you across,' he said, rising from his throne. 'I don't want you causing delays again.'

Again? Kember thought. The man seemed to have no empathy for anyone. Given the circumstances, Burnley might at least make a show of sympathy for the dead man and his family.

'Good.' Watson clapped his hands on his knees and stood up. 'The sooner this investigation can be concluded the sooner we can get out of your hair.'

Given Burnley's sharp-looking suit and tidy appearance, Kember was surprised when he took a tight-fitting threadbare flat cap to go with his thick raincoat instead of his homburg and pushed past towards the door. The secretary gave them no more than a glance as they emerged from the confines of Burnley's office, opened the outer door and ventured into the foul weather outside. The morning drizzle that had become proper rain as they'd arrived had now turned to sleet in the freezing wind and Kember understood Burnley's choice of headgear as he held his cap clamped to his head. Kember wished he'd risked taking his own fedora as defence against the stinging ice.

'I built this from nothing,' Burnley said, making a sweeping gesture that took in the main pit buildings, including the two winding houses with their headframe towers supporting giant wheels. 'There was little else but trees and fields when I arrived.'

Kember tensed his shoulders as a gust of wind threw sleet sideways at them. Burnley seemed not to notice as he strode along a path where coal-black water collected in ruts and potholes, never missing a step while Kember and Watson stumbled along as best they could.

'I got this place up and running in less than a year,' Burnley continued. 'Even though we had to use cementation.'

'Cementation?' Kember asked.

'It's a process to inject cement under high pressure into the shaft walls and tunnels to consolidate the ground and stop water leaking in. No one else could have done it quicker and we've been productive ever since.'

A vicious gust forced cold water into Kember's eyes and ice down his neck.

'We've even got our own fire brigade; did you know that?' Kember admitted he didn't. 'The Aylesham Mines Rescue Station is fifteen minutes away at best and I didn't trust them to respond in good time to prevent serious damage, so I invested in a water bowser and a second-hand Merryweather Hatfield trailer pump. Perfectly serviceable. Granted, they're a few years old but they'll work well enough until the Aylesham lot can get here.'

Now there's the measure of the man, Kember thought. *Willing to spend money on machines but not on human beings.*

As they approached the fan house, the deep thrum of machinery mixed with the exhaust from the fan outlet and the howling wind. Burnley opened a door and went through, leaving the door to slam shut rather than hold it open for the two detectives. *Charming*, Kember thought. He opened the door for Watson and they both stepped inside where the comparative warmth hit him, and he could feel the power of the machinery throbbing in his chest as it turned the huge ventilation fan. An engineer gave them no more than a cursory glance as he switched his attention from a console of gauges to the giant engine. Another sat in a small office-like structure in a corner of the building.

Burnley wiped away the water dripping from his moustache and gestured for Kember and Watson to follow. They kept close to the left-hand wall painted cream and maroon until they came to the office. Burnley went in without knocking, startling the man who was sitting with his feet up on a desk. The tea he was holding sloshed into his lap and he almost choked on his sandwich but Burnley waved away the man's apologies.

'This is Victor Young, fan house engineer and foreman,' Burnley said. 'Young, this is Detective Inspector Kember of Scotland Yard. You already know Detective Inspector Watson from Canterbury.'

Four in the office made for a tight squeeze but Watson managed to shut the door, cutting out most of the engine room noise.

Young, regaining his composure, wiped his fingers on his overalls and shook hands with the two detectives before he relinquished his chair to Burnley and offered Kember the only visitor's chair in the office. Kember declined and insisted Young sat instead. He explained the reason for their visit and his own fresh involvement in the investigation, looking for signs of unease in Young's face all the time.

'Can you tell me what you do here, Mr Young?' Kember said.

Young nodded in the direction of the green-painted machinery visible through the large windows. 'I'm in charge of making sure the fan keeps operating to ventilate the mine for the fore shift.'

'And how does that work?'

'You saw the two headframe towers with the winding wheels as you came on site?' Young said. Kember nodded. 'The cage in the downcast shaft takes miners to and from the coal seam deep underground. The coal comes out through the upcast shaft, which is connected to this fan house by a drift. That's a sloping tunnel at about a thirty-degree incline that meets the shaft near the bottom. The fan draws out stale air and dangerous gases and that sucks fresh air in through the downcast shaft, and keeps the air circulating.'

'Thank you. That was most succinct.'

Kember looked through the window at the fan engine. He always found it useful to get interviewees talking about their work, whether they liked their job or not. It put them on firm ground and lulled them into a false sense of security. Young was well spoken and articulate, and someone who didn't strike him at all as being a violent man. Then again, the victim had not met a violent death. Kember looked back at Young.

'Did you know the man who died?'

'Chris Morris? A little,' Young said. 'We shared a dorm and had the odd drink and game of cards but that was about it. He worked underground so our paths never crossed on shift.'

Kember's ears pricked up at the mention of cards.

'Do you have a pack . . . of cards?'

Young looked back suspiciously. 'Everyone does. Not much else to do around here.'

'Any missing?'

'No.'

'Any idea why Morris would have kept torn cards?' Kember pressed.

'Only if he'd been careless with them and couldn't afford a new pack,' Young said. 'Why?'

'What was Morris like?' Kember said, ignoring the question.

'How d'you mean? I already told the inspector everything.'

Kember noticed the glance he threw Watson's way. Why did he look so worried if he'd already told him everything?

'Just going over it for my own peace of mind,' Kember assured. 'Was he easy to get on with, for instance?'

'He was' – Young shrugged – 'normal.'

'Did he get drunk or into fights?'

'Not when I was with him. You can't get drunk when you're on shift the next day. Working a mine with a hangover is torture, not to mention dangerous.'

'Dangerous?'

'If you're thinking about the banging pain in your head and an upset stomach, you can't concentrate on the work, can you?'

'No, I suppose not.' Kember smiled. 'Did he seem under a lot of pressure or unduly tired?'

'Aye,' Young said. 'Chris moaned about being tired in the evenings. We all do, but he started getting headaches all the time and feeling dizzy. A couple of nights before he passed away, he said he felt sick.'

Kember remembered what Watson had told him earlier. 'Did anyone else get ill?'

'No, Inspector,' Burnley said, forcibly. 'Hard work can take its toll and any man can overdo things but that doesn't mean my men are a sickly bunch.'

Kember ignored the outburst and waited for Young to answer, wondering why Burnley had lied about the other miner who had been unwell.

'We all thought he had the flu or food poisoning,' Young continued. 'But he ate the same as the rest of us, and the doc checked him over and said he didn't have a high temperature so it couldn't be either of those. We think he stayed down there too long and too often. It happens.'

Kember nodded and thought of Doctor Headley performing his post-mortem. If anyone could establish the cause of death, he could. Kember saw Burnley fidgeting as though his time was nearly up and supposed he might have to do this again in a more formal setting. He decided to bring the questioning to a close himself. He wasn't making much progress in any case.

'Before we leave you to your sandwich, Mr Young, do you know of anyone who might have held a grudge against Christopher Morris? Did he have any enemies that you know of?'

'Enemies?' Young's eyes widened. 'I thought he died of a heart attack, pure and simple. Are you saying . . . ?'

'As I told you, I'm covering everything, just to make sure.'

Young shook his head. 'Like I said, he pretty much kept himself to himself, except for the occasional drink and card game. He was an overman, so I suppose he might have had an argument with any one of the other miners.'

'Sorry,' Kember said. 'What's an overman?'

'He checks the underground workings with the deputies every morning before the men go down for the fore shift, and they stay underground to manage the work. The back-overman and his deputies do the back shift each afternoon.'

'They're inspectors,' Burnley said. 'Much like yourselves. Morris was the overman for the fore shift. Instead of asking questions of people, they ask questions of the mine workings. What state are they in? Are they safe? Any explosive gases present? Are the pit props sufficient? Does flooding pose a problem? Those kind of things. And they're the foremen underground, doling out the work and keeping an eye on the men. All designed to keep my coal mine safe.'

Except that it isn't, Kember thought, but muttered, 'And profitable.'

'I prefer productive,' Burnley said.

He raised his chin, his walrus moustache quivering, as if challenging anyone to contradict his view of the perfect coal mine. But Kember saw the look Young gave the owner. For all his swagger, bluster and defiance, it seemed Burnley was out of touch with the feelings of his men.

'But you're right,' Burnley continued. 'However much people like me might go into business for the love of it, the bottom line is that it has to be financially worthwhile. England isn't a nation of shopkeepers for nothing, you know. You have to find your own way to make a living.'

Kember almost grimaced at the comparison and glanced at Watson, whose expression told of his own distaste. He didn't for one moment believe that Burnley ran a colliery out of passion for coal mining. While he might love the wheeling and dealing of private enterprise, as all businessmen did, it seemed more likely to be a way of achieving wealth and status, currying favour with those who could unlock the doors to the inner sanctum of high society. On the other hand, struggling shop owners eked out a meagre living, trying to stay afloat and feed their families.

Kember felt his brain tuning in to the thrumming of the fan machinery the longer they stayed in the office and it was beginning to give him a headache. Time to go.

'I think that's all for now,' Kember said, reaching to shake Young's hand.

Burnley nodded to Young and grunted before leading the way back around the fan house walls and out into driving sleet.

'And now for Terry Armstrong, if you please,' Kember said, pulling up his collar.

Burnley scowled and changed direction towards where the winding headframes stood like the skeletal remains of a dinosaur.

CHAPTER FOUR

Lizzie took a deep breath as Sergeant Wright turned his Wolseley police car in through the main gate of RAF Scotney and the white-stuccoed Georgian edifice of Scotney Manor loomed large, its windows crossed with tape to protect against bomb shatter and a shield of sandbags protecting the porticoed entrance. The main range and its two wings, along with several outbuildings and extensive grounds, had been requisitioned by the RAF as soon as war broke out. An airfield with its numerous associated hangars, blast pens, Nissen huts and half-sunken operations block had been added, turning it into an operational air station.

Lizzie waited for the tyres to stop crunching on a large semi-circle of gravel in front of the portico before she opened the passenger door and stepped out. The chill wind whipped the door from her hand and slammed it shut, and she bent to mouth *sorry* through the window. Wright waved away her apology and reversed the car before turning back on the driveway to the main gate.

She ascended the steps and entered through the front door to be met in the ornately decorated hall by Flight Lieutenant Ben Vickers of the RAF Police, who put his hand on her elbow and steered her to one side.

'How did it go?' he asked.

Her friends often touched the arm of the person they were comforting but the automatic gesture by a man, even one she knew meant nothing by it, seemed insincere and patronising. It annoyed her after what she'd been through that morning and she pulled her arm away.

'As well as you would imagine,' she said, with a shake of her head. 'I've been grounded, pending an investigation.'

Vickers made a face. 'Well, that's not the end of the world. Given what happened to the others, they'll have to clear you.'

Lizzie felt a lump form in her throat. The death of Amy Johnson, one of her heroines, had come as a huge shock to everyone. A pioneering woman and a giant in the world of aviation, her loss had affected women aviators far more than it had any man.

'Have they found her body?' she asked.

Vickers shook his head.

It had been over a week since that fateful day so she hadn't expected any other answer. She had never met Amy Johnson, but like many people she felt she knew her because of her exploits as one of the best pilots in the world, men included. She'd hoped that at least they'd find Amy's body, but hope was a state of mind that could drag you down as well as lift you up and she knew she had to let go.

Flight Captain Geraldine Ellenden-Pitt entered the hall from the officers' lounge and Lizzie felt her chest tighten with trepidation. She tried to gauge Geraldine's mood but the officer's face remained impassive. This wasn't a conversation she had been looking forward to.

Vickers glanced at his watch as Geraldine approached.

'Sorry, got to go. The radio boys have been picking up some kind of interference and Wing Commander Matfield wants me to check the perimeter.'

Geraldine and Vickers nodded to each other as he left and Lizzie waited for the expected tongue-lashing.

Geraldine inclined her head for Lizzie to follow and they took the short walk across the hall, along a corridor and into the seclusion of the ATA operations room.

'I see you made it back in one piece,' Geraldine said, moving to the other side of a desk as Lizzie closed the door behind them.

'Yes ma'am, but not for want of trying by the stuffed shirts of the AIB,' Lizzie replied. 'They tore me apart like pack hounds on a fox, not to mention the ATA women's section, and all women in general.'

'Yes, well, I suspect the death of someone as famous as Amy Johnson has caused adverse propaganda and shed unwanted light on the powers that be.' She pulled out the chair and sat. 'Group Captain Dallington took great pleasure this morning in conveying the outcome of your hearing and it's taken all my willpower not to say something to him I would undoubtedly regret.'

'I'm sor—'

'No need to apologise,' Geraldine cut across. 'I've read your report several times and I cannot say, in all honesty, that I would have taken any other decision myself.'

Lizzie's mouth almost dropped open. Of all the possible outcomes, she hadn't expected that one. Especially since Dallington, the commanding officer of RAF Scotney, seemed to be so pleased to hear of her grounding.

'I thought you'd be angry with me for putting our future here in jeopardy,' she said.

'Don't get me wrong,' Geraldine said, with a shake of her head. 'I'm still peeved at you for giving Dallington any excuse to gloat. But trust me, it would take more than a single hiccup to give him enough ammunition to have us posted elsewhere.' She pushed a pile of papers aside and rested her elbows on the desk top. 'The Air Ministry needs aircraft ferried to the front line every day and they are well aware we've been doing a bloody good job of it from the day we got here. I've even had Pauline Gower on the telephone telling me as much.'

Lizzie swallowed. If the head of the ATA Women's Section had taken the time to ring Geraldine, questions must have been asked at a high level. The death of Amy Johnson had certainly shocked the country.

'Common sense seems to be fighting back against misogyny and discrimination,' Geraldine continued. 'At least, it does in the War Cabinet and the higher echelons of the Air Ministry, despite the stance of many of the old school. That's not to say we can be complacent. We still have to be better than the men on a daily basis, and contend with the Dallingtons and Matfields of this world.' She looked across to the door. 'Talking of whom.'

Lizzie followed Geraldine's gaze and saw someone watching through the window set into the door. The bald, bespectacled head of Group Captain George Dallington, who hated having women on his air station and who had tried on numerous occasions to have them posted elsewhere, peered at them through the glass. He opened the door, removed the unlit pipe from his mouth and cleared his throat.

'I do hope I'm not interrupting something,' he said, his expression conveying no matching sign of genuine apology. 'The Air Ministry have informed me of the outcome of your meeting, Miss Hayes. My office, if you please. You too, Flight Captain.'

'Yes, sir,' Geraldine replied.

Lizzie seethed that he hadn't used her title of Second Officer, even though he was well aware of her recent promotion. She thought she saw Dallington smirk before he turned away but that would have been unusual. His face usually showed one of only three emotions: disinterest, anger and outrage.

◆ ◆ ◆

Kember followed Burnley as they retraced their steps back from the distant fan house and along walkways of slushy mud between the cluster of colliery buildings, Watson keeping pace beside him. The air had got noticeably colder since their arrival and the sleet no longer melted on their overcoats. The grey blanket of clouds seemed to have sucked the last vestige of life and colour out of the whole site while they'd been in the fan house; the blackened brick and grey corrugated iron of the buildings even grimier than before, and the coal even blacker. Burnley ducked in through a doorway, failing to hold it open for them once again, and Kember followed, hearing Watson close it behind them.

With the whistling wind and general noise of a busy coal mine shut outside, the cream and maroon-painted interior of the winding house was relatively quiet. Only the occasional hiss from the steam-driven winding engine gave any indication of the power on hand. A huge drum, wound with a cable that disappeared through an aperture in the wall to their right, stood in front of them taking up a large portion of the room. A few feet behind the drum sat the boilersuit-clad winding engineman, an operating handle near his left hand, his right foot next to a red-painted foot-pedal, and a tin of sandwiches on his lap.

Burnley made curt introductions and said, 'The winding engineman can stretch his legs but can't leave his post. He has to be ready to move men up and down the shaft at all times.'

Kember thought the upright chair, constructed from thick wood and painted green to match the machinery, looked most uncomfortable despite the addition of a thick cushion.

'Mr Armstrong,' he said with a nod, acknowledging Burnley's introduction. 'May we have a moment?'

Armstrong wiped his mouth on his sleeve and put aside his sandwiches. 'What can I do for you?'

Three sharp rings sounded from a bell and Armstrong's attention switched immediately to a large black dial about three feet in diameter on which were letters painted in white around the edge. A large brass pointer, like the big hand of a clock, indicated the position of the lift cage.

'The banksman at the pithead has signalled that someone is waiting to go down,' Burnley explained.

Three more rings sounded.

'That's the onsetter acknowledging. He operates the cage underground.'

Two rings.

'And that's the final signal to say those wanting to descend are ready and waiting in the cage.'

As if on cue, Armstrong took hold of the operating handle, wound the wheel and pressed the pedal. Kember watched the pointer move slowly as the cage descended, a few minutes passing before Armstrong turned the handle again to slow the descent until he brought the cage to a stop.

'I'm sorry, sir,' Armstrong said, turning to Kember. 'I'm all yours for the moment.'

'That was very proficient,' Kember said, truly impressed with the skill needed to raise and lower men hundreds of feet beneath the surface. 'But I'm afraid I need to ask you a few questions about the man who died. How well did you know him?'

Armstrong gave a facial shrug. 'No better or worse than anyone else around here. I sit here operating the lift cage so I don't see many faces while I'm on shift. I see dozens of men out and about every day, of course, but there's rarely any time to chinwag with them.'

'But you slept in the same hut,' Kember said. 'You must have known him better than a nodding acquaintance.'

'We ate, drank and played cards together but you only ever know as much about a man as he wants you to.'

Kember knew that to be true from experience but there were those cards again. 'I hear you all own playing cards. Did you play a lot?'

'There's not a lot to talk about other than the war and the mine when you live on site, and that gets boring after a few days. Then you go back to the eating, drinking, and five-card brag.'

'Do you know of any reason why Morris had two torn cards?'

Another facial shrug. 'There's no accounting for the things people keep. Perhaps they were reminders, or good-luck charms.'

Kember nodded, unconvinced. 'Did you see anything unusual on the night Morris died?'

'No, nothing. It was a normal day. We each came off shift, got cleaned up, did whatever we usually did and went to bed.'

Not that normal, Kember thought. One of their workmates had been sick enough to die that night and nobody had been interested enough to notice. 'How did Morris seem to you? Did he look ill?'

Armstrong shook his head. 'Tired, perhaps. I think he said he felt a bit headachy. Not surprising, really. Being winter, there's always a few head-colds about.'

'What about the rest of you?'

'Paul Ramsey wasn't feeling too clever neither but it's not that surprising. Sometimes you can spend too long underground and need a day off to get the coal dust out of your lungs.'

Kember decided to change tack. This line of questioning was getting him nowhere.

'Did Christopher Morris ever cause trouble in the mine or bad feeling among the men?'

'In what way?' Armstrong gave Burnley and Kember a sidelong glance.

'You tell me,' Kember said.

'Nah. Not that I know of. We all keep our heads down, get on with it and hope we're left alone. Those that go underground pray they won't die from a roof collapse, gas or explosion, I hope the cable doesn't snap and take my head off, and everyone else tries to make sure they don't lose a finger or an arm. If you make it out in one piece, you thank God you've lived to do it again tomorrow.'

'Doesn't sound like the kind of job your average man would like.'

'It's not about liking it,' Burnley interjected. 'For some, it's in their blood. There's a lot of men here from Wales and up north whose families have been miners for generations. Others have been drafted in from elsewhere but they haven't got the same coal dust running through their veins.'

'Does that cause bad feeling?' Kember directed the question at Armstrong.

'Not really,' Armstrong replied. 'The newcomers are good enough so you just have to get along, don't you?'

Kember detected something in the man's tone that suggested getting along wasn't always easy. In his experience, no organisation ran as smoothly as people would like or as harmoniously as the owners and managers portrayed. His own rocky relationship with Chief Inspector Hartson was a case in point.

Three bells rang again and Armstrong's attention diverted back to his job.

'As you can see,' Burnley said as he ushered Kember and Watson back towards the door, 'it's a close-knit community we have here at the colliery. Christopher Morris died of a heart attack so I can't see that there's anything further to investigate.'

'I understand that, Mr Burnley, but we're policemen.' Kember put the stress on *policemen*. 'We're paid to look at things differently.'

◆　◆　◆

Geraldine rapped on the door of Dallington's office and entered at the commanding officer's shout of 'Come!' Lizzie followed her in and stood stiffly by her side.

'Sit,' Dallington said, reaching for his tin of Old Holborn tobacco.

The two women complied and Lizzie watched Dallington make a show of filling his pipe. To her left, the gripped hands and clenched jaw muscles of Geraldine betrayed her rising tension. In contrast, Wing Commander Matfield, Dallington's second in command, was sitting casually to Lizzie's right with his legs crossed, idly picking imaginary fluff from the cloth of his peaked cap as if awaiting the arrival of his afternoon whisky in a gentlemen's club.

Dallington reached for his matches and elbowed a black and white cat out of his way. Tilly, the air station's mascot, glowered at him and jumped to the floor with a thump. Dallington scraped a match into life, sucked on his pipe stem until clouds of blue-tinged smoke engulfed his head, and blew out the match a split second before Lizzie was sure it would burn his fingers. The cloud drifted behind him, obscuring the display of personal memorabilia arrayed on the wall, and he aimed a stream of smoke at the ceiling before turning his attention to Geraldine.

'It seems the powers that inhabit the Accidents Investigation Branch are to conduct a full investigation, not only into the conduct of Miss Hayes, but also that of all the other ATA pilots who took to the air on the fifth of January.'

'Not all,' Geraldine said, with ice in her voice. 'I see the men are not included.'

'Of course they aren't,' Dallington snapped. 'Their judgement is beyond question. None of them crashed their aircraft, for a start.'

Geraldine glared at him across the desk. 'May I respectfully request that you address Second Officer Hayes by her given title? Sir? Especially if this is to be a formal hearing.'

'It's not a blasted formal hearing, as well you know,' Dallington snapped, almost choking on his pipe smoke. 'The matter is out of my hands and in those of the AIB. I merely wished to discuss the options.'

Blood pounded in Lizzie's ears. Her flight captain was treading a dangerous path by goading Dallington, even though Lizzie was entitled to be called by her proper rank. Dallington would take any excuse to berate the Air Ministry and War Office with further requests for their removal and he wouldn't wait for the outcome of any investigation if he felt he had the ammunition.

'Options?' Geraldine said, through gritted teeth.

'She's suspended,' Dallington said, not looking at Lizzie. 'There must be options with regards to what we do with her.'

Lizzie could see the colour rising in Geraldine's cheeks and wished for the ordeal to be over. Geraldine took a long breath and let it out slowly. Lizzie wanted to do the same, to forestall the feeling of panic starting to bubble in her chest. This was neither the time nor the place to have a full-on attack. It would confirm every prejudice Dallington had about letting women fly and allowing them to remain on *his* air station.

'Sir, Officer Hayes is merely suspended from flying activities temporarily,' Geraldine said.

Matfield uncrossed his legs, reminding Lizzie that he was still in the room, and she noticed he was smirking, almost as if he was enjoying the exchange.

'Thank you for sight of the interim decision from the AIB,' Geraldine continued, 'but I feel Officer Hayes—'

'I wasn't aware your feelings had any bearing on this, Flight Captain.'

Lizzie noticed the grip of Geraldine's hands tighten even further, thinking she might break her own fingers if this continued.

'I have been on the telephone to HQ at White Waltham, talking about recent accident reports across the whole of the ATA,' Geraldine said. 'The men are faring no better or worse than the women and most accidents seem to be the result of the poor condition of the aircraft, or the need to deliver to forward stations in bad weather or under the nose of Jerry. Either way, not usually the fault of the individual.'

'There, you've said it yourself,' Dallington said. 'Not *usually* the fault of the individual but distinctly possible nonetheless.'

'Sir?' Matfield said, sitting forward. 'If I might make a suggestion?'

Dallington looked taken aback.

Lizzie's heart sank. Geraldine's verbal sparring with Dallington was one thing but Matfield's interventions were never guaranteed to make any situation better. Often the opposite, in fact. Dallington had been Matfield's commanding officer in the Royal Flying Corps at the end of the last war. He had helped the young man, as Matfield had been at the time, survive the emotional aftermath of being shot down and the trauma of being the last man standing in a subsequent ground skirmish. Undoubtedly, that still engendered a certain amount of gratitude, even after more than twenty years. However, Matfield's opinion about the unsuitability of Dallington to command an air station was well known by almost everyone at RAF Scotney except Dallington himself, who thought he should be commanding an operational base for fighters or bombers.

'All we know is that Officer Hayes is unable to fly at present,' Matfield continued. 'I rather suspect there is little else for a pilot to do around the air station, so would you object to her taking two or three days' leave, perhaps?' Matfield said.

It was Lizzie's turn to be taken aback. She'd expected banishment rather than a 72-hour pass.

'Object?' Dallington said, sitting back in his padded leather, wing-backed chair. He pushed his glasses back up to the bridge of his nose with his forefinger. 'I welcome the opportunity to remove any liability from this air station, however briefly.'

'Thank you, sir,' Matfield said. 'I'm sure Officer Hayes would be delighted at the chance to return home to visit her family.'

Lizzie glanced at Matfield. She knew him as a calm, secretive and mistrustful loner who shared some of Dallington's reservations about women in the armed forces but was rarely hostile towards them. She turned her gaze to the left. Geraldine knew Lizzie's family were less than welcoming because of her anxiety and OCN, and because they disliked and disapproved of her job in the ATA. Returning home was out of the question. She'd rather be working on a case with Kember.

Her focus turned back to Dallington when she realised that he was speaking.

'. . . if I can leave the matter in your hands for now,' Dallington said to Geraldine. 'I have better things to occupy my time. The pair of you are dismissed.'

Lizzie stood up with Geraldine and they saluted the group captain, whose attention had returned to relighting his pipe that had gone out. As they turned to leave, she saw Geraldine give Matfield an almost imperceptible nod of appreciation that he failed to acknowledge. They were through the office door and closing it behind them when a call came from Dallington.

'And don't forget to surrender your flight authorisation card.'

As the three men braved the elements once again, Kember walked alongside Burnley.

'You mentioned a banksman, someone who operates the lift cage on the surface,' Kember said.

'Thatcher,' Burnley said, without turning.

'Does he sleep in the same hut as the others?'

'No, although he's on the same shift. He was allocated a bed in one of the other fore shift huts when he came to work for me a few months ago.'

Kember stopped walking. 'I'd like to speak to him.'

Burnley stopped a few steps on and turned, his eyes studying Kember. 'What for?'

Kember sighed. Why couldn't people just comply with his requests and answer his questions instead of always responding with a question? 'He belongs to the team who run the pit machinery on the fore shift so I assume he would need to be on duty while the rest of the safety team made their morning checks.'

Burnley took the few strides back to where Kember stood. 'He isn't part of the underground safety team and he didn't sleep in the same hut as Christopher Morris.'

'I'm aware of that,' Kember said, looking Burnley in the eyes without flinching, in spite of the stinging sleet. 'Inspector Watson, did you speak to the banksman during your investigation?'

Watson nodded and pulled his collar in tighter. 'We spoke to everyone and Mr Burnley's correct; neither the banksman nor the others at the pithead went underground or had access to the hut where Morris slept.'

Kember didn't doubt that Watson's men had carried out a decent and professional investigation but he hadn't been drafted in for nothing. His job was to kick over stones and lift logs to see if anything interesting crawled out. Having come down all the way from Tonbridge, he felt it would be remiss of him not to speak to the banksman at the very least. Despite Burnley's protestations, Kember insisted on taking a detour to the lift cage at the pithead. The mine owner let out what sounded like a growl and complied, his face looking like something unsavoury was being held underneath his nose.

Their course led them back across the slushy pit yard, through a doorway, along a corridor and past where helmets and head-torches were given out and collected. The chatter of men bantering at the top of the pit shaft was far below the volume of noise that Kember had expected and he assumed that to be due to the machinery being housed elsewhere. Burnley introduced a thin man wearing a donkey jacket and miner's helmet, but no head-torch, as Alastair Thatcher, the new fore shift banksman, and stepped away to allow Kember and Watson room to talk.

Kember judged the bespectacled Thatcher to be about half a foot shorter than his own six feet, short curly hair in evidence below the rim at the back of his helmet, and thought he looked more like a timid office clerk than a hardened miner, even if he did only work at the pithead.

'You're new here then?' Kember said.

'Not that new,' Thatcher replied. 'Been here a few months.'

'What did you do before?'

'I was banksman in a pit up north until the depression, then I was a delivery driver for a few years. The family's been in mining for generations so it's in my blood. When this job came up, I jumped at the chance.'

'Were you on fore shift duty the day Christopher Morris died?' Kember asked.

'I'm guessing you know I was,' Thatcher said, eyeing the detectives suspiciously. 'Why do you ask?'

'I ask, Mr Thatcher, because I've been brought in to re-examine the circumstances surrounding the death of Mr Morris.' Kember watched for a reaction but Thatcher only frowned.

'What circumstances? He told us the doc found Morris had died of a heart attack.' Thatcher nodded towards Watson.

'Nonetheless, I've been brought in to see if I can find anything that might suggest a root cause of that heart attack. Do you know of anything I should be made aware of?'

'Such as?' Thatcher's eyes narrowed. 'As you can see, I operate the lift cage at the top of the shaft. The only time I would have seen Morris is when he passed through here to go down the pit or on his way out.'

'You didn't see him socially?'

'I saw him in the club but everyone goes there. Most people round here know most others to nod at but that doesn't mean we know what goes on with them.'

Kember had to accept that as truth. How many times had he nodded to someone in New Scotland Yard without knowing the man behind the face? He was almost embarrassed to think of the number of occasions when he'd been recognised by someone who had then come over for a chat without him ever recalling their name or how they knew each other.

'Did you like Morris?'

Thatcher shrugged. 'I didn't know him well enough to like or dislike him. We played darts now and then, winner stays on and all that, but I'm rubbish at it. We weren't mates or anything.'

Kember noticed the slight flick of Thatcher's gaze down and to his left and wondered if the unconscious action told a different story.

'Did you notice anything unusual about him on the day he died? Either as he went down for his fore shift safety inspection or when he came back up at the end of the shift?' This time Kember noticed Thatcher look up before he spoke, a sign that the man was trying to recall a memory rather than construct a lie on the spur of the moment.

'He did look a bit peaky in the morning,' Thatcher said. 'Didn't really notice at shift's end though because everyone flooded out as usual, trying to get to the showers and canteen quick smart.'

Kember nodded. 'What about his friends?'

'What friends?'

'He didn't have any?'

Thatcher gave Kember a sidelong glance. 'I thought you were asking about someone in particular, but I told you I didn't know him that well. I'm in the club mostly, sometimes in the Volunteer pub in Bramling, and I saw him a few times drinking with his workmates. Apart from the odd bit of fishing, there's not much else to do around here to be honest, especially in winter. I don't know if he ever went to Canterbury with anyone. I don't go. It's a long way and the buses and trains don't run late enough to make it worthwhile more than every now and then. I stay here; save my money for better days.'

Kember thought it curious that Thatcher had said more about what he did rather than confirming anything detailed about what Morris got up to.

'Did Morris have any enemies that you know of?'

Thatcher's eyebrows shot up. 'What's that got to do with anything?'

'I'm trying to get a feel for who Morris was, what he was like.'

Thatcher looked at Kember suspiciously and shrugged. 'Everyone has disagreements, Inspector. Arguments, tiffs, squabbles; I'd be surprised if Morris had been any different.'

'Did you ever see Morris become aggressive or behave in such a way that it might have led to someone deciding to settle old scores?'

'Old scores? Are you suggesting someone did for him?' Thatcher shook his head when Kember didn't reply. 'By all accounts, he wasn't a nice man, if that's what you're getting at. I've seen him have a go at Ramsey, he's one of the fore shift firemen, but that's what promotion can do to you. Goes to your head.'

'Have a go?' Kember prompted.

'Shouted at him. Belittled him. As I said, not a nice man.'

'Nobody wanted to take him down a peg or two?' Kember saw a flicker in the man's eyes before Thatcher looked away.

'What people say with drink inside them can't be taken as gospel, can it?'

Again, a non-answer that said little but suggested something going on below the surface. Maybe Thatcher knew as little as he said but Kember decided he'd lay good money on the conversations and rumours he'd heard weren't of the benign kind.

'Ever see him with marks on him? From a fight, maybe?'

'We're not barbarians, Inspector,' Burnley interrupted, a frown on his brow as he glared at Thatcher. 'You can't go around fighting all the time. I won't allow it. We've all got to get along to a greater or lesser degree because you have to be able to rely on your workmates to get you out of a fix if the worst happens. We all get cuts and bruises at one time or another; that's just the nature of the work.'

Kember put a hand up to placate Burnley. He didn't want to antagonise him too much too soon. There would be time to put pressure on him later if necessary. There hadn't been a mark on Morris but it often paid to stir the pot.

'Did he ever seem wary or scared of anyone?' Kember continued.

'Not that I'm aware of. He was big enough and ugly enough to take care of himself, I reckon, though I never saw him as much as raise his fist. Although we're miners, we don't go around thumping each other willy-nilly. You can see from me that we're not all built like a brick outhouse.'

Kember smiled. That much was true. He'd seen other miners today who had the appearance of being able to give good accounts of themselves in a scuffle, but Thatcher didn't look like he could fight his way out of a paper bag.

'Is this getting us anywhere?' Burnley said. 'Thatcher clearly has little to impart about Morris that could help your investigation. They didn't even share a dormitory.'

'I'm sorry, Inspector, but Mr Burnley's right,' Thatcher said. 'I appreciate you're only doing your job but I didn't know much at all about Morris. We were never friends and I never took much notice of him. I'm not the best person to put these questions to. You should try his hut mates.'

A loud bell rang three times and a light came on, taking Thatcher's attention back to his lift cage control board. He pressed a button to answer with three rings. A moment later, the bell rang once and another light glowed. Thatcher pressed another button to answer with two rings.

'Sorry, work goes on,' Thatcher said, turning back to Kember. 'I've got a cage full of men coming up so I'll have to scoot you out of the way. They'll arrive at the surface in just a few minutes, tired, hungry and covered with black coal dust. I wouldn't want that nice overcoat of yours to get smudged with the black stuff as they push past.'

Kember could hear the cage ascending and see the taut cable moving up on its way to pass through the headgear high above the pithead, and be wound on the drum operated by Armstrong in the winding house. It was a slick operation and Kember decided he'd questioned enough for now. He followed Burnley and Watson back to the other entrance, well out of the way of stampeding miners, and halted.

'I'll be back tomorrow morning at nine o'clock, Mr Burnley, and I expect Mr Young and the other men to be ready for further questioning.' He saw Burnley's face redden.

'But I thought—'

'It would be a waste of everyone's time for you all to come to Canterbury Police Station.'

The threat stunned Burnley into enraged silence and he stormed out into driving sleet.

◆ ◆ ◆

Sitting with Geraldine in the officers' lounge, Lizzie handed over her ATA documents, a sinking feeling in the pit of her stomach at the thought of never flying again. The cockpit of an aeroplane was one of the few places she ever felt in control. The solitude, constant thrum of an engine, blue sky above and patchwork green below gave her a sense of peace she rarely experienced anywhere else, except perhaps when alone on top of a secluded hill.

'You'll need that if you intend going home,' Geraldine said, returning her travel warrant.

Lizzie shook her head. 'I'll not be going home.'

'Pop up to London, then, to see if any old friends are about.' Geraldine poured two cups of tea and splashed in some milk. She slid a cup towards Lizzie. 'I don't want you moping around here, feeling sorry for yourself.'

Lizzie avoided Geraldine's gaze. Was she that transparent? Moping around was exactly what she'd intended to do. Using a fork, she cut a bitesize piece from a thin slice of carrot cake, popped it into her mouth and grimaced. It had hardly any taste and you could count the sultanas on the fingers of one hand.

'Chin up,' Geraldine said. 'Pauline Gower won't let this go much further. If the pressing need for delivering aircraft in all conditions continues to increase, it's inevitable that there will be more accidents. I've told Pauline on several occasions that we should train for instrument-only flying, and be allowed to use the radios in an emergency. We don't want to let Jerry know where you are and all that, but still . . .' She took a forkful of cake, chewed, and swallowed with difficulty. 'Furthermore, ATA pilots have been attacked so many times I believe we should have the guns loaded.'

Lizzie had often thought so too, but that would mean even more training and she suspected it would never happen.

Geraldine ate another piece of cake and screwed up her face. 'Christ, it's like chewing cardboard. Tastes like it too.'

'They won't ever let us fly Spitfires and Hurricanes at this rate,' Lizzie complained. 'If the investigation goes against me, that'll be it for the women's section of the ATA.'

'That's total rot,' Geraldine said, putting her fork down. 'You heard what I said to Dallington. The men are faring no better than us. The ATA can't afford to lose good pilots and even Gerard d'Erlanger has been saying they need more.'

'He's the head of the ATA; he's bound to get his way and be given more *men*.'

'Listen,' Geraldine said, leaning forward conspiratorially. 'I don't want this to go any further because it hasn't been confirmed yet but I have it on the best authority, the *best* authority, that opinions are changing and you could all be flying fast fighters within a few months.'

'That will be fabulous,' Lizzie admitted. 'If I'm still around to enjoy it.'

'I'll see to it that you are.'

CHAPTER FIVE

Kember and Watson trailed behind Burnley as he strode angrily towards the sanctuary of his warm office and barged through the outer door. When the two detectives reached the office, they found no secretary keeping guard but Burnley turned and barred the way.

'I'm sure you gentlemen have important matters to attend to so we'll say our goodbyes here.'

It was a command that Kember didn't mind. He had no desire to stay amid the drab buildings, railway lines, piles of coal and spoil-heaps any longer than necessary. As it turned out, Burnley's idea of 'goodbye' was to disappear inside without another word and close the door with some force. Kember retreated to the car with Watson, glad to be out of the freezing sleet being thrown at him by the wind. The musty smell of damp clothing filled the car almost immediately.

'I'm afraid I can't stay with you tomorrow,' Watson said, as he started the engine. 'I can get someone to drop you back here in the morning, though, and collect you in the afternoon.'

'That would be fine, thank you,' Kember said, his mind still on the cool reception they'd been given as Watson drove out through the gates. 'Burnley's a pleasant chap, isn't he?' He glanced across and saw no humour on Watson's face. 'Was he like that during the investigation?'

'Worse. Griped about invasion of privacy and all sorts. We had the devil of a time getting to speak to everyone, and I got the feeling that word had got around to not cooperate with us.'

'Why do you think that was?'

Watson's mouth turned down. 'Like he said, to him, time is money and people don't matter. For every hour my team were there, halting production and pulling his men off shift for questioning, all he saw was a loss of profit. We found no evidence of malpractice, though.'

Seeing Watson's gaze flick to the rear-view mirror several times, Kember turned to look over his shoulder. A lorry, spanning almost the entire width of the narrow lane, was bearing down on their police Austin.

'A friend of yours?' Kember asked.

'Hardly,' Watson replied.

'Well, he's getting awfully close for a casual acquaintance. Better put your foot down and find a passing place before things get too cosy.'

'Christ almighty!' said Watson as he complied, fighting to keep the car in a straight line on the icy road as he accelerated. 'Do you have a gun?'

'No,' said Kember. 'You?'

'No.'

The Austin began to pull further ahead of the lorry, but any joy was short-lived as the shadow of the lorry loomed large behind them again.

'Jesus!' Watson shouted, spinning the wheel and steering into a skid as the Austin slithered on the tarmac slick with mud and sleet, forcing the car to right itself and shoot forward, missing a copse of trees huddled right next to the lane by inches.

The respite was brief. The lorry came again but there was nowhere for Watson to turn as the lane passed between thick hedgerows. Kember's heart pounded and he turned to squint through the water-streaked rear window. He couldn't see the number plates and the driver was wearing a cloth cap, its peak pulled low. Having arrived in the area that day, he was convinced it must be an old adversary of Watson's, but now wasn't the time to chat as the lorry drew close again and the police car shot past the safety of a farm track that turned off at the end of the line of trees.

'There's a humpbacked bridge over the railway line ahead,' Watson said as he leant forward, peering through the windscreen that the wipers were struggling to keep clear of ice. 'The lane's even tighter there so we might get the chance to turn the tables.'

'As long as nothing comes the other way,' Kember said.

He almost wished he'd brought his police-issue .38 Webley revolver, but remembering the last time he'd fired it and missed immediately expelled the thought. He took another glance back and saw the lorry lagging behind.

'Here we go,' Watson said, as the road rose and curved left.

They were crossing the bridge within seconds. Kember's stomach lurched as the car dropped down the other side and followed the lane into a right-hand curve through a corridor of small trees. The screen of foliage gave way to sodden fields of corrugated mud on either side, separated from the tarmac by water-filled ditches that would break axles and flip the whole car if they went in.

'Crossroads ahead,' Watson said. 'I've got an idea. Get my torch from the glove compartment.'

Kember retrieved the black Eveready torch, similar to the Bijou torch he often carried, its five-inch shaft a little thicker than a gun barrel. He saw the crossroads approaching, with its clusters of concrete dragons' teeth anti-tank obstacles on each corner ready to be moved to block the road should an invasion come.

Watson steered the Austin behind one set of tank traps, clipping the rear on one of the teeth as it skidded to a halt. He killed the engine and the two policemen leapt out of the car. The lorry was bearing down fast and showed no sign of slowing. Watson took up a shooting stance, holding his torch two-handed. Kember understood his plan and copied him. Sleet lanced down at forty-five degrees, stinging Kember's eyes as the lorry roared straight through the crossroads, its thick tyres spraying the policemen and the Austin with mud and slushy ice. Kember tracked the lorry with the pretend gun, just in case.

Once the lorry had disappeared around a bend in the lane, Kember lowered his hands, feeling ridiculous at the way he'd held the torch like some child playing cops and robbers. He looked across at Watson and saw he'd taken the brunt of the splattering, the front of his trousers and coat caked with mud. Kember hadn't escaped entirely unscathed, and the absurd situation got the better of him. He began to laugh with the release of tension and Watson joined him but the laughing soon subsided as they inspected the damaged bodywork and bumper, and the sleet drove them back inside the car.

◆ ◆ ◆

Standing beneath the shelter of the manor house portico with sandbags stacked into a protective wall between the columns, Lizzie enjoyed a drag on her cigarette as a vehicle sporting Air Force blue paintwork entered through the main gate. With the cab looking like a normal saloon car but the rear section covered in khaki canvas, she thought it a rather odd-looking beast as it trundled along the drive. Then again, she'd seen so many strange vehicles popping up all over the place that they almost seemed normal now. *Necessity is the mother of invention*, she thought, as the car, with its RAF roundel and lettering, reached the semi-circle of gravel and crunched to a halt. Flight Lieutenant Vickers left the cab and ran to get out of the sleet. Reaching the steps, he took them two at a time, and stopped by Lizzie as two other men emerged from under the cover of the canvas.

'Bloody awful weather,' he said, wiping his face with a hand-kerchief. 'But what do you think of Tilly?'

'The station's cat?' Lizzie said, and returned a lopsided smile. She knew what he meant.

'Ah, a bit more enthusiasm, if you please Officer Hayes,' Vickers said. 'Car, Light Utility, RAF, one. Known as a Tilly. Based on Kember's Hillman Minx, actually, although I accept mine's not quite as alluring to the eye.'

'I'm sure it's very – um – nice,' Lizzie said, feeling guilty at Vickers' disappointed expression. She offered him a cigarette, which he accepted and lit from the dying embers of her own. She flicked the stub into the driving sleet.

'I've waited months for it to arrive and I hope this is the first of many. The Tilly isn't going to set the world on fire but at least we won't have to use our two staff cars to supplement the work of the lorries, especially once the other one arrives along with a couple of other vehicles.' He perked up. 'It's not the car itself that's important right at this moment, though.' He pointed to his men carrying a box each around the side of the house. 'We found the source of the radio interference.'

Now Lizzie was interested. 'Whereabouts?'

'Deep in the woods over that way,' Vickers said, and pointed. 'We found transmitting equipment hidden in a dustbin buried in the ground and covered with branches. It wasn't particularly well camouflaged, in my opinion, but I suppose it did the job for a while.'

'How did you find it?' Lizzie said, puzzled. 'I know you said radio signals had been detected but if it was buried . . . ?' She let the question hang.

Vickers took a drag on his cigarette and watched the smoke being whipped away by a gust of wind.

'The radio boys have experienced signal interference before and thought it was an echo from the army, or the Home Guard mucking about with things they didn't really understand. Quite annoying when aircraft are landing or there's an air raid. This time they were listening out and picked up a transmission. They did a rough triangulation and told us where to look, but I agree it's a bit odd. I can only assume that whoever was using it either saw or heard us coming, hastily packed up and legged it as fast as they could before we found the dustbin.'

'Does that mean we have a spy in the area?'

Vickers gave an awkward laugh. 'For Christ's sake don't say that in front of Dallington or Matfield. They'll have a fit. No, the camouflage was a far from professional job. My guess is, a radio ham was playing about with his equipment, maybe listening in to control-tower talk. They used to do that before the war, you know? Chatted to each other, swapped weather reports, spoke to their counterparts all over the country and abroad. Quite a few societies about, dealing with that sort of technical stuff.'

Lizzie wasn't convinced. 'Why bury it at all?'

'I suppose they didn't want Jerry to get their hands on it if ever the invasion had come. It looks a primitive piece of kit to my untrained eye, but useful to have in an emergency, I suppose. I'll speak to Captain Brown to see if it's anything to do with his lot.'

That seemed more likely to Lizzie, although from what she'd seen of Elias Brown both before and after he became captain and commander of the local platoon of Home Guard, he wouldn't know a radio valve from a beer mug. Radio hams would want to keep their kit close, in a garden shed or cellar. If they did bury it, she didn't suppose they'd traipse all through a thick wood to do so, invasion threat or not.

'How did your encounter with Dallington go?' Vickers asked.

Lizzie gave him a wan smile. 'As you would expect. He delighted in the fact that I'd been grounded and didn't want me on his air station if I couldn't fly, even though the latter sentiment was prevalent from the moment the ATA arrived. I could see the glee in his eyes at the prospect of using the investigation as a way to lever out the rest of the ATA.'

'I wouldn't worry too much about that,' Vickers said, through exhaled smoke. 'He's tried many times before, even called on all his friends in high places, and hasn't succeeded so far. Actually, I think he's pretty much resigned to never being able to get rid of the ATA. He seems to consider you all a necessary evil which allows him to keep command of the air station until such time that it becomes fully operational again with its own squadrons.' He threw the remains of his cigarette over the sandbags and on to the sodden grass beside the portico. 'Fancy a brew?' he said, with a glance at his watch. 'It's a bit too early for the hard stuff.'

Lizzie nodded. She didn't want another cup of tea but the idea of being alone with her thoughts unnerved her. The prospect of never flying again weighed heavy and she could feel the tension at the nape of her neck and the beginnings of a tension headache forming at her temples. Ben Vickers had been a great support to both her and Kember in their previous investigations and chatting with him often alleviated any drift towards a panic attack.

They wandered through the main entrance into the hall, entered the almost empty officers' lounge and sat at the first table they found. She always thought it curious how Vickers, Matfield and other male officers avoided the soft settees and easy chairs arranged around a table at the centre of the lounge. That was where the ATA women always congregated at the end of a working day and sometimes when off-duty. They had created their own bar, named the Hangar Round club, in a disused cellar beneath the manor house to get away from the male-dominated lounge and the constant advances from certain officers, but the soft furniture still held the aura of being off-limits to men, who always sat elsewhere unless invited.

'Have you spoken to Kember?' Vickers asked.

'Not yet,' Lizzie said. 'He's in Canterbury on a case.'

'What do you intend to do while you're grounded, then?'

Lizzie shrugged. 'Geraldine wants me to go home or see friends.'

Vickers took a packet of Woodbine cigarettes from his jacket pocket and held it up to show Lizzie. She declined the offer of another smoke and he seemed to think better of it too. 'That's not what I asked,' he said, returning the unopened packet to his pocket.

Lizzie sighed. 'There's not much to do. I could go to see a film matinee in Tonbridge.'

'That's one afternoon taken care of. What about the rest of the time?'

'I'll try to keep out of Dallington's way for a start. And Matfield's. I could read or listen to the wireless but I might see what I can do to spruce up the Hangar Round club.'

'Sounds like fun.' He pulled a face.

Lizzie smiled. 'It's only during the day. The girls will be around each evening, assuming they make it home in time from their daily aircraft deliveries.'

She wasn't sure how well she'd cope with hearing about the flying exploits of her friends while her own wings remained clipped. She hoped the Accidents Investigation Branch wouldn't take too long over their investigation, whatever the verdict.

As Vickers signalled for a steward to bring tea, a communications orderly entered the lounge, came over to their table and addressed Lizzie directly.

'Officer Hayes?'

'Yes?' Lizzie replied, surprised it was her and not Vickers whom the orderly wanted.

'There's a telephone call from Canterbury for you.'

◆ ◆ ◆

'What was all that about?' Kember said, as he wiped his face.

'Your guess is as good as mine,' Watson replied, as he turned the Austin north towards Canterbury. 'Did it definitely strike you as deliberate?'

'It crossed my mind. See who it was?'

'Only the peak of a flat cap.' Watson made a face. 'I had sleet in my eyes. Maybe he couldn't see through his windscreen either and didn't even see us. All I saw was a small number five painted on the front but that could mean anything or nothing.'

'Do all the locals drive like that?'

'It has been known.'

A few minutes later, Watson stopped the Austin at a checkpoint and waited for one of the four Home Guard soldiers to emerge from the comfort of their covered sandbag enclosure. The unlucky soldier huddled against the inclement weather, his rifle not even held at the ready. Watson wound the window down a few inches and sleet lanced in through the gap. He held up his warrant card and the soldier gave it a cursory once-over before signalling to his colleagues. As soon as the red and white barrier no longer barred the road, Watson accelerated away.

'Bloody annoying pipsqueaks,' he complained. 'We used to be the law around here but now we have to play second fiddle to a group of old men, bank clerks and boys. Mind you, we could have done with a few of them at the crossroads.' He turned left at the next junction, almost without slowing. 'What did you think of Victor Young?'

'I've no doubt at all, he had something to hide,' Kember said. 'But that could easily be to do with his obvious dislike of Burnley rather than the dead man. I got the same feeling from Armstrong and Thatcher.'

Watson nodded. 'Burnley thinks the sun shines out of his own backside and all his workers should be grateful for the illumination. As far as he's concerned, they're paid enough and he can get them to do whatever job he likes during the working day. There's no place for sentimentality. On the other hand, the workers think he's a waste of fresh air who's got where he is on the backs of others.'

Kember sighed. 'Any chance you could come back with me tomorrow?'

Watson shook his head. 'Afraid not. As I said, I've been pulled away and you're in the hot seat. Can't even spare you a constable, except as a temporary taxi driver.'

'In which case, so I know what I've got myself into, did you come across any animosity between the groups of men?'

'How d'you mean?'

'You know how police forces can be, even sections within a force,' Kember said. 'They keep pretty much to themselves unless cooperation is absolutely necessary so it will be interesting to see to what extent a shared dislike of Burnley by the underground miners and surface workers makes them friendly enough to mingle.'

'The enemy of my enemy is my friend, sort of thing?' Watson said, giving Kember a sidelong glance.

'Exactly.'

Watson thought for a moment. 'The men of Hut Six are a mixed bag, if that's anything to go by. They all have important and specific jobs, and all have authority over others to some degree. Three work underground, as Morris did, and two on the surface. Not sure what you can make of that.'

'Me neither,' Kember said. 'Something for me to pick the bones out of tomorrow.'

They reached the Kent and Canterbury Hospital and parked as close to the entrance as possible. The wind had eased a bit but the sleet was just as bad. The forecast was for more of the same, then snow. Kember pulled up the collar of his raincoat and held his fedora on as he loped across the short distance to the entrance, leaving Watson in the car. The reception was warm and inviting, but the whistling wind still made a chilly impression on the relative quiet inside. The nurse behind the desk raised her eyebrows questioningly and Kember enquired about Dr Headley. She gave him an exaggerated frown and pointed to somewhere behind him. Kember turned and looked towards a line of seats against one wall and saw Headley slumped on a chair in a corner. He had the legs of the chair placed over the straps of his carpet bag and forensic instruments box, trapping them to prevent anyone light-fingered enough to try taking them. His glasses were askew and the overcoat draped over his arm trailed on the floor. The sound of gentle snoring drifted across, much to the displeasure of the nurse. Kember thanked her, apologised for his colleague's apparent fatigue and promised to remove him immediately.

At the shake of his shoulder, Headley awoke with a start.

'What the blazes are you doing, Kember?' he said, his speech thick with sleep.

'Sorry to interrupt your dreams but it's time you were getting back to Tonbridge,' Kember replied. 'Did you find anything interesting?'

Headley yawned and righted his glasses. 'Not in my dreams.' He stood up and donned his raincoat while Kember untangled the straps of his bag and box. 'In the post-mortem, on the other hand . . . You?' He put the strap of the box over his shoulder and left his carpet bag for Kember to carry.

'Only more questions and a thoroughly unpleasant owner,' Kember said.

The wind had picked up again, throwing sleet in their faces as they struggled to get the luggage into Watson's car. If Kember hadn't felt so cold himself, he might have laughed at the look of misery on Headley's face.

'Had a little coming together have you,' Headley said, eyeing the Austin's battered rear wing and bumper.

'Something like that,' Kember replied, as he ushered the doctor into the car. 'The driver of a farm lorry thought he was racing at Brooklands and nearly ran us off the road.'

'Nearly?' Headley gave him a wry smile. 'Looks like he succeeded.'

Kember got in next to Watson and closed the door. 'We had to get out of his way a bit smartish.'

'It seems you can't help antagonising people wherever you go.'

'I don't know what you mean,' Kember said, thinking that was a bit rich, coming from the often spiky pathologist.

'We've got time to pop in for a livener if we get a shift on,' Watson said, seeming to pick up on the mood.

As Watson started the engine and they began the short drive to Canterbury West station, Kember half-turned in his seat to glance at Headley.

'Now we're away from wagging ears, you said the post-mortem was – um – interesting?'

'More than,' Headley said, and yawned. 'As soon as I saw the body it was obvious, he hadn't died of a heart attack brought on by exhaustion.'

'He hadn't?' Watson said, frowning.

'I didn't even have to cut him open. Although I did, of course, for the sake of thoroughness.'

'Was he murdered?' Kember asked.

Headley gave a short laugh. 'You're the inquisitor, I'm the physician. I can only tell you what bodies tell me. The rest is your domain.'

Kember sighed, playing Headley's game again. 'And what did this body tell you?'

'The first thing I saw told me pretty much all I needed to know.' Headley sat up a little more and leant forward conspiratorially. 'Patches of the skin were cherry-pink.'

'That's lividity, surely?'

Headley shook his head. 'Livor mortis causes a deep-pink to reddish-purple discolouration of the skin where the blood has settled at the body's lowest point after death. The teeth can turn pink too. In the case of this man, other areas of skin were pink but Dr Paine's notes didn't mention any discolouration, which suggests he either didn't see it or judged it to be lividity. If he was adamant that his examinations had found nothing untoward, his certification of death would not have been questioned.'

'Except we did,' Watson said, grim-faced. 'We asked for a post-mortem.'

'If not lividity, what caused it?' Kember waited, but Headley strung out his moment.

'As I said, I opened him up, just to make sure, and there it was again,' Headley said. 'Cherry-pink lungs.'

'Inflammation from breathing all that coal dust?' Watson suggested.

'No, Inspector. I tested muscle fluid from his legs and found concentrations higher than fifty per cent. That's equivalent to over sixty per cent in the blood. A lethal saturation.'

'Sixty per cent of what?' Kember asked, becoming impatient.

'Carbon monoxide,' Headley stated. 'A very common poison gas in coal mines.'

'He was gassed?' Watson said, shocked.

'I would say so. There have been many tragic mining accidents recorded as due to poor ventilation. The risk of explosion is a constant threat. Burning coal releases carbon *di*oxide, but if there is insufficient ventilation to provide enough oxygen, then burning the coal or leaving it to decay releases carbon *mon*oxide.'

Kember rubbed the end of his nose in thought. 'The fan house foreman said two men had complained of headaches, dizziness and feeling sick in the days before Christopher Morris died.'

'All common symptoms of carbon monoxide poisoning.' Headley nodded. 'I'm very surprised that Dr Gunstone didn't mention it in his own post-mortem report.'

'But there were six miners from the same shift in the same dormitory, four who worked underground. How could only two of them display the symptoms and only one die?'

'If you insist on asking me to play detective every time we meet, I'll have to insist on taking a cut of your salary.'

As the station came into view, Watson parked at the side of the road outside the Unicorn Inn and assured Headley that his bags would be perfectly safe. To emphasise the point, he pulled a large card from the glove compartment and put it face up on the dashboard to show: ON POLICE BUSINESS. They got out of the car to be met by an icy blast of sleet, which hastened their entry into the pub.

Kember and Headley stated their preferences and found an empty table in a corner as Watson went to the bar.

A crackling log fire projected welcome warmth into the room, its dancing yellow flames mesmerising and soporific. The smoke from cigarettes, cigars and pipes formed a mist-like layer on the brown ceiling, giving the illusion of looking through an open roof to the real winter clouds outside. The buzz of conversation permeating the fug even seemed to emanate from the walls.

Watson returned with a pint of bitter each.

'I got you the last of the corned beef for your sandwich, Dr Headley,' he said. 'With a slathering of sweet pickle as requested. It'll take a moment to come. Sorry Kember, we have to make do with Spam. I'll buy you dinner later.'

Kember nodded his thanks. He wasn't bothered; he rather liked Spam. He liked corned beef more though, especially fritters covered in crispy batter. He glanced at the clock hanging on the wall behind the bar, rose from his chair and excused himself from the table. Moving to stand at the end of the bar, he caught the attention of the barman and beckoned him over.

'Do you have a telephone?' Kember asked.

'We do but it's not for customers, I'm afraid,' the barman said.

Kember wasn't one for casually abusing his authority as a police officer but the sight of his warrant card changed the barman's mind, and he was led through to a hallway behind the bar where a black Bakelite telephone stood on a tall thin-legged table. He waited for the barman to return to his duties before putting a call through to RAF Scotney.

❖ ❖ ❖

Lizzie took the call in the ATA ops room for privacy.

'Hello?' she said into the mouthpiece. 'Elizabeth Hayes speaking.'

'Lizzie, it's me.'

Her heart gave a jolt as she recognised Kember's voice. She knew he was away on police business and hadn't expected to hear from him for a while. That and her current predicament made his call all the more welcome.

'Oh. It's lovely to hear from you,' she said. 'How's it going down there?'

'First things first,' Kember said. 'How was the hearing?'

'Awful.' Lizzie grimaced to the empty office. 'They tore me and the ATA apart and grounded me while they investigate.'

'Waste of time, if you ask me. There's nothing to investigate. Are you all right, though?'

Lizzie didn't want to burden him with her woes when he was on a case. He might worry, and the quicker he solved the crime the quicker he'd be back.

'I'll survive,' she said, not convinced her job was safe. 'What was it you called for?'

'To ask how your ordeal went, mainly,' he said.

She heard him breathing as he hesitated.

'Is something wrong?' she asked, as a twinge of unease fluttered in her chest.

She listened as Kember gave a very brief outline of the day's events, frowning into the empty room at the mention of the playing cards, closing her eyes at the re-telling of the encounter between Watson's Austin and the lorry. The tension in her chest increased and she automatically reached to ping a rubber band on her wrist, like she always did to help stave off a full panic attack.

'Where are you now?' she asked. 'Are you safe?'

'I'm fine,' Kember said. 'We're all in a pub in the middle of Canterbury. Headley has a train to catch soon and then I'm off to do some work. I've a fat case-file to read and then Watson has offered to stand me dinner.'

'Lucky you. What are your plans for tomorrow?'

'I'm going back at nine in the morning to interview the men from the dormitory. I'll keep you posted.'

The telephone operator interrupted, warning that their three minutes were up.

'Time to go,' Kember said. 'I've a pint waiting and Spam sandwich starting to curl.'

'Jonathan,' Lizzie said, using his first name for emphasis. 'Do be care—'

The line went dead with a static click and she replaced the handset back on its cradle. She looked at it for a few seconds as if it would come alive again and tell her more. It may have been her imagination but Kember had sounded tense. Maybe he was worried about the outcome of the AIB investigation or the prospect of another altercation with the rogue lorry. Whatever it was, she was sure that returning to the mine without DI Watson wasn't one of Kember's better plans.

Some situations might be beyond her control but leaving Kember to go back to the mine alone wasn't one of them. She resolved to rectify that in the morning, by rising early and taking her Norton motorbike to Bekesbourne.

I've nothing to do and I'll go mad if I stay here, she thought to herself. *Another pair of eyes on the case won't hurt, will it?*

◆ ◆ ◆

After his call disconnected, cutting off Lizzie's warning in mid-sentence, Kember replaced the handset in its cradle and returned to the bar. Their food had arrived much quicker than Watson had feared and Dr Headley had already polished off his corned beef sandwich.

'Checking in with Miss Hayes, were we?' Headley said with a crooked smile. He took a swig of his beer.

'Seeing how she got on with the Accidents Investigation Branch, if you must know,' he said, checking between two unevenly cut slices of bread to see if there was evidence of any Spam inside.

'Ah, my apologies,' Headley said. 'It must have come as quite a shock to be investigated after suffering such a traumatic experience.'

Kember watched him down the rest of his pint and took a draught of his own. Lizzie didn't deserve to be hauled over the coals for what was basically an act of God, especially when others had taken off in good faith and been caught out by the bad weather.

'You'd better have this,' Headley said, handing Kember a folded sheet of paper.

He opened it and saw the summary of Headley's post-mortem.

'I thought it would come in handy if you had a copy,' Headley said. He held up his hand. 'You can thank me another time with a pint or two but I ought to be going if I'm to get back to Scotney before tonight.'

Kember refolded the sheet and secured it in the inside pocket of his jacket. He wished he was accompanying Headley back to Scotney, to Lizzie, but Chief Inspector Hartson was not in the habit of assigning him to quick and easy cases. He had no idea how long this one might take, and despite Watson saying that farm vehicles racing through the narrow lanes were not an uncommon sight around here, the incident with the lorry niggled at the back of his mind.

He sighed and downed his pint.

CHAPTER SIX

The following morning, Kember sat in the back of a police Wolseley being driven by a constable of the First Police Reserve, one of the police pensioners re-engaged for war service. They were supposed to be below the age of sixty but such was the leaching of young men from the police into the armed forces that many older officers had returned, while others already in service had remained beyond the retirement age. Kember suspected his driver to be pushing seventy.

A severe frost overnight and ominous-looking clouds hanging very low this morning had left the countryside looking like a monochrome photograph. The black filigree of leafless trees and hedgerows stood out starkly against fields coated with a white glaze, and the dark walls of houses and other buildings supported glistening white roofs from which protruded chimney pots belching black and grey smoke from fires burning coal and logs.

The twin winding wheels of Bekesbourne Colliery appeared in the distance and grew bigger as the car drew nearer. Soon, the forbidding spoil-heaps and harsh buildings of the mine works became visible as they approached the entrance and turned in. Ice from the puddles cracked like splintering wood as the car negotiated the track rutted by the previous comings and goings of numerous lorries and halted outside Burnley's office. An icy blast hit Kember as he opened the door and left the comparative warmth of the car.

The constable didn't wait. With a wave and a promise to return at about four 0'clock, he swung the car in a half-circle and took the Wolseley back towards the lane.

Kember knocked on the outer door and stepped into the office guarded by Mrs Wall the secretary, remembering that her soft-looking shell contained a hard centre, like a Paynes Poppets toffee. She looked up and glared at him through her glasses as though a stray dog had wandered in.

'You'll have to wait,' she said in a clipped voice. 'Mr Burnley is not in his office at present.'

Wall by name, wall by nature, Kember thought. He glanced at a clock to his right as the secretary went back to her typing. Ten to nine. He was early and Burnley was either a stickler for timekeeping or wished to keep Kember in his place. He wasn't bothered which. It was warmer in here than the car and gave him a chance to get full feeling back in his gloved fingers.

Burnley ducked in through the door at five to nine, bringing with him a blast of freezing air and the smell of coal before he shut the door. His hat and overcoat glistened with ice. *More bloody sleet*, thought Kember.

'Punctual, DI Kember,' Burnley said, water droplets sparkling on his walrus moustache. 'I like that in a man.'

Only because I don't want to let you off the hook, thought Kember, but he said, 'Just basic courtesy, Mr Burnley. I trust your men will be ready for me?'

Burnley's face clouded over. 'Wait here.'

Burnley hung his hat on the rack and disappeared through the door to his office, Mrs Wall giving him a warm smile as he passed her.

Kember thought for a second before he ignored the command and followed, brushing past Burnley's secretarial guard dog and ignoring her protestations.

'Impatient, are we?' Burnley said, and nodded to Mrs Wall that all was well.

Kember waited for the door to close.

'When DI Watson and I left here yesterday, we were followed by a farm lorry that was going too fast for the conditions.'

'I'm sorry to hear that,' Burnley said, sorting through a sheaf of letters.

'We were forced from the road and his car took a knock.'

'Again, I'm sorry to hear that.'

Kember doubted that and wasn't about to let Burnley off the hook that easily. Men like him were concerned when events directly affected their own wealth and well-being, and riling him a little might produce results.

'You don't seem surprised.' Kember watched Burnley put the letters in a box-file that he returned to a gap among other box-files on a shelf.

Burnley stared at Kember and sniffed dismissively. 'The whole of Europe's at war, fascists and communists are everywhere, the country's going to the dogs, and even though the RAF supposedly won the Battle of Britain, neither they nor Churchill can keep the Luftwaffe from closing us down every night. So, no, the erratic driving of some maniac behind the wheel doesn't surprise me. It's just another sign of the times, Inspector.'

'Would you be more interested if it had been one of your lorries?' Kember watched for a reaction.

'It can't have been one of mine. They arrive empty and leave fully laden with coal on a tight schedule. Either way, I suspect they tend not to fare well as racing cars, especially through the narrow country lanes. In any case, I don't have enough vehicles or manpower, despite our reduced working day, so I don't have the luxury of disciplining a driver for being a little enthusiastic in the execution of his duty.'

Denying with one breath, excusing with another, Kember thought. Burnley was just the kind of despot who would send a lorry to run him off the road as a warning to stay out of his business. Not that Kember could prove he was responsible, or even identify the lorry and its driver from among the dozens that must arrive and leave every day.

'I hope you realise that I've had to re-jig the shifts to accommodate all this nonsense?' Burnley said as they left his office. He took his old cap from the rack and turned to his secretary. 'Hold my calls, Mrs Wall. I'm hoping this won't take long.'

Mrs Wall flashed her boss another smile before glowering at Kember as he followed Burnley into the frigid pit yard.

The sleet seemed thicker and icier somehow, as if undecided whether to become hailstones or a full snowstorm. Kember turned up the collar of his overcoat and adjusted his fedora, preventing most of the sleet from reaching his neck. He thought a coal mine, especially this one, was a godforsaken place to be at any time of the year but a freezing day in January took the biscuit. He was about to follow Burnley to meet the men when a grumbling, cracking noise from their right stopped them in their tracks.

◆　◆　◆

Lizzie had risen at six o'clock while the shroud of night had still covered Scotney and the surrounding countryside. Her room had held a chill and she'd needed to wipe ice from the inside of the window where the condensation from her breathing had frozen. Outside, it had looked as if the previous day's rain and sleet had washed the colour from the world. Shivering, she'd dressed quickly, adding the leather motorcycle trousers she'd bought during a visit to Paris before the war, while on a flying tour of Europe with her father and brother. She followed up with gauntlets, her thick greatcoat, a silk scarf against her neck, and a woollen scarf to cover her nose and mouth. Descending the stairs to the warmth of the officers' lounge, where the fire had been kept going all night, she'd managed to grab a cup of scalding tea and a thick slice of hot toast and margarine for breakfast before venturing outside.

Her black Norton motorbike had looked almost invisible in the dark as she'd retrieved it from the motor shed, smiling at the sentry to ease her passage without awkward questions. Fearing being prevented from doing what she was about to do, she had wheeled the Norton as far as the gatehouse without switching on the ignition. A warder of the Air Ministry Wardens had stepped out of his guard post to offer assistance and she'd let him jump-start the motorbike for her. Her plea of being a woman lacking in strength and technique was readily accepted as the reason for her not having started it already. She'd got away quietly from the manor house and allowed the warder to feel as though he'd helped a damsel in distress. Satisfaction all round.

After pulling her woollen scarf over her nose and mouth, she had eased away from the gatehouse at a minute to seven and opened the throttle gently for the ride along Manor Lane down to Scotney village, taking care on the tarmac covered with thick frost. With first light due at around half past seven and sunrise at eight, if there was to be any sun, she hadn't expected any villager to be out and about but she'd known some would be breakfasting behind the dark shrouds of their blackout curtains and boards. After passing over the level crossing by the railway station, she'd ridden eastward until the village of Hawkhurst where the branch line terminated, then north towards Cranbrook. From there, it was a long drag north-east to Canterbury, passing through the occasional checkpoint manned by a local platoon of Home Guard.

It had been light for forty-five minutes by the time she'd reached the village of Challock at a quarter past eight, where a few souls were braving the cold, just as it had started sleeting. In contrast, many more people were abroad in their thick winter coats by the time she'd turned off near Chartham, to avoid all the checkpoints around Canterbury.

Now, as Lizzie negotiated the humpback bridge where Kember had said that he and Watson had escaped the killer lorry in the Austin, she spotted the twin towers of the colliery pithead in front of her. The temperature had dropped during her ride east, her leather trousers and gauntlets, thick greatcoat and woollen scarf barely able to protect her from the ice and wind chill. The sleet had thickened by the time she turned into the colliery entrance, used a wheel rut in the mud to navigate a path through the frozen puddles and drew up beside a Humber parked by an office building just as the door opened.

The two men leaving stopped as Lizzie lifted her goggles and pulled the scarf from her face, taking a lungful of cold air that seared her lungs.

With a jolt, she recognised one of them.

◆ ◆ ◆

'What the bloody hell—?' Kember said, recognising Lizzie at the same time, but unable to fathom why she was here.

'That's a nice welcome after the journey I've had,' Lizzie said.

'A colleague of yours?' Burnley asked, a soppy smile on his face.

'Excuse me one moment,' Kember replied, while glaring at her.

Burnley moved away as Kember approached Lizzie, who had already pulled the Norton on to its stand and stowed her helmet.

'What are you doing here?' he growled.

'I've come to help,' she replied brightly, with distracting flicks of her brown hair, coaxing it back into shape.

'I don't need your help.'

'That doesn't matter. I'm here to give it anyway.'

'I thought you were suspended,' Kember said, with a sideways glance towards Burnley who looked impatient.

'From flying, yes,' Lizzie said. 'Dallington wanted me gone and agreed I could have a few days' leave. So, I'll not be missed and I had nothing else to do.'

'Hartson will love this if he finds out you're here. The first time you helped me, he suspended me for a week and made sure I was kept on paperwork for a month. After the second time, he swore he'd keep me on traffic duties.'

'He didn't though, did he? I won't tell him if you won't. Your chief inspector will never know.'

Kember looked into her eyes. Perhaps it was the flat wintry light but they seemed bluer than he remembered and he couldn't look away.

'You can't send me back now,' she said. 'I got up early and came such a long way. You'll just have to get on with it . . . with me in tow.'

He looked at her in exasperation, trying to think of something logical and professional to say. The truth was, he was glad to see her and the prospect of working together again was one that brought some warmth on this freezing day. Her insights had been invaluable in the past and he found he was arguing with himself in his head, justifying why he should let her stay. But the decision was taken out of his hands as she brushed past him and introduced herself to Burnley.

The colliery owner seemed captivated by her, which gave Kember a strange feeling of annoyance, but at least everyone was now walking in the direction of the canteen, where Burnley had said the first interview could be conducted.

They entered the empty dining room with its unmanned servery and Kember hung his big coat over the back of his chair. He produced a small notebook and pen, and Lizzie, after tugging off her gauntlets, did the same.

'You didn't say where you're from,' Burnley said.

Lizzie smiled disarmingly. 'I'm an officer in the Air Transport Auxiliary, hence the uniform, but I've been seconded to the Kent County Constabulary for the duration of this investigation.'

Kember almost flinched at the ease with which the familiar lie left her lips.

'Officer Hayes possesses interpretive skills that have proved beneficial to us in the past,' he added, feeling both annoyed at her unilateral announcement of the extension of her involvement beyond today's interviews, and pleased at the same time.

Burnley gave Kember a quizzical smile. 'Getting a woman to do a man's job? I suppose that's the way of the world at the moment. Got a few of them in the screens building where the coal is cleaned and sorted, and doing other surface jobs. Needs must, and all that, but you'll never see a woman down the pit. All the same, might be worth you sticking to asking the questions, Inspector. I'm not sure the men will take kindly to being interviewed by a woman. I'll wheel the first one in then, shall I?'

Seeing Lizzie's jaw muscles tighten, Kember said, 'If you wouldn't mind,' before she could explode in fury.

'Bloody cheek,' Lizzie said as soon as Burnley had left.

'Outside of wartime, mining is exclusively male,' Kember said, realising his mistake immediately as Lizzie turned on him.

'Women have worked in mines for centuries. Whole families, in fact, children included. Do you know how many women were employed by collieries a hundred years ago?'

'No,' Kember admitted.

'Nor do I exactly, but it's more than a couple of thousand. Many of them went down the pit until the law changed banning children under ten and all women from working underground.'

'This isn't the time or place to have that argument. We've got a murder to solve.'

'I know that,' Lizzie snapped. 'It's galling, that's all.'

Kember reached into his jacket and drew out the cellophane-wrapped playing cards. 'Here. What do you make of these?'

Lizzie took the cards. 'I'm not sure.' She turned them over. 'If you found them on a table in a pub, you wouldn't give them a second look.'

'They were in Morris's belongings.'

Lizzie held them up to the light. 'It's unusual for a victim to have two of the same thing on them so they could be ritualistic, they could be calling cards, or they could mean nothing. Are you sure they're important?'

'DI Watson seems to think so; that and the unsatisfactory answers the men and doctors gave him,' Kember said, taking them back as the first miner brought a blast of cold air into the canteen. 'At any rate, he managed to convince Chief Inspector Brignull, which is why we're here.'

CHAPTER SEVEN

Lizzie looked the man straight in the eye as he clumped across the wooden floor in heavy boots but he failed to return the challenge and looked away as he removed his cap and sat.

Kember introduced himself and Lizzie as Burnley made a show of sitting nearby, scraping his chair out from under a table before sitting heavily.

'And you are?' Kember asked the man.

'Harold Quayle,' he replied. 'But everyone calls me Harry.'

'Harry,' Kember confirmed. 'What do you do here?'

'I'm a fireman.'

Lizzie made a note.

'Not the kind you're thinking of,' Quayle said. 'I'm one of the deputies who does the daily checks underground with Morris. Sorry, did.'

'You're one of the deputies,' Kember echoed, remembering Lizzie's technique for putting someone at ease. 'How many are there?'

'Two. Me and Paul Ramsey on the fore shift with Chris Morris the overman. Another team of three on the back shift.'

Lizzie saw Kember nodding his understanding as she made more notes.

'What can you tell me about the night Christopher Morris died?' Kember said.

'Nothing more than I told the other inspector.' Quayle's gaze did not deviate from Kember. 'We all went to sleep but he never woke up.'

She saw the man's grip on his cap tighten, the rest of his body frozen.

'Did he not cry out in the night?' Kember continued. 'Moan and groan, perhaps?'

'No. Nothing. Mining's a hard game and we're always exhausted. When we've got a rest day, we often have a drink and that puts us to sleep too.'

'What about the days leading up to that night?'

Quayle frowned. 'What d'you mean?'

'Any complaints about feeling unwell?' Kember said.

'Yeah, of course. They complained of being tired, having headaches all the time and being dizzy. Two nights before he died, Morris said he was sick. The doc said it wasn't flu or poisoning from the canteen food so we all thought they stayed underground too long, too often. Didn't expect him to have a heart attack though.'

Lizzie and Kember exchanged glances. She hadn't had time to read the case-file but his expression told her something was wrong about what had just been said.

'What did you do with Morris and Ramsey?' Kember asked.

'What?' Quayle's gaze flicked to Lizzie for the first time and back to Kember just as quickly.

Lizzie noticed a slight flush on the man's cheeks, even though it wasn't that warm in the empty canteen.

'What did your work entail?' Kember said.

'Oh, safety checks,' Quayle said.

Lizzie saw the muscles of the man's face relax now he was on familiar ground.

'The deputies have a district each,' Quayle continued. 'That's an area underground that they're responsible for. I would make sure the tunnels and drifts were safe in my district and the equipment was well maintained. Morris would go with Ramsey to do the same.'

'Did you all work the same shifts?' Kember asked.

Quayle nodded. 'Except the week before when I'd sprained my ankle. You can't work underground with an injury so I did surface work for a few days.'

'And that will be in the accident book, I suppose?'

'Yes, it will.' Burnley was on his feet. 'This is a legitimate and well-run operation, Inspector. Any incident, large or small, is meticulously recorded and kept. We have the best safety record of any mine in Kent. Everyone says so.' He raised his chin defiantly, his moustache sticking out like porcupine quills. 'If it wasn't for the odd niggle here and there, I'd say it was unblemished.'

What a ridiculous statement, Lizzie thought. The *odd niggle here and there* meant more than one, and more than one wasn't anywhere near being unblemished, especially when one of the niggles was a dead man.

Kember had paused to stare at his notebook and Lizzie could see his face creased with annoyance at the interruption. She suspected he wanted to eject Burnley from the room, a move she knew could prove counterproductive. They needed to speak to the other men from the dormitory and perhaps look around the mine workings, so antagonising the person giving them access wasn't a good strategy. Better to reset the ground rules in their favour than be ejected themselves from the colliery. That would delay the investigation until the wheel of legal machinery turned another revolution.

Kember looked over at Burnley.

'If you insist on interrupting my interviews, Mr Burnley, I'm afraid I'll have to conduct them without anyone else in attendance.'

A darker cloud than those outside covered Burnley's face.

Lizzie's expression was almost a match. She accepted that Kember was the detective but she wasn't sitting here beside him for her own amusement or health. She was taking notes, assessing the man's answers and body language, and interpreting his whole character for the benefit of the investigation. She had to accept that the bigots of the AIB could get away with suspending her, and Group Captain Dallington with wanting her banished, but she'd be damned if she'd let herself be ignored as if she didn't exist by a man like Kember, someone whom she'd helped solve two cases in the last few months. Lizzie could contain herself no longer and leant forward to block the line of sight between Kember and Burnley, remembering what Geraldine had once told her about using *womanly wiles*.

'I'm afraid we do need peace and quiet while interviewing potential witnesses, Mr Burnley,' Lizzie said, her voice a soothing balm. 'So that important details aren't missed or misconstrued.' With a slight tilt of her head, she flashed an encouraging smile and he sat down again, although his expression changed little. Lizzie turned back to Kember and could have sworn she saw him flinch under the stony look she gave him. That pleased her, almost making her laugh despite herself. *Point made*, she thought.

'Mr Quayle,' Kember continued. 'Harry. Did you get on with Christopher Morris?'

Quayle shrugged. 'He was a workmate, not a friend, but we did what workmates do. We had a beer, played cards and darts.'

'Cards ever get ripped, did they?'

'What?' Quayle frowned.

'Never mind,' Kember said. 'What was he like?'

'He liked a flutter on the gee-gees, on anything really, but hated losing. He could be a difficult man to get to play a straight game. A bit of a pillock, if you ask me.'

'But he was also your boss.'

'He was.' Quayle gave a thin smile. 'That doesn't mean he was the best man for the job. He used to be a fireman too but was promoted when another bloke, a reservist, was called up for the army.'

'How did that make you feel?'

'How d'you think?' He glanced at Burnley, who seemed on the verge of exploding. 'I wasn't best pleased, but you've got to get on with it, haven't you? Life is unfair. That's just the way it is.'

'That's enough,' Burnley said, leaping to his feet again. 'We've all been through this before with Inspector Watson and I can't see the point of repeating ourselves. I have work to do and important people to see.'

'I'd calm down if I were you, Mr Burnley,' Kember said, closing his notebook. 'Inspector Watson led the investigation into the death of Christopher Morris on the basis that it was probably the result of natural causes. Having now conducted a second post-mortem, it seems the victim didn't die of a heart attack brought on by physical exhaustion after all.'

'What?' Burnley's face fell.

'He died of carbon monoxide poisoning.'

Quayle looked at Burnley and back to Kember, his eyes wide and scared.

'But what about the mine?' Burnley flicked a look at Quayle, then Kember. 'What will you do now?'

'What I've been sent here to do,' Kember said. 'Establish whether the death was a tragic accident, or not, and whether anyone is culpable.'

'What do you mean, culpable?' Burnley said, a slight tremor in his voice.

'I need to know whether anyone was responsible in any way for the death of Morris, whether deliberate or through negligence and—'

'Deliberate?' Burnley cut in. 'Are you suggesting he was murdered?'

Lizzie noted that the mine owner had ignored the suggestion it could be negligence and his face had lost some of its colour.

'It may be something or nothing, Mr Burnley,' Kember continued. 'We don't want this to take any longer than it has to and I have many questions so we'd appreciate you getting on with your day job, while we get on with ours.' His voice and smile did not carry the warmth of Lizzie's.

Burnley stared at Kember for a few seconds, then gave a curt nod and ushered Quayle from the canteen. He paused in the open doorway, a flurry of what looked like snow swirling at his feet. 'This place will be gearing up to feed the hungry hordes shortly so you can't stay in here. I have a meeting with the mayor in Canterbury so you can use my office until this afternoon. Just make sure you leave it as you find it.' The door closed behind him as he left without waiting for a response.

Kember turned to Lizzie.

'I didn't mean to imply—'

'Never mind that,' Lizzie cut across him, not interested in his apologies or Burnley's attempt at a dramatic exit. 'All that about unblemished records and this being the safest mine in Kent. It's tommyrot, and if he can attempt to manipulate the truth so illogically and blatantly, what else might he try to distort? He's far more concerned about the so-called important people he has to see and about the reputation of the mine than the welfare of his workers.'

'Yes, I got that,' Kember said. 'Although a sizeable number of businessmen would think the same way. Profit and reputation are everything.'

'He can point his chin at us as much as he likes but did you notice what was missing?'

'What do you mean?' Kember frowned.

Lizzie's mind was racing in that way that often threatened to jumble her thoughts.

'Burnley didn't ask the obvious questions when you suggested Morris might have been murdered. In my time conducting criminal research with Oxford prison and the police, I learnt the first question a person asks about a murder is *How did he die?* which we know. The second is *Who did it?* or *Who do you suspect?* but Burnley wasn't interested.' Lizzie shook her head. 'After that, it's natural for shock to cause a person to slip into denial and try to offer an alternative explanation; *Are you sure he didn't slip?* rather than *Was he pushed?* but Burnley said nothing. Was that because he didn't care or because he already knew?'

'You think he's the murderer?' Kember said.

Lizzie sighed. 'I'm saying his behaviour is odd, even for a cold-hearted businessman. As for Harry Quayle, he looked scared and gripped his hat as if trying to keep it all in, although being under the glare of his boss wouldn't have helped. His body gave him away, though. When you tell the truth it can tumble out of you because you know what happened and you don't have to think too much except about specific details. If you really try to concentrate on something unfamiliar, like getting a lie right, you need to think about every part of that deception. Your brain has to use a lot of its power to the point it can almost forget it's got a whole body to run. Quayle's body went as still as a statue at one point.'

'Interesting,' Kember said. 'Quayle is the third mine worker I've spoken to and their stories match. I could almost swear some of the words and phrases they used are the same.'

'I thought I saw something cross your mind earlier,' Lizzie said. 'But it's not surprising that they've been talking to each other and comparing accounts since the death.'

'It's not just that.' Kember scratched the end of his nose. 'They seem *very* similar to the statements taken by Watson and his men immediately after Morris died.'

'Ah, that changes things. It's fine if the original accounts are similar but not exact because that could denote the recollection of a shared truth. People are notoriously bad at noticing and remembering. They pick up on different things, with some of those details seeming contradictory at the time while the majority will corroborate the others. Of course, if the details are too similar, or even too dissimilar, especially if they've become so after several days, that could indicate a shared untruth.'

Kember sighed. 'All I know is, I'm not being told everything at present and I need to know why. What is it that's missing?'

◆ ◆ ◆

Tiny flakes of white fell around them as Lizzie and Kember walked back to Burnley's office, the drab pithead slowly being whitewashed and the tops of the spoil-heaps already looking as though cream had been poured over helpings of leftover steamed pudding.

A chorus of wolf whistles drew Kember's attention and he saw three grinning, grubby-faced miners standing in the distance by a large rail truck piled high with coal, already jumping back to work after a gruff shout from a nearby foreman. Kember turned to speak to Lizzie but she'd strode ahead. As he caught up to her, he saw her tight lips, jaw muscles taut with clenching teeth, and eyes that threatened to ignite the coal spontaneously.

'What's wrong?' he asked.

Lizzie stopped and rounded on him.

'Why should anything be wrong,' she snarled, forcing him to take a half-step backwards. 'Why should three grown men making lewd noises be of any concern?'

'They didn't mean anything by it,' Kember said, already feeling the previously solid ground beneath him begin to shift in that way it always did when Lizzie was angry. 'Everyone does it,' he said with less confidence. 'They were paying you a compliment.'

'Compliment?' Lizzie snapped. 'I'm wearing a massive coat, thick boots and sporting wind-blown hair that looks like a bird's nest but they still think I'm fair game because I'm a woman, leering at me in broad daylight, in the open, in a workplace. If you had fifty-year-old dockers' wives calling out sexual innuendos to you, wouldn't you be embarrassed or worried?'

'I'd be amused,' Kember said, knowing immediately that he'd said the wrong thing again.

'And that's the difference between men and women,' Lizzie said. 'The perception of threat. The chances of you being whistled at, followed one night, dragged into a dark alleyway and raped are slim. To me and all women, it's a distinct possibility, especially in the blackout.'

'I don't think—'

'No, you don't,' Lizzie said. 'How many rapes have you dealt with in your time in the police?'

Kember couldn't recall off the top of his head, and wondered where this was going. 'I don't know. Two or three a year. Most never made it past the front desk through lack of evidence and only a couple went to court. It's hard to prosecute when it's one person's word against another.' Kember could hear the apologetic note in his voice.

'Exactly,' Lizzie said, her cheeks flushed with anger and cold. 'Do you know how many rapes are recorded every year? Around a hundred or so. For the whole country. That doesn't add up, does it, and do you know why? Because of all the others you didn't get to hear about when the woman was too scared, or dead. How many wives and girlfriends said *no* but were forced by their husbands and boyfriends? How many desk sergeants didn't take a woman seriously because they thought she was drunk or dressed inappropriately and asking for it?' She pointed to where the miners had been. 'You think a wolf whistle is harmless, and I admit most of them will be no more than embarrassing, but it's the thin end of the wedge that allows a rapist to walk free.'

With that, she turned on her heel and strode across the pit yard of icy, coal-black puddles and up the office steps, leaving Kember to hurry in her wake.

Kember was glad they'd be in the smaller, warmer confines of Burnley's office but the mood of Mrs Wall the secretary was little different to Lizzie's. Her frosty reception made it clear that she considered their presence an affront, her taut expression as grey as today's twinset and as bleak as the weather. She put down the paperknife she'd been using to slit open a large envelope and disappeared into Burnley's office, ostensibly to ensure it was ready, although Kember suspected she was moving things out of their way so they couldn't be interfered with. Lizzie laid her gauntlets on a small table near where a paraffin heater stood in the corner of the room, took a framed photograph from Mrs Wall's desk and looked at it for a few seconds before showing Kember. The familiar formal pose of a family photograph taken in a studio consisted of the mother wearing a bonnet, sitting on a chair with a young curly-haired boy on her lap. An older girl with her hair in curls was standing next to her mother with the father in his best suit behind them. All but the young boy had spectacles.

'Explains the prissy attitude, don't you think,' Lizzie said, hastily replacing the photograph as Mrs Wall returned.

As soon as the secretary had shepherded them into Burnley's office with a spare chair, she pulled the door closed with enough force to suggest being sealed inside a tomb. Kember opened his mouth to make a comment but Lizzie swept her arm around, indicating all the framed paraphernalia.

'Oh my God!' she exclaimed. 'Even from that short interview, I could tell the man is a fully fledged narcissist. Exaggeration, pride, inability to accept criticism, obsession with what people see and think of him and his achievements, lack of sympathy and empathy for his workers, a jumped-up opinion of himself and his own importance.'

'You liked him then?' Kember joked, glad Lizzie's focus had shifted.

Lizzie glared at him. 'Have you seen all this?' She waved a hand at the display again.

'Yes,' he said. 'I saw it yesterday and thought it a bit much.'

'A bit much? This place is second only to having his name up in lights in Piccadilly Circus.' She looked at the photographs. 'Even given the bigwigs and the rich and famous, the majority of the photographs are of himself talking, looking smug and receiving accolades. This is a man full of his own importance and achievements, but not accepting of the fact that both were probably reached through the efforts of others. As I said, a classic narcissist.'

'Does that make him a killer though?' Kember said, manoeuvring the visitor's chair next to Burnley's behind the desk.

'No, but it doesn't rule him out either,' Lizzie said. 'And it makes it much more difficult to break through that air of entitlement and invincibility. Even if he's not the killer, he won't want to admit that such a thing as murder could happen on his premises. In Burnley's mind, the death of Christopher Morris must have been the man's own fault.'

Kember positioned the chair from Mrs Wall's office on the other side of the desk. 'I must admit, he's been quite abrasive on the two occasions I've met him, and I say that knowing people like Group Captain Dallington and Chief Inspector Hartson. Even DI Watson had little good to say about the man. I can't see why he would want to kill one of his own men though. Why not just sack him?'

'Perhaps this was his way of doing that.' Lizzie studied another photograph.

Kember pondered that for a moment. Quite apart from the risk of being hanged for murder, it seemed ridiculous for a man like Burnley to court bad publicity on a national scale, as a murder would surely do, rather than endure a little local discomfort by sacking someone. Perhaps Morris hadn't been murdered after all. As Victor Young had said, staying underground for too long and too often was the logical explanation, and covering that up by coercing the colliery doctor into certifying a heart attack made much more sense.

Kember voiced his opinion to Lizzie but she shrugged it off.

'It'll be interesting to hear what the other miner has to say,' Lizzie said. 'The one who got ill but survived.'

'Paul Ramsey?' Kember said.

'Yes. He must be feeling scared that if someone did get to Christopher Morris, they might have been after him too.'

Kember kicked himself. He should have thought of that; he was the bloody detective, after all. One man had died but there had been two victims. Had it been Ramsey's misfortune to become collateral damage, or his good fortune not to have died as well?

A knock on the door announced the arrival of the next interviewee and a short, thin man in an ill-fitting suit entered. Mrs Wall pulled the door shut, leaving him stranded at the end of the office, clutching a knitted woollen bobble-hat in his hands.

Kember indicated the chair. 'Please do sit, Mr . . . ?'

'Ramsey, sir,' the man said. He walked forward and sat. 'Paul Ramsey.'

Kember exchanged a glance with Lizzie.

'Are you expected somewhere, Mr Ramsey?' Kember said, indicating the man's suit.

'No, sir.' Ramsey smiled and laughed nervously. 'When I was told the police wanted to speak to me, I thought I'd better spruce myself up.'

If the man respected the police enough to wear his Sunday best, Kember thought keeping names on a formal footing, rather than calling him Paul, might elicit better results. He smiled back at the miner and consulted his notebook.

'You're a fireman on the fore shift and you worked with overman Christopher Morris and another fireman, Harry Quayle. Is that correct?'

'That's right,' Ramsey said. 'We're the team on the fore shift.' He squeezed his woolly hat. 'Were.'

Kember noted the hesitancy in the man's speech, as though he was measuring his words before speaking them.

'Can you tell me about your work underground?' Kember asked.

'Of course. We carried out safety checks before the fore shift. Harry and I were responsible for separate areas of the tunnels and coal face.'

'The districts,' Kember stated.

'That's right, sir.' Ramsey seemed impressed by Kember's knowledge.

'And what did Mr Morris do?'

'He was in charge, making sure we did our jobs and double-checking here and there.'

'How long did he stay with each of you?'

'With me? All the bloody—'

The sudden swearing surprised Kember. Ramsey seemed such a timid man and had been relaxing as the questioning progressed. Now the miner sat up stiff, his left hand gripping his other wrist.

'Go on, please,' Kember soothed.

Ramsey took a deep breath. 'Let's just say, he didn't seem to like the way I did things. Harry was the more experienced anyway, so Morris always came with me to check my district.'

'How did that make you feel?'

'How did that make me feel? A bit pissed off, excuse my French, miss.'

Lizzie smiled.

'I bet,' Kember said, remembering Chief Inspector Hartson's scrutiny of his every case. 'What did you think of him, in general?'

'To be honest, he wouldn't have been my choice as an overman. He wasn't much of a mate, even before he got promoted over Harry. Harry was more experienced and ten times better at his job. You want to have a word with Vic Young, he's in the fan house, about an injury to his brother. Nasty bloke, was Morris. Ask Terry Armstrong in the winding house about his missus. And he was a card cheat, by all accounts. Took Eddie Pine for hundreds of pounds, so Eddie says, but he couldn't prove it.'

'A card cheat?' Kember said, thinking this sounded promising. 'Any cards ever get ripped in anger?'

'Ripped in—? What the heck are you talking about, sir?' Ramsey said, quizzically. 'You lay them on a table, not throw them at each other.'

Kember could see Lizzie scribbling in her notebook but she had seemed to keep her eyes on Ramsey all the while he was talking. For his own part, Kember had noted the animosity of Ramsey towards Morris and the suggestion that he was universally disliked. That wasn't unusual in any job. In Kember's experience, every workplace had the people you liked working with and those who rubbed you up the wrong way, intentionally or not. While there had to be leaders and followers, thinkers and doers, an imbalance could definitely lead to fireworks.

It was time to come to the crux.

'Can you tell me what happened in the days before Mr Morris died?' Kember looked Ramsey straight in the eye.

'Nothing much to tell, sir,' Ramsey said, his gaze fixed at a point beyond Kember's left shoulder. 'We did our checks, managed the work underground, came off shift, showered, ate, drank, slept and started again the next day.'

'I meant about feeling unwell.'

'Ah, well, we started getting a few headaches, that's me and Morris. It was the run-up to Christmas and the new year and we'd had a few bevvies so you expect the odd hangover, don't you?' Ramsey gave a slight shake of his head. 'Trouble was, new year had been and gone and we still kept getting headaches. Started feeling a bit sick too.'

'I understand there are a number of gases that can build up in a mine,' Kember said.

'The damps? Yes, sir.'

'Could those have caused your headaches?' Kember was wondering whether lack of safety care killed Morris after all.

'Any of them can give you a headache.' Ramsey rubbed the back of the hand holding his bobble-hat. 'We have Davy lamps and canaries to check for a build-up of gas to make sure it's safe for us and the men to work down there. Firedamp is methane gas, the one that causes the most explosions. The Davy lamp flame gets bigger. Black or chokedamp is carbon dioxide. It can suffocate you so the flame gets smaller. Whitedamp is carbon monoxide. It will knock over a canary before it does a man. Hydrogen sulphide is called stinkdamp because it smells like rotten eggs. It's very rare but it can make you keel over, suffocate you or explode. You can smell it's there, though.'

'You carried those, did you?' Lizzie asked. 'Lamps and canaries?'

The sudden question from Lizzie made Ramsey's eyebrows shoot up in surprise.

'Always,' Ramsey said. 'Harry and I had one each.'

'Was there ever any gas?'

Ramsey's shoulders twitched. 'Gas is always there but that's what the ventilation fan is for, to suck stale air and gases out one way and draw fresh air in the other. The Davy lamps and canaries are there to find any pockets the air flow has missed and to warn of any build-up of gas to a dangerous level.'

'Like the eddies in a river,' Lizzie said.

'Sort of.'

'Harry Quayle was on the same shift as you but he never felt ill?' Kember said, puzzled as to why only two of the three men would get headaches.

'That's right, sir,' Ramsey replied.

'Did that not strike you as odd?'

Ramsey rubbed the back of his hand again before answering.

'No, sir. The food here's rubbish and we've had flu going round so we just thought it was something to do with that.' Another shake of the head. 'Was it whitedamp that killed him and nearly killed me?'

Kember wondered whether the slight-looking man in front of him could cope with a murderer living and working at the mine, but the cat was out of the bag so there was no point in deception.

'We believe it was someone rather than something,' Kember said.

'Someone?' Ramsey's eyes widened almost imperceptibly and he swallowed hard. 'Who?'

'That's what we're trying to find out, Mr Ramsey.'

◆ ◆ ◆

Having escorted Ramsey from the office, Lizzie shut the door and turned back to Kember.

'Only half of that was the truth,' she said.

Kember nodded. 'I wouldn't be surprised. Few people tell the whole truth to the police because they all want to come across as good people, but we all have our secrets.'

Lizzie looked at Kember askance. *What did he mean by that?* At that moment she realised how little she knew of this man she was drawn to and how little that seemed to matter.

'But nothing Ramsey said seemed out of kilter with the facts,' Kember continued. 'Despite the tension between Ramsey and Morris, there was nothing in the case-file to suggest they ever came to blows. They and Quayle went underground together for the inspections on the fore shift and it sounded like Morris kept an eye on Ramsey for most of the day. They must have been near to each other for long periods so perhaps that's why they got ill within a few weeks and Quayle didn't. What if it was just the gas that killed Morris after all?'

'You don't believe that?' Lizzie said, trying to urge him to continue his good old-fashioned digging. 'Why did none of the other miners become ill? Yes, those three were together every day but there must have been others around them.'

Kember shrugged. 'Ramsey said gas collects in pockets and Victor Young implied exposure over time was lethal, like the old Chinese torture of death from a thousand cuts.'

'Maybe so, but Ramsey also said the Davy lamps and canaries weren't affected.'

Lizzie stood staring at him but he wasn't looking at her, choosing instead to doodle in his notebook. He'd already drawn a Davy lamp and was attempting a canary. She decided to say nothing else, just wait for him to fill the silence and say the next thing. He rubbed the end of his nose and Lizzie relaxed, recognising the gesture of concentration.

He looked up at her eventually. 'All right, I agree it doesn't add up.'

She'd thought he'd succumbed to the obvious solution, but was relieved he hadn't resigned himself to accepting a simple explanation after all. In her opinion, there wasn't one.

'Rather than keep it to yourself,' she said, sitting opposite him, 'why don't you tell me what's in your detective's head and I tell you what's in my psychologist's brain? Before the next man arrives.'

Kember looked at her quizzically for a moment and sighed.

'All right. It's clear that Ramsey was rankled by being under daily scrutiny from a man he disliked, on top of the promotion of Christopher Morris over Harry Quayle. Quayle wasn't enamoured with Morris either, and it came across quite starkly that some of the other mine workers also had reasons to dislike him. For the sake of thoroughness, I think we need to discover more about the problems Ramsey hinted at regarding Victor Young's brother and Terry Armstrong's wife. They mentioned nothing when I first spoke to them, but I suppose Burnley's presence was an effective gag. And we should ask Eddie Pine about those card games.'

'I've been thinking about those cards and I still can't fathom why he'd have two the same,' Lizzie said. 'Perhaps they were reminders, or even mementoes of big wins. Nothing to do with the case at all.'

Kember tapped his notebook. 'One other thing nobody has mentioned yet is the relationship between Burnley and Morris.'

Lizzie heard a noise behind her and turned but there was nothing there. She heard it again and motioned for Kember to carry on as she stood.

Kember frowned but continued. 'Burnley doesn't seem the kind of boss who gets overly concerned with people unless they have a direct impact on his business or personal life, like Morris dying.'

Lizzie had reached the door and she quickly turned the knob, whipping the door open. Mrs Wall stood there, holding an empty glass the wrong way up and looking startled and guilty.

The secretary recovered, waving the glass in the air. 'Would you like something to drink before the next man arrives? We have Ribena.'

'Thank you, that's so kind,' Lizzie said, unable to keep a hint of sarcasm from her voice.

Mrs Wall gave her an embarrassed smile and retreated. Lizzie closed the door and returned to her seat, lowering her voice as she spoke.

'We'll have to keep an eye on that one.'

'I suspect she's been told to do the same to us,' Kember said. 'Ignore her.'

Lizzie thought that keeping an eye out was one thing but eavesdropping with your ear to a glass against the door was tantamount to spying. Was Mrs Wall acting the loyal secretary, doing as she was told? Perhaps she was hoping to impress her boss for a pay rise or some kind of advancement? Could her actions be as basic as a mercenary listening in for extra cash? Or was there another reason? Something at the back of Lizzie's queue of thoughts niggled away, vying for attention. Secretaries were the gatekeepers to the inner offices of businesses, government ministries and even royal chambers. They always knew more about what went on than anyone else, so Lizzie thought it best to keep Mrs Wall in her sights for now.

'Anyway, you were going to unload your psychologist's brain,' Kember said.

Lizzie looked at Kember, having almost forgotten she was in the room with him, took a breath and refocused her mind.

'You have to look for the signs, not just the language,' Lizzie said. 'It's what the body says without your knowledge, your consent or your control, rather than the words it speaks. For example, when Ramsey arrived, wearing his suit instead of his ordinary clothes, he clutched his bobble-hat in his lap, like a child clings to a teddy bear for comfort, and you could hear the nervousness in his laugh. The man seemed scared, although I don't know whether that was because of us or what he knew.'

'*Did* he know anything?' Kember asked.

'More than he told us,' Lizzie said. 'Straight after he swore for the first time, he did this.' She gripped her right wrist with her left hand. 'That's as defensive as crossing your arms and legs, forming a barrier across your front. He did it just after he revealed his dislike for Morris. Of course, he couldn't go back after that and had to explain himself. When you asked how he felt, he repeated the question before swearing again.'

'The swearing is significant?' Kember asked, looking puzzled.

'No.' Lizzie sighed, irritated that Kember had learnt nothing from her. 'Repeating a question makes it sound as though you want to make sure you've heard right but what it really does is give you time to think. It indicates a lie is coming.'

Kember consulted his notes. 'Feeling "a bit pissed off" doesn't sound like a lie to me.'

'But it could be,' Lizzie said. 'What if it's an understatement and Ramsey was a little more than that? What if he'd come to the end of his tether and had enough? Enough to kill Morris?'

'With mine gas? How?'

'That's your domain, as Headley would say.'

Kember made a disapproving face. 'Don't you start.'

Lizzie let out a little laugh but her mind refocused again just as quickly. 'After Ramsey repeated the question, he went on to voice his opinion of Morris, telling us about the possible grievances of the other men on the fore shift. Then he talked about the gases and what they were called.'

'Surely that was in response to my questions?' Kember said.

'Yes, but it was the high level of detail,' Lizzie explained, trying to remain patient. 'When he was on firm ground and imparting his knowledge, he over-explained, but at other times he glossed over, as though there was more that he didn't want us to know. Did you notice him rubbing the back of one hand with the other some-times?' Kember nodded as Lizzie demonstrated. 'That's like patting someone on the back to encourage them before they do something difficult or unpleasant. Rubbing someone's hand is reassuring, and he was comforting himself to keep himself calm.'

'You got all this from a wrist grip and hand rub?' Kember said, with raised eyebrows.

'Of course,' Lizzie said. 'I've told you before that the rest of your body talks as much as your mouth. When he described drinking at Christmas, he shook his head. His brain was telling his body that his mouth was lying. When you asked whether they ever detected gas, his shoulders twitched. That was his brain giving the game away again. A mini-shrug revealing he wasn't sure he was saying the right thing, or too much.'

At that moment, a knock on the door halted their discussion.

CHAPTER EIGHT

The door to Burnley's office opened and Mrs Wall brought in a jug of blackcurrant Ribena and two glasses.

'Mr Pine is here to see you, Inspector,' she announced, ignoring Lizzie as she left.

Lizzie re-took her seat next to Kember as the miner was shown in and the door pulled shut again. Kember saw her smile at the man, and marvelled at how quickly she could change her demeanour to fit the occasion.

'Is it still snowing, Mr Pine?' she asked.

'No, ma'am,' Pine said, undoing the buttons of his donkey jacket which was speckled with ice. 'Sleeting again.' He gave her a puzzled look. 'No offence, but I didn't think women could be detectives.'

'I'm not a detective,' Lizzie said. 'I'm a psychologist helping the police.'

Pine stiffened and his face took on a look of suspicion. 'I didn't think they could be head doctors neither. To be honest, I'm not keen on having my noggin examined, especially by a woman. No offence.' He looked at Kember. 'And I bet you're the bugger that got my shifts changed. 'Scuse my French.'

To establish his authority and forestall any resistance to Lizzie staying in the room, Kember completed the proper introductions and pitched straight into his questioning. He established that Pine was the fore shift onsetter, the man responsible for the cage at the bottom of the pit shaft. He had been present during the safety checks, the fourth member of the underground team that everyone else had failed to mention. Like the others in the dormitory, Pine had seen nothing suspicious on the night Morris had died, nor anything unusual in the days and weeks leading up to it.

'Each day seemed normal enough,' Pine said, shaking his head.

'Normal, as in . . . ?'

'After checking with the fan house that the fan had been running to clean the air, Chris Morris, Harry Quayle and Paul Ramsey would ride down with me in the cage. Quayle would go off to check his district, Morris would go with Ramsey to check his.'

'Always?' Kember asked, remembering the interviews with Quayle and Ramsey.

Pine nodded suspiciously. 'Yeah.'

'Wasn't that unusual?' Kember said. 'Shouldn't he have divided his time equally between Ramsey and Quayle?'

Pine's gaze flicked nervously between Kember and Lizzie. 'I suppose so, strictly speaking,' he said, crossing his arms.

Kember noted the movement. Another defensive gesture, perhaps? Pine's lips were pressed into a thin line, a clear sign that he thought he'd said something out of turn.

'Then why did he neglect his safety duties to stay with Ramsey?' Kember said.

'I suppose it was because Quayle was the more experienced fireman,' said Pine. 'I don't know, really. I wasn't with them because I stayed at the shaft bottom, operating the cage. I'm good at my job, keep my head down and just get on with it.'

The little shoulder twitch and minute head shake that accompanied Pine's statement surprised Kember. If Lizzie hadn't pointed them out in Ramsey, he would never have noticed. Kember decided to not play games.

'Or was it because they didn't like each other?' Kember stared at Pine until the miner looked away.

Kember let the silence work its magic.

'Quayle didn't like him either,' Pine said. 'Nobody did.'

And there it is, Kember thought, exchanging a glance with Lizzie. That confirmed what Quayle and Ramsey had said. Morris had it in for Ramsey on a daily basis, which would have ground anyone down over time. On its own, was that motive enough for murder, if murder it turned out to be?

'What did Morris do that made him so unlikable?' Lizzie said, in the soft encouraging voice Kember had heard her use on suspects before.

Pine looked at her and sighed, seemingly resigned. 'Morris was a bully to Ramsey, always nagging at him and pulling him up for tiny things, but it was more about what he didn't do. For as long as I've known him, he's always been crap at his job – sorry, I meant slapdash – and I think he got promoted above his ability, if I'm brutally honest.'

'Slapdash in what way?' Lizzie pressed.

'Always cutting corners. Neglectful. Being on shift with Morris was always a worry because he didn't do things the right way, he did them the quick and easy way. Everyone else had to take up his slack just to keep themselves safe.' Pine looked at Kember. 'Look, I don't understand why we're going over this again. Morris died of a heart attack, didn't he? What's all this got to do with it?'

'We're going over it again, Mr Pine, because Christopher Morris didn't die of a heart attack as first thought,' Kember said, watching Pine's face for a reaction. 'He died from whitedamp poisoning.'

'He died from whitedamp?' Pine said, his eyes widening.

There was the repetition preceding a lie but Kember saw none of the other signs of shock he'd expect to see if the revelation had been news to him. So, Pine already knew something else had killed Morris.

'The cause of Morris's death was confirmed by a second post-mortem,' Kember said.

'That's impossible,' Pine continued. 'None of the other miners, the hewers and so on, were taken ill.'

And there was the lie.

'That's not true though, Mr Pine. Is it?' Kember said. 'Ramsey, with whom Morris stayed most of the time, was also ill.' He saw a flash of fright in the man's eyes.

'I – I know Ramsey was under the weather but Quayle and I were fine,' Pine recovered. 'We all thought it was flu. How could it have been whitedamp if it affected no one else?'

Bugger, thought Kember. That was the big question he couldn't answer, and Pine and the others knew it.

Lizzie was tapping her pencil on the desk, appearing absent-minded. 'What happened between Chris Morris and Terry Armstrong?' Lizzie said.

Again, that flash of fear in Pine's eyes.

'Nothing much,' Pine said. 'Armstrong thought Morris was mucking about with his missus.'

'And was he?'

Pine shrugged. 'Morris liked to wind people up and often boasted that he could have any woman he wanted, any time he wanted. It was something and nothing, if you ask me. You'll have to ask Armstrong.'

'We will,' Kember said. 'And while we're at it, we'll ask about the money he allegedly swindled out of you at cards.'

'How did you—?' Pine's mouth dropped open.

So, that's true too, Kember thought. 'Did you ever tear up the cards and throw them on the table, or at him, in anger?'

'I'm not that kind of man, Inspector.'

'How much did you lose?'

'That's between me and Morris.'

'Was. In case you'd forgotten, the man who cheated you is dead, possibly murdered.'

'You think it was me?' Pine said, leaping to his feet and knocking a glass. Fortunately, it didn't tip over and splashed only a little Ribena on Burnley's desk.

'Mrs Wall has a cloth,' Kember said to Lizzie. 'Please,' he added, remembering she wasn't his subordinate.

Lizzie hurried to the door.

'I didn't have anything to do with it, honest,' Pine protested.

Lizzie returned in seconds with two dusters and threw one to Kember. 'She's not there but I found these in a drawer. The only clean ones.'

'I wouldn't murder anyone for a few quid.' Pine looked really scared now, not knowing which of them to look at.

His whiney voice had already begun to irritate Kember, so he banished him to the outer office while he and Lizzie ensured the purple drink didn't stain Burnley's desk.

With the door closed, Lizzie said, 'Well?'

'More half-truths,' Kember replied, wiping stray drips from the edge of the desk. 'I noticed those nods and shoulder twitches you said to look out for. He knows more than he's saying, although he corroborated the bullying of Ramsey, the adultery with Armstrong's wife, and suffering himself at the hands of Morris the card cheat.'

He'd have to speak to Young and Armstrong again, with Lizzie present this time, but that hadn't been arranged. No matter. If Burnley or his secretary weren't around, they'd have to go in search of the two men themselves, with Pine to lead the way.

'I'm not sure that Pine was telling the truth about his involvement,' Lizzie said.

'Why not?' Kember stopped wiping.

'Because he emphasised that he was good at his job,' Lizzie said. 'Without prompting, he said "I keep my head down and get on with it", which is positive affirmation. By saying it out loud to us, he's trying to convince himself of his own good character while also putting distance between his own, supposedly good, actions and those, supposedly bad, of Morris.'

Kember knew she was right, of course. He'd witnessed villains distancing themselves from people they'd been in cahoots with for years. Even family members. Honour among thieves was mostly a myth. He'd known burglars dividing up the streets and seen criminal gangs stay out of each other's way but that had more to do with expediency, pragmatism and profit than anything that could be called honour.

'I'll get rid of these,' Lizzie said, taking the cloths. 'We don't want to upset Mrs Wall by returning stained dusters, do we? Besides, she's got plenty more.'

◆ ◆ ◆

At Kember's request, Eddie Pine took them in search of Victor Young and Terry Armstrong but their journey was made arduous by the spiralling snow that had replaced the morning's driving sleet. They tried the canteen, where weary-looking mine workers occupied the previously empty tables, tucking into what Kember thought looked like some kind of vegetable stew served with bubble and squeak and chunks of bread. Kember's mouth watered. He'd eaten breakfast hours ago and he was partial to the fried potato and cabbage concoction.

They tried the on-site social club next door but found only a bored ancient-looking barman and a few off-duty surface workers. Two were playing dominoes, one was reading a newspaper, one was dozing in a corner and two were nursing half-pint glasses as they smoked and chatted.

They returned to the bleak outdoors and with backs bent and shoulders hunched they followed Pine on a course through the haphazard array of grimy buildings. The occasional cluster of black-jacketed men sporting miners' helmets hurried by. Through a narrow gap between two buildings, Kember caught sight of two figures. The short one saw him glance their way and hurried out of sight, the much taller one dropped the corner of a tarpaulin sheet and followed his colleague.

After a couple of minutes, Pine led them to the one other place they might find Young and Armstrong, their dormitory on the edge of the colliery site where Morris had breathed his last.

As they stood on the steps of Hut Six, Pine said, 'You should know your way around by now,' and pulled his collar up against the flakes of snow that seemed to be multiplying by the minute. 'Looks like someone's in there but if they're not, I'd grab a cup of tea in the canteen, if I were you.' He looked up and squinted. 'This is gonna settle.'

As his form retreated into the clouds of swirling white, Pine responded to their shouted thanks with a wave of his hand in the air.

'We'll speak to whoever's inside before going to the canteen,' Kember said, feeling his stomach growl. 'I spoke to Armstrong and Young yesterday so I'm not expecting them to be any more forth-coming, although that said, Burnley's not breathing down their necks today.'

'They'll want to reinforce what they said to you already,' Lizzie said, opening the door. 'But if they lied yesterday, they'll find it more stressful as they try to remember.'

A movement caught Kember's eye and he glanced to his right along the line of dormitory buildings. As someone emerged from Hut Eight and turned to close the door, he recognised Thatcher, one of the men he'd spoken to the day before. Kember brought him to the attention of Lizzie with the briefest of explanations while they watched him walk in the direction of the canteen and club.

Kember turned his attention back to Hut Six and held the door for Lizzie to go first, through the outer door into a small vestibule. He knocked on the inner door and opened it to find Armstrong the only one in the hut, lying on a camp bed in the near corner on the right, smoking a cigarette and sending smoke rings up to the rafters. He announced himself and beckoned for Lizzie to follow. Armstrong sat up and swung his legs off his bed, motioning for them to sit on the next one.

The air smelled of cigarette and coal smoke, sweat from discarded clothes strewn on the badly made beds, cheesy feet from boots and shoes that lay underneath, and damp. Although a fire burned in the stove at the far end of the hut, its flue disappearing through the back wall, Kember could feel a draught and wondered how Burnley got away with treating his workers so badly, even if there was a war on.

While Lizzie went to the fire to rub the warmth back into her hands, Kember sat on the bed next to Armstrong and took out his notebook. Although he suspected this might be a short interview, Lizzie's input would be invaluable when he questioned Armstrong about his wife.

'What's she doing here,' Armstrong said, with a nod of his head towards Lizzie. 'Can't cope on your own?'

Kember decided to play along.

'Officer Hayes was at a loose end so the powers that be seconded her to me.'

'Ah, you're babysitting?'

Kember smiled at the angry glance he saw Lizzie flash his way. 'Sort of, although she has her uses.'

Armstrong grinned. 'I bet.' He took a last pull on his cigarette and crushed it with the remains of others in some kind of upturned lid on the floor. 'What can I do you for?'

Kember ignored the quip and opened his notebook. 'I've spoken to the other men from this dormitory and that has created some loose ends that need tying.'

'What kind of loose ends?' Armstrong eyed Kember suspiciously.

'The last time we spoke you said you all play cards; five-card brag, I believe?'

'That's right. Nothing serious, mind. Just a bit of fun to relieve the boredom. We play for farthings, unless it's Friday payday and our shifts mean we have Saturday off. Then the stakes could be higher.'

'High enough for Eddie Pine to lose heavily?' Kember raised his eyebrows.

Armstrong gave him a sideways look. 'Sometimes.'

'Pine seems to think his misfortune was down to cheating by Christopher Morris.'

'Yeah, well.' Armstrong shrugged. 'We all thought that but could never catch him or work out how he did it. Four of us would jack it in early on a Friday night after we lost a couple of quid, but not Pine. We knew we were in for a hiding if we stayed in the game and preferred to spend our hard-earned on a few bevvies. For someone to win at cards there has to be a loser and he should have stopped when he'd lost what he could afford.'

Kember nodded. *Sage advice for anyone*, he thought. 'Did that make him angry?'

'Of course, but without proof, what can you do?'

A lot, thought Kember, *if you take matters into your own hands.*

Kember looked up as Lizzie walked back from the stove and sat next to him on the bed. She'd undone her coat to reveal her ATA uniform beneath and Armstrong looked her up and down with a smirk. Feeling irritation rising within himself, Kember hoped she'd keep calm and let him continue to lead the questioning. Playing the dumb sidekick to him was the best strategy for the time being, however annoying for her that might be.

'You told me that Morris and Paul Ramsey had felt ill,' Kember continued. 'But you're all miners, so I find it hard to believe the possibility of gas inhalation never crossed your minds.'

Armstrong opened a tin of tobacco, teased out some strands along a cigarette paper, licked the edge and rolled it into an uneven cigarette. He offered it to Lizzie, who declined, before striking a match and lighting it in a flicker of flame and a puff of smoke. Kember noted that the offer was not extended to him, even though he hadn't said he didn't smoke.

'Gas did cross our minds, as it happens,' Armstrong said at last. 'But we have procedures for that.' His shoulders twitched. 'Before they went underground, Quayle checked with Young that the fan had been running for an hour. Ramsey and Quayle were in the fore shift safety group and it was their job to inspect the districts. Everyone carries or can see safety lamps and canaries, and when the next full shift goes underground, it's also their responsibility, and in their best interest, to keep an eye out for signs of gas.'

'Sensible precautions,' Kember said.

Armstrong took a puff on his cigarette and exhaled noisily. 'What's all this, anyway? What've cards and headaches got to do with Morris dying? I thought he had a heart attack?'

Kember shook his head. 'A second post-mortem showed that he died from what you call whitedamp.'

Armstrong frowned. 'How can that be?'

'That's what we're trying to find out,' Kember said, thinking Armstrong's tone had sounded convincing enough but the man's expression lacked sincerity as if forced. Perhaps this was what Lizzie had described as the brain concentrating on one thing to the exclusion of others.

'It's not my work area,' Armstrong continued. 'I'd have helped if I'd known.'

Kember doubted that. 'You said last time that Morris never caused bad feeling among the men, but we know about the card cheating, the bullying of Ramsey, and Quayle being overlooked for promotion in favour of Morris. In my experience, any one of those can rub someone up the wrong way.'

'I didn't see any bullying from my seat in the winding house and the promotion was Burnley's doing. Any one of us would have taken it if offered.'

Kember nodded. He probably would have done in the same situation.

'Did Morris have a temper?'

'No more than any man but he had a chip on his shoulder about the bosses of big business,' Armstrong said. 'He always went on about what they did to the miners and other workers in the general strike.'

'That was 1926, fifteen years ago,' Kember said, as he made a note in his book. 'A long time to hold a grudge.'

'He lost his job and had to leave his family in Yorkshire to work in the Kent mines. Many others did the same. We've got miners here from Durham, Yorkshire, Wales, all over. Then more miners up north and in Wales lost their jobs during the depression. There was work in Kent but they had to walk here because they couldn't afford train tickets. His uncle was one of them. Worked here for a few years but died with two other men when a tunnel collapsed and flooded.'

'Hard times,' Kember admitted. 'Sounds like he had a lot to be angry about.'

Armstrong shrugged. 'We all have our cross to bear.' He took a drag on his cigarette and blew a smoke ring.

Not a man who looks under the weight of a cross, thought Kember.

Lizzie, who had been listening while becoming increasingly fidgety, leant forward with her elbows on her knees.

'What went on between Morris and your wife?' she asked.

Her sudden intervention took the men by surprise. Kember threw her a warning look as a shadow of anger crossed Armstrong's face like a storm cloud.

'Nothing went on. Why d'you ask that?'

'Because it's been reported to us that there may have been more between them than was appropriate?'

'Rubbish, who said so?' Armstrong snapped. 'Morris fancied Sheila but she was a good wife, a loyal wife, and didn't want to know. He kept on at her so I had to have a word with him. Friendly, like. I don't do fisticuffs.'

'How did Morris take it, this *word*?' Kember asked.

'How did he take it? All right, I suppose.'

There was that repetition again. Perhaps Morris did take it well but he might just have laughed in Armstrong's face, knowing the man wasn't the best physical specimen.

'What do you know about Victor Young's brother? Did he come to Kent?'

Armstrong gave a facial shrug. 'I think he was injured in a mining accident up north somewhere. You'll have to ask Young.'

'Oh, we will, Mr Armstrong. Thank you, I think we'll leave it there for now.'

'Good, 'cause I fancy a kip.'

Kember stood up from the bed. 'Where could we find Victor Young, do you think?'

Armstrong let air out through puffed cheeks. 'If he wasn't in the club or canteen, you'd better try the fan house. He's not on shift but it's his pride and joy and he can't keep away.'

They left Armstrong pinching out his cigarette and emerged from the warmth of the hut to be confronted with worsening weather outside. Lizzie buttoned up her coat against the snowflakes falling in large clumps and Kember raised his collar.

With low cloud blanketing the sky and visibility already diminishing, the snow-covered roofs and dark forbidding walls of the mine buildings had taken on an eerie presence, like the standing stones of Stonehenge in early morning mist. A thin covering of white now obscured the paths, making navigation through the site difficult, and Kember indicated what he thought was the general direction of the fan house. As they picked their way across the site as best they could, Kember noticed the rumble, hum and clank of machinery and the shouts of mine workers had become muffled, as though he was listening to a wireless from another room. He hoped Watson's constable would be able to make it back to them later because a hotel in Canterbury was more alluring than a night at a coal mine.

'Do you know where you're going?' Lizzie asked, her cheeks glowing red with the cold.

'Of course,' Kember lied, realising he'd become disorientated and only had a rough idea of where they were in relation to the fan house. 'It's through here.'

He saw the look of doubt on Lizzie's face but she followed him anyway, across a yard and along the side of a storage building.

A sudden blow to his back sent him sprawling in the snow.

The noise of crashing and splintering wood came from behind as a weight fell across him, knocking the breath from him.

His vision blurred, blood rushed in his ears and his heart raced. He panted, freezing air searing his throat as he tried to force oxygen into his winded lungs. Thankfully, the weight lifted, allowing him to breathe again. He turned over and lay on his back, gasping, feeling the shock of snow on his neck, waiting for another blow. As his sight cleared, he saw a shadow standing there, reaching for him. He prepared to fight but the hands were gentle, supportive, taking his elbow and helping him to sit up. Only then, with the cold and wet soaking through the seat of his trousers, did he see Lizzie bending over him, splatted with mud and snow.

'Are you all right?' she said.

He saw worry creasing her face and took a deep breath. 'I'll live. More importantly, how are you?'

'Shaken up but otherwise fine.'

Kember got to his feet. 'What happened?' he said, brushing at his coat and pulling his wet trousers away from his skin with a grimace.

'I heard a noise and looked up in time to see something falling,' Lizzie said. 'I'm afraid I tumbled on you after I barged you out of the way.'

That explains the winding, Kember thought, patting his coat over his ribs. 'Thank you.' He smiled. 'It seems you've come to my rescue once again. It's becoming rather a habit of yours.'

Lizzie smiled. 'Your turn next time.'

Kember looked up at the second storey where an open loading door banged in the wind. A jib protruded from the wall but its pulley was empty. He expected to see the concerned and apologetic face of the operator in the doorway but there was nothing but an empty black hole. A rope lay on the path next to the cargo it had carried. Several wooden boxes had shattered on the hard ground, sending wooden shards in all directions and spilling out greased machine parts.

'I'm touched by the concern for our health,' Kember said, looking around for signs of human activity but seeing none amid the worsening snowstorm.

Lizzie picked up the end of the rope, which still had a leather cover over a whipping knot. 'It's not frayed but it wasn't cut either.'

'Released deliberately, I'd say. Waited until we were underneath the pulley.'

'Someone tried to kill us?'

'A warning,' Kember said, trying the door beneath the pulley but finding it locked. 'The trouble is, warnings pique my interest because they always mean I'm ruffling the right feathers.'

'We should call the police,' Lizzie said.

'What am I then?' he said, aware they were in a place unfamiliar to them but known intimately by everyone who worked there.

Lizzie's sardonic laugh wounded his pride.

'A single unarmed detective whose life has just been threatened,' she said.

'Well,' Kember said, putting his hand up to catch snowflakes. 'I'm beginning to doubt that Watson's constable will come out in this, so you're stuck with me.'

Lizzie brushed mud from the shoulders of Kember's coat but the snow was falling more heavily and sticking to their clothes and hair. It had already coated the boxes and machine parts, and reduced visibility to a few feet.

'Better get inside then, before you become a snowman,' she said.

◆ ◆ ◆

Lizzie heard the muffled throb of an engine before the outline of the building materialised out of trees and the snow. It was smaller than she'd imagined for such a large mine but there was no denying the power of the machinery. It may have been freezing outside but the heat hit her as soon as she followed Kember through the door. The engine driving the fan's huge blades threw out more than enough warmth to heat the room and condensation fogged the windows. An engineer did a double take when he saw Lizzie but quickly recovered his composure, nodded a greeting to Kember, and returned to tinkering with a control. Another engineer sat in the foreman's corner office, hunched over a desk, making entries in a log book.

Kember rapped on the door and the engineer looked up. He turned out to be the fan house foreman for the back shift and, after introductions, he left the office, slipped through a side door and returned a few seconds later behind Victor Young.

'Inspector,' Young greeted, closing the office door on the other foreman and eyeing their dirty coats. 'Bit slippy out there, is it?'

'The sky's falling down,' Kember said, no hint of mirth around his eyes.

Lizzie saw no reaction to the quip in Young's face, but his eyebrows did flicker when Kember introduced her. Young indicated a chair for her to use and she thought about declining. It may have been one of the many gestures that men thought chivalrous but she found the idea that a woman was too delicate or didn't have the strength to remain standing absurd. Being offered a seat always felt like a deliberate act of dominance and submission. Men saw the size and quality of their desk or chair as representing their value and importance in the power hierarchy. Those without a desk or big chair who remained standing used the height differential to reflect what they saw as their place in the natural order.

Not wishing to antagonise Young before they'd begun by appearing churlish, Lizzie accepted the offer but sat at an angle, all the better to keep both men in her sights.

'You're an elusive man, Mr Young,' Kember said, as Young took the seat behind the desk. 'As your shift was changed, this was one place I didn't expect to see you.'

'I'm always working, even when I'm not,' Young said. 'I prefer the company of machines to people. You know where you are with machines. When they work, they work. When they don't, there's usually a good and simple reason. People are too complicated.'

Lizzie didn't disagree, but that was where her expertise came in.

'Do you get on with your workmates, Mr Young?' she said.

'You have to if you work in a colliery,' Young said, eyeing her suspiciously. 'I get on well enough.'

'Not everyone does though, do they?' Kember said.

Lizzie noticed Young's jaw muscles tighten. An involuntary reaction he'd probably not even noticed himself.

'You told me last time that Morris was easy enough to get along with,' Kember said. He checked his notebook. 'Kept himself to himself, according to you.'

'If you say so,' Young said.

'We've been asking around and it seems no love was lost between Morris and the others in your dormitory.'

Young crossed his arms. 'And?'

'Bullying, cheating at cards, an adulterous affair, undeserved promotion. Doesn't sound like the shy retiring type. I was wondering whether one of those issues came to a head.'

'What do you mean?' Young threw a glance at Lizzie. 'Did they cause his heart attack?'

'I mean that we believe Morris could have been murdered.'

'You're joking?' Young's eyes widened. 'Have you found something?'

Lizzie heard his words but they didn't match her observations. He sounded taken aback, almost shocked, but his head had made the tiniest of nods, as if the announcement had not been a surprise.

'Morris died of carbon monoxide poisoning,' Kember said. 'Whitedamp, I believe it's called. Isn't that one of the gases your fan helps to suck out of the mine?'

'That's right,' Young said. 'But I thought you said he'd been murdered.'

'Can you think of any way that Morris could have succumbed to whitedamp?'

Young frowned in silence for a few seconds and Lizzie watched as he uncrossed his arms and gripped one wrist with his other hand. From one defensive gesture to another. No lie coming but he was setting a barrier between himself and the death.

'Gases are an occupational hazard in mining and many men have died because of them,' he said. 'The air flows through the mine in a certain way, d'you see? Have you ever heard the expression *put the wood in the hole* when you want a door shutting? That comes from the airlocks underground that direct fresh air around the tunnels. Trouble is, if there's a spur tunnel, hollowed-out chamber or natural cavity, the airflow passes by and all sorts of gases can build up in there.'

'The gases that safety lamps and canaries detect?' Kember said.

'If you use them properly, yes.'

Kember made a show of consulting his notebook. 'I understand it was standard practice for one of the fore shift safety team to check the fan had been running for an hour before they went down the pit.'

'That's right,' said Young.

'Who checked with you on the morning before the night Morris died?'

'I'm not sure. Ramsey, I think.'

Kember made a note in his book and Lizzie knew he'd recognised the lie too, but whose was it? Armstrong had told them that Quayle had checked with the fan house. She leant forward and Young gave her a wary glance.

'I was sorry to hear that your brother was injured in a mining accident,' she said, with the best look of concern she could muster.

Young's body stiffened and his face hardened. 'An avoidable accident.'

Lizzie nodded. 'When did it happen?'

'In the May of '26.'

'Was it serious?'

Young didn't answer.

'Please tell us what happened?' Lizzie's voice soothed.

Young looked at her, thinking. Then, with eyes glistening with unshed tears, he sighed.

'We worked in neighbouring pits in Yorkshire, about a mile apart. Wally, that's my brother Wallace, told me that Roy Jackson, one of the firemen from his pit, was more intent on bossing people around than doing his job properly, so I warned him to look out for himself. One day, there was a build-up of methane gas and it went up like a powder keg. It's not called firedamp for nothing. Two men died and several were injured, including Wally. He broke his leg in two places and walks with a stick now. Jackson got away with it because the general strike started two days later and the incident was swept under the carpet. Occupational hazard, they called it.' He shook his head. 'The mine bosses had enough to contend with.'

'How did that make you feel?' Lizzie said.

Young looked sharply at Lizzie. 'How do you think it made me feel? Sad, angry, helpless. There was nothing I could do. I went back to work after the strike because I needed the money but the fireman had already got the sack for being a ringleader.'

'You stayed in Yorkshire?'

'Yes, for a few years. I came down to Kent when the depression hit the north hard and I lost my job.'

Lizzie nodded her understanding. 'We believe Chris Morris did the same. Did you know him back in Yorkshire?'

Young gave her a grim smile. 'Do you know how many coal mines there are in Yorkshire, and how many miners there were back then?'

Avoidance, Lizzie thought. In not answering her question, he'd inadvertently given her the information . . . and more. She noticed Kember rubbing the end of his nose, something he unconsciously did when thinking, and knew he'd picked up on something too.

'Do you know why Mr Burnley promoted Morris instead of Quayle?' Kember asked.

Young shook his head. 'I really don't. That's one you'll have to ask Burnley.'

'Did they clash at all? I don't mean fighting. I mean, did they disagree about things?'

'If they did, Burnley wouldn't have promoted him, would he?'

Lizzie saw the shoulder movement and frowned. So, they *did* disagree but Burnley promoted Morris anyway. Why would someone like him do that when he was so strict about the way he ran his mine and so miserly about improving conditions for his workers? She looked at Kember and decided she couldn't rely on him to ask the questions she wanted answers to. *In for a penny, in for a pound*, she thought.

'When did you realise that the man you blame for your brother's injury was working here?'

Young looked stunned. 'He – he's not.'

The stutter, a slight widening of the eyes and an immediate flush of the cheeks told Lizzie she'd hit the mark. 'Come on, Mr Young,' she said, her voice firmer now, like a hospital matron. 'Your description of Roy Jackson from the pit explosion matches everything we've been told about Christopher Morris.'

Lizzie saw Kember give her the same look he always did when she'd annoyed him by overstepping the boundary of her role. He'd probably come to the same conclusion about Jackson being Morris but she didn't care. He'd been too slow and she'd got the desired reaction. She inclined her head almost imperceptibly towards Young and raised her eyebrows at Kember, inviting him to take up the baton. He pressed his lips together disapprovingly before looking at Young.

'You mentioned Jackson was sacked for being a ringleader in the general strike,' Kember said. 'If he is Morris, does Burnley know?'

'I – I don't know.' Young glanced through the office windows to where the foreman and engineer were chatting, as if willing them to come to his rescue. 'All I do is manage the fan house on the fore shift. Everything else is none of my business.'

'Even though he's the man responsible for the explosion that injured Wally?'

Young's head snapped back at the use of his brother's nickname and he glared at Kember. Lizzie noted steel in his eyes and thought he looked angry, but even though her research experience in Oxford prison had taught her that most killers didn't look like they could harm a fly, he still didn't strike her as being a murderer.

She saw Kember tense beside her and her senses heightened, watching Young for the unconscious, uncontrollable, physical signs of impending aggression or lying. She need not have worried. Young relaxed and all the tension dissipated, as though he'd come to a decision.

Young's gaze dropped to the desk. 'Many of us drink in the Volunteer, the pub down the road at Bramling, because the miners from Snowdown Colliery drink there too. Birds of a feather, and all that. The landlord keeps pigs in a sty opposite the pub and sometimes they're so loud at feeding time that you can hardly hear the darts scores being called out.'

Young looked up and Lizzie expected the next utterance to be a lie, but he displayed no twitches, no defensive gestures, and no indications of concealing the truth. His body hadn't adopted an unnatural stillness of the kind that often came over liars concentrating hard on an untruth. She frowned. Was Young about to confess?

'I'd never met Jackson but I knew of him, about him, of course,' Young said. 'One Friday evening, Morris was three sheets to the wind, having had a few jars, and he started telling me stories of his mining days up north. "Worked in Durham and all over Yorkshire," he said. Survived roof falls, flooding and an explosion. "Tell me more," I said, and he did. I soon realised he was talking about the day my brother was injured and he had been the fireman on the same shift. The overman was in charge but it was a big pit with several districts. The overman couldn't cover them all so it would have been left to Jackson, or Morris as I now knew him, to check for gas in his own district before the hewers and other miners of the shift went down. I don't know what happened for certain but if Morris had done the proper checks, there wouldn't have been a build-up of methane and my brother wouldn't have been caught in an explosion.'

His gaze lowered to the table again, his body slumped like a partially deflated barrage balloon.

'Realising that Morris was Jackson must have been quite a shock,' Lizzie said. 'Did you tell him who you were?'

Young shook his head. 'What would have been the point? What would I have said to make myself feel better? What could he have said to satisfy me?'

'Did you tell the police?'

Young shook his head. 'It would have been a waste of time. There'd been no investigation or inquiry and he'd been sacked already because he was a strike leader and suspected communist, not because of the explosion.'

Lizzie nodded. 'How did that make you feel?'

Young sighed. 'It was bad enough that Morris got away with it but knowing he was here, and sleeping in the same dorm, that was almost unbearable.'

'Enough to kill him?' Kember asked.

Young gave Kember a wry smile. 'I sleep in the dorm, eat in the canteen, drink in the club, and work the fan. I have all the reason and opportunity in the world but I'm not the murdering kind. Am I glad he's dead? Abso-bloody-lutely. Did I gas him? How on earth could I do that without killing everyone else down the pit at the same time?'

'Paul Ramsey was also taken ill,' Lizzie said.

'But not Harry Quayle or Eddie Pine, and they all went down there together. Day in, day out.'

Lizzie had to concede the point but something didn't sit right. Everyone in the dormitory had a reason to dislike Morris, perhaps to kill him, but even though only Ramsey had been alone with him regularly for any length of time, giving him clear-cut opportunities, he'd become ill too. Mine damps were naturally occurring gases that could be controlled through ventilation and detected by safety lamps and canaries, but surely they couldn't be harnessed in the pit tunnels in order to quickly, easily and effectively administer them to a single victim as a murder weapon? Was it just an accident after all, the result of Morris cutting corners like he had in the Yorkshire pit?

'I think we'll leave it there for now, Mr Young,' Kember said. 'Thank you for being a little more truthful on this occasion. We might have a few more questions so please don't leave the colliery.'

Young laughed dryly. 'Have you seen it out there? Nobody's going anywhere for the foreseeable.'

CHAPTER NINE

He's right, thought Kember, as he and Lizzie left Young in the warmth of the fan house and stepped out into the swirling white. The biting wind took the temperature down even further, searing the exposed skin of his face and neck.

'We should get something to eat but I want to check something before this gets too bad,' he said.

Lizzie waved her assent and pulled her scarf up to her nose, giving her the look of a cat burglar, if it hadn't been for her hair being whipped across her face by the wind. Her clear bright eyes looked even bluer amid all the monochrome as she looked at him questioningly, and he had to tear his gaze away to concentrate on their task.

He took the lead back along the path but the low, snow-laden clouds caused a grey flat light that took all the contrast and shadows out of the landscape, and he blundered forward, hearing Lizzie stumbling along behind him. They reached the main buildings and turned away from the direction of the canteen. The spot where he believed he'd seen the two miners acting suspiciously at the opposite end of the narrow alley lay just around the corner of the next building, not too far from where someone had tried to drop a stack of goods on their heads. He didn't know what he'd seen, it could have been completely innocent, but the furtive actions of the miners had niggled at the back of his mind and he needed to satisfy his curiosity. He realised it was a trait that Lizzie also exhibited, often to his annoyance or concern, and wondered whether that was one of the connections that drew them together.

It was a question for another time as he reached the position that allowed him to look along the alley. No one there now, as far as he could see.

'What are you looking for?' Lizzie asked, shielding her eyes from the driving snow.

Kember described what he thought he'd seen earlier and saw the familiar faraway look that came into her eyes when she was placing herself into a scene. It was something he didn't understand but knew often worked. It didn't this time and he saw her eyes refocus.

'I need to see what's at the other end,' Lizzie said, leaving him open-mouthed as she shuffled through a drift into the gap.

Kember followed her track through the several inches of previously undisturbed snow until they reached the end of the alley where an access road zigzagged its way to their left through more buildings. To their immediate right stood the bulky outline of the front of a large vehicle. Almost fully concealed down to the ground by a dark tarpaulin, the tyres of its large wheels were still visible. It had been reversed into a gap between the wall of the three-storey building and a low, corrugated-iron Nissen hut. Snow settling on the hut and lying on the tarpaulin and drifts beginning to pile against the walls and wheels camouflaged the vehicle further. Whoever had parked it there had meant it to be well hidden. From whom? Him?

Parked no more than a foot behind the end of the tall building, it was a corner of the tarpaulin covering the nose of the vehicle that Kember had spotted being held up. If the two miners hadn't caught his eye, he would never have known there might be something here of potential interest. He lifted the bottom of the tarpaulin and flung it over the bonnet of what was now revealed as a lorry.

'I saw two men doing something here earlier and they disappeared smartish when they saw me looking.'

'It's a lorry,' Lizzie said, blinking away snowflakes. 'Is it important enough to be out in the freezing cold for?'

He pointed to a small number five painted in white near where a piece of cloth covered the registration plate. 'I'll bet you a week's wages, this is the lorry that almost ran us off the road.'

'I thought you said it was a farm lorry,' Lizzie said.

'It had no markings except a white number five and the number plate was covered. It looked like a farm lorry to us but we'd just left the colliery so there always was a strong possibility someone had sent it after us.'

'Do you think Burnley's behind it?'

'He might not know what his lorry was used for, but then again, he's as likely a suspect as any,' Kember said. 'The incidents with this and the falling stores are proof that someone working in this colliery doesn't want us poking our noses into how Morris died. Which gives me every reason to poke a bit more.'

A gust of wind blew snow at their faces and they turned their backs to it.

In that moment, with the light still washing out any definition, leaving everything looking as flat as a charcoal drawing on white paper, Kember thought he saw a shadow. He blinked and the shadow moved.

He touched Lizzie's arm. 'We're being watched,' he said, and tilted his head for her to follow as the shadow ducked behind the caterpillar tracks of a large crane. Kember reached the crane a few seconds later, the top of its boom and jib obscured by the falling snow. He squinted, trying to cut out some of the strange glare making his eyes hurt, and understood now why Scott of the Antarctic always wore snow goggles.

The shadow disappeared around the corner of a large hut and Kember set off in pursuit, his shoes providing no traction on the slippery ground. Slithering around the end of the hut, he saw the shadow ducking to the left and followed. With a glance behind to ensure Lizzie was still with him, he darted alongside a line of railway coal trucks that looked out of place with the rails obscured. *Where is everybody?* he thought. He realised the snowstorm would have driven most men inside but surely there were hardier souls whose jobs outside demanded they stay at their posts? Muffled hums and clanks told him those men were around somewhere, operating the necessary machinery to keep production going until dusk.

The shadow disappeared and Kember resorted to tracking it through its footprints left in the snow. This did not prove easy, as they crossed the tracks of other unseen mine workers. He reached the end of the line of trucks and rounded the corner of the weigh-bridge house. Nothing stood on the weighing platform, not that the man sitting inside the weighbridge house could have seen much. The windows were so obscured by snow on the outside and condensation on the inside that he might just as well have been looking through frosted glass.

Kember hurried on, shoes crunching on soft new snow but slipping and sliding on ice caused by snow compacted under miners' work boots. Veering to the left then turning to the right, he found himself in the pit yard where miners scurried from one building to another, the small huddles of men with their black helmets standing out starkly from the accumulating white. He spotted a smaller figure leaving the yard in the distance and set off after it, steadying himself with a hand against the wall. Following between two more buildings, places that now seemed familiar, he saw the figure disappear through the door of the canteen and he rushed forward to catch up.

Just as he reached the door, a figure rushed at him from his left and he flinched, throwing up his left arm in defence.

◆ ◆ ◆

Lizzie saw Kember glance at her just before she stumbled over a step beneath a snowdrift and had to put both hands out to stop herself falling. By the time she'd recovered and hurried forward, Kember had disappeared and she couldn't determine in which direction he'd gone. Thinking that the figure would be weaving in and out in order to lose them, she made a decision and turned left.

It soon became clear that Kember had taken a different path but tracks in the snow suggested their quarry had gone this way. Lizzie crept forward at each turn and junction, trying to peer through the swirling white as it stung her eyes. The clouds filtered the light in a way that kept everything translucent, as though being viewed through tracing paper, and she continued to trip over things hidden beneath undulations of snow that she couldn't distinguish from the flat.

At one point, thinking she spotted Kember scurrying between two buildings, she gave chase but he was too quick and she became disorientated. Perhaps it had been him, but her heart gave a hard thump when the thought occurred that it might have been one of the miners he'd seen, someone now tracking him, or her. She looked around, suddenly anxious. She'd lost Kember and now stood alone among a cluster of tall dark buildings, snow caking her hair and forcing its way inside the collar of her coat, acutely aware of how vulnerable she was.

The only problem with walking through a busy colliery should have come from the inherent danger of such a workplace. Right now, her greatest problem was the isolation caused by the snow-storm, the diminishing visibility removing the safety of numbers as miners took shelter. With a potential killer at large, she felt alone, fearful and small. Her fingers were too cold to ping the rubber bands on her wrists or twist the lid from her jar of Vicks VapoRub and she wished she hadn't left her motorbike gauntlets in the office. Apart from the buildings surrounding her, there was nothing for her mind to latch on to, even to employ her countermeasure of counting up and down.

She began to pant as her chest tightened and her breathing became shallow. *Not now!* she screamed inside her head. Her throat constricted as her eyes darted, searching for a danger she couldn't see. That should have reassured her but it only served to heighten the fear. Lizzie doubled over, trying to breathe normally and had a sudden thought. She grabbed a handful of snow and threw it at her face, but all that did was sting her eyes. She took another handful and pulled down her scarf, shoving the clump of freezing flakes under her chin and against her neck.

The sudden cold had the desired effect of shocking her and she gasped, knocking her thoughts out of their negative spiral. Her fingers burned, her head throbbed and her neck tingled but her breathing slowed and she began to see much clearer. Visibility was still poor but at least that wasn't of her own mind and body's making.

The fast-falling snow had covered any tracks she might have followed so she picked her way carefully alongside a building and around another, wary of any movement around her, until she saw the bottom of the headframe towers. From there, she got her bearings and headed for the canteen where she hoped Kember would meet her once he realised they'd become separated.

As the canteen came into sight, she saw a figure scurry towards it and disappear inside. She saw a larger figure following and she hurried to intercept it by the door.

The figure stopped and raised an arm, and with relief, she saw it was Kember. Having recently felt so small and afraid, she laughed at his reaction and saw his already cold-flushed cheeks turn a deeper shade.

'It's only me,' Lizzie said.

'Where did you come from?' Kember said, lowering his arm. 'I thought you were behind me.'

'I stumbled as you gave chase and when I looked up, you'd disappeared.'

'I'm sorry. I thought—'

'Don't worry.'

'Are you—?'

'I'm fine, but we'd better get out of this quickly because I saw the person you were following go inside. Let's see if anyone looks wet and guilty, shall we?'

With that, she opened the door and stepped through. The canteen was now half-full of miners, a warm fug hitting her after the chill of the snowstorm and the ice-cold emergency countermeasure she'd employed against her panic attack. Kember followed and every one of the miners glanced towards them but none stopped their eating, drinking and conversations. Lizzie scanned the room for signs of the newly arrived, but it was difficult to tell. Melting snow was evident on the donkey jackets of three men collecting food at the counter, the boots of men sat at the tables nearest to Lizzie were wet with slush, and the floor was awash with meltwater.

Kember gave her a nudge and she followed the line of his nod to his left.

'That's Thatcher, the banksman,' he said.

Kember followed this with a nod towards the far corner, where the only two people in the room who had not looked their way were sitting. Burnley was nursing a steaming mug of tea in front of him on the table, listening intently to Mrs Wall sitting opposite.

Lizzie noted the glistening wet on the shoulders of both their coats, and their cheeks as flushed as her own with the sudden warmth of the room. She made her way around the men at the counter, past a rack of damp jackets and stood next to Burnley's table.

'You'll not feel the benefit—'

'I beg your pardon?' Mrs Wall said, starting to frown up at the intrusion.

Burnley's look of guilt, as if caught with his trousers down, was almost comical.

'If you don't take your coats off,' Lizzie said. 'You'll not feel the benefit when you go back outside.'

'I could say the same to you,' said Mrs Wall.

'Miss Hayes, please sit,' Burnley said, smiling, his composure having returned. 'Inspector.' He nodded to Kember. 'Can I get you a cup of tea?'

'I'd love one,' Kember said. 'And something to eat, if that's all right? My stomach thinks my throat's been cut.'

Burnley held up two fingers to the watching canteen staff and pointed down to the table. Lizzie, who had already removed her coat, saw two of the serving women exchange looks that said *what did his last servant die of?* She removed her coat, placed it over the back of the chair on the far side and Kember did the same as he took the seat opposite.

'Should you both be in here at the same time?' Lizzie asked, wondering whether this was a clandestine meeting, a chance encounter, or something more sinister. *But why meet here?* she thought. *Are they hiding in plain sight?*

'I came to find Mr Burnley to tell him about you, actually,' Mrs Wall sneered.

'What about us?' Lizzie asked.

'I went to run an errand, and when I returned, you had both left the office. I didn't see you leave the site.'

'I didn't realise you'd been told to spy on us.'

'Not spy, Miss Hayes. Mr Burnley asked me to look after you while he was away. He telephoned just before he left Canterbury on his return journey, to ask me to warn you that the lanes would be treacherous and it would be a good idea for you to leave before the roads became impassable. I couldn't find you, and Mr Burnley has just arrived back.'

'Ladies, please,' Burnley said, smiling at Lizzie again.

His attempt at a sly wink did not go unnoticed by Mrs Wall, and Lizzie could feel the hostility radiating from her. It was as clear as a summer's day that she wanted to be something more than just his secretary.

Two mugs of steaming tea delivered unceremoniously by a sour-faced middle-aged woman broke the tension.

'When I arrived back, I wanted to let you know that your chances of reaching Canterbury this afternoon were fast diminishing,' Burnley said. 'Mrs Wall told me you'd gone off on a jaunt around the colliery so we both went looking for you.'

'We needed to speak to Young and Armstrong,' Kember said.

'Again?' Burnley raised an eyebrow.

'To confirm a few details after our interviews with the other men. Nothing more.'

Lizzie watched for the slightest twitch as she said, 'I think you mentioned that your safety record was unblemished, Mr Burnley. Is that still the case?'

'Why, has someone made an accusation?' Burnley shot back. He regarded them through narrowed eyes. 'I told you this morning, it's second to none.'

'I merely wondered whether the snowstorm had affected the smooth operation you have here.'

Lizzie could detect no telltale signs of deception and it was obvious that Burnley believed every word he said about how well the mine ran and how great he was at running it. Did that equate to knowing nothing about how a stack of goods had almost dropped on their heads? Or had he ordered someone to get rid of the problem they posed, having asked for the details to be kept from him? She gave Burnley a warm smile and saw both the secretary and Kember clench their jaws.

Burnley took a few mouthfuls of tea and wiped his walrus moustache. 'The trains and lorries will have difficulty if it doesn't let up and we may be stuck here for a day or two, but the snow can't reach underground so it shouldn't affect prod—'

'I wonder whether we might have a word in private?' Kember interrupted, glancing towards Mrs Wall.

Burnley looked taken aback. 'You can speak freely in front of Mrs Wall,' he said. 'She's my right-hand man – er – woman.'

Lizzie noted the slight upward tilt of Mrs Wall's chin at the compliment given in front of strangers.

'In that case,' Kember said, 'I think you ought to reassess your method of recording incidents and accidents.'

'What do you mean?' Burnley frowned.

'Ten minutes ago, Officer Hayes and I narrowly avoided being crushed under a stack of stores falling from a second-storey jib not two hundred yards from here.'

Lizzie saw Burnley's expression of shock but was more intrigued by the look of horror on the face of Mrs Wall. Her reaction felt more in keeping with her being a mine owner rather than a secretary, and Lizzie couldn't help staring, even though she avoided her gaze.

'Impossible,' Burnley said, his face now a picture of puzzlement. 'I would have been told if something that serious had happened.'

'Clearly not,' Kember said. 'The door to the storehouse was locked but the loading bay doors were open. Someone inside either failed in their job, or tried to kill us. Either way, we could have died.'

Burnley's lips were parted and his head was moving in a slow shake. Mrs Wall was studying a breadcrumb on the table.

'I'll speak to the men, Inspector,' Burnley said. 'I'm sure it was a complete accident. It'll be because of the snowstorm, nothing more. They probably didn't even see you.'

Lizzie watched as Burnley's mouth kept moving but the words stopped coming. Exposing his safety record as a sham was one thing but the suggestion that it might have been deliberate had clearly shaken him.

Kember consulted his notebook.

'When we first met, why didn't you tell me that Morris was a known militant leader in the general strike, and a suspected communist?'

'Who told you that?' Burnley's eyes narrowed.

Kember and Lizzie remained silent.

Burnley sighed. 'Because I didn't think it was relevant.'

'Or maybe, with your own personal gripe against Morris, you thought it would make you a suspect?'

'Tommyrot,' Burnley snapped. 'Morris was a communist who believed in the redistribution of other people's wealth,' he continued. 'Did they tell you that, Inspector? He hated all businessmen, so I'm told, and all authority, despite being in charge of men himself. How do you square that, hmm? Never did trust the fellow, but not nearly enough to want him dead.'

'So, why did you employ him?' Kember said.

'Because I didn't know at the time. We were gearing up for this to be the great mine it is today and we needed men, simple as that.'

'So, few questions were asked?'

'I would say we weren't as rigorous in our recruitment procedure as we might have been. Morris seemed solid enough but we got to know the darker side of him over time.'

'What do you mean?' Lizzie asked, thinking there might be something deeper she could latch on to.

'All the militants and ringleaders from the general strike were arrested and blacklisted,' Burnley explained. 'Many miners came south and changed their names to find work after the strike, but Morris didn't turn up until a few years later, during the depression, so we didn't put two and two together for a long time.'

'I assume he did well, given that you promoted him?' Lizzie said. Even if he had changed his name to get the job in the first place, it seemed odd to her that someone arrested for leading a damaging strike would be kept on by a man like Burnley and then promoted. Was the man's arrogance and lust for money and power so great that he'd risk major disruption to squeeze the last drop of energy and mining experience out of a known troublemaker and communist?

'Not a bit of it,' Burnley said. 'He was mediocre at best, a slacker. He started complaining, whipping up the men to make demands, never drawing attention to himself by leading from the front like he had before. At least, not at first. We looked into his past a bit more and found his details and description matched those of Roy Jackson, a man who had spent time in prison as a strike ringleader.'

'Why not sack him?' Lizzie asked.

'Because by then he'd become the head of the union branch here and was always causing minor problems that cost me money. The Kent coalfield has suffered damaging strikes in the past. In addition to 1926, the strike at nearby Snowdown Colliery in 1921 forced it to close and it wasn't reopened for two years. Betteshanger Colliery, also not far from here, suffered a damaging strike in 1938. I couldn't afford to sack Morris in case he took everyone out with him.'

'But the government passed a law banning strikes during wartime,' Lizzie said, noticing Mrs Wall still worrying at the breadcrumb.

'Order 1305, yes,' Burnley said. 'What good would that do if the whole colliery ground to a halt and, God forbid, it spread to the others? The government would wade in and arrest everyone, and I'd still be left without a workforce. No production for the war effort, and a massive loss of money for me. There aren't enough prison beds for every miner so they'd have to let them go and then they'd be even more unsackable than they are now. I didn't want Bekesbourne to go the way of Snowdown.'

'Then why even promote Morris over Harold Quayle?'

'I suppose you've heard the saying, keep your friends close but your enemies closer?' Burnley said, and Kember nodded. 'I thought if I gave him more responsibility and money by making him an overman, he'd have more to lose.'

'Did it work?' Kember asked.

'To a degree,' Burnley said. 'Didn't stop him getting himself killed though.'

'You think it's murder too?'

'Don't be ridiculous. The man had a heart attack. Whether that was caused by exhaustion or exposure to gas is neither here nor there.'

The miniscule nod of his head alerted Lizzie to the lie. The words were confirmatory, the gesture was contradictory. But how much did he really know?

Burnley recovered his composure and leant back in his chair with that aloof air of the rich and powerful who expect you to come to them. Kember copied the movement, sitting back casually but flicking the pages of his notebook theatrically. He stopped at a page and looked at Burnley.

'Our investigation has confirmed that you weren't the only one with a reason to dislike Christopher Morris,' Kember said.

Burnley shrugged. 'Wherever men gather there will be differences of opinion.'

'Quayle was the man ignored for promotion – in favour of Morris. Ramsey was bullied – by Morris. Pine was cheated out of hundreds of pounds at cards – by Morris. Young's brother suffered injury in a mining accident because of negligence – by Morris. Armstrong's wife was having an affair – with Morris. You can't abide blacklisted communists – like Morris. Those aren't differences of opinion, Mr Burnley. Those are motives for murder.'

Burnley studied Kember for a few silent seconds before laughing.

'I'm sorry, Inspector, but your suggestion is absurd. Whatever disagreements I or my men had with Morris, there is absolutely no way that any of us could have killed him in such a fashion. You said it yourself; he was negligent. The man simply cut too many corners and put his own life, and those of my men, at risk. He died and we can count ourselves fortunate that he took no others with him.'

Lizzie narrowed her eyes. Burnley's laugh sounded spontaneous; his sitting posture, as if he was lounging in his office, was relaxed; the sips of tea followed by wipes of his moustache seemed entirely natural. *And that's the problem*, she thought. Everything appeared naturalistic, but even for a hardened businessman like Burnley, having himself and his men under suspicion for murder should have caused him more consternation than he'd displayed throughout the day. Here in the canteen, his whole performance was overly calm and confident, like an actor on stage. *Is that for the benefit of the others in the room?* she thought. *Or is he hiding something?*

Lizzie had also been watching Mrs Wall out of the corner of her eye and the secretary had kept calm through everything Burnley had said. Truly, his right-hand woman. Kember was rubbing the end of his nose and Lizzie knew the time was right.

She opened her mouth to speak just as their food arrived and bowls of vegetable stew with chunks of bread were plonked on the tabletop with a clatter of cutlery. Two plates of crispy-topped bubble and squeak followed. Her mouth watered but she kept her eyes on Burnley.

'I want to see the district,' she said, leaning forward. 'The one where Morris and Ramsey worked together.'

'The district?' Burnley echoed; eyebrows dipped in a frown. 'Whatever for?'

Kember raised his eyebrows at her and forked a piece of bubble and squeak into his mouth so sharply that Lizzie thought he might stab himself in the lips. She knew she'd overstepped the mark again – she was only here to advise after all – but Kember understood more than most what she had to gain by putting herself at the heart of where victims had been.

'I'd like to get a feeling for the conditions underground,' she said.

She saw Kember bite his lip and knew in that moment that he would support her again if Burnley proved reluctant.

'The coal face is no place for a lady.' Burnley shook his head.

'Women have worked in mines before,' Lizzie said, her look as cold, hard and sharp as a shard of flint. 'And what makes you think I'm a lady?'

A strange expression of amusement and intrigue settled on Burnley's face. Mrs Wall glared at Lizzie.

'You can't see gas, Miss Hayes, although in the case of stink-damp, you can sometimes smell it,' Burnley said. 'I can think of nothing else you might see that's relevant to the death of Morris.'

'Maybe not,' Lizzie said. 'But if I don't look, I'll never know.'

Burnley sighed and shook his head resignedly. 'The back shift finishes at six o'clock tonight and the safety team at seven but you'll have to wait until the fore shift safety team go down at six o'clock tomorrow morning.'

'Can't we see it tonight?'

'Absolutely not. I'll need time to make arrangements for you to be escorted.' He stood up and glanced towards the windows, steamed up and running with condensation. Someone had wiped a patch through which snow could be seen falling in clumps. 'You'll need somewhere to stay tonight but I suppose you won't want to sleep in Morris's bed, Inspector. If you don't mind sharing a dormitory, Hut Two is empty at the moment. As a rule, we don't have room for overnight guests but we moved the men out because it had a leaky roof. It's all shipshape and Bristol fashion now. If you take beds on opposite sides, I'm sure propriety and decorum can be maintained. I'll get someone to light the stove and check the bedding.'

'Thank you,' Kember said. 'I'll telephone Inspector Watson from your office when we've finished, if I may?'

'Of course. Enjoy your meal.'

Lizzie watched Burnley doing up the buttons of his coat as he left with Mrs Wall. Was another affair going on there or was the attraction all one way?

◆ ◆ ◆

'That was interesting,' Kember said, spearing a forkful of bubble and squeak. 'Have you noticed how no one denies there were tensions on site but everyone rejects the possibility of murder?' He chewed the potato and cabbage, savouring the addition of a hint of onion, and followed it with bread dipped in his stew. His years in the Metropolitan Police had taught him to eat whatever was on offer and whenever possible because you didn't know when you might be able to grab the next bite.

'Methinks the gentlemen doth protest too much,' Lizzie replied.

'I beg your pardon?'

'I'm paraphrasing from *Hamlet*.' She put down her knife. 'Everyone is insistent that Morris can't have been murdered, but why? All right, I accept the method and opportunity are lacking a bit of definition but we've got motive coming out of the walls. Why can't he have been murdered? What makes everyone in that dormitory so sure that their workmate in the next bed or sitting across from them in the canteen couldn't have found a way?' She shook her head. 'There should be at least one of them who doubts it was natural causes. There should be at least one who accepts the possibility of an outside influence, even if they believe that it was an accident. All these men are too emphatic with their opinions.'

Kember had seen Lizzie's skills and knowledge at work, enabling her to get inside a criminal's mind, and he welcomed the psychological insights that complemented his detective work. The problem was, whereas she might have good reasons to believe that subterfuge was being employed as a smokescreen, all he had was Headley's post-mortem results that showed the colliery doctor and local pathologist had made the wrong diagnosis, deliberately or not, and answers from the miners that pointed to them all hiding something, none of which had been tantamount to admissions of guilt. It wasn't a crime to hate someone, and lying to the police wasn't exactly a rare phenomenon. Unable to put his finger on an answer, the only things that didn't take him back to square one were the torn playing cards. He had learnt enough from Lizzie to suspect they had a meaning yet to be deciphered and that Morris had died by the actions of another. His mind flicked through his mental file of possibilities.

'They all had a reason to hate Morris so his death is of no consequence to them.' Kember pushed his empty plate away and drew his bowl closer. 'It's a possibility they're covering for the murderer because they all agree that it's a good thing that Morris has gone. They might genuinely not know who the murderer is. It's also a possibility that it was an accident caused by Morris's own negligence, something that would trouble Burnley because he wants to keep the mine running. If the men are worried about losing their jobs, which means they'd be eligible for a call-up to fight, they might believe that keeping their mouths closed about what really happened is the best option. Morris has gone, the mine stays open, their jobs are safe. Everyone wins.' He sighed. 'I still don't know where the torn playing cards fit into all this, but if there's one thing I've learnt from you, it's that anything can have a deeper meaning. Have you any ideas on that front?'

Lizzie had wolfed the last of her food and took a mouthful of tea to wash it down. 'No, but I have been thinking about that and you're right. There might well be a perfectly rational and simple explanation but it's too unusual to ignore until we find one. And while my subconscious is doing its job, I need to see that pit tonight,' she said. 'Then, with any luck, we can get out of here and find a hotel in Canterbury.'

Kember sighed. *Here we go again.*

'Why tonight?' he said. 'Can't it wait until morning? You heard what Burnley said.'

'I see no reason why we can't go down at the end of the back shift and watch the safety team at work. It would give us some idea of the conditions that Morris and Ramsey worked in.'

'Maybe,' Kember said. 'But they inspected the mine every morning before the fore shift. Wouldn't it be better to wait so we get to see the pit at the same time of day that they did?' Even as he finished speaking, he could see from the steel in her eyes that he'd lost this argument.

'By tomorrow morning they'll have made sure everything's tidied away,' Lizzie said in lowered tones. 'If we go at six tonight when the safety team starts its rounds, we might spot something out of place.'

Kember laughed and regretted it immediately when he saw her jaw tighten. 'Sorry, didn't mean to be rude, but we're not miners. How will we know if something is out of place?'

'Like I told Burnley; if we don't look, we won't know.'

Once again, he knew she was right. It couldn't hurt to look tonight, just in case there was something to see that might not be there in the morning.

'We should speak to Ramsey or Quayle,' Kember said. 'If we ask Burnley, he'll refuse point-blank, and if we turn up unannounced at the cage, they'll turn us away. I could make demands but I have serious suspicions about this mine owner who thinks he does all the hard work and nobody else. If we're going to do this, I'd prefer he didn't find out until we're back up.'

Lizzie got to her feet and grabbed her coat.

'Come on then.'

She was halfway to the door by the time he'd gulped the last of his tea and started to follow. He recognised this behaviour too. She had the bit between her teeth and it would take something momentous to deflect her from her task.

Remarkably, the clumps of snow had become bigger, as though whole snowballs were falling from the sky, and the tracks made by Burnley and Mrs Wall had already started to be ironed out of the blanket underfoot. The poor light still failed to provide any definition and perspective, making progress across the site somewhat treacherous. The sun would have been visible low on the horizon by now, were it not for the all-obscuring clouds merging with the ground, and it wouldn't be long before the light would begin to fade.

They rounded the corner of a building and the office came into view. The warm light shed through its windows gave the pristine snow the yellowish hue of a custard tart, and cast an elongated shadow beyond Lizzie's snow-capped Norton. The face of Mrs Wall appeared at one of the windows before a blackout board was hoisted into position, cutting off some of the illumination.

Kember let Lizzie climb the steps and enter the office before him, stamping their boots free of ice as they went. Mrs Wall turned at the noise and wrinkled her nose.

'Mr Burnley insisted on arranging your accommodation himself,' she said.

'No problem,' Kember said. 'I've just popped in to use the telephone.' He indicated the door to Burnley's office with his open hand. 'May I?'

'You can use mine,' Mrs Wall said, picking up another blackout board.

'Thank you.'

As she turned her back, Kember made a sign for Lizzie to wait. He could hear the secretary protesting as she realised that he'd ignored her instruction and entered Burnley's office. As he shut the door, he heard Lizzie start a conversation about leaving her motor-cycle gauntlets there a bit longer to dry out. Within moments, he'd rung the operator, been connected to Canterbury Police HQ, and had waited for DI Andy Watson to be called to take the call.

'Can you delay our car for a couple of hours,' Kember said, keeping his voice down. 'I'm going down the pit at six o'clock with Officer Hayes to have a look for ourselves.'

'Can't that wait?' Watson's voice sounded tinny and distant.

'We were offered an escorted tour tomorrow but we thought a surprise visit might be more beneficial.'

'You don't do things by halves, do you? I'll do as you ask but the road conditions are bad and getting worse.'

'Thanks. We've been offered accommodation on site in case it's needed but a hotel would be more comfortable.'

Watson chuckled. 'I'll see what I can do. Telephone me later when you're d—'

The line went dead and Kember replaced the receiver. The odds were shifting towards them spending the night at the colliery, whether they liked it or not. But first, they had to keep Burnley and Mrs Wall in the dark, persuade Ramsey or Quayle to escort them underground, and convince everyone at the pithead and under-ground to keep their visit a secret, all under the nose of whoever the real murderer was.

And that could be anybody.

They left the secretary still seething and went in search of Ramsey and Quayle, the two firemen who had worked underground with Morris. Lizzie considered them the best options for agreeing to take her and Kember underground. Victor Young the fan house foreman and Terrance Armstrong the winding engineman hadn't actually been underground during Morris's last stint on the fore shift safety team. Edward Pine the onsetter had, but only at the bottom of the shaft to operate the lift cage.

The snow had now obliterated everything to such an extent that Lizzie wasn't sure whether following Kember's determined course was wise. She sort of got her bearings from the headframes but still considered it pure luck when they made it back to the canteen. While Kember checked the social club next door, a quick poke of her head around the door confirmed that neither man was eating. Kember returned with the same result. Another tramp through the deepening, foot-dragging, energy-sapping snowdrifts, fighting against the wind that had picked up again, brought them to the steps of the dormitory.

They found the two men inside, along with Armstrong and Pine, sitting on beds nearest the stove. Apparently, Young had elected to stay in the fan house all day. *Now that is dedication*, Lizzie thought.

'It's certainly warmer at this end of the room,' she said, rubbing her hands together.

'Aye,' Armstrong said. 'That it is.'

'The initial police report said this room was warm on the night Morris died,' Kember said. 'Why is it so chilly in here now?'

Armstrong shrugged. 'Got to be the snow, hasn't it? That white stuff might look like a bedspread but it don't act like one.' He indicated a nearby bed. 'If you've more questions, you can take a pew,' Armstrong said.

Kember held up a hand. 'A kind offer but we've no time I'm afraid. We need to visit the underground workings.' The men didn't flinch. 'Tonight.'

That raised eyebrows and caused glances.

'What does the big boss say?' Ramsey asked. 'We don't do tours down the pit.'

Lizzie saw Kember give the men a gentle smile.

'Mr Burnley has agreed to provide us with an escort but he is adamant that we go down tomorrow morning. We don't want to be here any more than you want us here, and as the pit will shortly cease production for the night, we saw no reason to delay.'

'What's that got to do with us?' Quayle asked.

'Ordinarily, nothing, but you're the men who worked with Morris so if one of you could show us around, we could probably get out of your way a lot quicker.'

The men looked sceptical and Lizzie could see that Kember's approach, as calm and measured as it was, didn't seem to be getting them very far. None of the men were unconsciously displaying any guilt through their gestures, speech or body language, but perhaps that was due to the pack mentality. Safety in numbers engendered confidence. She took a half-step forward and clasped her hands together, hoping the gesture would make her seem like a damsel in distress to these hardened miners. Even some of those who knew her considered her to be *not quite normal* but she could put on an act as well as the next person.

'Gentlemen,' she began. 'I'm afraid it's my fault.' She ignored Kember's curious glance. 'This place is too harsh and too cold for me and I desperately want to get back to Canterbury by late this evening.' She saw their expressions soften. 'We need to see the underground workings to show we've been thorough and checked everything. That way, DI Kember can drop me at a nice warm hotel and the police won't need to bother you again.' She saw Kember nod his head, playing the part she'd hoped he'd pick up on. 'We both have duties to attend to elsewhere. I have warplanes to deliver for the RAF and the inspector has to get back to his police head-quarters in Tonbridge. The roads will be impassable by tomorrow and it would be beastly if we were to be stuck here for days.'

Lizzie gave them her best tilted-head, wide-eyed, fluttery-eyelash look and saw two of the men smile. She hated playing the helpless little girlie, pandering to the prejudices and expectations of a certain type of man she encountered, but it so often worked.

'Why did Burnley agree at all?' Quayle asked. 'No offence, miss, but it's dark, dirty and smelly. No place for a girl. None of the women who work here go underground. Burnley doesn't allow it.'

'I think he agreed because I'm not here to dig coal,' Lizzie said. 'He did insist that we have an escort though, which is perfectly sensible.'

Out of the corner of her eye, she noticed Quayle flick a glance at Pine then away. It lasted a split second but she was sure something unsaid had passed between them.

'What are you looking for?' Quayle asked. 'Morris died in his sleep.'

'He died of carbon monoxide poisoning so we have to take a look at where the gas occurs naturally,' Kember said. 'His death might have been no more than a tragic accident.'

'That's as may be but we could lose our jobs if Burnley finds out we took you tonight,' Pine said. 'None of us can afford that.'

'I'm sure it won't come to that if we're quick,' Kember said, looking at each man in turn. 'All we need is . . . ?'

'Half an hour,' Lizzie said.

'Half an hour.' Kember nodded. 'I'm not at liberty to discuss my investigation but it would be better all round if we went tonight . . . and Mr Burnley didn't find out.'

Ramsey had continued to stare at Kember from the moment the conversation started and his face now carried a look of concern. 'You don't think it's a tragic accident at all, do you? You could order him to let us take you down but instead you're asking us to do it on the QT.' Kember stayed silent. 'What have you found? Do you think Burnley killed Morris?'

Kember glanced at Lizzie. 'It's one possibility,' he admitted.

'You must have good cause to think that so why should we put our lives at risk for you?' Ramsey said. 'If Burnley killed Morris, and I wouldn't put it past him, and he finds out we helped you tonight, it won't just be our jobs on the line, any one of us could be his next victim.'

'The way things stand, any one of us could be next anyway,' Kember said. 'That's the point. But if we can get down there tonight, chances are we'll find all the answers we need, one way or the other, and be gone before you know it. As Officer Hayes said, the weather is getting worse and the last thing anyone wants is for us to be stuck here, possibly for days.'

Lizzie noticed Quayle and Pine look at Ramsey as though waiting for his lead.

'Go on then, I'll take you down,' Ramsey said. 'Eddie can operate the cage, Terry can have a word with the winding house, and Harry can warn Vic in the fan house.' The men nodded. 'Best go down when the safety team have done their stuff, so we don't get in their way, but before the power goes off.'

Lizzie had hoped to go down before that but didn't want to push her luck. Instead, they agreed to meet at the lamp room later that evening.

She left Hut Six with Kember in search of their own beds but with no plans for spending the night at the colliery. She intended to leave as soon as Watson's car arrived. Seeing the underground mine workings had become her priority, and avoiding their accommodation would make Burnley suspicious before they'd had a chance to go down the pit.

'Beastly?' Kember said, turning his shoulder to the wind. 'Who do you think you are, Bertie Wooster?'

'I had to get them on our side somehow,' Lizzie said. 'Something's going on between Quayle, Pine and Ramsey, for certain.' She huddled behind Kember for meagre shelter. 'They exchanged glances in that furtive way people do when they want to keep something hidden but still can't resist taking a full look.'

'Like a criminal returning to the scene of a crime to gloat?'

'Not quite, but similar.' Lizzie leant into a gust and let it pass. 'Why did you tell them that Burnley might be the killer?'

'Because he might. The man at the top is always in the best position to do bad things and get away with it. Besides, they needed an extra push to persuade them to take us down without Burnley interfering.'

Lizzie couldn't argue with that and was grateful the ploy had worked.

They arrived at Hut Two, which turned out to be a converted utility hut with the bottom half of brick, the top half built of solid wood, and a new timber roof covered in bituminous roofing felt. To Lizzie, it looked little more than a large shed, not dissimilar to the motor shed back at RAF Scotney.

Kember opened the door with a key already in the lock, flicked a switch and a single lightbulb on a flex hanging from a rafter shed pale light throughout the dormitory, blackout boards already in position covering the windows. True to his word, Burnley had seen to it that a coal fire was roaring away in the stove at the far end of the room and the six beds had been made up, with a shallow mattress, one pillow and two rough blankets each. One bed looked like someone had taken an earlier nap. The Ritz it was not. Lizzie stood by the stove rubbing her hands as she had in the other hut, and was struck by how much colder the whole room felt. Although recently lit, the stove was doing its best against the lack of insulation in the roof and the draughts coming in through air bricks. It had yet to reach its full potential but Lizzie doubted it had the heating ability to take more than the chill off the room.

'I've stayed in worse, but not much,' Kember said. 'All the same, I could do with forty winks.'

'You carry on,' Lizzie said, watching as he slipped off his shoes and got under the blankets of a bed near the stove, fully clothed.

She turned off the light and returned to her bed by the light of the fire. She sat on the thin mattress with her knees drawn up, one blanket over her legs and the other around her shoulders, staring at the flames.

It had been a long day already and she could have done with a nap herself, but her mind was racing. Each of the men they'd spoken to had displayed a tendency to lie, illustrated through their words and gestures. At the same time, the unspoken language of their bodies demonstrated that all of them had spoken some truth.

She knew all the best lies were based on truth because the closer you kept to what really happened the easier it was to maintain the deception without faltering, and any slight slip up could be explained and laughed away.

Her troubled mind kept returning to the fundamental requirements of murder; motive, means and opportunity. All of them had reasons to a greater or lesser degree, but how could any of the five men – six if you counted Burnley – have murdered Morris with the administration of poisonous gas in sufficient quantity and concentration without killing someone else or themselves as well? Even if that was possible, how could they get away without leaving one witness? Ramsey had almost succumbed to the same fate and hadn't been able to tell the police anything apart from describe the symptoms he'd experienced. That pointed to the inhalation of gas in the mine, but why did Ramsey not die? Why did others in the tunnels not experience symptoms? Why did Morris, unwell but alive at bedtime, die in the warmth and comfort of his own bed in the middle of the night?

She took a deep breath, let it out and relaxed her eyes, seeming to stare right through the fire and beyond. She allowed her mind to begin sliding into an almost meditative state where images could be recalled, replayed and imagined. As a small child, her schoolteachers had chastised her for habitual daydreaming but it was so much more than the idleness they thought they'd seen on the surface. Studying for her psychology PhD and researching the criminal mind had taught her to combine her experience and unique skill. Taken with the known facts of a case and what she was able to glean from a crime scene allowed her to think and feel as though she were the murderer. Unfortunately, providing profiles of killers relied on crimes being committed first. The more crimes, the better the insight.

She took another deep breath.

Not quite normal.

CHAPTER TEN

Kember woke with a start to find Lizzie bending over him, one side of her face in deep shadow, the other given a satanic quality in the orange glow from the fire. He blinked, pushed himself up and swung his legs off the bed.

'You were driving them home, there,' Lizzie said.

'Bloody cheek,' Kember replied, his voice still thick with sleep. 'I don't snore.'

She grinned and disappeared, the dormitory light coming on a few seconds later.

'It's time to go,' she said.

Kember looked at his watch and donned his shoes, the cold of the leather penetrating through his socks. 'Did you sleep?' he asked.

'No.' Lizzie shook her head as she laid her blankets over the bed and sat down. 'I had too much to think about.'

'Any conclusions?' he said, aware that Lizzie's mind worked in a different way to his when mulling over what was known, and especially the unknown. He needed to stitch together hard facts through diligent detective work. Quite often, her extraordinary skill would enable her to explore the gaps and fill them in. He was grateful that on two recent occasions their methods had complemented each other.

'It's curious,' Lizzie said. 'No one seems to have ever been in a position to murder Morris and get away with it.' She paused for a second. 'Did the police report or post-mortem suggest a time of death?'

Kember reached into his coat pocket. 'This is a summary of the police report given to me by Watson.' He pulled a creased sheet of paper from his pocket and opened it. 'It gives the estimated time of death between one and three in the morning.'

Lizzie stood and took the paper from him. 'According to some doctors I've spoken to in the past, the number of deaths by natural causes increases between those times. It's probably complete nonsense but some ill patients have been known to set an alarm clock so they're awake during what they consider to be the danger hours.'

'Hmm.' Kember rubbed his nose. 'I must admit, many of the murders I've dealt with have occurred under the cover of darkness, and quite a few of those after midnight and before sunrise, but that's just my experience.'

'So, if you had a way of killing someone without extreme violence and wanted to make a death look like natural causes, the early hours would be a perfect time to murder.'

'You could say that.' Kember took the paper back from Lizzie. 'In which case; remind me why we're braving a snowstorm to go down a deep dark pit in the evening, a time when the miners have only just finished work?'

'Because how it's left now will be similar to how it was left after Morris's last shift,' Lizzie said. She moved to the door and put her finger on the light switch. 'Hadn't we better get a move on?'

Kember sighed and led the way out into the snow, the white flakes thrown sideways by the wind straight into his ear the second he set foot beyond the lee of the hut. The last light of day had given up the ghost and disappeared, leaving the colliery barely lit by lamps heavily masked under blackout regulations, affixed almost haphazardly to the side of various buildings. He heard the switch and door click in quick succession behind him and Lizzie handed him the key as she strode past. He performed a quick shuffling run to catch her and they manoeuvred between the now familiar buildings back to the pithead. Even with the snowfall and such paltry illumination, they saw a lot more miners than before, walking in different directions away from the pithead and shower block.

'The last of the fore shift, I hope,' Lizzie said.

They reached the main pithead building, with its siren boxes on the wall just inside the entrance, one for mine emergencies and one for air raid warnings, and entered the lamp room where Paul Ramsey and Eddie Pine waited with helmets already on. Kember saw a third miner standing by the cage operator's board.

Pine followed Kember's gaze and then looked back. 'I'm the onsetter,' he explained. 'I work the cage underground. Thatcher's the banksman who operates the cage from here.'

Kember nodded. 'We've met.'

Pine seemed unperturbed. 'To you, this is a quick look underground. To us, it's as important that everything's as safe as if this was the beginning of a shift. We had to have Thatcher here to do his bit.'

'Fair enough,' Kember said.

'Are you sure you want to do this?' Ramsey asked.

'It is necessary for the investigation, I'm afraid,' Lizzie said with a nod. 'If I— we don't see for ourselves then DI Kember cannot honestly report back to his chief inspector that every avenue of inquiry was explored.'

She shrugged apologetically and saw Pine return the shrug before he handed them two short donkey jackets and two helmets. Ramsey helped fit and test two battery lamps. Kember retrieved his tiny Bijou hand-torch from the bottom of his overcoat pocket but Pine held out a deep wooden tray.

'Contraband, please,' Pine said.

'Pardon?' Kember replied, taken aback.

'Only essential kit and equipment are allowed in the mine, so you can't take anything down there that might cause a spark. That includes torches, lighters, matches and cigarettes.'

Kember exchanged a glance with Lizzie and began checking his pockets just in case. Lizzie placed a box of matches and a crumpled packet containing two cigarettes into the box. As crime fighting equipment went, it was a meagre haul.

Pine then switched on and adjusted two safety lamps while Ramsey retrieved a square metal box with windows on three sides and a circular door with a window on the other, open to reveal a mesh screen. It had a tiny oxygen canister fixed to the top that also served as the handle. A bright-yellow canary twittered on a wooden perch inside.

'That's an odd-looking box,' Lizzie said.

'Haldane cage,' Ramsey explained. 'Canaries fall off their perch before we do. He lets us know the gas is there and when we're safely out of the way, we turn on the oxygen and revive the little beggar.'

Ramsey gave Lizzie a grin that Kember wasn't sure hit the mark.

'We've only got a few,' Ramsey continued, 'and we had to buy those ourselves because that skinflint Burnley wouldn't cough up.'

Pine handed Ramsey a metal disc with a number stamped on it, explaining in answer to Kember's raised eyebrow that it was a miner's check, issued as a tally to show how many men had gone underground. Kember and Lizzie weren't given one in case Burnley dropped by and asked awkward questions.

Suitably kitted up, Ramsey handed Kember the Davy lamp and Lizzie the Haldane cage before they proceeded to the lift cage. Thatcher pressed a button to give three sharp rings to the winding engineman. He then raised a curtain of steel mesh held in place by chains and metal bars, allowing Kember, Lizzie, Pine and

Ramsey to duck into the lift cage. With the mesh lowered once again, Thatcher slid a folding shutter until it closed, rang twice and the cage dropped a few inches with a jolt before it started a smooth descent.

With the only light coming from the head-torches on their helmets, Kember tried to keep his breathing steady as the beams picked out the sides of the pit shaft passing by. He'd never suffered with claustrophobia or a fear of the dark before but the rapid descent through solid rock into the bowels of Hades was not his idea of a good time. He'd been in cellars, basements, crypts, bunkers and shelters. He'd even had cause to chase a villain through one of the Victorian sewers beneath the streets of London. None of them had come anywhere near the depth below ground they were heading for now. None had come close to giving him the sense of foreboding one might feel if travelling toward the centre of the Earth for advance sight of one's own coffin in situ.

Kember felt the hairs on his neck and arms rise as he considered that every man now helping them explore the pit tunnels was a suspect in his murder inquiry. The extent of the danger they could be facing, and the backlash when Hartson found out, was not lost on him. With any luck, if any of the fore shift safety team was a murderer, the presence of the others would put him off making a move. They could have used the back shift safety team but he and Lizzie didn't want word getting back to Burnley before they'd finished. He took a deep breath. A quick inspection to satisfy Lizzie and have a look for himself, and then back to the surface where, hopefully, a car would be waiting to take them to a nice hotel in Canterbury.

The minutes passed as the air got colder and the canary sung its heart out. Kember wondered whether there would be enough cable, then dismissed the notion as stupid. How else would all the miners get to and from work every day? Eventually, the cage slowed until Kember supposed they were near the bottom. Then it began to rise and fall as if bouncing in slow motion, giving the sensation of standing on the deck of a ship.

As soon as the cage steadied and came to a stop, Pine lifted the mesh cover with a rattle that seemed louder underground and slid open a shutter with a clatter, letting yellow light flood in. Ramsey led them to a large double-door fitted into the rock nearby. Electric light lit a tunnel stretching away into the distance both left and right, and the floor underfoot, where two parallel rails had been set, had been smoothed by the everyday tramp of miners' boots. Wooden crossbeams held in place with enormous wooden pit props, looking as industrial as the metal machinery around them, braced the ceiling a few feet above his head. Kember felt damp air on his skin and imagined the sweat he could smell to be emanating from the rough walls. He looked at Lizzie but she was engrossed in her surroundings, taking everything in.

'This is the airlock,' Ramsey said, rapping on the wooden door with his knuckles. 'There are two doors and we keep one closed at all times so the air circulates the way we want it to. If we left it open, all the good air would whip through here, bypass most of the tunnels and flow straight out through the fan drift, doing nobody any good.' He pointed down the tunnel. 'That way's the district run by Quayle. This way's my district.' He opened the door and stepped through. 'Stay with me at all times, don't wander off and don't dilly-dally. It's a maze down here. Ask what you like and I'll answer what I can.'

They followed Ramsey and were ordered to shut the door behind them before he opened the next one. As Kember stepped out of the airlock into a tunnel similar in size to the one that they'd just left, he felt cold fingers snake around his hand and give it a squeeze before letting go. He looked at Lizzie, almost blinded by her head-torch as she gave him a smile.

'You can turn your head-torches off because we have electric light and we're not down here to work the coal. Keep them for emergencies.'

Kember and Lizzie complied.

In front of them stood an empty coal truck, next to the end of a conveyor belt that disappeared into the distance. White stencilled lettering on a long box fixed to the wall to their left declared it held a stretcher. Above it was a smaller box that contained first-aid equipment, and a cylinder of oxygen rested on the floor, held in place by a bracket fixed to the wall next to two red-painted fire extinguishers.

'Follow closely,' Ramsey said, taking the Haldane cage and Davy lamp from them.

They followed him through the wide tunnel alongside the conveyor belt, past a cavity hollowed out of the rock in which an office had been constructed from pit props and slats of wood, and into a slightly smaller tunnel leading to the right. Kember could see irregular-shaped lumps of shiny coal along the bottom edges of the tunnel and could smell the strong aroma of coal dust hanging in the air. They branched off a couple more times before Ramsey stopped and turned.

'This is part of the original coal face before we tunnelled further in,' Ramsey said. 'You can see where the seam was cut out and the rock above felled to open up the tunnel before the men moved forward to cut the next bit.'

'Why can't you just cut the lot out and be done with it, instead of digging all these parallel tunnels?' Kember said. He realised by the sad shake of the miner's head that Ramsey thought he was mad.

'If we took out a whole seam in one go the roof would fall in and the whole kit and caboodle would collapse,' Ramsey said. 'It would come down with such force that it would crush anything down here.'

Kember smiled, grateful that the yellow tunnel lighting washed out any sign of his embarrassment.

Ramsey continued. 'How we've been getting it out these past few years is by longwall mining, where we cut the coal, prop up the roof, put any rock spoil in the goaf – that's the cavity we've left behind us – and let the roof cave in. There's always a wide roadway tunnel propped up between us at the coal face and the collapsed rock behind.'

'Interesting but what's your job?' Kember said, knowing he'd asked that during the morning interview.

'It's the safety team's job to look for anything that could pose a danger,' Ramsey said. 'That's anything from dodgy pit props, a sagging roof, unsecured kit, stuff left in the way and so on. We also have to hold the cage and lamp up to the roof, on the floor and inside nooks and crannies. You never know when a pocket of gas might build up.'

'What do you do if you find gas?' Lizzie asked.

'Get everyone out safely,' Ramsey said. 'See if we can get some ventilation in. Maybe set it off in a controlled way. If it was left to build up too much it could ignite and cause an explosion big enough to cause a collapse. That in itself might release other gases equally as dangerous. Safest way is to not let it get to that stage at all.'

'What did Morris do down here?'

Ramsey laughed bitterly. 'Got in the way, mostly. He pecked at me all the time when he should've been checking all this with me, and sharing his time with Harry. God knows why he was promoted over him. He wouldn't even carry these.' He held up the cage and lamp. 'Always said, "as long as one of us has got 'em".'

'You must have breathed in a lot of whitedamp to get so ill,' Kember said.

Ramsey shrugged. 'A small whiff over a long period builds up in the body and has the same effect as a few lungsful of concentrated gas in a shorter period.' Kember almost missed the end of the sentence as Ramsey turned away and his last words tailed off.

They moved quickly through a sequence of much tighter tunnels, Kember smacking his helmet on the roof on several occasions, and emerged into another that opened out dramatically. Thick pit props formed a channel stretching left and right, with a black seam of coal visible on one side and a grey tumble of rock on the other.

Ramsey glanced nervously along the tunnel as a muffled call from Pine reached them, sounding distant in the maze of mine workings. 'Sorry, but do you mind waiting here while I see what the matter is?'

'Go ahead,' Kember said, seeing the look of alarm on Lizzie's face.

'This is one of the roadways,' Ramsey said. 'You're welcome to look around but for God's sake, don't touch anything.'

They watched Ramsey move nimble-footed along the channel until he turned past the angle of another tunnel and disappeared.

'I'm not sure it's a good idea to let him leave, or for us to stay here,' Lizzie said.

'Don't worry,' Kember said. 'If we're close enough for him to check in with Pine, we must be close enough to get out of here.'

'We're seven hundred and fifty feet underground,' Lizzie said, her face creased in concern. 'But as we're alone, let me take advantage of this peace and quiet for a minute.'

He nodded, knowing what she was about to do, and watched her take a few long deep breaths, slow her breathing and relax her eyes in that bizarre way that always gave her the expression of a Victorian porcelain doll. The warm artificial light from the string of bulbs brought out the tone of her skin in a way he hadn't noticed on any occasion before and he felt mesmerised. After a moment, realising he was staring, he managed to tear his gaze away from her face and glanced at the shovels, spades and pickaxes lined up against the wall. Pneumatic drills, with their umbilical cords snaking away into the distance, lay on the ground where the men of the back shift had left them, ready for the morning's fore shift to take them up and begin again. The air felt thick and dry with coal dust and he could taste it at the back of his throat. *How can men work and breathe down here?* he wondered.

'Where are you?' Lizzie said, her voice splitting the silence and giving Kember a jolt. 'I feel queasy,' she said, placing the palm of one hand on her chest. 'And my head aches.'

He opened his mouth to respond but realised she wasn't speaking to him. She'd allowed her mind to guide her thoughts in a way that the possible actions and intentions of others could become accessible. It wasn't a trance and it wasn't mind reading. Kember often joked that it was witchcraft but it wasn't that either. It was a skill, a talent f0r using her experience and expertise to the full, and one that he was grateful to tap into.

Kember watched her eyes refocus on him. 'Do you want to sit down?' he asked.

Lizzie took a deep breath. 'Whitedamp, and most of the other damps, are present all the time,' she said, her eyes fixed on him. 'The fan sucks them out constantly to prevent explosions and to avoid poisoning the men so nobody gets ill, but Morris and Ramsey did get ill so something must have gone wrong.' She put her fingers to her temples and half-turned away.

Kember watched her look at the seam of black coal as if it were the blackboard at Scotney Police Station where she'd find the answer chalked.

'If I were a miner, I'd do everything I could to monitor the ventilation myself, even though there are men whose job it is to keep the fan running, so I don't think it could have happened here by accident. It must be deliberate.'

'What are you saying?' Kember said. 'That the poisoning began down here? But how, when they have Davy lamps and canaries to sniff out the gas?'

Lizzie lowered her arms and turned back. 'Ramsey said he and everyone else carried a lamp or canary but Morris never did. He would never have known something was wrong if nobody told him.'

'Ramsey would have known.'

'Precisely. Either he knew and didn't say or the lamp was tampered with.'

'But—'

Suddenly, the tunnel lights died.

CHAPTER ELEVEN

Lizzie felt the total darkness wrap around her as if buried alive in a coffin. She had never been claustrophobic but when everything is invisible and every point of reference is erased, how do you know the walls aren't closing in or how small the space has become? How many times in their life does someone with perfect eyesight experience the complete absence of light with their eyes still open?

She felt the tightness in her chest constricting her breathing and her heart quickened.

Not here! The words screamed in her head.

She heard Kember curse and his fingers scrabbling before the blinding beam of his head-torch seared into her eyes, leaving a floating white dot in her vision. She fumbled for her own switch and the second beam pierced the dark. The harsh light from their torches created shadows that danced wildly and the effect shook Lizzie. She felt as though the seam of coal and wall of jumbled rock were waiting to move in. For one moment she feared they might encroach further if she looked away, but squeezed her eyes shut for a moment, shutting out the irrational thought.

'Where the hell is Ramsey?' Kember said, positioning his head so his torch shone along the tunnel.

At the turn of her own head, Lizzie caught her breath when their combined lights failed to penetrate more than twenty yards, as though the beams themselves were being absorbed by the grey rock and black coal.

'Ramsey!' Kember shouted. 'Pine!'

No answer came except his own voice bouncing off the rock walls.

'If the power's off and they're gone, we're trapped down here,' Lizzie said, her voice croaky as it left her dry throat. 'How do we get out of this?'

'By going that way.' Kember's beam bounced as he nodded in the direction Ramsey had left. 'I don't know how far we've come or where we are but there must be some way of finding out.'

Lizzie felt her wrist becoming sore from the rubber band she hadn't realised she was pinging. Anxiety level rising, she unbuttoned her donkey jacket, plunged her hand into her tunic pocket, and almost cried with relief as her fingers wrapped around the familiar shape of a small glass jar. She'd almost surrendered this to the contraband tray but her panic at the thought had prevented her from parting with it. She unscrewed the lid, took a deep sniff and came alive as the camphor, eucalyptus and menthol kick from the Vicks VapoRub shocked her mind out of its unnatural rhythm.

She replaced the lid when she saw Kember turn his head to look at the jar, his nose wrinkled against the pungent aroma. He'd seen her do this before but it still embarrassed her when someone watched. He moved closer to put his arm around her, as she suspected he might.

'Chin up,' he said, with more than a hint of awkwardness.

Detecting no patronising undertones, Lizzie allowed him to give her a reassuring squeeze before she pulled away, swallowing to moisten her throat.

'I don't fancy staying here so we'd better find out what's happened,' she said.

'I'm hoping there's an innocent explanation.' Kember started to lead the way. 'Maybe the generator failed. Maybe the lighting and power has been switched off because of an air raid.'

Lizzie wasn't convinced they'd have been abandoned for an air raid, and the colliery was bound to have back-up generators. She followed Kember along the channel between the pit props and turned the corner where they'd seen Ramsey disappear. A conveyor belt coated in black coal dust ran along one wall of the tunnel and she said nothing as Kember stated the obvious; that following it might take them towards the rail trucks and pit shafts.

As they stumbled along the uneven floor with darkness at their feet, Lizzie's thoughts returned to what had just happened. Kember's reaction to her show of anxiety was one she loved and hated at the same time. She was a grown woman, a modern woman, doing her job in the ATA as well as any man, the intellectual equal of Kember and his partner in this investigation. The implication that she'd needed a man's guiding hand and protection irked her.

But.

She knew the gesture had been another of old-fashioned chivalry, not control. She knew he had intended to comfort and reassure – and he had – so what was it that had disquieted her? Confused her? Knowing he was there to defend and protect when necessary was quaint and actually a great comfort, and she loved him for it.

She caught her breath and frowned, the beam from her head-torch sweeping left and right across Kember's back as she shook her head to clear it.

'Are you all right?' he called.

'Keep going,' she insisted, hoping it wasn't much farther to the shaft.

Lizzie thought her wish had been granted as a line of coal trucks on a curve of iron rails came into view but the flood of relief was short-lived.

They had reached a junction that led off in five directions, not including the way they had come. Four of them contained rail tracks. If they chose the wrong tunnel to follow, they could find themselves walking deeper inside the pit and even more lost in the warren of burrows and passageways.

'Look for some indication of where they might lead,' Kember said.

They shone their head-torches around the wide chamber and inside the entrances to the tunnels until Lizzie noticed something high on one wall.

'Look at this,' she said, pointing to some white lettering. 'Herne.'

'Hm, I wonder what that means?' Kember said. He checked the next tunnel. 'Canterbury.'

Lizzie moved clockwise to the tunnel they'd just left. 'Ramsgate.'

'Ashford here.'

'This one says Dover.'

'And Folkestone,' Kember said at the last tunnel. 'Place names in east Kent. I suppose that's better than calling them Tunnel One, Two, Three, and so on.'

'I'm not so sure the men are being fanciful,' Lizzie said. 'I've spoken to many soldiers who returned from the Great War suffering from what people generally still call shell shock. They often referred to place names like Piccadilly and Leicester Square, and it took me a while to realise they were talking about the nicknames given to areas in the trenches of the Western Front.'

'They didn't correspond to real directions, though, surely?' Kember said.

'I know, but these do not look random,' Lizzie said. 'If we were driving and came across such a junction, wouldn't these be in the right order at least?'

Kember looked at the signs again. 'You might be right. When we left the cage at the bottom of the downcast shaft and went through the airlock, we turned left along a wide tunnel with rails. At a guess, based on the pithead alignment, I'd say we'd headed north-west in the direction of Canterbury. If that corresponds to the tunnel marked Canterbury, the one marked Dover might take us south-east back to the pit shafts.'

'It's worth a try,' Lizzie said. 'I don't want to stay here while our batteries and air run out so I'm willing to take a gamble. As long as we don't branch off the main tunnel, we can always retrace our steps to here and try another one.'

Kember agreed, and Lizzie let him take the lead into the Dover tunnel. Their heads bobbed and swayed as they made stumbling progress, making the beams from their torches appear to dance on the floor, walls and ceiling with haphazard shadows as their partners. Lizzie found following the smoother floor around and between the iron rails a little easier than the rough edges near the walls. They passed the odd coal truck waiting to be trundled to the coal face, shovels and spades laid to one side, pneumatic drills and other hewing equipment stacked in clusters, and small side chambers with metal pails and a jumble of other equipment inside, their lights picking them out before they disappeared into the total darkness behind them.

Lizzie wondered whether the chill in the air was something to do with the ventilation system, but with eerily silent machinery abandoned for the night by the dozens of men who operated them, the heat that would normally have forced the men to strip to their waists to keep cool in the stifling tunnels was also absent. The Dover tunnel neither dipped nor rose but did have the occasional kink to right and left, forcing them to reassess whether they should continue or return to the junction. The decision was always to move forward and the discovery of a series of coal trucks on the rails encouraged them to carry on.

As they passed another stack of tools, Lizzie looked back at the spades and shovels, frowning as images of playing cards fluttered across her mind and something as yet indefinable slid closer to its allotted place.

Passing a longer line of trucks on a curving section revealed the downcast shaft lift picked out by the light from their head-torches and Lizzie's relief was palpable. Only then did she feel her hands clenched so tightly into fists that her fingernails had dug into the palms of her hands, and a tightness holding her chest in its grip. Taking a deep breath drew the smell and taste of coal dust into her nose, mouth and lungs, and she coughed. She hadn't realised how anxious and tense she'd become since they found the junction. An attack often manifested itself within a few minutes but this had crept up, wrapping her in layers of worry and concern, weighing heavier and becoming more constricting with every step she'd taken.

She forced herself to regulate her breathing and flexed her fingers to relieve the tension.

Ramsey, Pine and the cage had disappeared and it was obvious they had returned to the surface. Kember's head-torch picked out the controls and he pressed the bell button.

Nothing.

'If the bell isn't working, Ramsey and Pine can't have signalled to Thatcher and the winding house after the power and lights went out,' Kember said. 'Which means they must have got out beforehand.'

'Burnley must have come back, found the pithead occupied and ordered them to shut it down,' Lizzie said. 'We did ask them not to say anything.'

'I didn't ask them to leave us down here.' Kember jabbed the bell button twice more, as though repeating the action would result in the desired outcome.

'They'll come back,' Lizzie said, unconvinced. 'They must.'

◆　◆　◆

'Maybe we can climb up,' Kember said, his torch beam angling up into the shaft. 'There must be a ladder or some other way out.'

Lizzie's hollow laugh betrayed her opinion about the absurdity of the suggestion. Ramsey and Pine had not returned as they'd hoped and the power had not been restored. Time had started to distort, and even though Kember's wristwatch told him only twenty minutes had lapsed, it felt as though they'd been down there for hours.

'I won't be able to climb a ladder over seven hundred feet high,' Lizzie said. 'And what about your old back injury? What if that gives out halfway up?'

Kember kept looking around the area where the cage should have been, pulling this and pushing that, but as far as he could see, there were no levers, cranking mechanisms or other power sources that could get them out of this mess. He tried hard to contain his rising concern. They weren't in dire straits just yet but he could see that Lizzie was struggling to contain her own anxiety caused by their predicament. If being stranded was the result of innocent circumstances, all would be well and they'd be rescued. If not, their deaths might be no more than a couple of hours away. With power to the cage and lights having been cut, it was probable that the fan had shut down too, halting ventilation, and he knew the poisonous mine gases would have begun seeping into the air from the coal.

Watson was due to pick them up later, if the roads were still passable, but they could be dead by the time he arrived. He tried to remain calm and focused, believing there had to be a way to get out. They could try the upcast shaft, where rail trucks laden with coal were taken up to the surface, but that was likely to look no different to the downcast shaft that transported the men. They could try signalling but was there any safe way to do that, and would anyone be watching and listening? *No point*, he decided. If the mine had suffered a simple power cut, people would know they were trapped and would be working to free them. They hadn't been given miners' checks, so if they'd been left to die, no one would know or be up there to answer anyway.

He sat on a neat pile of pit props stacked against the wall.

Lizzie joined him.

'What are you thinking?' she asked.

'I'm thinking that our best hope is Watson,' Kember replied, realising the implication of that conclusion as soon as he'd uttered it.

'So, you think we've been abandoned?'

He sighed and watched the pale cloud of his breath drift through the beam from his head-torch. They'd been underground for more than half an hour already and he suddenly felt colder. *What symptom of gas inhalation will manifest first?* he wondered. Sitting side by side in silence for some time, Kember tried to concentrate on unlocking that one solution he knew must be there. Burnley might be a skinflint but his men wouldn't allow corners to be cut to such an extent that all their lives were forfeit if trapped after an accident.

He felt Lizzie shivering as she slipped her arm around his waist and pulled him closer, resting her head against his neck. It felt nice, but in any other situation it would have felt great. He shook his head to clear it and was rewarded with a few pounding throbs from a headache. Was that a sign? *Christ*, he thought. *That was quick.* He'd expected two hours before any symptoms arrived and they'd been underground for maybe an hour. What was it in the air they were breathing? *Carbon monoxide, most likely,* he thought, *but it could be anything.* His thoughts drifted to his son, a fighter pilot in the RAF, and his daughter in the WAAFs, the only good things remaining from his marriage. He hoped they were safe and vowed to call them if he got out of this alive. Although he thought about them often, he wondered why being faced with death always made him want to pick up the telephone. *Perhaps my life is flashing before my eyes,* he thought, his wry smile lost in the gloom. Lizzie's breathing seemed shallower than he remembered and he gave her a gentle nudge. She raised her head and put her free hand to her chest.

'I feel dizzy and slightly queasy,' she said. 'Is this it?'

'Not if I can help it,' he said. 'Stand up.'

He wasn't sure that standing was any better than sitting. Maybe it pumped the gaseous poison around their bodies faster but at least their noses and mouths were higher off the ground. *Is that even any good in an enclosed tunnel?* he wondered. *Is carbon monoxide lighter than air?*

Lizzie remained sitting on the pit props and he studied her face, full of shadows and angles created by his head-torch, and of worry lines.

'How do we get out of here before we're gassed to death?' she said. 'Burnley thinks we're coming down here tomorrow, we have a whole dormitory to ourselves, and we've already eaten in the canteen. If he's told the men to shut the pit down for the night, Watson might arrive too late to save us.'

Kember clenched his fists and forced himself to concentrate, making his heart and head thump. Miners were prepared for every eventuality so he knew something must be down there with them that could help. 'Wait here,' he said, and moved back to the shaft, where he looked in every nook and cranny near to the closed shutter. Something tried to get through the fog engulfing his brain like candyfloss and he squeezed his eyes tight to grasp at it.

'Airlock,' he said, stepping across to the wooden doors.

He found them heavier to open than before and an unexpected wave of vertigo made him as unsteady and nauseous as a Saturday night drunkard. He closed the door, tensed his arms and opened the next, revealing the black void beyond.

The beam from his head-torch zigzagged across the wall opposite the conveyor belt as he sought something he'd seen earlier. His eyes followed its passage until it passed over the long box containing the stretcher. The small first-aid box was there too but where was—

He fell to his knees in front of the black-painted cylinder and yanked it from its clip. The cold metal clanged on the rock floor and Kember ran his hand across its curves. His right hand grasped at the valve knob as his left pulled the leather mask to his face. The valve hissed and he breathed deeply, relief flooding into him with the life-giving oxygen. He knew it would take more than this to rid their bodies of the poison but at least they had a lifeline.

Two more gulps and he closed the valve, grasped the heavy cylinder and picked it up as awkwardly as someone carrying a salmon while wearing rubber gloves. He had to get it to Lizzie.

Fumbling back through the airlock, he found her on the pit props with her head in her hands, and crouched in front of her. He placed the mask over her nose and mouth and turned the knob. She began breathing deeply as the gas hissed and he insisted the mask stayed in place for several breaths.

Lizzie removed the mask. 'Where did you find that?'

'Through the airlock,' Kember said. 'I remembered it from earlier.'

'Are you all right?' She pushed the cylinder towards him.

He took another breath of oxygen. 'I'm fine, now.'

With their faces inches apart, the glare from their torches went over their heads, bathing their faces with an ethereal glow that made Lizzie's eyes sparkle. They stayed like that for a few seconds, until the look she gave drew him closer.

He could smell her perfume and feel her breath on his face. His heart thumped and he held his breath. Shivering in a coal mine, wearing donkey jackets and helmets, and being gassed to death seemed neither the right time or place to be feeling whatever *this* was. Her hand went to his shoulder and she leant forward. He met her halfway and their lips touched. The kiss was as warm and soft and tender as any he'd ever experienced, and he forgot for a split second that they were dying in the dark.

She pulled away. 'Sorry I—'

'No need. It was—'

'All the same . . . Thank you.'

'Thank . . . ?'

They looked at each other and laughed; the moment and the awkwardness already in the past. Kember got up from his crouch and sat next to her.

'Lizzie. Things have been difficult these past few months, what with my wife and marriage and everything, and I wish things could be different for us.'

'You don't have to—'

'I do. I really want it to be different, better, and I think you feel the same.'

She smiled and gave a little nod.

He took a deep breath from the cylinder and let it out slowly, his heart thumping as he feared what Lizzie might think. If their fate was to die together hundreds of feet underground, he wanted her to know what she meant to him and why he'd never shown it.

'We married when I was eighteen and have been together for almost twenty years,' he began. 'Even though it's been over for a long time, divorce hasn't been possible. I had an uncle who made a lot of money from manufacturing but he couldn't have children and he saw me as the son he always wanted. When he died, he left me the house in Tonbridge and all his money.' Kember offered the oxygen mask to Lizzie and waited for her to take a few breaths. 'He was very religious and a stickler for the sanctity of marriage so he put stipulations in his will about who could inherit and when. His house came to me immediately but it only remains mine if I stay married for twenty-five years, and I won't see a penny of the money until then.' He felt a bit giddy and took another breath from the mask. 'I tolerate my wife's indiscretions and avoid antagonising her because it's the children's inheritance too and I'm loath to give her any grounds for initiating a divorce out of spite. I don't care about the house or money but I do care about my children's future, and you.'

'Wouldn't she stand to lose everything too?' Lizzie said, looking up at him.

'She's well off enough to consider it a fair price to pay to see me suffer.'

He was secretly pleased when he felt her arm snake around his waist.

'When my mother had her riding accident, I went to bits,' Lizzie said. 'I became anxious, fearful that she was going to die. The anxiety got worse and I started to wash my hands excessively and keep things clean in the hope that no germs would get to her. I developed little rituals that I convinced myself would keep her safe, but only if I repeated them a number of times in exactly the same way. My school friends thought I was mad or a witch, judgements that have followed me ever since. I studied psychology to find out

179

what was wrong with me and realised I could only fix myself by achieving the impossible, going back in time and preventing my mother's accident. People have always considered me not quite normal and I've had to hide who I am from strangers every day of my life. I do care for you too but how can I inflict that, my anxiety and OCN, on any man, especially a married one?'

'I'd cope,' he said, his heart thumping so hard he thought she must feel it through his chest.

'That's sweet,' she said, and surprised him by leaning forward and planting another kiss on his lips, before drawing back to take a pull of oxygen. 'But I can't allow you to throw away your inheritance for someone like me when you've only six more years to go. Anyway, it could be immaterial.' She tapped the cylinder. 'I don't suppose this will last very long. We're just delaying the inevitable.'

As they sat together in silence, Kember wondered where they could go from here. He wanted to say something comforting but knew she was right.

His professional mind slipped into gear and started cycling through their options. He feared that Watson might not realise they were trapped underground, even if he were able to reach the colliery through the snowdrifts. There were two mine shafts, one for men and one for coal, but the power to the cages was off. Whether that was deliberate – most likely – or an air raid precaution – unlikely – remained to be seen. Their headaches and dizziness proved that gas was seeping rapidly into the air from the coal seam and at the moment they had one small cylinder of oxygen between the two of them. It was enough for now but they might be trapped until the fore shift. Seven hundred and fifty feet below ground; it might as well have been the centre of the Earth.

Kember's mind often acted like a large paper room in a government ministry where all the files were kept, and something Kember had mulled over had stirred the man in a tan overcoat and flat cap who he imagined worked there. All he needed to do was wait for the little man to reach for a dusty shelf to retrieve a memory, and for his brain to make the connection.

He didn't have long to wait.

'We should try the other shaft,' Kember said, his torchlight bobbing as he stood. 'I've got an idea.'

CHAPTER TWELVE

Lizzie followed Kember with reluctance as he headed into a tunnel they'd yet to explore. He was a detective, a man, and would believe it possible to escape up the other shaft until the facts proved otherwise. Gas was seeping into the mine, that was undeniable, but the district run by Quayle might be worse and moving to there could be putting them in greater danger. She remembered the two head-frame winding towers on the surface being close together, which gave her hope that the distance through the tunnel would not be too great.

She was right.

It seemed an eternity of bumping, scraping and tripping along the long straight tunnel but it could have been no more than five or so minutes. The width and height of the tunnel and its slippery rails underfoot suggested a major thoroughfare for transporting coal hewn from the main seam, and that assumption proved correct too as the opening of the upcast shaft came into the range of their lights. The closed shutter of the cage opening seemed twice as big as that of the downcast shaft and a line of empty coal trucks stood nearby. Shovel and pickaxe handles protruded from one of the trucks ready for use on tomorrow's fore shift. The rails leading from the opening curved away towards the tunnel and into the coal-black void beyond.

'I thought so,' Kember said.

Lizzie heard Kember put down the cylinder with a clang and saw his beam directed towards another standing next to fire extinguishers and wooden boxes of emergency medical kit. As pleased as she was, she wondered whether it was worth prolonging the agony.

'Was that your idea?' she asked, still convinced their fate lay at the bottom of this pit.

She was surprised at how resigned she sounded, tinged with bitterness, but Kember seemed not to have noticed.

'Partly,' he said. 'With two districts, there had to be more than one cylinder of oxygen. I suspect there are more nearer the coal face, which means we might be able to hold out for a few hours longer than I'd feared.'

He retrieved the new cylinder and set it down beside the other. It clanged with a different note and Lizzie saw the frown on his face.

'What's wrong?'

'It's the same size but much lighter,' he said. 'Someone's been using it a lot because I think it's almost empty.'

'Quayle,' Lizzie said, matter-of-factly. 'He'd have been safe with the fan off if he used this oxygen while he did his safety checks. Pine wouldn't have needed the other cylinder because as we said, he knew how long the checks took and could ride up to the surface for fresh air, coming back down at the last minute.'

Kember tapped the sides of both cylinders and Lizzie heard the difference in notes.

'This one from Ramsey's district is only half-full as well,' he said. 'He must have been sneaking sniffs whenever he could give Morris the slip.'

'That doesn't help our current predicament,' Lizzie said.

Kember looked up at the point of the roof where the upcast shaft disappeared towards the surface. 'I don't fancy getting get lost hunting fresh cylinders. If we're low on oxygen, I'd prefer to not take any chances.' He took hold of the shutter handle and gave it a yank. It remained in place.

Lizzie watched as he fumbled with the handle and found a second catch. The shutter slid open and he stepped inside the large opening where rail trucks piled with coal would be trundled into the cage during the working day.

'You shouldn't be able to open these shutters when the cage isn't there,' Kember said. 'The fact that you can makes me hope that this is our escape route.'

Lizzie shook her head. She was a young, healthy, fit woman but even if the shaft contained a ladder, she feared climbing vertically for seven hundred and fifty feet could be beyond her abilities and strength. She wasn't a miner, she flew aeroplanes.

'As I suspected,' Kember said.

Lizzie's heart sank.

She heard the scrape of shoes on metal rungs and the glare from Kember's head-torch disappeared, leaving a faint glow at the base of the shaft. She wondered whether she should try to follow but the thought of falling to instant death, or even worse, breaking her back and dying in agony made her nauseous. She squeezed her eyes shut and concentrated on her breathing, trying to ward off panic, but the urge to vomit increased.

Her eyes opened wide. *The carbon monoxide!* She hurried to the cylinders, grabbed a mask and took a few deep breaths of oxygen, almost laughing at the absurdity and danger of their situation.

Kember's light reappeared as he descended to the floor and she was reassured by his presence. He came over to her and grabbed the mask of the other cylinder, taking a few long breaths.

'I think it's possible,' he said.

'I can't climb all that way up,' she said. 'It's too far.'

'It's not straight up.' He leant against a coal truck.

Lizzie felt a prickle of irritation. She'd seen him climb straight up.

Kember scratched his nose. 'When I first spoke to Victor Young, he told me about his job in the fan house and how the fan works. It sucks stale air out through this shaft which draws air in through the other one, creating a through flow of fresh air.'

'I know but I don't see how that helps us,' she said, unable to keep a tremor of frustration from her voice.

'It's been at the back of my mind and now I realise; the fan house is – what – a little over four hundred yards from the pithead winding gear. Why so far?'

Lizzie thought. 'In case there's an explosion at the pithead?' she suggested, not knowing where this was going.

'Not the pithead: underground,' Kember said, clearly enthused by this knowledge. 'And not just explosions but any kind of emergency.'

'I don't see . . .' Lizzie shrugged, the black shoulders of her over-size donkey jacket bunching like a bat testing its wings before flight.

Kember patted the rough-hewn rock wall nearest to him. 'Quayle said he was responsible for the drifts in his district, as well as tunnels. Young said the upcast shaft was connected to the fan house via a drift tunnel with a thirty-degree incline. Given the depth of this shaft, that would tally with the distance the fan house is from the pithead. I believe the fan drift is not just a ventilation shaft but was designed as an escape route.'

Lizzie wondered whether the oxygen was working on Kember as it should. 'But I saw you climb straight up.'

'True,' he said. 'I went up a few yards to see if I could see anything, and the ladder does go on, but the fan drift is a much better option. I was never very good at trigonometry at school, but by my reckoning, it's about fifteen hundred feet to the fan house.'

'Fifteen hundred feet?' Lizzie couldn't help throwing her head back with a laugh. 'We'll never make that. What do you think we are, mountain goats?'

Kember stepped towards Lizzie, his face suddenly solemn, and put his hands on her shoulders.

'Trust me,' he said. 'If we stay here, we could die, even if we could find more oxygen, which in the dark and this maze of tunnels I think would be a grave risk. The entrance to the fan drift is just through that opening, where the cage comes to rest. The incline is quite sharp but it's a lot better than going straight up. It's lined with concrete and I remember Burnley mentioning a process he called cementation, which they used to keep the groundwater from seeping into the pit shafts and tunnels. There are iron rungs set into the floor to help us climb but they're only about a foot wide, and we can stop for a breather as many times as you like.'

Lizzie laughed again and wondered if the gas was getting to her again.

'Breather?' she said. 'Those cylinders are too heavy to carry very far, never mind lug up a concrete hill.' She took a mask and tried to keep her breathing normal as she inhaled, aware of her mind trying to betray her. As the life-giving gas worked its magic again, she calmed herself further by touching the rubber band on her wrist. Realising Kember was talking again, she tuned in.

'. . . and I'd rather die getting you out than watch you die slowly down here. I don't know how carbon monoxide behaves in the air but the higher we climb, the farther we get from the coal and the nearer we get to fresh air.'

It annoyed her that she knew he was right again. If they tried climbing straight up, there was no telling who or what awaited them at the top, even if they could make it. If someone realised that they were climbing, that someone might restore the power and send the cage down to scrape them off the wall like mud off a boot. If someone really was trying to kill them, they stood a better chance of survival by taking a longer but slightly easier route to reach the surface away from the pithead, somewhere they wouldn't be expected.

They spent a few moments tying their laces tight, buttoning their donkey jackets and ensuring the lamps were secured to their helmets. Snagging a loose piece of clothing or equipment during the climb was the last thing either of them wanted. At best, it could delay and tire them; at worst, it could precipitate their death.

'If we can't take these with us, we should make good use of them before we go,' Kember said, tapping a cylinder. 'To give ourselves an extra boost.'

Lizzie agreed and they both covered their noses and mouths with the leather masks for the final time, taking a few deep slow breaths. She could sense Kember's impatience to get going and she suspected there was more to it than the simple desire for escape and survival. Even in the harsh glare of the head-torches she could see the hard edge to his jaw either side of his mask and the steel in his eyes. He tapped the cylinder with his fingers, deep in thought. To say that Kember abhorred murder and attempted murder was an understatement. Lizzie knew that when the intended victim was one of them, the desire for revenge and retribution could be as strong as any emotion. Had their last two cases not demonstrated that?

Kember pulled the mask from his face. 'Are you ready?'

Lizzie dropped her own mask and nodded. The extra oxygen had begun to make her feel giddy and she suspected it was a case of having too much of a good thing.

'No time like the present,' she said.

Kember led the way past the open shutter to the large cage space at the bottom of the upcast shaft and turned sharp right. Lizzie tipped her head back and looked straight up, feeling her mouth open in dismay. Whatever she'd expected, it hadn't been the total absence of light beyond her torch beam. She thought there should have been a pinprick of light at the top of the shaft at least. Panic waited in the wings at the realisation of how far seven hundred and fifty feet really was, but then she remembered the cut power and the blackout regulations and felt slightly better.

Kember had waited at the opening to the fan drift and now gestured for her to go in front of him.

'You go first,' he said, his face looking like a charcoal sketch in the harsh light of her head-torch. 'If I'm right, it's going to be a long drag to the top, and from what I can see, it's quite steep and the rungs are smooth. If you slip, I don't want you tumbling all the way back to the bottom.'

This wasn't the time and place to argue but Lizzie felt a twinge of irritation at his assumption that if anyone would trip, it would be her. After all, he was the one with the old back injury. If anything, she thought it would be her own mind that would trip her.

She moved her head left, right and down, her eyes following her torch beam in search of any guide rail, handhold or carved steps. In addition to the rungs, iron loops had been set into the concrete walls every few yards on one side, but the rope she supposed they once held had long gone, if ever it had been threaded through at all. The scale of the task struck her as she took the first tentative steps in to the maw of the tunnel. Even though the almost smooth concrete floor afforded little by way of grip beneath her boots, the walls were rough enough to threaten to tear the skin from her palms. She tugged at the arms of her oversize donkey jacket, pulled them lower and kept the cuffs gripped in place with her fingers. Now she could use the thick material to protect the heels of her hands as she braced herself against the walls and stepped nervously from one iron rung to the next.

She heard Kember enter the drift behind her, the shadow of her body cast by his torch dancing ahead of her. As it stretched away, seemingly independent of her body, she imagined the shadow belonged to Hades escorting her to the mouth of the underworld. But were they leaving hell behind or climbing towards it?

Lizzie tuned in to the scrapes of their boots on the rungs as they started to acquire the rhythmic quality of a ticking clock. Her breathing settled down to its own pattern and her mind started to function like a turning, whirring clockwork mechanism, going back over what they'd learnt in the last few hours, trying to separate the lies from the truth and piece together what might really have happened. She had only a passing concept of time as they inched up the sloping drift tunnel, the foot of the upcast shaft receding, but her thigh and calf muscles burned as if on fire from within and she hoped this reflected good progress.

A score of steps later, just as she realised that she could no longer feel her toes, a dark line across the dull concrete appeared up ahead. She thought it might be a crack in the tunnel's floor and prayed it would prove wide enough for her to sit on for a while. Her fingers groped for it as she approached and relief made her catch her breath. A foot-deep platform created in the cement stretched tunnel wide.

'What's wrong?' Kember said as Lizzie halted, his voice thick with concern and fatigue.

'I have to stop,' she said. 'There's not much call for climbing up mine shafts when you're a pilot. My bloody legs ache.'

She proceeded to turn herself with awkward movements until she felt the ledge beneath the seat of her trousers, and lowered herself warily.

'What are you doing?' Kember asked.

'There's a small ledge with enough room for us to sit side by side,' she replied, her head pounding in time with the thumping of her heart. 'We must be above the gases now, so we can afford to rest.'

He uttered some kind of guttural acknowledgment and manoeuvred himself on to the ledge, breathing heavily.

'Is anything wrong?' Lizzie asked, noticing him grimace as if in discomfort. 'You don't sound too good.'

'It's a bit of a strain on the old back injury,' he said. 'I'm fine when upright but this prolonged hunching over is killing me.'

Expending all that energy on the climb while wearing the thick donkey jacket had made her feel warm to the point of sweating. Now, sitting still, she noticed her body already felt cooler, except where she and Kember were pushed together.

He angled his head downwards and the beam from his head-torch illuminated a short section of the tunnel. 'I wonder if this marks the halfway point?'

'I bloody hope so,' Lizzie said.

Their beams illuminated little more than twenty yards of tunnel, the black-looking iron rungs and loops standing out against the grey, water-stained cement, and the bottom of the black void possibly over a thousand feet below. She reached for her rubber band in dismay, and a squeeze of panic threatened to engulf her when she realised her left wrist was bare. *It must have broken and dropped off,* she thought. Although she drew some comfort from feeling the band on her other wrist, her heart skipped a beat when she patted her pocket and found it empty. She plunged her hands into the donkey jacket's pockets and patted all her other pockets in turn but the VapoRub jar had gone.

'What's wrong?' she heard Kember say and she looked at him accusingly but realised he would be the last person to take any of her countermeasures. He was still speaking, his voice muffled and distorted now as though heard through water. She felt hot, her throat tight, and she clutched at her neck to tear away whatever was strangling her. Her fingers found bare skin. As she looked back along the tunnel, the steep incline stretching down into darkness, her eyes began to play tricks, creating flares of red and orange from the light of their head-torches. She felt drawn down and tried to stand, to turn and get away. Her foot slipped from the iron rung and her boot scraped against the rough cement. Her fingers scrabbled for a handhold but she couldn't see beyond the dancing head-torches that flashed like bolts of lightning, the roaring in her ears providing the thunder. Her other foot slipped, threatening to send her tumbling back to certain death at the bottom of the fan drift, but her fingers caught one of the iron rings and gripped hard, on fire with the effort. She twisted, something pawing at her jacket like bindweed and bramble. Her breaths came short and shallow, her chest unable to expand as though someone had their arms around her, constricting. She was shaking, sweating, the narrow walls of the drift tunnel closing in further. She shut her eyes and a tear squeezed out, trickling down her cheek.

That simple feeling of salt water tickling her face distracted her mind for a split second. It was long enough. She realised the arms weren't constricting, they were comforting and she heard Kember's soothing voice reaching her through the fog. She fought hard to regulate her breathing, and slowly each breath became longer and deeper, her eyes refocusing as her mind relaxed and regained control of itself.

As quickly as it had started, the panic attack stopped.

She felt stupid. This was the first time Kember had witnessed a full attack, and all because she'd lost the little blue jar. She thought back and suspected she must have dropped it when she'd last used it, when the lights had gone out. She looked at Kember and saw his face creased with worry.

She smiled in reassurance and rested her head against his shoulder.

They sat with their thoughts for a few moments, Kember's silence confirming that he understood her need for recovery. The solution to all their problems wouldn't be found on a cement platform in the dark. They had to get to the surface and out of danger first. From fresh air and freedom would come new hope, renewed energy and clearer thinking.

She shuddered, feeling the cold more acutely now her flushes and sweating had dissipated. Having stopped because of complaining muscles, Lizzie now found her ankles, knees and hips ached from their cramped and unnatural sitting position. Despite the warmth along her left side which pressed against Kember, her right side was chilled to the bone. If they were about halfway to the fan house, they must still be several hundred feet underground. That would have made it chilly in summer but cold air sinks and the surface was several feet deep in fresh snow. She thought of the hours she'd spent delivering Tiger Moth aircraft, with their cockpits open to sweeping rain, being buffeted by skin-freezing wind, and like as not, shot at by tired and over-zealous anti-aircraft crews mistaking her for the enemy. Aloft in the clouds was what she knew best, where she felt most at home, where she could relax and be free of the anxiety that dogged her, and where she wished she was right then.

Lizzie flattened herself against the wall as best she could to allow Kember to manoeuvre himself off the platform and take up position behind her again. He moved easier than when he'd sat down and Lizzie was thankful that at least the rest had given his back some respite.

This time, Lizzie counted the iron rungs as she took each step. She'd estimated they were about a foot apart which meant a thousand steps should take them to freedom. After five hundred, a weary misplacing of her left foot caused a jarring pain to shoot up her leg, jolting her tired mind from its train of thought. Something about the hut had been bothering her but now the pain in her joints took her attention. She waved away Kember's concerned enquiry, took a deep breath and trudged ever upward.

Lizzie estimated they'd been underground for maybe two hours before they entered the fan drift and had been climbing for around three-quarters of an hour, including their breather. Her body said longer.

Six hundred rungs came and went. The muscles of her legs ached with effort and cramp.

Seven hundred, and a breath of air flicked her hair.

Eight hundred steps, and the breath had become a breeze.

'The bastards have turned the fan on,' Kember called.

She swore inside her head and concentrated on finding each iron rung as the air being drawn from the deep mine became a howling wind that rushed up and threatened to lift her off her feet. She felt as though she were standing on the seafront at Hastings in a force eight gale, her ears aching from the wind whipping by, the breath being sucked from her and the skin of her hands and face dried and chilled. Her clothes billowed around her like an overstuffed Guy on fireworks night and she could smell the stink of engine oil, stale air and sweat from below, coal dust coating her nostrils and feeling gritty in her mouth.

Nine hundred steps and Lizzie noticed the slope of the tunnel decreasing until she had to lean back to stay upright and not rush headlong towards the tunnel's end. The space began to open out, the walls and roof receding from her touch. She reached for the wall on her left and felt for the iron loops, working carefully towards where she could now make out a whirring and thrumming through the noise of the wind.

One thousand steps. She progressed as if stalking some kind of prey and saw a flashing up ahead. Curiosity getting the better of her, she eased forward and realised she'd moved close enough for the fan blades to reflect the beam of her torch.

She heard a noise behind her and turned to see Kember squinting at her through watery eyes, his hair dancing around his head like a dark halo. Kember tried to say something. She could see his lips moving but heard no words. She pointed to her ears and shook her head. He nodded and tapped to his chest before pointing towards the fan. She held his arm and shook her head. Weren't they too close to the fan already? What if it sped up and drew them on to its deadly blades? He gave her a hug she supposed he thought was reassuring and worked his way past her. Her chest tightened at the thought of losing him and her mind shouted at her to stop him, but her feet were rooted to the spot. All her psychological training and experience were no match for the fear of death.

Kember had advanced about twenty feet before he stopped, turned and beckoned to Lizzie. Her hair lashed at her face and eyes and she could barely make out his gestures indicating that he'd found a door. She felt for the iron loops and moved forward to join him, every muscle tensed. He grasped a lever fixed to the door and pushed hard. The strain told on his face as he heaved against the flat piece of metal but it didn't budge. He tried again and she added her own weight behind it.

It remained stuck. Or locked.

Kember had abandoned the lever and looked like he was searching for something. Wind whipped at his clothing, making his trousers billow like sails. The beam from his torch bobbed and zigzagged, reflecting off the fan blades, and she saw for the first time that a steel mesh stretched across the tunnel, protecting the fan from flying debris.

She watched Kember tugging at something on the wall and he returned seconds later with a long-handled fireman's axe. She moved back at his waved instruction and he swung the axe in an arc. Metal clanged loud above the other noise as the flat end of the axe struck the lever. It didn't budge. Given that this was supposed to be an emergency escape route, Lizzie concluded that someone had deliberately locked the door or jammed the lever on the outside.

Kember swung again. And again.

The next swing did the trick and the lever moved. Kember pushed it open and put his shoulder to the door, axe held defensively in his right hand. Lizzie had expected snow-chilled air to be sucked in through the doorway but it was as dark and enclosed beyond as the tunnel. Her heart sank. *Are we ever going to get out of this?* she thought. Fearful of entering an even smaller place, she reached for Kember's outstretched hand nonetheless and allowed herself to be pulled into the chamber. It was very cramped and only Kember's body pressing against her stopped her reaching for her rubber band. Their time underground had taken them into spaces of decreasing size and she couldn't bear to think about what might come next.

Kember shouldered the door closed and patted the walls until bright light seared into Lizzie's eyes at the flick of a switch. Blinking as her vision adjusted, she saw they were in a room about four feet wide and six feet long. Two chunks of splintered wood lay at their feet, bearing testimony to the fact that someone had jammed the door and sought to keep them from escaping. The artificial wind remained on the other side of the door but she suspected the ringing and aching in her ears would take time to dissipate.

'Thank Christ for that,' Kember said, breathing heavy with the effort of opening the door in such a brutal fashion. 'That fan was sucking the very breath from my lungs and I couldn't have stood much more.'

She looked up at his concerned face and into his marvellous blue eyes. Her head, ears, muscles and joints ached but she was alive, for now. He'd seen to that and she'd be eternally grateful.

Despite her recently confessed convictions, the urge was too great to pass up the chance to plant one last kiss on his lips, taking him by surprise. His face reddened, and she hoped she hadn't over-stepped the mark after what had been said in the tunnels.

'Where are we?' she said, to hide her own confusion as well as his embarrassment.

'It's an airlock like the one in the pit,' he said. 'The engineers can get in and out but the fan only draws stale air from the mine rather than fresh air in through the doors.' He manoeuvred around her to get to the outer door. 'Let's get out of here.'

CHAPTER THIRTEEN

Kember's mind was on full alert. The power had been switched on, to the fan house at least, but that didn't mean the cavalry had come to their rescue. Despite the cramp in his lower back muscles, Kember focused on what might lie beyond the outer door of the airlock. If someone had guessed they might work out how to escape a slow death in the mine, they must also have realised that jamming the fan drift door was not guaranteed to keep them in for long.

He switched off his head-torch and motioned for Lizzie to do the same before he reached back and switched off the airlock light, plunging the small space into total darkness. He then tested the outer door, convinced it too would be jammed, but the well-greased lever and hinges allowed him to open it with the faintest of sounds. He wondered why it hadn't been wedged shut too and concluded it was too visible from the path and the fan house entrance for anyone to risk time fiddling around outside the airlock. Also, it might have drawn unwelcome attention if anyone had noticed a chunk of wood braced against the door lever. The door swung outwards without a sound and his brow wrinkled in a frown at the scene that met his eyes. He'd expected almost impenetrable dark, caused by the government blackout and clouds made dense with unshed snow that blocked the moon. Instead, masked lamps cast their downward glow along the path leading to the pithead creating circles of bright sparkling snow. His eyes were drawn upwards and he noticed more faint glows around the pithead, suggesting all the colliery lighting had been switched on. *Curious*, he thought.

He hesitated, trying to detect any movement beyond the snow that still fell steadily, whipped into a flurry by an occasional gust of wind, until the light touch of Lizzie's hand on his back prompted him to move down the steps. The many layers of white flakes should have made a soft muffled crunching sound, like that of cotton wool being squeezed, but ice cracked beneath his shoes suggesting that someone else had stepped here this evening after the snow had begun to lie. He bent awkwardly, his back muscles complaining about being worked again, and brushed the top layers of snow from the patch in front of him. The impression of a small round-toed boot emerged, captured in snow compressed into ice. It confirmed his suspicion that the door had been jammed recently but told him nothing about the owner. He pointed it out to Lizzie, who bent and touched it with her hand, fingers splayed. The thrum of machinery drew his attention back to the fan house, where he could see from the line of rounded depressions leading from the path to the door that someone had returned there. Had they left?

Kember turned to Lizzie and motioned for her to wait but he wasn't surprised when she ignored him. He made a stern face and whispered, 'Stay behind me.' She nodded and he moved to the fan house door. Dark coverings obscured the windows, although light seeping around the edges suggested they were makeshift rather than intended for the blackout.

He crouched by the door and tried the handle. It opened easily.

He peered inside, squinting against the harsh light of the room, and saw a man in the corner office looking bored. He stood upright and walked straight in, as though he'd walked along the path like normal. The man looked up in surprise but made no attempt to move from the chair. It was the same man they'd seen earlier when they came to speak to the off-duty Young. Kember opened the office door and stepped in. Lizzie followed and shut the door to reduce the noise.

'Didn't expect to see you two here,' the man said.

'And why's that?' Kember replied.

'Because you've been gone a while and they've been looking for you over at the pithead and dorms.'

Kember glanced at Lizzie.

'I'm the fan house foreman for the back shift,' said the man. 'We met earlier.'

'I'm afraid I didn't catch your name,' Kember said.

'Gordon Collins, sir. Call me Don; I don't like Gordon.'

Kember noticed the man wore an armband with the letters ARP. 'I see you're an Air Raid Precautions warden. What's happening, Don? There's a lot of light showing out there and I thought the mine didn't work at night because of the blackout.'

'The likes of me don't get told anything, sir.' Collins gave a heavy sigh. 'I keep my head down, do as I'm told and do my job. There are three designated ARP wardens, one each for the fore and back shifts, and one for the night-time.' He pointed to himself. 'I'm the only ARP warden that lives on site so I got the night-time, but when I was ordered to hurry over and start the fan, that's what I did. I guessed they'd gone down the pit to look for you, although why you'd be underground at all, never mind at this time of night, is beyond me.'

To Kember, Collins seemed less surprised by their visit and more disgruntled at having to work the fan outside of his shift hours. It wasn't the reaction of someone who'd deliberately trapped them in a mine shaft and tried to kill them.

'Have you seen anyone else over here this evening?' Kember asked.

199

'No, sir,' Collins said. 'I've not long got here and there were no other footprints that I noticed.'

From the depth of snow over the boot mark and what Collins had said, Kember thought the door must have been jammed not long after Ramsey had taken them underground. That didn't help at all. It could have been anyone, including Ramsey after he abandoned them at the bottom of the pit.

'Thank you,' Kember said, opening the office door. 'I might need to speak to you again later.'

Collins shrugged. 'Fine by me.'

Once outside the fan house, Lizzie looked at Kember and spoke in a quiet voice. 'He's either a very good liar or telling the truth. My money's on the latter because he didn't flinch, hesitate, or make any telltale movements.'

'Hmm,' Kember said, pulling the collar of his donkey jacket tighter around his neck.

'What's the matter?' she said.

'We've just escaped certain death but we're away from the pit-head and have no idea who might be lying in wait for us along that path. Up to six people we know of had a motive to murder Morris and any number of them might be involved in trying to kill us. And that's not all; starting the fan must mean they're looking for us but if they think we're down the mine, why are *all* the lights on?'

'If they sent someone down who couldn't find us, maybe they started a search party,' Lizzie said.

Kember remained unconvinced. Even if Burnley wasn't involved in the death of Morris, a man like him who complied with the government blackout regulations and a specific order to cease mining operations during darkness, wouldn't switch all the lights on just to find them. He'd be unlikely to risk attracting the wrath of ARP wardens or the Luftwaffe by lighting up the whole area. If he was involved, it seemed sensible that he'd wait until morning, send the fore shift safety team down and only then form a search party.

He became aware of Lizzie staring at him.

'I think we should see what Burnley has to say for himself,' he said. 'But for God's sake, keep your eyes peeled for anyone on the path or in the trees. If you see anything at all, give me a sign.' He went to move off but stopped. 'And don't switch your head-torch back on.'

He surprised himself with the firmness of his command and the depth of his concern. Despite his initial shock at her arrival, he'd welcomed Lizzie's presence, knowledge and help before their ordeal underground. But he was a policeman used to chasing villains through badly lit alleyways in the dead of night, usually with a sergeant or constable with him, and they knew and accepted the risks of the job. For all her bravery as a wartime pilot, and even after all they'd been through in the past few months, Lizzie was still a civilian woman who had neither the training nor the strength to combat tough miners who might be out to attack them in the dark. There was nothing he could do now to ensure her safety except stay alert and keep her close.

As the sound of machinery receded behind them, the path seemed interminably long compared to earlier, wending its way through snowdrifts either side. The cotton wool sound of snow being compressed under their shoes seemed so loud to Kember that he thought no one could fail to hear them coming. It was scant comfort that he and Lizzie would also be warned of anyone approaching.

On the outskirts of the maze of buildings, Kember recalled their last encounters; dodging death by crushing and an exhausting pursuit through deepening snow. Lamps affixed to the sides of some buildings, their blackout masks allowing only a downward spread of illumination, created small islands of light that accentuated the deep shadows between. The knowledge that one murderer had been on the loose since his arrival had heightened Kember's sense of danger in the colliery, but the thought that there were more killers waiting beyond the swirling wind-blown snow increased his trepidation. They reached the familiar ground of the canteen and clubhouse, and Kember was grateful to have done so without further incident. He opened the door of the canteen and carefully pulled aside the blackout curtain. Total darkness. He switched on his head-torch at the same time Lizzie switched on hers and the twin lights revealed rows of empty tables and an empty servery.

'Eaten and retired to their dormitories or the social club,' Lizzie said, stepping back and switching off her head-torch.

Kember exhaled, suddenly realising that he'd been holding his breath, and switched off his own head-torch. The canteen returned to pitch black and he left, signalling with an incline of his head for Lizzie to follow him next door. A fug of warm bodies, coal-fire smoke, tobacco and stale beer met them in the crowded club. A hubbub of conversation drifted towards them from the men seated at tables and standing at the bar. He couldn't be sure, but he guessed more men than normal were in here tonight because of the weather preventing travel to nearby pubs or Canterbury.

A few men turned their heads to give them looks of curiosity and a few grinned or pointed. Kember felt self-conscious, as though risen from the dead, but then realised both he and Lizzie still had their miners' helmets on. The men soon lost interest as the novelty wore off and they returned to their conversations and games of darts and dominoes.

'I can't see Burnley,' Lizzie murmured.

'Neither can I,' Kember said, scanning the room for anyone paying particular interest to them. 'Let's have a word with the barman.'

He approached the bar and waited for the barman to pull a pint for one of the miners before beckoning him over.

'Have you seen Mr Burnley this evening?' Kember said.

The barman shook his head. 'He usually only comes in once a week to make himself look like a man of the people, unless he wants something.' He pulled a dimpled pint mug from a shelf and began polishing it with a glass cloth.

'What about Paul Ramsey and Edward Pine?' Kember said.

The corners of the barman's mouth pulled down for a few seconds. 'A bit earlier, maybe.'

'Harold Quayle, Terrance Armstrong?'

The same hesitation and look from the barman. 'Aye.'

'Alastair Thatcher or Victor Young?'

The barman put the beer mug back on the shelf and held up a finger for his next customer to wait. 'Might have done. I've had a lot in tonight, with the weather and all.'

'I take it, then, that you won't know where they are now?'

'How would I know? They don't tell me and it's more than my job's worth to leave the bar on a night like this.' He inclined his head towards the waiting miner. 'Do you mind?'

Kember shook his head and let the barman get on.

'Looks like we'll have to do a bit of searching of our own,' he said to Lizzie. 'We'll need to watch each other's backs until help comes. It's not letting up out there so I'm not banking on Watson riding to our rescue tonight.'

'They must be together somewhere. Birds of a feather, safety in numbers, and all that. I'd guess the dormitory's our best bet.'

He nodded. 'But first, Burnley.'

Ushering Lizzie out in the freezing air again, he led her on a trudge through the snow until they reached the colliery office, where the blackout boards were shielding the windows but a masked lamp outside still cast enough light to pick out tracks to and from the steps. Kember guessed that several shuffling feet had created the deep gouges in the snow, obscuring individual foot-prints. He climbed the steps and entered without knocking, with Lizzie close behind.

The only illumination within Mrs Wall's domain came from Burnley's office where the door stood ajar. Kember crossed in a few strides and pushed it open. The light from a banker's desk lamp showed the office was empty.

'Where is everybody?' he said, frowning. 'I'd expect to see someone, anyone, especially Burnley.'

'Has something else happened, do you think?' Lizzie said. She reached for the lamp on Mrs Wall's desk and switched it on.

'Like what? We must be the hottest news at the moment. Barring a pit accident or an air raid, and there's no hive of activ-ity or blackout to suggest either, I can't see what else could have happened.'

'Well, they can't have abandoned the place.' Lizzie riffled through papers left in the secretary's in-tray. 'If they still think we're underground, they'll be over at the pithead, surely?' She put the telephone to her ear, tapped the plunger on the cradle a few times and shook her head at Kember. 'Dead,' she said. 'The snowstorm must have brought down the telephone lines.'

Kember felt a knot in his stomach. That finally put paid to the chance of any reinforcements. They could be outnumbered by potential villains and he wasn't hopeful that other miners would come to their aid. In his experience, even good men stood by, not wanting to get involved in case the bad people took note and came for them next. The weather was a double-edged sword; if no one could get in, the killer, or killers, couldn't get out.

'There's no use waiting here for someone who might never come,' Lizzie said. 'Shall we take a look at the pithead? It might give us some idea of what's been going on these past few hours.'

Kember agreed and they left the office as they'd found it. Back out into the cold, their breath formed white clouds around their heads. The snow had eased off a little and the flakes floated like seeds from a dandelion. Lights still lit up the colliery and they soon found their way to the pithead and through to the lamp room. No one tended to the rows of helmets and head-torches or manned the office where the miners' checks were issued and contraband held. Kember scanned the board of numbered metal discs and found none missing from their pegs.

'It seems that nobody's underground at the moment,' he said.

'And our things have gone,' Lizzie said, holding out an empty wooden tray as proof.

Kember went through the next room to the downcast shaft, where no one stood by at the signal board and the shutter was closed. He pulled the handle and the shutter opened, revealing the empty lift cage through the mesh. He closed the shutter, moved along a short corridor and emerged back in the pit yard.

'Apart from the lighting and the fan being on, it's as though this is a normal evening like any other. No one's in the office, the pithead is closed, I can't hear any clanking of cranes and railway coal wagons, and the clubhouse is full.'

'If we assume Thatcher and the men from Morris's dormitory are involved in some way, and maybe Burnley, it's unlikely any of the other men except Collins will know anything's wrong,' Lizzie said. 'To them, it *is* a normal evening. If any of them do have any inkling that something's up, they won't want to rock the boat and risk getting their pay docked. Like Collins said, they'll want to keep their heads down and get on with it.'

'Right,' Kember said, fed up with being hunted and chasing shadows, and with his patience wearing thin. 'Dormitory next.'

Lizzie struggled to keep up with Kember as he forged ahead, retracing their steps and passing near the office. Everything was covered with at least a foot of snow, maybe more, including her Norton motorbike, or disguised behind sweeping drifts that changed the look of everything she'd seen on her arrival. Even the roof of an Austin car carried several inches of the white stuff, and its wheels were similarly embedded.

She followed close on Kember's heels towards where the dormitory huts were marked by more cones of light, and stopped by the steps when he did.

'What's wrong?' she said, looking around for danger.

'It seems there's been a lot of coming and going here this evening,' Kember said, looking at the ground.

She looked at the snow, churned up around the steps of Hut Six and with multiple tracks leading off in all directions. That could mean anything. The barman said the men had been in for a drink, which wasn't surprising, and they might have come straight back to the dormitory, taken a different route through the colliery, or gone for a walk, although the latter was unlikely given the weather.

'What are you thinking?' Kember asked.

'That it's bloody cold and there are a lot of tracks,' she said. 'I'd say they're all inside trying to keep warm.'

'Let's find out, shall we?'

Lizzie gripped the handrail as she climbed the icy steps and was grateful when they had negotiated the two doors to stand in the warmth of the hut. Six heads turned their way in surprise and there followed a comical pause as she and Kember stood dripping melting snow on to the floor and several miners' mouths dropped open.

Of all the men huddled around the fire at the far end of the dormitory, Burnley was the first to recover.

'Where the bloody hell have you been?' he snapped, jumping to his feet. 'We've been out looking for you.'

'You, of all people, must have known where we were?' Kember said, his tone laced with sarcasm.

'Me? I was only told an hour or so ago that you'd persuaded my men to show you the pit tunnels tonight instead of tomorrow. They've already been given a rollocking, let me tell you, but where did you get to?'

Lizzie was intrigued when Kember sat on the end of a bed in a relaxed manner, deliberately placing himself lower than Burnley. This took the wind out of the mine owner's sails by showing him that his confrontational stance was of no consequence and that Kember did not feel threatened by his attack-dog reaction.

'We had a little underground adventure, that's all,' Kember said, brushing the left cuff of his coat free of water drops that had once been snowflakes.

'Underground ad—? Do you know how much time we've wasted searching those tunnels? I know you didn't come up in the lift cage because I waited at the pithead the moment I knew you'd gone against my wishes, but my men could find neither hide nor hair of you.'

'I can only assume you had some kind of emergency on the surface,' Kember said, ignoring Burnley's implied question about their escape, 'because after Ramsey left us, the power went off and we were left down there in the cold and dark for hours.'

Burnley's eyes narrowed. 'So how *did* you get out?'

His expression and emphasis did not bypass Lizzie. Any normal person would have shown concern for their welfare, maybe anger at those who might have caused or contributed to the situation, and perhaps even been contrite that the state of affairs had arisen at all. By showing interest in how they'd escaped from the pit rather than relief that they had and any shock at how long they'd been underground, Burnley had reinforced Lizzie's view that he saw men as a commodity to be saved for another day to continue the drive for profit, rather than the human souls they were.

'Through the fan drift,' Kember said, with a shrug. 'If you remember, Mr Young told us about it the first time you showed us the fan house.'

'Well, that's excellent,' Burnley said, turning his head to give Young a nod. 'The emergency escape route works after all. No need for a practice drill.'

'Where's Thatcher?' Kember turned his head to look at Pine. 'Why didn't he tell Mr Burnley sooner that we were down there?'

Pine indicated Burnley with a nod. 'It's like Mr Burnley said: he came by and saw Thatcher at the pithead. You'd persuaded us to take you down tonight because of the weather and because you thought Mr Burnley could be the killer. That's why Thatcher kept quiet about it and told Mr Burnley it was an additional safety inspection—'

'I thought that was ridiculous,' Burnley interrupted. 'I ordered Pine and Ramsey to come up and shut down the fans and pit for the night.'

'I didn't want to get in any more trouble, so I did as I was told and warned the others,' Pine said.

Lizzie saw him glance at her with a flicker of his eyebrows and she noticed Kember had seen it too. The men believed Burnley capable of murder and Pine was trying to ensure none of them were held responsible for any decision taken by Kember and herself.

'We came up in the cage expecting some emergency,' Ramsey said. 'It fair panicked me when I saw Mr Burnley standing there. His face was like thunder so I just went with what Pine said.'

'I expected Mr Burnley to leave us to it,' Pine continued. 'I thought we could get you out smartish like, once he'd gone, but he waited until we'd shut everything down and gave us a talking to about all the goings-on.'

'It displeases me to have my men lie, Inspector,' Burnley said. 'It dismays me that an officer of the law would do so too, but I understand they did it to save your blushes and theirs. The power of the police is a persuasive force. If I'd known you were down there, I'd have ordered you up too. Why couldn't you wait until morning like we'd agreed?'

'I don't understand,' Kember said, his eyes fixed on Burnley. 'If you really ordered your men to shut down the pit because you didn't know we were underground, why did you switch the power, lights and fan on again several hours later? Did you think we'd be dead by then?'

'Good Lord, no.'

Burnley's face looked shocked but Lizzie thought the way his body stiffened told a different story.

'You hadn't been down there long enough by the time we came looking,' Burnley said.

Didn't answer the why? *question*, Lizzie thought, but Kember seemed not to notice.

'What did you think when we weren't waiting at the bottom of the pit as expected?' Lizzie said.

'I thought you were both heartily stupid,' Burnley said, his gaze flicking between Lizzie and Kember. 'Why in God's name didn't you stay put?'

'I think you can guess why,' Kember said. 'Firstly, we were abandoned in tunnels we'd never seen before and had little idea of where we were or how to get back to the cage. Secondly, with the power off, we had no lights but our head-torches and no way of ringing up for the cage. Thirdly, we could feel the effects of mine gases and knew we had to get out. Fortunately, we found the emergency oxygen cylinders to keep us going until I remembered Young telling me about the fan drift. What he failed to tell me was that the airlock door would be jammed with a chunk of wood.'

'What? B-but—' Burnley spluttered. 'That's impossible.'

'And then the fan was switched on as we approached, trying to suck whatever heat we had left from our bodies,' Kember said, his gaze never leaving Burnley's eyes. 'It seems the person who murdered Morris hasn't finished killing yet.'

Lizzie's mind churned. Burnley had said he'd been told only an hour ago that they were in the pit but he hadn't said who by, and neither had the men. When she'd arrived that morning, a Humber car had been parked by Burnley's office, but she'd seen a snow-covered Austin there since their escape from the pit.

'Mr Burnley,' Lizzie said. 'What make of car do you drive?'

'My car?' Burnley frowned. 'A Humber Snipe. Not that it has anything to do with anything.'

'And where is it now?'

'I moved it to the shelter of a motor shed near my office because of the bad weather.'

Realisation hit Lizzie like a punch to her stomach. She turned to Kember and said in a low voice, 'Didn't you say DI Watson had an Austin?'

'Yes.' Kember eyed her curiously. 'And . . . ?'

'A Humber was parked by the office when I arrived this morning but there's an Austin there now. We passed it on the way here, near where I left my motorbike. It had a few inches of snow at most so it hadn't been there long, and it was definitely an Austin, not a Humber.' Lizzie turned back to Burnley. 'If you've already spoken to your men, why are you here? In fact, why are you all together in here?'

'Because of that damned fellow detective of yours,' Burnley said. 'Do you think I'd be stuck in here by choice?'

'I guessed as much,' Lizzie said.

'Inspector Watson?' Kember said. 'Why didn't you say he was here?'

'You didn't ask,' Burnley said.

Kember thought twice about hitting him. 'Did *he* tell you we were underground?'

'He turned up about an hour ago and asked where you were, which I knew nothing about, obviously. He suggested you were down the pit, which I thought was absurd, but Pine and Ramsey were getting worried for your safety and decided to come clean. I was shocked, to tell the truth. Annoyed and shocked. Watson demanded that the power and fans be switched back on and I didn't need telling twice. I saw Collins and sent him to get the fan going, and I ordered Ramsey and Quayle to go underground to bring you up.'

'Where is he now?' Kember asked. 'We haven't seen him.'

The corners of Burnley's mouth turned down and he shrugged. 'I thought you might know. He demanded the colliery lighting be switched on so he could search for you, even though I said it was against blackout regulations. I offered our help but he said any of us might be in danger so we should stay together. He's been gone a while so I would guess he's still out looking.' He inclined his head towards the men. 'Watson told us to stay put but I must say, locking the outer door didn't much seem like protecting us; more like imprisoning us. The roads are blocked anyway so there was nowhere outside the colliery that we could we go. I'm surprised he got through from Canterbury, to be honest.'

Lizzie exchanged a glance with Kember.

'After I'd spoken to the men with Watson, I suggested we repair to the canteen or club but they were packed at the time so this was the next best place,' Burnley said, matter-of-factly.

Lizzie detected no unnatural movements of his head or shoulders, and no gripping of his wrists or hands. She knew that truth tellers tended to summarise events but recall conversations, the

211

opposite of those telling lies, which suggested Burnley's account was correct. The last part, anyway.

'Where is Thatcher?'

'I don't know, Inspector,' Burnley said. 'His own hut, I expect. Watson said something about him being in the clear because he didn't sleep in the same dormitory. I have no idea what he was talking about.'

'Officer Hayes and I need to speak to my colleague urgently,' Kember said, his face serious. 'Is there anywhere in the colliery other than the club, the canteen and your office where DI Watson might have gone?' Burnley and the others shrugged, shook their heads and looked unhelpful. 'For your own safety while we're gone, I'd continue to follow his advice and stay put, if I were you.'

Burnley looked unperturbed and nodded to Kember's right, towards the bed nearest the door. 'You might want to swap those jackets for your own before you go.'

Lizzie looked across and saw her greatcoat laid on the bed. Watson must have retrieved them from the pithead. She checked the pockets and found her things there. Kember checked his overcoat but came up empty-handed. They changed into their own coats and went out through the first door into the vestibule.

'Where the hell do we look for Watson first?' Kember said.

Lizzie had no suggestion that would satisfy him and they stepped outside, still with their miners' helmets on, back into the freezing night.

CHAPTER FOURTEEN

Kember waited for Lizzie to join him outside before he closed the outer door and checked below the knob. The end of a key he hadn't noticed on the way in protruded from the keyhole and he turned it to lock the door, pocketing the key.

'Why do you suppose they thought it was locked when it wasn't?' he said.

Lizzie shrugged. 'Perhaps Watson told them that to keep them quiet, hoping they wouldn't check. Perhaps he was distracted and forgot to lock it when he left.'

Kember wasn't convinced that a seasoned detective like Watson would have done either of those things. He also wasn't enamoured with the idea of traipsing through more deep snow. Their climb up the drift tunnel, the skin-chilling wind whipped up by the ventilation fan, and their travels around the colliery in the snowstorm had aggravated his old back injury almost to the point of spasming. But Watson was out there somewhere. They closed the top buttons of their coats and pulled their collars up, as tight around their necks as they could. As night wore on, the temperature seemed to be dropping further. *What fool ever said it was too cold for snow?* he wondered.

The masked lights within the colliery grounds still offered meagre illumination and guidance as Kember made the first move, towards Burnley's office. Lizzie kept at his elbow, uncomplaining. The snow seemed to be petering out but sudden gusts of wind picked up powdery crystals from the drifts and threw the stinging ice into his eyes. They rounded the edge of a building that he recognised from their earlier fruitless chase, where the deep and pristine snow proved no one had come that way for hours. Beyond another building, ploughed channels through the snow indicated recent activity and his hackles rose.

A figure detached itself from a building to their left, hurrying as if on some urgent task. Silhouetted and back-lit against a cone of masked light, the shape froze momentarily when it saw them approaching. As it recovered and edged closer, Kember almost pulled up in surprise himself when he recognised Burnley's secretary. She was hunched over, holding the collar of her coat together with one hand and the knot of her headscarf with the other.

'Hello again, Mrs Wall,' Kember hailed, relaxing at the sight of the sour but familiar face. His call galvanised her into hurried, jerky movements along the icy path towards them. 'Working late again?'

Mrs Wall stopped in front of them. 'I was on my way to speak to Mr Burnley,' she said, and dabbed at her eyes with a small white handkerchief.

'Is everything all right, Mrs Wall?' Lizzie asked.

Mrs Wall sniffed. 'No, actually. I thought I saw someone following me.'

Kember's ears pricked up. 'Saw who?'

He stepped forward to put a comforting hand on her arm but the sudden movement made her flinch and pull away. A fleeting look of shock passed across her face and was gone. He saw Lizzie frown and her lips press into a thin line.

'I was mistaken,' Mrs Wall said as she looked over her shoulder and tugged at the knotted scarf. 'I changed course and ducked back in case. When I stopped, no one was there. It must have been you I saw.'

Kember looked in the direction she'd glanced at, not expecting to see anything. 'Are you sure? You seem a bit jittery.'

'It's dark, I was scared, I just wanted to get away.' Mrs Wall's voice was tense and sharp. 'The death of Morris was a shock to everyone. That and this weather play tricks on you, especially at night.'

'Shouldn't you be at home by now?' Lizzie said, as frostily as the air around them. 'I do hope Mr Burnley's paying you well.'

'I'm snowed in like everyone else.' Mrs Wall sniffed and wiped her nose with a handkerchief. 'Might as well catch up on things.'

Kember threw Lizzie a warning glance before asking Mrs Wall, 'Have you seen Inspector Watson on your travels?'

Mrs Wall looked away. 'I can't say that I have,' she said, with another sniff and wipe of her nose.

'That's very odd. Mr Burnley said he arrived an hour ago but he seems to have vanished.'

'I believe he's been all over but I haven't seen him recently.' Mrs Wall hunched as a sudden gust passed over and around them. 'Not since he arrived back here, at any rate.'

Kember had a feeling that she was avoiding his gaze but that could have been the cold wind funnelling between two buildings making all their eyes water.

'I must get on. I'll let the inspector know you're looking for him, if I see him.'

'If someone is prowling about tonight, one of us should go with you,' Kember said.

'That won't be necessary,' Mrs Wall said. 'The hut's just over there.' She pulled a neck-scarf up over her nose and mouth, and turned in the direction of the dormitories.

They watched the secretary's back as she shuffled away.

'She must have seen Watson after he put the men in the dormitory,' Lizzie said, once she was out of earshot. 'Otherwise, how did she know in which direction to go to speak to Burnley?'

'Good point,' Kember said. 'Let's check the office again while she's out of the way. If Watson's not there, we'll have to try the club, the canteen and surrounding buildings as well.'

'I don't fancy another trek to the fan house, though,' Lizzie said.

As they trudged towards the office block, Kember went over the conversation with Mrs Wall. Lizzie had seemed less than generous during the exchange, considering the secretary's fright. Against his better judgement, he said, 'I thought you women stuck together. You don't seem too sympathetic about her recent scare.'

'Did you get the impression she was feigning being scared?' Lizzie said, without stopping. 'I did. Yes, I know she seemed different to the battleaxe we encountered this morning but she seemed more distracted than frightened.'

'Distracted by what?'

'If she's on her way to speak to Burnley, we should ask him later.'

'She won't get in,' Kember said. 'I have the key.'

Within minutes, they stood dripping melting snow on to the floor of Mrs Wall's office, the smell of polish still thick in the air. It was as they'd left it, with Burnley's door open and the desk lamp still on, but no Watson.

They went outside and Kember sighed, his ghostly breath whipped away by a gust. All this in-the-warm, out-in-the-cold malarkey had started to play havoc with his sinuses too.

They had no joy over at the pithead; the canteen remained in darkness, and the barman in the club was still selecting glasses at random to polish. The dartboard had been abandoned, although groups of men were still playing cribbage and dominoes, and the number of customers sitting and standing in the smoky fug nursing dimpled pint mugs of beer seemed not to have changed since their last visit.

Kember followed Lizzie back outside, where the wind had almost stopped, allowing complete silence to descend, the like of which he hadn't experienced since being trapped underground. Fortunately, the lights were still on, reflecting off the white snowflakes and confounding a full comparison with the total darkness of the tunnels.

'If he's not in the main buildings, where would he go?' Lizzie said.

Kember indicated the route they'd taken after their encounter with the falling stores. 'If I were Watson, I'd start looking around some of the lesser buildings to see if anyone had become trapped or locked in.'

'But there are dozens,' Lizzie said.

'The coal mine version of house-to-house inquiries,' Kember said with a wry smile.

They trudged off, following a track in the snow, assuming it to be their own from some time ago as it skirted around a bulldozer that Kember remembered from earlier, then two old carts.

'You take me to the nicest places,' Lizzie said, her voice close behind him.

He traversed diagonally across a courtyard, head down against the snow, and took the right of two brick arches. Having passed more equipment and between two colliery buildings, he paused to get his bearings. He didn't recognise the row of brick-built huts with flat roofs, nor the two coal trucks he assumed stood on rails hidden beneath the snow, and realised the track he'd been following must have branched off the one they'd made earlier.

'Well, that's me lost,' he said.

He expected some kind of comment from Lizzie, either help-ful or sarcastic, but she didn't answer. He turned and realised with horror that she wasn't behind him.

'Lizzie?' he said, as if she might be hiding just out of sight. 'Lizzie!' he called louder.

Cold fingers gripped his heart and he began a stumbling slith-ering run back the way he'd come, shouting her name, his con-science screaming that he should have taken more care and looked after her. His heart thumped with effort and panic, a condition not allayed by reaching the carts where he'd last heard her speak.

He called her name again. No reply.

Lizzie had disappeared.

Following Kember across the colliery in the dark reminded Lizzie of a similar trek made only a few weeks before. That time, the route had been between tall trees in a wood, the cold just as bitter and the shadows just as impenetrable. The bushes that had brushed her legs and the tree roots that had sought to trip her had been replaced now by energy-sapping snowdrifts and slippery ice. Passing a large bulldozer, its paintwork chipped and scuffed with age and con-stant use, and a pair of even older carts, she almost wished she was back in the warmth and safety of the RAF Scotney officers' lounge, drinking sherry and sugarless tea with the ATA girls.

'You take me to the nicest places,' she said to Kember's back, aware that she had arrived at Bekesbourne without his invitation, approval or knowledge.

She followed him across a courtyard, turned her back momen-tarily against a flurry of snow, and passed beneath a brick arch. Having narrowly missed walking into two tractors parked in deep shadow, she realised she could no longer see Kember's shape through the falling snow. Everything around her was silent and monochrome, as if she were at the flicks watching a black and white film on the big screen, or the sole actor in her own silent movie.

Assuming she had fallen behind rather than strayed off course, Lizzie continued to follow a track in the snow and emerged from the end of an arched-roof passageway into a courtyard. Several large, indefinable pieces of equipment, either stored or dumped out of the way for good, stood rigid like the dinosaurs she'd seen in Crystal Palace Park before the war. Several routes promised egress from the courtyard but only one cone of masked light offered any illumination, creating bizarre shapes out of shadows.

Lizzie wasn't one for being scared of the dark. She neither believed in otherworldly demons and ghouls that were said to haunt secluded places at night nor feared foxes, rats and other nocturnal scurrying creatures. She had, however, encountered the worst that mankind could present and it was the thought of more of this that made the breath catch in her throat. She felt rooted to the spot, unable to breathe properly, hearing the buzz of uncertainty inside her head, feeling her insides twist.

She stamped her feet, as much against the cold as for distraction, her fingers hurting as she fumbled with the buttons on her coat. She managed to reach her jacket pocket and almost sobbed as she remembered she'd lost the tiny jar of cobalt-blue glass that contained her saviour. Instead, she reached for the remaining band on her wrist, and pain exploded inside her head.

◆ ◆ ◆

Kember experienced a moment of panic when he realised Lizzie had disappeared.

He looked around, as if she would be standing a few yards away, mocking him for being anxious or scolding him for leaving her, and mentally kicked himself for being stupid. He tried to focus. She had spoken to him at the carts so she must have been following at that point. He was certain he'd heard her muffled footsteps behind him as they'd entered the courtyard but that was the last thing he remembered. She must have taken the other arch by mistake.

He turned to hurry back to the courtyard as the wail of an air raid siren began rising.

'For Christ's sake, not now,' Kember said.

All the lights went out.

'Damn.' Kember grimaced. When the siren petered out, he knew the bombs would soon fall. 'Trust the bloody Luftwaffe to fly in this.'

He reached up for his head-torch and switched it on. Bright and effective in the confines of a mine tunnel, it proved barely more use outdoors than a candle, even in the pitch black. That said, Kember knew it could be a draw for German aircraft, if the pilots could even see such a small light through the thick cloud, but he had to find Lizzie and Watson.

Reaching the courtyard, he saw Lizzie's tracks and turned through the left arch, a weight of dread settling on his chest as he hurried past two tractors and stopped at the opening to an arched passageway. Two sets of footprints converged, which meant one of three things: either two people had passed here at different times, two people had met, or one had started following the other. He hoped it was the first one. By the meagre light of his head-torch, the short passageway looked like a smaller version of the pit tunnels but without the accumulated layers of coal dust.

All the moisture left his mouth.

The whole site suddenly seemed a far more sinister place to be spending his time, especially running around in the cold and dark and snow. After his shock and initial pleasure at seeing Lizzie arrive that morning, he'd had one eye on her all the time from that moment on.

Almost.

He knew she could take care of herself, to a degree, but their escapades so far provided justification for his concern over her safety. He cursed himself for losing her, not least because someone else had been here too. Recently.

The siren stopped and silence descended once again.

He checked over his shoulder before easing along the covered passageway, conscious of the sounds his shoes were making on the ground. As the end approached, framing some kind of industrial machines in the arched entrance, no other sound came from behind or beyond. *Am I being paranoid?* he wondered. *Has Lizzie found Watson or returned to the warmth of the clubhouse?*

His questions were soon answered as he reached the far end and his head-torch briefly picked out the shape of a figure as it disappeared around a far corner.

'Hey!' he called, hoping it was her but fearing the worst.

He gave chase but skidded to a halt before he'd reached even the closest of the snow-covered machines. His bobbing, weaving light had picked out a miner's helmet lying a few feet away from a dark bundle on the ground to his right, and he reeled in shock when he realised what it was.

'Lizzie!' he shouted, as if the sound itself would wake her.

He ignored the snow and knelt at her side, the groan from her lips telling him she was conscious. He touched her cheek with the back of his hand, wiping away the snowflakes, praying she wasn't badly hurt. She opened her eyes and he thanked the god he didn't believe in.

She gasped and took a deep breath, raised her head and said, 'You took your time.'

He almost laughed with relief as he helped her sit up. 'I didn't think you'd miss me, playing snowballs out here with your friend.'

'Friend?' She rubbed the back of her head with her hand and tilted her head from side to side.

'I saw someone running off before I almost tripped over you having a nap on the ground.'

'Cheeky sod – I was only stunned. Good job I was wearing that helmet.' She put her hand up to shield her eyes from Kember's torchlight. 'Do you mind?'

He helped her stand and made sure she was steady before retrieving her helmet.

'That's staying on,' she said, and switched on the head-torch. 'Although I'm not planning to get clouted again anytime soon. Why do they always hit me on the head?'

'I should get you to the office or the clubhouse, anywhere you can be safe,' he said, intending to keep her as far from any more harm as he could. 'You might have concussion.'

'Don't be stupid,' she said softly, but with steel in her look. 'All I've got is a headache, and where on this site do you really think it's safe, especially when it's about to start raining bombs.'

He realised with annoyance that she was right, again. Their best bet was to carry on, hope the bombers would pass over, find Watson and catch the murderer. Simple.

And whoever had hit her was going to pay.

CHAPTER FIFTEEN

Lizzie's head pounded as though someone was beating time with a wooden mallet but she couldn't let on to Kember. They had to find the murderer and she couldn't afford for him to be distracted by worrying about her even more than he did already. Her miner's helmet had taken the brunt of the smack to her head but it had been delivered with enough force to make her see stars. Even while falling to the ground, her thought had been to stay down and still. A certain type of murderer will attack you again to make sure. A smaller number will take pleasure in it and sometimes take their time over ensuring that you die slowly. Thankfully, she reflected, most people aren't seasoned killers and won't even check your demise if you look dead enough.

She had lain as still as she could, breathing as little as she dared, hearing what she thought sounded like a curse. Then the assailant had fled at the sound of Kember's approach and his voice shouting her name.

Kember seemed caught in two minds. He set off in the direction the figure had left the courtyard but soon stopped to check she was following. Then he urged her to the front but that didn't satisfy him either. She guessed that having her in sight in front was marginally preferable to having her out of sight and vulnerable behind him, but leading could mean being the first to face whatever danger lay around the next corner. In the end, she allowed him to grasp her hand and they proceeded side by side like an old married couple holding on to each other for dear life.

The courtyards created by the groups of old buildings, built at some time in the distant past and for some forgotten function but now revived for colliery business, gave way to the larger modern utilitarian structures of corrugated iron. Lizzie started to recognise certain buildings and views until she believed she knew where they were. Working through the colliery, they turned at the end of one building and found their earlier steps to the alley, where Kember pointed out fresh tracks yet to be obliterated by new snow.

'Watson might have come this way,' Kember said.

Lizzie stopped, making Kember turn back towards her, concern in his eyes. An earlier conversation and images from underground swilled around in her head, filling her mind with a shocking realisation. They'd discussed the impossibility of committing murder deep underground without witnesses seeing and she'd declared that no one could have got away with it.

No one.

No. One.

'Show me the playing cards,' Lizzie demanded.

'What, here?' Kember looked puzzled but handed them over.

'How stupid of me,' she said, turning them over in her hands. 'I should have realised, it's so simple.' She regretted the phrase when she saw the peeved expression on Kember's face. 'Both cards are the six of spades and the spade is a tool used in mining, so each card represents six miners.'

Kember nodded his understanding, his heart thudding at the possibilities. 'The five remaining men in the dormitory plus Burnley. What about the other six?'

'There are only six. The cards are defaced; one torn a third of the way down the centre and the other two-thirds of the way.' She paused a second for Kember to pick up on her meaning but he was waiting for her to continue. 'I think the cards were a warning to Morris from the six men. I'm guessing there were a few angry words exchanged as well, but the first card was torn one third to see if he'd get the message to go. He didn't so they left the second with the longer tear. The more I thought about it the more I realised it must be all of them,' she said. 'In every interview I've been present at, those men have displayed lying behaviour through their speech, their mannerisms and their body language.'

The dim illumination of a nearby cone of light threw half his face in shadow and revealed the other half in conflict.

'When Ramsey told us earlier, about gas building up in the body over a long period, he said it in a way that bothered me,' Lizzie continued.

'What way?' Kember took the cards back.

'He looked away and his voice became faint, as if he'd made a mistake and let the cat out of the bag. He worked with Morris every day and they both got ill. Quayle was in the same safety team and he never got ill. That could be because he has his own district but . . . do you remember he said he'd had time off for a sprained ankle?'

'You think he was shirking?' Kember slipped the cards inside his jacket pocket.

'Maybe, maybe not, but it got him out of conducting underground safety checks, which is convenient, don't you think? Spending a couple of days in the fresh air, where the gas in his body would begin to dissipate rather than accumulate, would have given him a chance to recover, at least a little bit. Maybe that's how they did it, and tampering with the Davy lamp helped them expose Morris to the gas.'

Kember touched his nose. 'What about Pine?'

'He operates the cage at the bottom of the downcast shaft,' Lizzie said. 'It would be easy for him to take a ride back up to the surface for a few breaths of fresh air while the others carried out their checks, especially if Thatcher was accommodating.'

'And the whitedamp?' he said. 'It's the canary that sniffs out carbon monoxide, keels over and dies.'

'Not necessarily. Those cylinders in the mine gave me an idea. What if the door to the canary cage was pushed to and the valve released just enough to let a trickle of oxygen through? That would keep the canary alive and unaffected, wouldn't it?'

'But the men would die.'

'One did,' Lizzie said. 'And Ramsey became ill. Think about it. Quayle was safe in his own district during the fore shift inspection but Morris always stayed with Ramsey in his. If they were exposed to whitedamp and the canary cage had been tampered with, they would never have known they were being exposed over time.'

Kember shook his head. 'The same cage would need to be used every day for that to work. Either that or a different cage tampered with each day. That's quite an undertaking, to keep it from all the other men.'

'Not if the man doing the tampering was Ramsey,' Lizzie said. 'He carried the lamp and canary and could control both. Morris wouldn't know anything was going on because he was a slapdash and arrogant bully.'

'He'd be poisoning himself.'

'Yes, but that knowledge would give him the edge. He'd have the opportunity to stop it at any time if he got too ill. Maybe he took a whiff of oxygen when he could or acted sick to get fresh air.'

Kember shook his head again. 'You're forgetting the fan. It runs for an hour every morning to clear the mine of gases and suck fresh air in for the men to breathe.'

'I know,' Lizzie said, feeling certain now. 'That's what I'm saying. Young must be involved as well.'

'That means he must have had to keep the engine on but the fan disengaged for the hour the others were underground,' Kember said.

It was a preposterous notion but Lizzie mentally kicked herself for not having given it her full consideration before. There must be other explanations but at the moment it did seem the most logical.

'That only leaves Armstrong from that dormitory.'

'If I'm right about the cards, it would make sense, wouldn't it?' Lizzie said. 'Far easier to keep a secret if everyone's involved.'

Kember raised his eyebrows as if not entirely in agreement with her statement. 'I think you're right about all of them being a part of it in some way but apart from the playing cards we have little except conjecture based on what we've been told by men who are already suspects. No one has made a formal statement and they could deny everything in a trice. They want to keep their lives, their freedom and their jobs, and that's a powerful motive for them to stick together.'

Lizzie started to shiver again with cold, which made her head ache. 'We can speculate all we like about who disliked who and for whatever reasons but Morris died in the early hours while sleeping in a dormitory with five other men. There were no opportunities for one man to get him alone and give him a fatal dose of poison gas and the other man, Thatcher, doesn't live in the same dormitory. All the men in Hut Six played a part, they must have, and Thatcher and Mrs Wall helped by keeping quiet.'

Lizzie took a long breath and waited for Kember's response. She had to admit it wasn't as solid a case as he would like. Her theories were based largely on her skill as a criminal psychologist, and she knew how that had been received by their superiors in the past.

'Regardless of who it was, we come back to the same question; how did he, or they, manage to get Morris to inhale the final lethal dose of carbon monoxide in a room full of sleeping miners without him or anyone else noticing and with no one else dying?'

Lizzie knew he was right. They still had little to put to a judge and jury that couldn't be explained away as coincidence, the product of circumstance or the result of accident or war. Her eyes bored into him and her mouth pressed into a thin line. She was far from finished but they had Watson to find.

It was easier to let Kember take her hand again than to argue but her mind sensed something awry as they got closer to the end of the alley where she knew the lorry should still be parked. The scene didn't look quite right and Kember's tighter grip told her he'd noticed too. Although in partial shadow, the snow looked discoloured, darker, not dirty but as if disturbed. Reaching the end of the alley confirmed her suspicions. The snow had been gouged and displaced as if kicked aside. The end of the tarpaulin covering the front of the lorry had been thrown back the way Kember had done some time earlier, but this time it had not been replaced, allowing a layer of snow to settle on the bonnet and windscreen. A track of depressions on the ground, made within the last hour or so judging by the amount of infill by the clumps of silently falling flakes, led in the same direction they had taken after first discovering the lorry.

'Maybe someone came to check the lorry hadn't been discovered,' she said.

'Then why leave it exposed?' Kember said. 'My money's on Watson having been here.'

Lizzie noticed a few spots of something spattered on the snow in the sheltered area behind the front wheel. It remained frozen there, looking black in the meagre light. She took a step forward. 'Is that oil?' She bent to look closer at the ground.

Kember followed her gaze and shone his light at the spots. He crouched to get a better look, but Lizzie recognised it before he even touched the substance and rubbed it between his finger and thumb.

'Blood,' he confirmed.

Lizzie took a glance around for safety's sake before she got on her hands and knees beside him, almost oblivious to the freezing snow, and bent low to shine her light under the lorry. Her head thumped in time with her heart.

'There's a body,' she said.

It looked like it had been rolled once on to its side from where it had fallen, a poor attempt at concealment, even in this weather. Kember reached across the body and gave the coat a tug. The body rolled easily from beneath the lorry, on to its back and into the open. A dark patch where the head had been lying told its own story.

'Jesus Christ,' he said, 'it's Watson.'

The pain in her stomach was like a punch to the gut as Kember felt Watson's neck for a pulse.

'He's alive,' he said. 'Help me sit him up.'

They propped the unconscious Watson against the wheel, making sure he wasn't about to topple sideways, and Lizzie noticed Kember's Bijou torch lying just under the lorry. She picked it up, flicked the switch – it still worked – and handed it to Kember. Watson must have found it at the pithead.

'We must get him somewhere warm before he freezes to death,' she warned.

'The dormitory's nearest,' he said.

Her heart sank and concern must have shown on her face.

'We've no choice in this weather,' he said, with a flicked look skyward. 'Anyway, those footprints are too small for Burnley's size twelve feet and the big work boots the men were wearing. Take his right arm, I'll take his left.'

She gritted her teeth, admitting he was right, and prepared to take the strain.

By putting their arms around Watson's back and holding his arms around their necks as if taking a drunkard home from the pub, they supported the weight of Watson's limp body and shuffled forward, dragging the detective's feet through the snow. Their slow and faltering progress was further hampered as the curtain of falling snow began to thicken, bringing visibility down to a few yards again.

'I'm surprised he made it to the colliery in this,' Lizzie said, the effort of carrying a dead weight evident in her voice.

'He said he'd send someone to fetch us and probably didn't want to let us down,' Kember said.

They both stumbled over a hidden step and almost dropped Watson.

All Lizzie's concentration and energy went on helping to get the unconscious policeman to the dormitory, which seemed farther away than she remembered. Eventually, the line of huts came into view and they steered towards where they'd left the men.

'I told Watson we were going underground today,' Kember said in a low voice, as they reached the steps of Hut Six. 'He must have guessed we'd been left down there when he checked the pithead and found our things but saw the power had been switched off.'

Lizzie caught her breath. 'Burnley must have known we were down there as much as the others,' she replied in a whisper. 'I think he'd have left us down there to die if Watson's arrival hadn't galvanised him into action.'

They managed to negotiate the steps – icier than Lizzie remembered – and navigate through the two sets of doors, glancing at each other in surprise that the outer one was unlocked again. All the men were standing there, wearing their donkey jackets and mixed expressions of anger and surprise. They moved aside as she and Kember placed Watson on one of the beds near the stove.

Burnley burst in through the door.

'Is he all right?'

'Do you have a first aid kit?' Lizzie snapped, too tired for niceties.

'Not in the huts,' Burnley said, sheepishly. 'There are some at the pithead, and we have the hospital block, of course. Three beds and well equipped for small emergencies.'

Lizzie gave a heavy sigh. 'Water?'

'Y-yes,' Young said, grasping a nearby tin jug.

'Sit down,' Kember demanded. Only Burnley complied, his face pale and drawn.

Lizzie took a small handkerchief from her pocket as Kember offered her his. 'Pour some on this.' She held out Kember's handkerchief as the man splashed water over it. She then turned Watson's head and cleaned away the blood from his matted hair as best she could. The wound was not as bad as she'd feared, being two inches long but shallow. The blow rather than blood loss was responsible for Watson's unconscious state but she knew from bitter experience how fickle the human body could be in coping with such trauma.

'Here, use this,' Kember said, draping his own coat over Watson's body. 'It'll warm him quicker.'

Pine opened the stove door and placed another large chunk of coal on the fire.

'What the devil happened?' Burnley said, his voice unsteady.

'I'd have to say, one of you got to him first,' Kember snapped.

There was a chorus of denials that Lizzie had little time for and she could see that Kember's patience was well and truly at an end.

'I locked the door when we left so where were you and how did you get out?' Kember said to Burnley, his voice cold and curt.

'It wasn't locked,' Burnley protested. 'All I did was go to the office to see if the telephone had come back on and I was on my way back when I saw you.'

'And what about you lot?' Kember growled at the other men. 'Where do you think you're going?'

'We're pissed off, to be honest,' Quayle said. 'We keep getting locked in for no good reason and that's not fair. All we want is to go for a beer at the club.'

'I'll tell you what's not fair,' Kember spat. 'We've been run off the road, had goods dropped on us, been trapped and gassed underground, and barricaded inside the fan drift,' he said, stony-faced. 'Officer Hayes was attacked a few moments before we found Inspector Watson lying in the snow with his head bashed in, so you won't mind if we take your protestations of innocence with a pinch of salt. Sit down before you give me more reasons to doubt you all.'

Lizzie wasn't sure what reactions she'd expected but they weren't the looks of horror, incredulity and panic now displayed on the men's faces. The body language seemed defensive; crossed arms, shoulders turned towards Kember, chins up in defiance. Hardly the gloating, bravado or hiding in plain sight of men guilty of malice aforethought.

Despite being outnumbered six-to-one, Kember stood his ground and the grumbling miners slowly shed their jackets and returned to their seats and beds. Lizzie continued to minister to Watson's wound until satisfied it was clean, dry and unlikely to bleed any more. She then took her handkerchief, placed it over the wound, folded the silk scarf from around her neck into a headband and tied it around Watson's head as a makeshift bandage.

Kember stood close by, brooding.

'I know what you think of us, Inspector,' Burnley said, breaking the silence that had descended on the hut.

'I doubt it,' Kember said.

'We aren't monsters in league with the devil, you know. I had nothing to do with the attacks on you, Inspector Watson, Miss Hayes or Morris. In fact, if it hadn't been for my swift actions in restarting the power and the fan, the outcome of your illegal and ill-advised adventure underground could have been even more unpleasant.'

Kember laughed bitterly. 'And there was me thinking it was due to Inspector Watson turning up in the nick of time.'

'Nonsense,' Burnley said. 'We can't be held responsible for your actions when it was you who'd moved from where my men expected you to be.'

'Turning the fan on when we were in the fan drift, when the airlock door had been wedged shut, is not the actions of a rescue party.'

'I've already told you; I know nothing about the wedge but turning on the fan was designed to give you fresh air and keep you alive. I'm a pillar of the community. Morris, on the other hand, was a wastrel, a communist who drew enjoyment from striking and disrupting wherever he went.' Burnley's voice cracked. 'If you're looking for a devil, Inspector, that would be your man. If it wasn't for his negligence towards his own safety and that of his men, Morris wouldn't have allowed himself to absorb a fatal dose of deadly mine gases, you wouldn't have needed to interfere in the operating of a critical facility of the war effort, and nobody else would have been hurt.'

Lizzie continued her nursing duties, confused by what she was hearing. Burnley was once again exhibiting all the behaviours of a narcissist but something he'd said had flicked a switch in her mind. The main problem was, his unrealistic expectations and preoccupation with himself wouldn't allow anything to dent his self-image and pride, not even the gross exaggeration of the part he'd played in their survival, which he no doubt believed to be understated. If

Kember persisted, Burnley's narcissistic confidence could be undermined and threatened, causing the kind of mood swing that could lead to violence.

'Where is Mrs Wall?' Lizzie asked, more to defuse the situation than any real desire to know.

Burnley looked confused. 'Mrs Wall?'

'We saw her earlier. She said she was coming over here to see you.'

Burnley shook his head. 'She hasn't been here.'

Lizzie looked at Kember, who was rubbing his nose in thought.

'Are you and Mrs Wall . . . ?' Kember let the question hang.

Burnley looked affronted. 'Good Lord, no. Whatever gave you that idea! I'll have you know that I am a happily married man, Inspector. I'd look to your own, if I were you, if you want to talk about shenanigans on that front.'

Lizzie resisted the urge to glance at Kember, feeling a burn in her cheeks and knowing they were reddening. Her attempt at deflection had backfired and brought the attention back to them.

'Nice try, Mr Burnley,' Kember said, 'but I think we'll concentrate on finding whoever among you is the murderer.'

Burnley's face clouded even more and the other men shifted uneasily.

'What the inspector means,' Lizzie interrupted, 'is that even if one of you in this dormitory is not the murderer, there is someone working and living in this colliery who is capable of taking a life without compunction. He's had a hand in the murder of one person already and attacked me and two policemen. He will know that you have spoken to us individually and he will suspect that we are closing in on revealing his identity. In my judgement, he will not allow that to happen. Sooner or later, he will become paranoid about what you know, what you've said, and what you intend to do next. He will begin to see you as a threat and you will become a target.'

'My apologies,' Ramsey said, by way of interruption. 'I just wanted to say, sir, there are no bombs.'

Lizzie saw him clasp his hands together as if in plea, his head held in a slight bow but his eyes looking up at Burnley. He seemed completely subordinate and she realised the others had the same air about them.

'What?' Burnley snapped.

'The siren went off but I haven't heard any explosions,' Ramsey continued.

'Thank God,' Burnley said, in a way that suggested God had nothing to do with his affairs. 'Gone over to London, I expect.'

Lizzie realised she hadn't even heard any aircraft, despite the complete silence around the colliery due to the air raid warning and the weather. The thick clouds were laden with snow and may have muffled the engine noises, especially if the Luftwaffe had flown at high altitude, and she did have a thumping headache. That did not stop her wondering if she should have heard something, even if that was another siren from a nearby village. She realised what Ramsey was getting at. If the raiders had passed, the all-clear should have sounded.

'How is he?' Kember asked.

'We really need to get him to a hospital,' Lizzie said. 'I've cleaned the wound but if he develops a blood clot or a bleed on the brain . . .' She shook her head.

'I'm afraid you're stuck here,' Burnley said. 'The roads are impassable and the telephone lines are still down.'

Kember retrieved his coat from Watson and replaced it with a blanket from one of the other beds. 'In that case, I have time to ask Collins a few more questions.'

Lizzie suppressed a frown. They'd questioned those they needed to, so what was Kember up to? 'Can I speak to you?' she said.

Kember nodded and led them through to the vestibule.

'What are we really going to do?' Lizzie asked.

'We? Nothing,' he said, doing up the buttons of his coat. 'Watson can't be moved in his condition. One of us should stay with him in case he wakes up. He might have seen who attacked him and if it's one of the men in there—'

'And why does that have to be me?' Lizzie's face turned to stone as she glared at him. Was this another clumsy attempt at gallantry, a matter of police legality or an underlying bias that a woman wasn't as capable?

He sighed and glanced at the men through the window set into the door. 'You know as well as I do that miners are a tough breed with a lot of traditional views on a woman's place. Whatever you or I think, the men in there will find it less suspicious if you look after Watson and I act like a detective.'

'It wasn't that long ago that you were agreeing that all of them could be in it together,' Lizzie said, knowing he was right but feeling irritated anyway. 'Now you want me to stay in a room with them, alone?'

'To be honest, I'm not sure any of them are capable of cold-blooded murder.'

Quayle pushed open the inner door and stepped into the small vestibule with them.

'Sorry to interrupt,' he said. 'We keep being left in here with Burnley, even after you said he might be the murderer, and we don't like it.'

'You're all still suspects, Mr Quayle, but the murderer won't take any of you on if you stay together,' Kember said. 'The best place for you is in here, with Officer Hayes, watching over Inspector Watson. I assure you, a dead policeman is the last thing any of us want.'

Lizzie saw a flicker of fear in Quayle's eyes. She glanced through the window and saw Burnley looking at them.

'Inspector Kember is right,' she said. 'I could do with some help looking after Inspector Watson.'

Quayle hesitated for a moment before giving them a curt nod. 'You'd better be right,' he said, and pushed open the inner door.

Once the door had closed, Lizzie said, 'I know you only led the men to believe the killer could be Burnley to get them to take us down the pit but I'm still concerned about him,' hating the admission that she was worried about anything. 'I'm starting to doubt he's capable of bashing anyone over the head but that's not the problem. He could still end up doing something stupid. His inflated sense of importance and obsession with how he looks to others is no concern in itself, but the flip side of the coin is his inability to accept any criticism, his lack of empathy for others and his dehumanising of Morris.'

'Does that make him dangerous?' Kember said, with a raised eyebrow.

Lizzie shrugged. 'I've seen many successful businessmen with similar traits but Burnley's deep-rooted need for attention, admiration and any kind of approval is sated by his addiction to fantasy, whereby the world he's created in his head means that being ordered by Watson to open the pit translated into him riding to our rescue.'

'He's mad, then?'

Lizzie shook her head. Why did everyone think everyone else was mad?

'Not mad, a narcissist. He can't see any connection between exploiting his men and taking them for granted and the troubled relationship it causes between them. While he was speaking to us, all the good was "I", all the bad was "we", and he seemed oblivious that his men might have noticed. Did you see how cowed Ramsey seemed when he tried to tell Burnley about the air raid, even though no bombs falling is a good thing? I think this situation is making Burnley unstable and he needs to be watched.'

'As Lady Caroline Lamb once called Lord Byron: mad, bad and dangerous to know,' Kember said, and took another glance through the window. 'They're becoming agitated again. I should go, but you should keep your wits about you.'

'Where are you actually going?' she asked, a wave of anxiety breaking across her chest.

'To search the hut Burnley put us in earlier,' Kember said.

'What for?' She frowned. This wasn't what she'd expected. Had she lost her touch for reading people?

'Burnley told us that the dormitory had been out of action for a while for repairs but I noticed one of the beds had crumpled bedclothes. It didn't strike me as odd at the time but now, looking back, I think someone has been in there without his knowledge.'

'Sleeping on the job?'

'Not necessarily.'

'Could be any one of the colliery workers.'

'True, but I want to know which one, and why. I said I wanted to see Collins to deflect the killer from where I'm really going.'

Kember opened the inner door and called to Burnley. The mine owner joined them in the vestibule and stood with his back to her, looking Kember up and down.

'Look here, Inspector. I'm the owner of this place and I've done nothing wrong. People are dropping like flies and I need to get to the bottom of it as much as you. If you want to keep me locked up, you'll have to arrest and handcuff me.'

Lizzie was grateful as Kember gently moved Burnley to one side out of her way.

'Now I think of it, there is something you can help me with,' Kember said.

Lizzie saw Burnley raise his chin.

'While I'm busy, I need you to find out who pressed the air raid button and why they haven't signalled the all-clear.'

'Is that all?' Burnley looked crestfallen.

'Trust me, it may be important.'

Burnley nodded. 'Very well,' he said, and left through the outer door.

'Are you sure that's a good idea?' Lizzie whispered.

'You and Quayle convinced me it's better to keep Burnley and the others apart for now,' Kember said. 'After all, if he is the killer, all his potential victims are in here.'

'Except you,' Lizzie said, feeling a tightening of her chest.

'It's like Burnley himself told me earlier; keep your friends close but your enemies closer,' he said. 'I have to go before they start asking questions. Stay here and stay alert until I get back.'

'Take care,' Lizzie said. She noticed another key in the lock of the open door as Kember turned away, which explained their earlier easy entry. Thinking ahead, she pocketed it before calling to him. 'I think you should lock us in.'

CHAPTER SIXTEEN

Kember touched his lips, thinking back to the kiss in the tunnels, and allowed himself a small smile as he waited for his eyes to become accustomed to the dark. Then his smile faded. He was still married, even if his wife had kicked him out months ago. That he had been ejected from the house he owned perhaps meant that her latest in a long line of lovers was a serious proposition for a long-term relationship. Marriage? He thought not. His wife didn't do marriage very well. Definitely not loyalty or fidelity, come to that. He wasn't exactly the laughing stock of Tonbridge Police HQ but he knew many of his fellow officers felt pity for him. And embarrassment. And empathy, because many of them also had troubled marriages due to the nature of the job. Yes; pity, embarrassment and empathy.

His thoughts turned to Watson, his head crudely bandaged and the very real possibility of a deadly brain haemorrhage hanging over him. Even if he survived and awoke, the chances were that he hadn't seen who hit him and couldn't help them. His attacker might not know that though, or decide it wasn't worth the risk in letting him live. Leaving him there in a hut full of suspects, even with Lizzie watching over him, wasn't his best option; it was his only option.

He sighed and his breath hung around his head like a shroud, the wind having all but disappeared for now. Silence still blanketed the colliery like the snow, and in any other situation it would have been eerily beautiful. Keeping his miner's helmet on for protection, he considered switching on his head-torch, but as they'd discovered, the power wasn't sufficient to be much use in the open. In any case, Lizzie and Watson had been attacked in the dark and he didn't relish the idea of giving away his position to anyone abroad who might wish to do him harm.

The dark didn't seem to bother Burnley. His indistinct shadowy shape was already many yards away on the track towards the pithead as Kember locked the dormitory with his key. He put it in his pocket and hesitated, wondering if this was the right thing to do. Preventing the men from separating all over the colliery also ensured safety in numbers and was no bad thing, but had he incarcerated Lizzie with a whole group of madmen while another roamed around the colliery? In addition, he'd enrolled someone who Lizzie thought a narcissist to help him in his nocturnal investigations and then let him go off on his own. *Am I losing my touch?* he thought. Whatever the pros and cons, their lives would remain in danger until the killer was identified and caught. However helpful Lizzie could be, that was *his* job.

With weak moonlight starting to find fissures in the cloud but no colliery lamps to assist because of the air raid warning, Kember thought the snow resembled a counterpane draped across a bed in the small hours of the morning. He remembered Lizzie's words about when Morris had died: a perfect time to murder.

So was this.

On a bedspread the ripples, waves and depressions could have revealed the path where a cat had sauntered in search of a soft place to sleep. Here, it hinted at human tracks and footprints, any one of which might belong to the killer. Hut Two, the dormitory in which he'd spent a short time with Lizzie, lay near the far end of the row of identical huts. All had tracks that spread out from their steps like the indentations of crows' feet.

At least the snow has stopped, Kember thought, but the increase in visibility it brought could be a double-edged sword. He knew he might get a glimpse of someone if they tried to attack from the shadows, but in return he would be easy to follow and ambush. Wanting as much night vision as possible, he waited for his eyes to adjust. The moon found a gap in the clouds and a sliver of silver swept over the colliery like a rolling wave searching for the shore. The band of light caught no activity on its passage across the site except his own and the whole place might well have been abandoned, for all the life he could see or hear.

Too impatient to wait any longer, his throat as dry and rough as the coal dust in the tunnels, the snow crunched underfoot as he stepped off the steps of the building, sounding like boots on gravel in the otherwise complete silence. The shortest distance between two points is a straight line and Kember followed the existing track in the snow between each dormitory building.

He stopped suddenly.

Deliberately.

And listened for the sound of anyone following whose reaction might have been a split second too late. The silence reassured him and he carried on. He started to wonder again what the hell he was doing, tramping all over a coal mine at night, no doubt being tracked by a vicious killer. He was a detective. He should be the one doing the tracking but at least he felt sure something important remained to be discovered inside that hut.

Lizzie composed herself and refocused her mind on what lay on the other side of the door. You could never be certain how someone would react in any given circumstance. They might become stoic or emotional, resigned or resistant, passive or aggressive. Her experience told her that any change to a situation – such as locking her and Watson in the same room where the men's freedom had been restricted – might trigger a negative response. The compliance the six mine workers had shown so far, even allowing for Burnley's narcissistic bluster, was as insufficient a gauge of their potential for violence as licking one's finger, putting it in the air and declaring that a storm was coming. Lizzie knew that while all the men were together, she needed to keep things calm and not say or do anything antagonistic, but that didn't sit well with her desire to get to the truth. She had an almost irresistible urge to dig deeper and find out if any of them really were capable of murder.

She returned to the warmth of the dormitory room where the scene had changed little: Ramsey and Quayle stared at the flames through the open door of the stove, as though communicating through daydreams; Armstrong was deep in thought and occasionally frowned or shook his head; Pine picked dirt from beneath his fingernails; and Young rested his chin in one hand with his elbow supported on one knee.

Lizzie checked on Watson but he showed no signs of regaining consciousness, although her bandaging skills seemed to have done the trick as far as bleeding went. His pulse appeared strong and regular, and his chest rose and fell with rhythmic breathing. There was nothing more they could do for him but wait and hope.

The moment she sat on the end of the bed and tried to look calm and relaxed, her stomach began to churn and her headache made a comeback. Knowing she dared not lose control in front of these men, she concentrated on the detail of a woodgrain knot in one of the wooden floorboards and used that focus to fight and regulate her breathing. *Why does my mind do this to me at the worst possible moments?* she thought. She flicked a glance at the group of men but their minds were elsewhere, lost in private thoughts. She took the opportunity to ping the rubber band on her wrist, and as the delicious wave of release coursed through her, she ignored all her experience and training, threw all caution to the wind and decided attack was the best form of defence.

Lizzie cleared her throat.

'While you're all here together,' she said.

When Young and Pine looked over, she knew she had their interest, so she chose Quayle to be first instead.

'Mr Quayle, can I ask you about your experience in the tunnels?' she said.

Quayle looked away from the fire and straight at Lizzie with a stare that could intimidate even the strong-willed. 'You can ask.'

Lizzie didn't flinch. 'While you were down there with Morris, did you ever argue?' She noticed Ramsey's gaze flick towards Quayle.

'Not really,' Quayle said. 'But then again, he didn't bother me in my district, and I'm not the arguing kind.'

'You didn't like him, though?' Lizzie said. 'A pillock, I think you called him.'

Quayle smiled. 'Yeah, he was. And no, I didn't particularly like him.'

'What did he say when you sprained your ankle and needed time off?'

Quayle's smile faded. 'He had a bit of a go. Shouted, like, but there wasn't much he could do. A man can't work down the pit if he's injured. He becomes a liability in an emergency. I saw the doc, who bandaged my ankle, gave me Aspirin and signed me off. "You're a lazy git," Morris said. I laughed and called him over-promoted. He laughed back.' Quayle shrugged. 'As I told you, life is unfair, but I didn't kill him. A few days later, I was as right as rain.'

Quayle went back to staring at the fire and Lizzie turned her attention to the next man.

'Mr Ramsey, I recall you said that Morris was a nasty man, a bully who ridiculed you and who thought he was too important to carry his own canary.'

Ramsey turned away from the fire. 'Pissed me off no end, excuse my French, miss. I've already said he was always in my ear or on my shoulder. "It's your job to carry the bloody canary," he used to say. Do this, don't do this. Do that, don't do that. "Keep an eye on the Davy." Still, you got to earn a living, haven't you? Oh, and I didn't kill him, neither.'

Lizzie let the men go back to their own thoughts, aware they would now be alert to her intention to ask more questions. Quayle and Ramsey had both recalled specific conversations which, in her experience, was the behaviour of those telling the truth. In almost the same breath, the two men had denied murdering Morris, which made it likely that was true too. Liars usually generalised rather than quoted, not least because it made it easier for them to remember later. Lizzie studied Young for a while, a man who never ventured underground, or even visited the pithead.

'Mr Young?' she said.

'I was wondering when my turn would come,' he said, with a smile that almost reached his eyes.

'Morris indirectly caused the injury to your brother.'

'And that means I killed him?'

'I didn't say that, but did you?' She held Young's gaze until the man broke the spell and looked at the fire.

'Everyone in this room had cause to dislike Morris but we all value our freedom too much to want to kill him,' Young said. 'So, no, I didn't do it. I remember once, when we were drinking and playing cards, he said, "What's done is done. You stick to your job and I'll stick to mine." That was fine by me. Having a beer when he was in the club, or trying to fleece a few quid out of him at cards was no hardship because I didn't need to see his face at work.'

'And what about you, Mr Pine?'

Pine looked up in surprise, as if he hadn't really been listening, having progressed from cleaning his nails to exploring the contents of his left ear with his little finger.

'I'm not sure Morris could be fleeced at cards,' Pine said, showing he'd been alert all along. 'He'd be the one doing the fleecing, and not the honourable way.'

'Cheating?' Lizzie said.

'Of course. Always. I thought we'd been over this.' Lizzie kept her face blank and Pine continued. 'I could never catch him at it but there is no way a man of small mind such as Morris could ever be that good. "It's all down to Lady Luck," he would say, but no one I know ever got that lucky except him.'

'You lost a lot of money to him?'

'Quite a bit, but I didn't kill him because of it. I could never put my finger on how he did it, and if you've no proof then it can't have happened, right?'

Lizzie shrugged, not sure whether he was talking about cheating at cards or murder. Either way, both Young and Pine sounded as genuine in their denials as Quayle and Ramsey had been. She had noticed no defensive grasping of hands or crossing of arms and legs, and no small nods or shakes of their heads to contradict what they were saying.

She sighed. She had believed Burnley to be capable of murder, someone who would then blame everyone else and play the victim when things went wrong. But how could he have killed Morris on his own, and would he have jeopardised his reputation, business and freedom just because Morris was a habitual strike leader?

She looked sideways at Armstrong and saw him looking back at her, no longer lost in his own thoughts. *How long has he been watching?* she wondered. The thought that he might have been observing for a while unnerved her and she reached for her wrist. Armstrong's eyes followed the movement and she stopped short of pinging the rubber band, feeling her heart thump and her embarrassed face flush with warmth. His eyes sought hers again, but this time they held resignation, a sadness she'd not seen in them before. Lizzie glanced at the other men but they had all resumed their fire-watching and thinking. She turned her attention back to Armstrong, who still looked at her like a man who had known pain and suffering. There was a softness in his features where before there had been stony determination.

The men had been wary and defensive during the questions put to them by herself and Kember, and Watson's investigation had got nowhere either. *Can the attacks on me and Watson have been a watershed?* she wondered. *Has some unwritten code been broken or an invisible line crossed? But by whom?* They all seemed so subdued and troubled that Lizzie began to find it difficult to imagine any of them capable of the attacks, never mind the murder of Morris.

Armstrong still watched her, his eyes never leaving hers as he pulled back the left sleeve of his jacket. Lizzie watched, unable to tear her eyes away as he unbuttoned the cuff of his shirt and slowly began to roll up the sleeve like a pub drunkard or bare-knuckle fighter preparing to take on an opponent. His hand, closed into a fist, was turned down, exposing the back of his arm as the material peeled away. The urge to move away and find something with which to defend herself was strong, but she felt compelled to stay and watch whatever ritual was playing out in front of her. She was confused. The move itself felt threatening but Armstrong's expression did not. Either the man was a psychopath in full control of everything he did and projected or something else lay beneath the action that others could only ever see on the surface.

His sad eyes remained fixed on her face.

Lizzie took another glance at the other men but they were oblivious to Armstrong and herself. A band tightened across her chest and she wanted to ping the rubber band or inhale from her medicinal jar. When she looked back, Armstrong's gaze remained locked on to her but his hands were still. She glanced down and saw that he'd turned over his fist, exposing the flesh of his inner forearm.

A neat ladder of equally spaced pale scars stood out in relief from the surrounding darker skin from near his wrist to the crook of his elbow. The two largest scars, longer and thicker, extended across his wrist where veins bulged blue. Lizzie realised she had almost stopped breathing and all the moisture had disappeared from her mouth. She recognised those scars as belonging to someone in torment, someone whose experiences weighed so heavily that they had felt the need to cause themselves physical pain to take their mind away from their emotional anguish. The two biggest scars would be where cutting the ladder had failed to ease the suffering and Armstrong had tried to take his own life. Had that been a cry for help, perhaps unrecognised by the supposedly strong men around him? Had they ignored him, maybe made jokes without realising the seriousness of what he had tried to tell them unconsciously through his behaviour? Had someone saved him, or had he just got lucky? Or unlucky?

She raised her gaze to his and he gave her an almost imperceptible nod before rolling down his sleeve. She reached for the band on her wrist, as if Armstrong's revelation had freed her from her own self-constraint, and gave it a ping. The rubber snapped against her skin and sent a jolt through her system. She did it again and felt a wave of relief as the tension left her body. Armstrong gave her the flicker of a smile and another nod before he too looked into the fire glowing inside the open door of the stove.

In that moment, Lizzie doubted that Armstrong could be the murderer. She could not say for certain but her research experience in Oxford prison had taught her that those who turned against themselves rarely turned against others.

She had seen men and women cut themselves as a way of relieving sadness or anger. Unfortunately, the relief often gave way to shame and guilt at having been overwhelmed by their initial feelings and she'd lost count of how many times those sufferers then felt sadness and anger at having resorted to harming themselves. It was a vicious cycle that was difficult to break, even with the help of others, and she'd seemed to be the only one in Oxford capable of recognising it for what it was. Those who harmed themselves often sought a measure of control or to express their inner pain. They sometimes wanted to be punished for perceived slights committed to others, to distract themselves with an immediate and external pain, to feel fleeting moments of pleasure, amongst the painful chaos, or to feel anything at all.

If many of Armstrong's scars hadn't appeared so old and well-healed, Lizzie might have suspected his wife's affair with Morris to be the cause. Anguish at her infidelity might have resulted in the latest scars, but that some of them were much older suggested former traumas. Perhaps his wife had strayed before. While in Oxford, Lizzie had uncovered myriad causes: abuse of every kind imaginable, trauma of the body or mind, an unshakable feeling of unworthiness, deep-rooted family problems of every kind, bullying by anyone and everyone, and sometimes an uncontrollable desire for members of their own sex. It could be any of those reasons or others, or several, or all.

Despite her growing feeling that taking the life of another human might be beyond this group, the notion that all these men were involved in something still niggled at the back of her mind. They had been too evasive and defensive during Watson's investigation and now Kember's. If they hadn't murdered Morris and couldn't have attacked Watson and herself, what were they concealing?

◆ ◆ ◆

Kember approached cautiously, taking frequent looks around and straining his ears for sounds of occupation. He could neither see nor hear anything unusual and so ascended the steps of Hut Two in slow movements. At the top, he tried the door and found it locked. That reassured him a little and he felt in his pocket for the key Lizzie had removed earlier as they'd left the hut to take their ride down in the lift cage to the bottom of the pit. He unlocked the door and eased it open, stepping through and shutting it before opening the inner door and switching on the light. The glare hurt his eyes for a moment but as they adjusted, he could see nothing had changed since their visit. The bed in which he had taken forty winks still lay unmade, the bed Lizzie had sat on had crumpled blankets, and the bed to his right still showed signs of having been disturbed when the hut was supposed to be unoccupied.

Kember gave the hut a quick sweep, for peace of mind rather than any other concrete reason, and returned to the suspicious bed. He took his time looking at the floor around and under it, checking the cabinets on either side, looking at the walls for signs of any marks made there. He checked under the covers, beneath the pillows and under the mattress. Also, nothing. So why was his detective's sixth sense telling him there was something here he was just not seeing? He smoothed the covers and sat down, wondering how a simple case had come to this; him sitting on a dormitory bed as people were attacked or killed around him. He sighed and stood, deciding to do one more check to satisfy himself.

Kember's second sweep gleaned no more than the first. It was a clean, freshly renovated hut that held the faint aromas of paint, furniture polish and coal smoke; the floor was made of polished wood; there was no ceiling, giving a view of the inside of the roof beyond the rafters.

Looking at the beds, he stopped as the little man in his head rose from his chair and flicked through a file. Lizzie's blankets were crumpled and creased where she had laid out the blankets and sat on the edge. He frowned, looked at his own unmade covers flung aside and went back to the bed that had first aroused his curiosity. He saw the creased blankets where he'd sat moments earlier and realised that the indentation of his backside on the edge, and that of Lizzie's on her bed, did not match what he'd seen here earlier. When he'd arrived, and before he'd disturbed the bedclothes, the indentation in the blankets had been in the middle.

He reached across and pushed down with his fist, making a crumpled depression. Looking closer, he found tiny flecks of soil where mud had been brushed from the blanket. The man in his head closed the file with a flourish and Kember looked up. The rafters were just out of reach of his fingertips. A smaller man would need to stand on the bed to reach them.

Kember smoothed the blankets, put his foot where his fist had been and stood wobbling on the bed. He reached up to the rafter directly overhead to steady himself, felt along the top with his other hand and almost recoiled when his fingers met something cold. He took a breath, felt again and retrieved an adjustable spanner from its hiding place, holding it delicately with one finger and a thumb.

He studied the foot-long tool, turning it in the light. It looked like it had been given a wipe but the dark blood and hairs caught in the wheel mechanism were as clear as day. A sick feeling, gone in a moment, left him with his jaw clenched in anger.

I must find this bastard, he thought.

Kember noticed the smell of coal smoke seemed stronger than when he'd entered and he looked towards the stove. Had someone blocked the flue from outside? By turning his head, a noise he'd heard in the background became louder and sounded like running water, but he knew this to be impossible because they'd had snow, not rain. Then the sound changed, to the rattle of hailstones on glass, like a handful of gravel thrown against the window. He went to the blackout boards, lifted one and looked out through the glass. The pane was clear except for a build-up of snow in the corners and he couldn't see any hailstones, but a flickering light played against the side of the next hut along, which had been in total darkness before. He sought a latch on the window but remembered that they weren't the opening kind.

On turning back to face the room, Kember found the sound had got louder and the smell had become stronger. He moved across to inspect the stove, wondering whether someone might have stoked the fire before he'd arrived, but as far as he could tell, more coal hadn't been put on the fire since he and Lizzie had been here. He held the adjustable spanner, felt the weight, and tried to think about who might have wielded it as a weapon before standing on the bed to conceal it. *Why hide it?* he wondered, and remembered when Lizzie had once described how any object could become a personal weapon for a killer and something they might become irrationally attached to. If she was right, maybe the spanner had acquired some kind of importance for the colliery murderer, like a lucky charm or a talisman.

Then he saw a waft of smoke roll into the dormitory from beneath the inner door.

Fire!

Kember realised the sound was the crackle of flames and the smoke smelled of wood not coal. His heart thumped and he looked around for an escape route. The only way out was through the front entrance but smoke flowed through gaps around the door and light flickered through its window, suggesting the vestibule was ablaze. He ran to the wall and stamped the heel of his shoe against the wood fixed above the level of the brickwork. Pain jarred up to his knee and he realised it was too solid to contemplate kicking his way out.

He hauled the blackout board from the window and a jolt of alarm shot through him when yellow light from flickering flames poured in through the glass. He ran to the other side of the room but that window was no different. It was as if fire had taken hold of the whole of the outside of the hut. He scanned the floor but that appeared as solid as the walls. Burnley may have skimped on the air bricks and opening windows but the rest of the construction seemed as solid as anything he'd seen on the air station at RAF Scotney.

Smoke had started to force itself through the roof panels and pour through the cracks around the door, along with the crackle of burning wood and a choking oily smell. Kember guessed the heat of the fire had taken care of the snow on the roof, and he imagined the bituminous roofing felt beginning to melt and disintegrate. Fearing the roof might start to collapse at any moment, and no longer worried about fingerprints, he swung his arm until the adjustable spanner connected with the window. The crash of shattering glass was barely discernible above the roar of flames from beyond. He felt as though the air was being sucked from his lungs as the flames sought fresh oxygen to burn. He glanced up. The layer of thick smoke had descended another foot and he knew he would soon be forced to the floor just to breathe.

The window was his only hope.

Stepping on the bed beneath the window, Kember could hear the urgent sound of a fire bell but couldn't risk waiting a second longer. He gripped the handle of the spanner and used it to knock away the vicious shards of glass protruding from the window frame until satisfied he wouldn't be lacerated. He then raised his leg and kicked his heel into the thin centre post of the window frame. It gave a loud crack but held. He tried again, feeling a twinge in his lower back. One more kick and the post came away from the frame, sending splinters in all directions. Kember was coughing now, smoke swirling around his head as he stepped down, putting the spanner in his pocket. He ripped the sheets and blankets from each bed and dragged the bare mattresses to the window. Flames had encroached from above, lighting the interior of the hut with an eerie glow that seemed to shimmer and move like sunset reflected on waves on a beach.

Kember took each mattress and threw it out of the window, hoping they and the snow would break his fall, then stepped back on the bed. He placed one folded blanket along the bottom of the frame and braced himself, praying his back injury would hold out, as well as his nerve. He hesitated as a chunk of flaming roofing felt fell past the window, and wondered whether he should go head or feet first, or sideways. He was fit enough, apart from his back, but no athlete. The crash of the roof collapsing near the door made up his mind. He stood on the end frame of the bed, gripped the already burning blanket, and launched himself sideways through the broken window like a high-jumper straddling the bar.

Kember tumbled as he fell and landed heavily on his left shoulder, winding himself and knocking his miner's helmet flying. Fortunately, the mattresses and snow did their job and he continued in an unplanned and awkward roll until he came to rest in a deep snowdrift. Pain lanced down his left arm and for one frightening moment he thought he'd either broken his arm or dislocated his shoulder. He lay in the cold for a moment, letting his breath return and his lungs fill with fresh air, before making tentative movements to test his arm and shoulder. The initial jarring had left behind a dull ache but he'd escaped serious injury.

The heat from the blazing dormitory had warmed the air around him and he realised his coat was wet from melting snow. This galvanised him into action and he stood up, testing to assure himself that the rest of his body was in one piece. The back of his left hand was sore with a small burn but nothing that couldn't have been suffered by careless tending of a garden bonfire.

He realised the adjustable spanner wasn't in his pocket and made a sweep of the area around where he had fallen. A hole in the snow gave away the tool's position and he retrieved it. His pocket wasn't the right place to keep evidence but he had no choice, given the circumstances. He found his helmet nearby and emptied it of snow before jamming it back on his head. Lizzie's helmet had saved her life and he wasn't about to take a chance on the thickness of his own skull.

Kember's priority right then was to get away from the building as it continued to burn to the ground, see if he could identify fresh tracks that might suggest who the arsonist might be, and return to Lizzie and the miners. He stumbled around to the hut entrance and saw that the melted snow around the front had obliterated any tracks. However, a new trail he hadn't noticed on his arrival stretched away at an angle to his own. Perhaps the killer had got careless and failed to follow other tracks to conceal his own. Maybe he didn't care any more. Maybe he'd seen an opportunity and had to throw caution to the wind, to trap Kember inside before he realised what was happening. Either way, the track was there, the disturbed snow highlighted with shadows cast by the fire.

Kember ploughed across the snow to the trail and took out his Bijou torch. In its light, he saw the small imprints of compressed snow and knew straight away that it was the same as the footprint he'd seen outside the fan house. Whoever the killer was, he had

255

stayed both one step ahead of the game while following Kember's every move. A commotion nearby made him look up and he saw men from the nearby dormitories, those who hadn't sought the refuge of the air raid shelters, using buckets and shovels to scoop up snow and throw it on the fire. Over his shoulder, an approaching bell announced the arrival of the Bekesbourne Colliery Fire Brigade with their water bowser towing a trailer pump, both emblazoned with BCFB.

As the bowser jerked to a halt and three men jumped from the cab, three more men arrived on foot. Looking like the miners they were, but wearing rubber-handled fire-axes on their belts, thick leather boots, and steel helmets bearing the same red letters, each had a role to play. Two men uncoupled the water-pump while two others connected the fire-hoses with brass nozzles and unrolled them towards the hut. Another fireman took the largest-diameter hose already attached to the pump and screwed it to a connector on the bowser. The remaining fireman waited until his colleagues were in position before cranking a starting handle, nodding with satisfaction as the noisy but powerful pump began to chug.

With two men now holding the hoses steady as the water began to flow, one team used a spray to send a deluge over the walls and roof, and the other directed a constant, high-powered, concentrated jet of water through the doorway into the inferno. But it was a hopeless battle from the outset, against orange flames that licked malevolently from every window and through holes in the roof. The colliery lights remained off because the air raid all-clear hadn't been sounded, but the fire reflected off the nearest huts, the snow and a few of the nearest buildings of the pithead, making the darkness beyond even deeper. *If the Luftwaffe can't see this then they aren't coming tonight*, Kember thought, as the choking smell of smoke, charred wood and bitumen pervaded the air and caught at the back of his throat.

He studied the footprints again and realised the track through the snow consisted of a single line, meaning whoever had tramped this way to the hut had not left by the same route. *Where have you gone?* he thought, looking around with no idea where to go next.

He saw Burnley stagger towards him from the direction of the bowser, panting and wheezing. The big man stopped and bent over, his hands on his knees.

'Thank . . . God,' Burnley said, between gasps for breath. 'Saw . . . the fire . . . raised . . . the alarm.' He waved an arm in the direction of the pithead. 'Collins . . . is dead.'

Kember was confused. The size of the spanner had given him pause for thought about the attacker's intentions, and Burnley couldn't have killed Collins and set the fire.

Then he saw the fire in Hut Six.

CHAPTER SEVENTEEN

Lizzie became aware of a draught around her ankles and glanced over at the door, expecting a visitor. No one had entered. She looked back at the men, still moaning about being locked in their own hut and threatening to break out, and realised all of them were at the end of the room nearest the stove, like before. Her mind shifted on to a different plane, imagining herself in the hut on the night of the murder. The police report said the room had been warm when they had arrived, despite an overnight frost, so why was it colder at one end now?

A thought struck her. She'd felt a draught at floor level in Hut Two, from the air bricks designed to ventilate the room. Hut Six also had a draught, but only at the end nearest the door.

Watson gave a barely audible groan, knocking Lizzie off her train of thought, and she checked his pulse and breathing, which both seemed normal. The heat of his forehead had dissipated too. All good signs, except that if the killer was in the room and watching them and Watson looked like recovering enough to identify his attacker, his life could be in more danger than if he remained unconscious and at death's door.

'I'm sure that was a fire bell again,' Quayle said, looking quizzically at Ramsey. 'That's twice now.'

Ramsey turned his head, as if doing so would give him greater hearing. 'How can it be? There's been no bombs, the pit's shut down for the night, and it's been snowing for hours.' He looked at Young.

Young shook his head. 'You're right. It can't—'

Pine and Armstrong had already got to their feet by the time Quayle shouted 'Fire!'

Lizzie looked towards the entrance in alarm, and saw smoke rolling through the wide gap beneath the door. She gasped. She had the key Kember had left with her but that door was the only way out and Watson hadn't regained consciousness. Pine strode to the door and touched the knob, recoiling with a yelp when the hot metal seared the skin on the palm of his hand. Armstrong rushed to the door but stopped, Quayle and Ramsey behind him.

'What're we gonna do?' Young asked, fear evident in his wavering voice.

Lizzie knew that alongside gas, the risk of explosion and fire were miners' greatest fears. Being injured or trapped underground came a close second. Those fears were etched on every man's face now.

'Smash the windows,' Young shouted.

'What about Inspector Watson?' Lizzie said, her throat already feeling constricted. She swallowed hard. 'We can't leave him.'

Armstrong gave her a look of anguish. 'This place will go up like a tinderbox. We haven't got time.'

Pine had already moved across to a window and ripped down the blackout board. Ramsey grabbed the fire poker and shattered the glass with it, shards of glass reflecting the orange of flames as they tumbled through the air.

Lizzie went to Watson as the men gathered mattresses and blankets. He was still unconscious but his breathing had been strong and steady for some time. Could she move him herself? She thought not, and looked for any other possible way out.

Hissing came from the direction of the front door and every head turned in surprise, including Lizzie's. The men by the window stopped trying to throw mattresses outside and watched as blackened water ran into the dormitory from under the door.

'Thank Christ,' Quayle said. 'The fire brigade.'

'They were quick,' Armstrong said, throwing a balled-up blanket back on a bed. 'How did they get here so fast?'

'Who bloody cares?' Ramsey said. 'Just thank your lucky stars they did.'

Lizzie could hear water hitting the roof and cascading down the sides of the hut, and the feeling of relief after the moment of panic made her equally as breathless. She turned away from the miners to tend to Watson and squeezed her eyes shut. Now, more than any other, was not the time to show any weakness in front of the men. Despite the fear that had manifested on their faces, they wouldn't admit to being scared and she shouldn't either. It would be expected of her as a woman but appearing stoic would stand her in good stead if things got worse.

How can things get worse?

As choking smoke swirled in through the broken window, Lizzie covered her nose and mouth with her arm, concerned about what a lungful of smoke would do to the unconscious Watson. Every part of her body seemed to be screaming for her to get out of the hut but she clenched her jaw and fists, telling herself that help had arrived. Men were shouting, her heart thumped and her headache pounded. *Will this nightmare never end?*

Shouts and bangs came from the entrance and the men stood back. The door suddenly crashed open and drooped on one hinge, water spraying into the room. Frantic shouts from the fire brigade miners galvanised those in the hut into action. Quayle and Ramsey ensured Lizzie was the first to leave, hurrying her towards the shattered door being held out of the way by Young. She looked over her shoulder, worried they might leave Watson behind, but Pine and Armstrong had picked the unconscious detective off the bed and carried him to the door.

Lizzie emerged into the cold fresh air, unable to contain a sob of relief, and was guided away from the doorway by Ramsey. A water bowser and pump fed two hoses being held by firemen, spraying water over the roof of the hut. She couldn't see any flames, just a column of smoke and steam as they doused the charred wood and roofing felt.

Then she saw Hut Two with flames licking around the remains of its wooden frame as a dozen men threw snow at it. The wooden roof and walls had collapsed, leaving blackened posts sticking up from the level of brickwork like spent matches. Kember had gone there to search but the murderer had struck twice, trying to kill them both.

Kember is dead!

A crushing feeling of dread flooded her chest the like of which she had never experienced before and she felt Ramsey stiffen and take her weight, holding her up as the power to her legs switched off. She recovered quickly and thanked him.

'Lizzie.'

She heard the call and spun around to find Kember standing there, his expression a cross between pain and elation, and for a split second she didn't know whether to kiss him with relief or slap him for making her think he was gone forever. Instead, she stepped forward and gave him a hug, putting her head on his chest and knocking her helmet askew. Fighting back tears of relief as his arms wrapped around her, she wished they were back at Scotney, having a pint of bitter in the Castle pub.

Conscious that the miners might be watching, Lizzie pulled away. The mine owner was staring at the men who had just been rescued as they placed Watson on a stretcher, and the firemen were tending to the pump and bowser that had run out of water. No one was paying her any attention and she looked back at Kember's smoke-blackened face.

'How's Watson?' Kember asked.

'He started making sounds in there and I thought he was coming round,' she said, keeping her voice as steady as she could. 'He was looking a bit better, until this.' She indicated the smoking hut. 'I think he's going to pull through but he needs to get to a proper hospital. What happened to you?'

'Arson,' Kember said flatly, and nodded in the direction of the destroyed hut. 'Attempted murder, actually. The killer got to me and then you, so I guess we must be getting close.'

Lizzie flicked a look at Burnley and saw Kember take the hint.

'I don't see how.' He shook his head. 'He called out the fire brigade when he saw Hut Two on fire and was with me when your hut went up. It couldn't have been him.'

If all of the men they'd suspected from the beginning were not to blame for the fires, who, out of all the colliery workers, had the opportunity to kill Morris and attack her and Watson? That didn't sound to her like they were getting close. 'They're all in the clear, then,' she said, wondering where they went from here.

'So is Collins,' Kember said. 'He's dead.'

Oh God. Not another one, she thought as her heart sank. 'In the hut?'

Kember shook his head again. 'The pithead. Burnley found him when he went there to check the air raid siren.'

'But you don't think he killed him?'

'Why would he kill Collins but save us from burning to death?'

Lizzie had to concede that made no sense. Kember pulled something from his pocket.

'I found this in Hut Two.'

Lizzie recognised it as an adjustable spanner and saw the signs of blood on the mechanism. She put her hand to her head and felt the indentation in the helmet that had saved her life.

'That's not all,' he said, pocketing the spanner. 'I found more footprints leading to the hut, like the one we saw at the fan house.'

'Inspector.'

Kember turned at the call from Burnley.

'Should I sound the all-clear and let the men out of the shelters?'

'Not at the moment,' Kember said.

'It's best if we all go over to the canteen,' Burnley said. 'When Mrs Wall turns up, she can find the men somewhere to sleep. Inspector Watson will be looked after in the hospital block. Thank God the fire was put out before all their belongings went up in smoke. I knew my decision to have my own fire brigade was the right one.'

He raised his chin as if daring him to contradict his assertion.

'Where did you find Collins?' Kember asked.

Lizzie saw Burnley's mask of bravado drop away, revealing the face of a man whose carefully crafted facade of always being in complete control of his destiny had taken a battering these last few weeks, and especially today. It was a mask she used herself on a daily basis to avoid the taunts of being *not quite normal*.

'In the office the ARP wardens use,' Burnley said, in a voice too small for the size of the man. 'He was sprawled on the floor.'

'I need to see that office right away,' Kember said.

'Nothing's flying tonight. We could get the lights back on if you wish?'

Kember glanced towards where Watson lay on the stretcher. 'If you can get Inspector Watson in the warm and have someone look after him, I'll press the all-clear as soon as I've checked the pithead. Then I'd be grateful if you could arrange for Collins's body to be kept somewhere secure and cool until we can get a doctor to certify death. There will need to be a post-mortem.'

Burnley nodded resignedly. 'Cool won't be a problem,' he said, looking around at the snow. 'It's going to be a struggle to keep any-where warm while the temperature's dropping further.' He turned away and started to issue instructions to his men.

'You go with Watson,' Kember said to Lizzie.

'No,' Lizzie replied, flatly, not the least bit amused by his sur-prised expression or the idea that she would willingly play nurse again. 'I'm here to help you solve this case, not tend the wounded and sit around waiting for the killer to make toast out of us. He'll have someone by his bedside all the time.'

'But I thought . . . after you . . .'

She pressed her lips into a thin line and inclined her head in the direction of the pithead. The movement sent a pain lanc-ing through her temples but she kept her eyes on Kember's as his expression went through a cycle of surprise, anger and frustration, finally settling on resignation.

Kember sighed, a cloud of breath making his head ghostlike. 'Come on then, but stay close.'

Despite a stab of resentment at being spoken to like a child, Lizzie knew Kember had her safety at heart and she didn't need to be told twice. She had no intention of straying off course like last time and getting smacked over the head with a spanner, even if she was still wearing her miner's helmet.

They took the path Burnley had trodden not long ago and Kember could hear Lizzie close behind, but he still took frequent glances over his shoulder to make sure. He didn't want to lose her again, with potentially fatal consequences.

As they progressed towards the pithead, he wondered why anyone would have wanted to kill Collins. As far as he could tell, the men in the hut all had reason to want Morris out of the way, not Collins, but the likelihood of any of them being a killer had faded in the last couple of hours. Burnley was right; the Luftwaffe wouldn't fly in this weather so why had Collins sounded the air raid alarm?

As they got closer, Kember could see where the snow had been churned and trampled, no doubt by the many men seeking refuge from the non-existent air raid in basements and shelters. He approached the main pithead building again, signalled for Lizzie to keep behind him, and stopped just inside the entrance by the two siren boxes. He ignored the one for mine emergencies and concentrated on the other. The air raid warning box installed on the outside wall of Scotney Police Station had a lockable cover, and one switch that could be turned to the appropriate air raid state to activate the siren. The cover to this one stood ajar, revealing two buttons inside, a red one marked *Alert* and a white one marked *Raiders Passed*. Pressed once, these buttons would activate the siren fixed to one of the winding gear towers for a set period before automatically switching off. If any German aircraft had really flown overhead tonight, the white button should have been pressed by now. Collins being found dead by Burnley explained why that hadn't happened.

Kember switched on his Bijou for more light, and a shiver travelled down his spine. A dull, dark-red smear of blood stood out on the metal cover. He touched it with his fingers and found it to be dry, but given that the air raid had sounded some time ago, that meant nothing.

He entered the pithead, which seemed as empty as before, and Lizzie followed. They searched the lamp room, shining their lights on the walls and into cupboards, and looked in the places where the helmets and contraband were kept, checking every nook and cranny. They checked a series of three small offices with papers piled on desks, jackets hanging on pegs, and notices pinned to boards on the walls. The lift cage area and a series of store rooms brought no joy either. They returned to the entrance and checked in the other direction.

Almost immediately, Kember nearly went flying as his foot sank into something large and soft. He saved himself from falling with an outstretched hand on a desk as Lizzie lurched forward to help him. He shone his Bijou down at the bundle on the floor and saw a body sprawled across it.

He bent down and felt the man's wrist for a pulse. Nothing, but that wasn't a surprise, given the amount of blood that had pooled around his head. His hair was matted with it and Kember guessed he'd find a large gash if he looked harder. He shone the Bijou over the man's attire and spotted the ARP armband, confirming who it was before he shone the light on the man's face.

'Collins,' he said. 'That definitely takes him out of the running for the title of Kent Colliery Killer.'

Now he was standing over the most recent victim, Kember felt a little more exposed. Morris had died unnaturally, but not violently like Collins. Lizzie had got away lightly because of her helmet but Watson had come off worse and might yet succumb to the blow to the back of his head. Kember was sure that the two fires had been set to kill him and Lizzie and he'd be damned if he'd let that happen again. Besides, if all the attacks were by the same person, which seemed probable, the killer had abandoned subtlety for desperation. It seemed probable that whoever was bringing terror to Bekesbourne Colliery and had killed Collins had also pressed the button while the men were locked in the hut, but was that to ensure everyone else was out of harm's way, or merely out of the way?

Kember checked the room and discovered what he hoped he would find; the ARP wardens' rota and a map of the colliery site, both on the far wall of an open office. The rota confirmed what Collins had told them about him being the night warden. He'd never heard of the two other names listed. He wrote these in his notebook. The map showed the site's fire station to be located around the back of the building he was in now. That made sense. Its location was central for everything except the fan house, and that would have its own fire equipment similar to that which he and Lizzie had found just inside the top of the fan drift.

'Time to press the all-clear button, I think,' Lizzie said. 'If we're going to find this person, we need more light, even if that means the whole colliery workforce traipsing around.'

Kember knew she was right. He automatically took a glance over his shoulder to satisfy himself there was no other way in before he moved across to the doorway and counted to sixty in his head. Taking a deep quiet breath, he leant forward and checked the corridor both ways before easing himself out from the relative safety of the office. He motioned for Lizzie to stay inside and headed straight for the siren box. It was as he'd left it and he pressed the *Raiders Passed* button. The long, rising wail of the all-clear sounded across the colliery and he waited for what seemed like an eternity for the external lights to come on. He'd hoped the sudden illumination might catch out anyone lurking in the dark but nothing stirred. He switched on the internal lights and returned to the office.

'What now?' Lizzie said, as Kember crouched to re-examine Collins's lifeless body in the better light.

Kember didn't answer. He had no idea what to do next, where to go or who to talk to. He closed his tired eyes and pressed them with a forefinger and thumb.

'Ah, Inspector. Are you ready for us?'

Kember looked up at Burnley standing in the doorway. The mine owner's voice sounded as steady and confident as ever but his eyes stayed fixed on Kember, never straying to Collins lying in a pool of blood on the floor. Kember had seen this type of reaction before. Burnley seemed as though he'd retreated into himself, somewhere he could control events. If he didn't look at the dead body, he didn't have to acknowledge it existed. If it didn't exist, nothing bad had happened. As a way of coping, it avoided reality for a while, but delayed acceptance and consequence would only make the truth all the more devastating down the line.

Kember stood. 'You can have your men take Collins away now but you should send someone for the key. This office should remain locked for now.'

Burnley shouted something over his shoulder before turning back to the room. 'The brigade assures me that the fires are out. Hut Two is destroyed, of course, but Hut Six suffered no more than superficial damage. The window and door are being repaired as we speak so the men can return shortly.'

'I found Mrs Wall and she suggested putting you in the bar of the social club, with Miss Hayes taking the office at the back.'

The look Burnley gave Lizzie suggested to Kember that he thought everything so far had been nothing more than an inconvenience. *Perhaps that's how businessmen become successful*, he thought, *by glossing over the truth when it's incompatible with their goal.*

'The outside lights are back on and the rest of the workers have come out of the shelters,' Burnley continued. He glanced back at Kember, still avoiding looking at the body. 'Have you any clues?'

Kember wondered whether Burnley's image of a detective was predicated on his reading of Conan Doyle mysteries in which the great Sherlock Holmes studied clues with a magnifying glass. Any sarcastic response Kember might have contemplated was stifled by the three men who entered the office with a stretcher, a tarpaulin sheet and a bucket from which protruded the handle of a mop. He stood aside as two of the men, their faces solemn, carefully lifted the body of Collins on to the sheet, wrapped him as though serving a pound of loose sausages, and laid him on the canvas stretcher. They then took hold of the wooden handles at either end and left the office with their human cargo. Kember dismissed the third man before he got to work on the blood with the mop and saw him drop a key into Burnley's palm.

'There may be evidence we haven't discovered yet so I don't want the floor mopped or the office tidied until we've had a chance to go over it.'

'What kind of evidence?' Burnley asked.

'I won't know that until we've looked,' Kember said.

It always amused him when asked such a question. In his experience, you knew what you were looking for in only a small number of instances. The rest of the time, you knew it no sooner than you saw it and very few were born with the ability to see something of importance in the midst of nothing of consequence. Sometimes, even the best detectives took years to hone that skill. He ushered everyone into the corridor and waited for Burnley's man to lock the door, taking the key as the mine owner went to pocket it.

'What now, Inspector?' Burnley asked.

That was the same question Lizzie had asked, and he still didn't know. He glanced at her and noticed her staring at the pocket in which he'd dropped the key.

'Why didn't you leave Hut Six after Inspector Watson put you there?' Lizzie asked.

Both men looked puzzled.

'Because he locked us in,' Burnley said.

'Yes, you mentioned that before,' Lizzie said. 'The thing is, we recovered two keys from the same lock but at different times, and the door was unlocked both times.'

'What are you saying, that someone kept unlocking it?'

'There are two keys,' Lizzie said, as if that explained everything.

'Of course, there are, but who unlocked the hut and why didn't they tell us?' Burnley said. 'Every key has a spare. The men have both keys to their own cupboards in the dormitories but every other spare is kept in a box in my office.'

Kember saw genuine puzzlement on Burnley's face and was inclined to believe he was telling the truth. That meant Burnley and his men hadn't left the hut after Watson because they had truly believed they were locked in, whereas when Burnley had left the hut after Kember and Lizzie went looking for Watson, he must have tried the door and thought they had left it unlocked, even though Kember had deliberately locked them in and taken the key.

'Somebody obviously tried to help you escape,' Lizzie said, staring at Burnley's face.

'That's ridiculous,' Burnley replied. 'As I said before, where would we have gone?'

This was getting them nowhere so Kember ushered Burnley and Lizzie outside the pithead building. The snow had stayed away and the air was clear but the temperature had dropped further. He could feel the skin on his cheeks and hands tighten in the searing cold.

'What time does the social club close?' Kember asked.

Burnley looked at the watch on his wrist. 'About now. We keep to national licensing hours so there's two minutes drinking-up time left. Any stragglers should be making their way back to their huts.'

Kember nodded. 'Good, that means no more surprises tonight. Do you have a nightwatchman or other security on site?'

'No. Never needed it before the war because we operated three shifts around the clock. We get the odd visit from local ARP wardens to check our procedures, and the local Home Guard sometimes patrol the lanes, which is why we should get these lights off again soon.'

Kember looked at his watch. 'Keep them on until eleven o'clock to ensure everyone is safely inside. I'm convinced it's myself and Officer Hayes who are the targets here so I will be keeping a vigil tonight, but I don't want to take the chance of anyone else getting killed by being in the wrong place at the wrong time, like Collins.'

The mention of the dead man's name had Burnley frowning again.

'I have a lot of paperwork to do, Inspector. You'll find me in my office until midnight, then I'll retire to my overnight room next to the motor shed.'

Kember raised an eyebrow. He hadn't thought about where Burnley would be staying.

'I didn't realise you had a bedroom here.'

'It's a room in a storage building that I had converted at the start of the war, just in case the bombing prevented me from going home. It has a basement I use as a shelter if the siren goes off. A direct hit and they'd be picking bits of me out of the slag heap for weeks but it's safe enough otherwise.'

Kember nodded.

They said their goodnights and Burnley left Kember and Lizzie standing outside the pithead.

Kember recognised annoyance and concern in the look Lizzie gave him as the bulky shape of Burnley receded towards his office.

'Get it off your chest,' Kember said, bracing himself for a barrage.

'I shouldn't have to,' Lizzie said. 'You're going to let him switch off the lights at eleven while you stand out in the cold waiting for someone, possibly Burnley, who has attacked and killed before to try again? Is that your best plan?'

Kember sighed, a cloud of breath wreathing his head before it drifted away.

'It's my only plan.'

CHAPTER EIGHTEEN

'Are you serious?' Lizzie fumed. 'We haven't been targeted enough already that you want to tether yourself out in the open like a sacrificial goat?'

Kember put his hands up defensively. 'I can see no other way to draw the killer out in the open. Up until now, we've been following him around from one crisis to another, being subjected to whatever he thinks will do us most harm. He's trying to get to us and he doesn't care if he hurts anyone else who gets in the way. The fires prove that. If everyone else is inside for the night, the only people outside should be me and him.'

'Assuming he falls for it.'

'Of course, but with daylight and the prospect of help from Canterbury, out will go his best chance of getting rid of us once and for all. We've got half an hour before the lights go out again and I want another look at the ARP office.'

'What about me?' Lizzie said. 'What am I supposed to do while you're putting your head above the parapet?'

'I want you safe inside with Mrs Wall when the lights go out,' Kember said, as he stepped back inside the corridor. 'The fewer people standing around in the dark, the better I'll feel and the more chance I'll have of drawing him out.'

Lizzie tried to free her mind as the feeling of being excluded started to build but the cold and her headache conspired against her. They had been going around in circles, believing one man from the dormitory, a combination of several, or all of them guilty of murder, but so far all they'd established was how wrong they were on all counts. Her instinct, experience and training told her she was missing something important and she wasn't convinced that standing up like an Aunt Sally at a fete, waiting for someone to throw things at him, was the best way to bring it to light.

Kember had reopened the ARP office and was studying the area around the pool of congealing blood on the floor when Lizzie entered. She'd often seen him concentrating on the minutiae, trying to find that one piece of physical evidence to reveal and condemn a killer. Her technique favoured looking at the broader picture, trying to see the patterns in what was left behind, and sometimes what was not.

'I don't think it's Burnley,' Kember said.

So, he thinks the same, Lizzie thought. 'What's changed your mind?' she said, and watched him move further around the desk.

'The spanner I found is a foot long and very heavy. If someone had tried to kill you and Watson with it, you'd be dead. There's no doubt that his was a nasty blow but not fatal, yet. The killer must also have known hitting your helmet wouldn't kill you. I think someone wanted Morris dead, and only Morris. Everything else has been about diverting attention away from whoever the killer is, perhaps even trying to frame Burnley, who isn't popular among the entire workforce. The driver of the lorry wore a flat cap like the one Burnley wears and the attacks and fires happened when Burnley wasn't actually locked in the dormitory hut. I think those were deliberate ploys and the spanner was left for me to find. Why else would he have put it in such an odd place instead of keeping it close to hand?' Kember rubbed his nose. 'Despite the killer's best efforts, I haven't arrested anyone so he's getting desperate, which is why I think he killed Collins.'

'For what it's worth, I don't think any of the men in Hut Six are killers either,' Lizzie said. 'Yes, Morris is dead, but surely Watson would have found a final playing card torn completely in half to complete the sequence? The fact that there isn't suggests they got cold feet about committing murder or that was never their intention.'

'Well, he didn't kill himself.'

Lizzie's mind slipped into a different gear. *If you're not Burnley or one of the men from Hut Six with a grievance against Morris, why did you kill him?* She understood that Collins had probably got in the way, as had she, Kember and Watson, but why Morris?

'Wait,' Kember said. 'What's this?' He crouched to examine a dirty mark on the floor.

Despite being a colliery, the floors of the offices and other buildings were kept as clean as possible and signs advocating cleanliness at all times for safety reasons were pinned everywhere. Kember and Lizzie had walked through here, as had Burnley and Collins, and there was ample evidence of that in their muddy footprints, but this mark was over to one side of the desk and looked out of place on its own. She crouched down beside him and examined it closely, measuring it with the span of her spread fingers before standing and placing her foot next to it for comparison.

'From the size and shape, I'd say it's a woman's work or winter boot with a flat heel,' Lizzie said. 'And it looks similar to the one we saw outside the fan house and the one near to the lorry where we found Watson.'

'I saw the same size footprints leading to Hut Two,' Kember said. 'That is the mark of our killer, but a woman?'

Lizzie gave him a sharp look. 'We don't always go around in French heels.'

She took a few seconds to think. As far as misogyny went, Burnley was cast in the same mould as Group Captain Dallington, the CO of RAF Scotney, and had openly admitted to not being one who employed women to do a man's job unless absolutely necessary. But this was war. Even so, there couldn't be that many on site.

'Burnley admitted he employs women in the colliery, including the screens building to sort the coal,' Lizzie said. 'We know they work in the canteen too but I can't see how any of the women here would have the knowledge and opportunity to do what this killer has done. I can understand how we and Collins might have got in the way, but if it is a she, why would any of the women have wanted to kill Morris?' Then it came to her and she shook her head. 'Even though the grievances of those men in the dormitory may make it seem as though one of them is the murderer, I don't think we need worry about them any further. We should look closer to home.'

Kember frowned. 'What do you mean?'

'Mrs Wall.'

'Burnley's secretary?' Kember said, eyebrows raised. 'I know you found her a bit prickly but are you saying she could be a vicious murderer? I'm not so sure she has the know-how and strength to kill with gas and spanners,' he said.

Lizzie gave him a look as stinging as a physical slap.

'I know your work relies on tangible facts and evidence but you're ignoring the obvious,' she said, beginning a slow pacing of the narrow office as her eyes assumed that faraway look she often displayed when she placed herself in the mind of a killer, working through the possible explanations suggested by body language and expressions that Kember wasn't trained to notice.

'You can go anywhere on this colliery that you please,' she said, in a quiet, almost envious voice, speaking as though Mrs Wall was there with them. 'Few notice a woman in a man's world such as this, except to whistle and leer. Even fewer see a secretary.' She narrowed her eyes and smiled. 'I bet you hear all the goings-on among the miners, and visitors. You know who comes and goes, and why. You see what goes on, who are friends, who are not. You keep all the secrets; it's in the title, after all. Mr Burnley knows you're loyal,' she said. *Are you loyal enough to kill for him?* filled her mind.

'You guard his office . . . ferociously.' She smiled, her eyes still looking through and beyond the walls. 'You keep it scrupulously clean, and I know you stay late of your own volition.' She tilted her head to one side as if in contemplation. 'Ah, it's all to please him. Of course, he knows you'd be willing to do anything for him and I think he appreciates that, although I'm sure he has to be discreet.' Her face became solemn. 'Those absolute idiots he employs may have muscle but they haven't enough brain cells to rub together to start a fire. How could he ever have expected them to solve his problem?'

Lizzie took a deep breath and her eyes refocused on Kember as he led her to the only chair. She didn't sit.

'Are you all right?' he asked, leaning his backside on the edge of the wooden desk.

She rubbed her temples with the tips of her fingers, knowing that doing what she did always left something of her behind. She often wondered how long she could keep doing it without losing the best part of herself.

'I should have realised sooner by the way she looks at Burnley and protects him,' Lizzie said. 'I thought it was because she's in love with him, not superficially but deeply and destructively.' She shook her head. 'That may be true but it's more than that. She wants to – needs to – control everything around her and has a compulsion to protect him. If he looks good, she looks good, and it's her job to ensure that happens. She sits at her desk in both silent and vocal judgement of everyone who comes through the office door. Anyone deemed a threat gets short shrift. Anyone but you, me and Watson, that is. We couldn't be turned away because of what we represent; the law. She also doesn't believe in imperfections. That's why the office is pristine and she cleans it constantly. Someone like that tries to change people and their surroundings to fit their ideal, to make themselves happier.'

Lizzie began pacing again, the way she often did when her thoughts came thick and fast, tumbling into her mind.

'That business with holding the glass up to the door? She can't bear not knowing what's going on because that would mean relinquishing some of that control, and she can't let that happen. I think she's obsessed with Burnley but he's a narcissist who expects that anyway and almost doesn't notice the attention. That would upset someone like her but what better way to get noticed and gain his approval and affection than to help get rid of the one person who has become a thorn in his side and threatened his business by disrupting his workers?'

'That makes sense but something doesn't sit quite right,' Kember said, with a slow shake of his head. 'I've met women killers before and in my experience, the majority get the better of their male tormentors by using poison or surprise to overcome any disparity in height and strength. Bludgeoning from behind comes into that category but a woman still needs the strength to wield anything as a club. Indiscriminate gassing and arson seem unusual and extreme methods to use just because of unrequited love or a need to be in total control. And I find it hard to believe that Mrs Wall is a cold-blooded killer who could have done all this by herself.'

Lizzie looked up at him. 'I know why you'd think that but women can be very resourceful. Perhaps the men came to Burnley with a plan to force Morris out, maybe teach him a lesson and frighten him into leaving, and he supported their aim with the hope that Morris would decide to leave of his own accord, rather than be sacked. Mrs Wall is a secretary and secretaries are always in the perfect position to overhear conversations. If she realised what the men were up to, she could have decided to get in on the act.' She watched Kember's face and could almost see the train of thought in motion behind his eyes. 'I won't be spending the night alone with her in the social club office, I can tell you that.'

'All right,' Kember said. 'Let's suppose you're correct and Mrs Wall is involved in some way. We know she drives and could have taken Burnley's hat to cover her hair, but why would she try to frame him by bashing people over the head if she idolised him and thrived on controlling him?'

Lizzie looked away, taking a few seconds to allow her thoughts to realign, before turning back.

'Her lack of height, strength, and perhaps even the resolve to kill with her hands might explain why only one in three blows were fatal, making it look like someone was framing Burnley.'

She waited, watching him digest this new perspective. He gave her one slow nod, as though he accepted the possibility but wasn't convinced.

'Even if we could fit together how we think Morris was killed, the only piece of physical evidence that could have linked her to the crime is the spanner, but I've handled it far too much for any of her fingerprints to have survived, assuming she didn't wear gloves in the first place.'

The scrape of a boot reached them from the corridor and Kember cautioned for Lizzie to be quiet. She tensed, wondering who else would be in here at this time of night, when one of the men from the colliery fire brigade appeared in the doorway.

'Sorry, sir, miss,' he said, with a deferential nod. 'I was looking for Mr Burnley but I can see he's not here.'

Lizzie saw the man's gaze drop to the blood on the floor.

'Is there anything I can do for you?' Kember asked.

The man hesitated and looked up. 'I don't know, sir. We found these, that's all. Stuffed into some of the air bricks.' He held out a bundle of dirty yellow dusters for Kember to take. 'Dangerous, is that. If you don't get a through draught of fresh air when you've got the stove lit it can give you—'

'Headaches,' Lizzie said.

'Yes, miss. Can cause mould and wood rot in buildings too, if you're not careful. Had terrible trouble with that in the first three huts the colliery converted to dormitories, until they forked out for more air bricks, that is.'

'Thank you,' Kember said. 'I'll hold on to these if I may?' The man turned to leave. 'You're limping.'

'Yes, sir,' the man said. 'Tripped over a stepladder covered with snow round the back of Hut Six. A couple of those dusters came from there, near the flue.'

When the man had gone, Lizzie touched Kember's arm.

'The police report said their hut had been warm when they arrived on the morning Morris died,' she said.

'Six bodies in a small hut for several hours with the fire going is bound to keep it warm at night,' Kember agreed.

'Yes, but I noticed it was draughty in their dormitory tonight, but only at one end.'

'Perhaps they only blocked half to keep the air flowing,' Kember suggested.

'Why weren't half the bricks in our dormitory blocked then?' Lizzie said. 'You must have felt the draught in there as well as I did.'

'I don't know. Perhaps it got too warm, or maybe it was because no one was living there while it was being repaired?'

'Many of these men have worked here for ages and stayed in those dormitories,' she said. 'Even if they do plug some of the air bricks with dusters when it's cold, which seems bizarre when you think of the care they usually take underground, it begs the question as to why Hut Six left most of them unblocked when snow is thick on the ground, don't you think?'

Lizzie took the dusters from Kember, turned them over in her hands and sniffed them one at a time, a recent memory churning at the back of her mind and vying for attention.

'What's wrong?' he asked.

'Smell these,' she said, brandishing the dirty yellow cloths.

He sniffed the dusters she held in her left hand, frowning. 'What am I smelling?'

'Now these two.' She held out her right hand.

'Furniture polish,' he said. 'As you'd expect.'

'That's right,' Lizzie said, with a narrow-eyed look of concentration. 'Remember when Eddie Pine spilt Ribena on Burnley's desk and you asked me to fetch a cloth?' He nodded and she continued. 'I found two clean dusters in Mrs Wall's desk drawer.' She put her hand out and pulled, miming the opening of a drawer. 'There were other dusters in there – dirty ones – and I thought nothing more than she'd been over-zealous in cleaning the office.' She shut the imaginary drawer.

Kember's eyes narrowed. 'What are you getting at?'

Lizzie's thoughts had started to tumble again, the solution so clear and simple that it irked that she hadn't realised before.

'The ventilation fan switched off while we were underground, stopping the crucial air flow and causing the mine to fill with poison gases given off by the coal. We were down there long enough for it to affect us and if you hadn't found that oxygen . . .' She held her hands out to illustrate the potentially fatal consequences. 'Morris, Ramsey, Quayle and Pine were always the first ones in the mine in the morning, meaning that if the fan had not been run properly beforehand, they would have inhaled some of the gas. It wasn't enough to kill them outright, or even make them ill in one go, but it would have built up in their bodies over time. Morris always made Ramsey carry a Davy lamp and canary rather than take his own down. It would have been easy for Ramsey to manipulate both, keeping the flame out of sight of Morris and keeping the canary singing by giving it bursts of oxygen from its cage cylinder.'

'We know all this, but Ramsey didn't die and Morris did,' Kember said. 'Not deep underground at work in the mine during the day but asleep in the dormitory at around half-two in the morning.'

'As I've said before; a perfect time to murder. Burnley and all the men in that dormitory admitted they wanted Morris to leave but they've all vehemently denied wanting him dead. If they'd continued risking their own lives, especially Ramsey, by using the natural mine gases, surely Morris would have died underground and any investigation would have ruled it as the result of Morris's own negligence. That didn't happen so let's consider for a moment that whatever their initial intention, they baulked at the idea of killing another human being. Someone still hated Morris enough to want him dead and that person must have blocked the air bricks deliberately.'

'And you think that someone was Mrs Wall?'

'With all that accumulated poison swilling around Morris's body,' Lizzie continued, 'and with him sleeping closest to the stove while it was lit and blasting out heat, blocking the air bricks that night could have given him the last fatal top-up of carbon monoxide. Yes, Ramsey got sick but he survived because he'd been taking oxygen from the emergency supply to dilute the effects. As we said, Quayle could easily have taken reviving breaths from the emergency oxygen cylinders as well as faking a sprained ankle, which is how I believe he never became ill at all. He was in his own district with his own oxygen. No one else was affected because Pine probably nipped to the surface, aided by Thatcher, and the rest came on shift after the fan restarted and were never exposed to more than

282

the odd whiff here and there, which is normal. Did you notice the air flow once we were away from the shafts?'

Kember admitted he hadn't.

'Neither did I. We'll never know for certain but I wouldn't be surprised if Morris was so arrogant and intent on putting Ramsey down that he failed to realise that the fan hadn't been engaged.' She put her hands on her hips, waiting for him to contradict her reasoning.

He didn't, but he did throw a spanner in the works.

'You took two dusters from Mrs Wall's drawer so who's to say someone else didn't take some too?' Kember said, with an apologetic shrug.

Lizzie bowed her head and rubbed her temples again. He was right, damn him. Everything was circumstantial, but why did Mrs Wall keep some of the dirty dusters in her drawer? Perhaps there had been no time to get rid of them.

'Is that why you want to use us as bait?' she said. 'To catch the killer in the act or get them to incriminate herself in some way?'

A jolt went through Lizzie and her chest tightened. Flight Lieutenant Ben Vickers had given the ATA women instruction in the art of self-defence, but the idea of jumping out at the appropriate moment to apprehend a murderer before she killed Kember filled her with dread. What if she missed her cue and Kember was badly injured or died? What if Mrs Wall was stronger than she looked and overpowered her? She realised Kember was speaking and lifted her head.

'. . . With *me* as bait,' Kember emphasised. 'It's dangerous and certainly not foolproof, but if I tether myself out like a goat, I think that's what you said, she might see it as her final opportunity.'

Lizzie felt her cheeks flush at Kember's arrogance. 'That's the thing about tethered goats, they get killed,' Lizzie said, suddenly finding it difficult to breathe. 'You can't do this on your own. Look what happened to Watson, and me.'

'But I'll know what's coming and won't be taken unawares.'

'I bet this isn't how you worked at Scotland Yard, is it? You'd have a constable to back you up at the very least, if not a sergeant too. What makes you think you can do this alone?'

Kember shook his head. 'I have no choice,' he said, and left the office.

Despite her own misgivings, the insinuation from Kember that she wasn't capable enough to be involved in the trap only served to make her determined to be a part of it. She followed him into the corridor and watched him re-lock the door.

'I'm staying with you,' she said in a tone that brooked no argument. 'You can't watch your back, be the lure and spring the trap at the same time. If it is Mrs Wall, she is more likely to come looking if I'm not keeping guard on her. Let me be the bait—'

'Inspector,' Burnley said, closing the outer door behind him as he entered the corridor from the pit yard. 'I can't let you stand vigil on your own.'

Lizzie thought she heard Kember emit a low groan.

'Mr Burn—'

'I know it's dangerous,' Burnley cut across Kember, 'but this is my colliery and I can't let some madman remain on the rampage, killing my workers and visitors. I want this over with. Tell me what I can do.'

Lizzie saw sincerity behind the bravado and was secretly impressed that the mine owner had finally shown some backbone. In contrast, the look on Kember's face was one of exasperation. His idea for going it alone in tatters, the plan now included two unwanted accomplices, one of whom had been a suspect until very recently.

'Very well.' Kember frowned. 'I think the best way we can do this without one of us getting hurt is for me to take up position in one of the offices, sitting with my back to the open door, and Mr Burnley keeping out of sight elsewhere. Officer Hayes will need to hide behind the door and slam it shut as soon as M—' He stopped with a glance at Lizzie and cleared his throat. 'As soon as the killer enters the office. That will trap and distract him and give me time to turn and defend myself. The three of us should be enough to overpower him before he has time to react. We'd better be. The telephone lines are down, Watson is incapacitated, and no one from Canterbury will come looking for him until daylight, assuming the roads are opened. We're on our own.'

'Not quite,' Burnley said.

Lizzie saw Kember's eyebrows twitch as a man wearing the boots, trousers and donkey jacket uniform of a miner entered the corridor at its farthest end and walked towards them. As he came closer, she recognised him as Alastair Thatcher from Hut Eight, the banksman who operated the lift cage on the surface. *At least he's not from Hut Six*, she thought.

'What's he doing here?' Kember asked.

Lizzie detected barely controlled annoyance in his tone of voice and hoped he wasn't about to lay down the law. As Burnley had said, this was his colliery and the thought of him and his men being excluded from its defence might result in the full withdrawal of cooperation. At this point, that would be a very bad development.

'I met Thatcher outside the hospital block after they'd taken Inspector Watson in for treatment,' Burnley said. 'He wanted to help and I thought it a good idea. The lights are due to go out in a couple of minutes.'

'The more people about tonight, the less chance of the killer making his move,' Kember said.

'Tommyrot,' Burnley scoffed. 'If we take the biggest office, the one used for keeping tabs on the comings and goings of our workers, lorries and coal, Thatcher can crouch behind the filing cabinet and I can hide by the side of the bookcase.'

'I'm here to help, sir,' Thatcher said, with a slight bow of his head. 'Any way I can.'

Lizzie noticed Kember grit his teeth. The tight rein he'd sought to maintain was slipping as the simple plan got more complicated with the addition of more bodies. As Police Sergeant Dennis Wright of Scotney village might say, it seemed like using a house brick to crack a cobnut.

She felt the familiar grip tighten across her chest and touched her rubber band for comfort. She felt Kember's reassuring hand on her shoulder and she nodded to signal that she was ready.

She was not. Not with such a bad feeling inside her.

Kember saw Lizzie nod as she played with the band on her wrist but wondered whether she was up to the job. Neither of their previous two cases together could be deemed a piece of cake and her experiences would have left their mark, as they had on him. The miners might be physically strong, and Lizzie's occupation delivering RAF warplanes was most certainly dangerous, but he was the policeman and this was his domain. To employ civilians to do the job of coppers wasn't ideal but the current circumstances were far from ideal and they were running out of time.

Burnley led them through to a spacious office two doors down from the smaller ARP office and pointed out the hiding positions. Kember had to agree, it was as good a place as any to set a trap for the killer. After all, if it was Mrs Wall, he had her weapon of choice in his pocket and she was shorter than Lizzie's five foot six. No match for the three of them.

'Is there any paperwork I can pretend to be reading?' Kember said, as he pulled the swivel chair away from the desk.

Burnley took a ledger from one of the shelves and opened it on the desk. 'It's not fascinating reading for the likes of you, Inspector, but it'll look the part.' He then hesitated and picked up a brass paperweight the size and shape of a tennis ball, engraved with a map of the world.

Kember switched on the desk lamp and a small pool of light spread no farther than the edge of the desk. That was good. The hiding places would remain in shadow, unless the ceiling light was switched on. He looked up. 'Have you a handkerchief?' he asked Burnley. 'I gave mine up for Inspector Watson.' Burnley passed him a folded square of clean linen and he used it to reach up and unscrew the hot lightbulb.

The effect was immediate, and eerie, and Kember looked across to ensure Lizzie was all right. She returned a thin smile and drew a stool behind the door, wedging it in the corner of the two walls.

'We might be in for a long wait,' she said. 'I'll be damned if I'm standing behind a door all night.'

Kember flashed her a grin and looked at his watch. 'Five past,' he said. 'Time to check the outside lighting has switched off, turn out the corridor lights, and take up positions.'

'I'll do the corridor, sir,' Thatcher said.

Kember made sure Lizzie was comfortable on her stool behind the open door and Burnley had settled in beside the bookcase, before he stepped into the corridor and moved along to the entrance. He looked over his shoulder waiting for Thatcher, who took a few seconds to emerge from the office and give him a nod. Kember eased the door open. A pale wash of moonlight that had made it through the clouds shed just enough light to see across the pit yard. As far as he could see and hear, all was quiet and still. The snowstorm had passed, to be replaced with a severe frost that nipped at his fingers.

Kember needed to advertise his presence but had the unnerving feeling of being watched and hoped the killer hadn't witnessed the arrival of Burnley and Thatcher or any of their preparations. He also prayed, to no god in particular, that whoever was tending to Watson had their wits about them. He feared for the policeman's life but had no one to rely on to keep him safe except the miners themselves. Not the best bedfellows right at that moment. Watson, having been felled by a crack on the head and survived, might not live through another visit from someone determined to end his life.

With an intake of breath, he opened the door wide and stepped outside, his exhalation condensing into a thick cloud that drifted up and dissipated. He took a few steps forward, swung his arms and stamped his feet against the biting cold, and coughed loudly. He waited a few seconds and repeated his actions, the coughs echoing off the pit-yard buildings in the still night air. *That's enough*, he thought. He could always try again a bit later, if necessary, but he rather hoped for a quick result.

Kember went back inside and closed the door with a yank designed to make a noise. He then heard the click of a switch as the corridor lights went out, plunging it into darkness except for a faint glow from the door of the office. He saw the dark shape of Thatcher entering the office and waited for his eyes to adjust. Lizzie was well out of sight behind the door and neither Burnley nor Thatcher could be seen in their respective hiding places. *As perfect as it's going to get*, he thought, and took up his own position in the swivel chair by the desk.

All they could do now was wait and hope.

CHAPTER NINETEEN

From her position low down, Lizzie could see nothing more than a yellowish glow through the window set into the door. Hers was a simple task. All she had to do was stay awake, keep alert and slam the door shut, but it had been a long and exhausting day and she desperately needed a cigarette.

Thatcher had paused by the door as he waited for Kember to complete his performance outside, baiting the trap. He'd told her the door needed to be fully open and had leant on it until it touched the wall to create a triangular space. The feeling of being enclosed and restrained by someone had unnerved her but she felt calm return, having taken a few long deep breaths and let them out slowly, before silence enveloped the office. She'd heard Kember cough as though he had Spanish flu or tuberculosis and knew this was his call to Mrs Wall. *Here I am, alone. Come and get me.*

The trouble with sitting silently in the gloom, even with people close by but out of sight, was the sense of being alone with her thoughts. *What if I stuff this up?* she thought. *What if I'm too late and she kills Kember?* She knew the idea was preposterous, of course. Her job was to trap Mrs Wall so she couldn't escape. It was up to Burnley and Thatcher to intervene before any physical harm could come to any of them. *What if I react too soon and she gets away?* She dismissed that outcome as improbable. Thatcher was young enough to have the legs to chase down a woman like Mrs Wall, even if Kember and Burnley were slow off the mark.

Her mind tuned in to Watson, lying in a bed in the hospital block. He had someone there to care for him tonight but being knocked unconscious was not as inconsequential as the Hollywood films made out. It might serve the story for someone to be incapacitated, and maybe even for them to recover in the nick of time to affect the outcome, but the after-effects were rarely as mild as going to sleep for the merest of moments. She'd sometimes stifled a laugh when someone hit on the head in a film had got up within half a minute, rubbed the back of their head as if nothing had happened worse than being hit with a football, and leapt back into action, exchanging punches and slugging it out with the bad guys.

When you got hit on the head, you stayed hurt.

She rubbed her temples in an attempt to ease the headache she felt making a resurgence, thinking about her own injury. Although the blow from the adjustable spanner had been deflected by her miner's helmet, the patch at the back of her head where the shock wave had penetrated still felt tender. She'd witnessed the aftermath of blows to the head and it didn't matter whether the victim had been rendered unconscious or not, brain damage, blood clots and the symptoms of concussion could often manifest days or weeks after. She began to worry about whether she had concussion and started recalling events from her recent past just to see if she had memory loss. With events rushing through her mind, as her thoughts often did when she was assimilating and juggling all the information from an investigation, she started to worry that she had brain damage.

The thought of losing her mental capacity and spending the rest of her life in an asylum brought a tightness to her chest that she barely noticed as her thoughts tumbled on. She recalled the initial encounters with Burnley and his men, all of whom had been dismissive of her and wary or critical of Kember's insistence that she be involved. All of them so much like Group Captain George Dallington of RAF Scotney. To be a woman was to start at a disadvantage. God forbid that you were intelligent too. To be young and attractive as well was almost tantamount to committing a crime in some men's eyes. In fact, what was attractiveness? Was it physical, psychological, spiritual, ethereal? Something else? Wasn't beauty supposed to be in the eye of the beholder? What did that say about some beholders?

She went over her encounter at the AIB again, analysing what was said, working through what she could have said, rehearsing what she should have said. Then she did the same with her first meeting with Burnley and felt the band across her chest tighten even further and her throat constrict. Despite the snow lying thick on the ground outside, her hands had become clammy and the clothes she wore seemed heavy and all-enveloping. She imagined she could feel every point at which the cloth touched her skin, irritating and chafing. The stool suddenly felt hard and uncomfortable and her rising anxiety told her she was heading for a panic attack. *Why does this keep happening today?* she wondered. Could her crash and the AIB investigation be affecting her that much? A lot could be riding on this trap but she tried to tell herself that it wouldn't be the end of the world, that there would be other opportunities to get the evidence they needed to catch Mrs Wall and send her to the gallows.

It made no difference.

Without her little blue jar and unable to break the silence with a snap of her band, Lizzie knew she had one chance to nip this in the bud before it got any worse. She braced herself and pinched the skin on the back of her hand as hard as she could bear.

The effect was as immediate as it was dramatic. All her negative thoughts dissipated. All the doubts and worries that had threatened to drown her in self-recrimination vanished like breath dispersed by winter wind. Her headache remained a dull throb at the base of her skull but her heart no longer raced and her attention refocused on the room and task at hand.

And not a moment too soon.

She heard the tiniest of sounds from outside the office and held her breath, unable to identify what had caused it. She heard another brief sound, this time like the rustle of clothing. It had to be Mrs Wall. Lizzie tensed, ready to push the door and spring the trap. The glow through the door's window dimmed and she looked up, seeing the shadow of someone approaching the other side of the door. She heard the rustle of paper as Kember turned a page, playing the part of a detective engrossed in the details of the ledger.

The shadow moved on and a few seconds more of total silence passed before an explosion of activity beyond the woodwork made Lizzie jump. She stood up and shoved the door but it didn't move.

Mrs Wall screamed as Thatcher rushed at her at the same time as Burnley, knocking Kember aside. Lizzie saw a flash of metal and shouted, 'Kember!' through the window.

'Get—'

'Argh.'

'Hold her—'

Thatcher had the spanner from Kember's pocket in his hand and Lizzie saw it arc towards Mrs Wall and Burnley.

'Ouch.'

Burnley's head snapped back and Kember's hand reached for what looked like a knife.

The men seemed to be doing all the struggling, the diminutive Mrs Wall lost among the waving of arms and weapons.

'What's th—'

Burnley's paperweight hit the floor with a thud at the same time as the knife spun away and clattered against the filing cabinet.

'You—'

'Stop!' came Kember's voice. The struggle ceased. 'Enough. Let's all calm down.'

The door swung away from Lizzie and slammed shut, as it should have done at her first push. Thatcher stood there, offering his hand. She declined and felt her cheeks flush, not at the gesture but her failure to carry out the simple task as her contribution to the trap. No one else seemed bothered. Kember, breathing heavily from the encounter and touching a scratch on his neck, bade Mrs Wall to sit on the chair previously occupied by him and moved to the filing cabinet to retrieve what Lizzie recognised as the paperknife from Mrs Wall's desk. Burnley stood next to Mrs Wall, wiping the perspiration from his forehead with the cuff of his shirt and touching a red mark on his cheek very gingerly. Thatcher stood poised, the adjustable spanner in his hand.

Before anyone could say anything further, the creak of an opening door preceded light flooding the corridor and the noise of many hobnail boots scratching the floor. The office door swung back open and Ramsey appeared in the doorway.

'What's happened?' he asked, eyes darting left and right.

The faces of Young and Quayle appeared over his shoulders.

'We were talking and thought something smelled fishy,' Young said.

'Aye,' Quayle agreed. 'Went to have a word with you but you weren't in the club so we came looking.'

Jostling from behind the three men brought Armstrong and Pine into view. 'Thought we'd take a look in here, see what was happening, like,' Armstrong said.

As they all crowded into the office, making it feel quite small, Pine pushed to the front. 'Didn't want to leave you out in the cold with a madman on the loose.'

'Turns out it was a mad woman,' Thatcher said.

'No. Not Mrs Wall,' Armstrong said, and a chorus of murmurs signalled agreement from the others.

Kember held out his hand and took the spanner from Thatcher. Mrs Wall's eyes, already wide with fear, flicked between him and the miners from Hut Six. Lizzie frowned. The secretary appeared smaller, diminished in some way, almost as if the hands of Kember and Burnley on her shoulders offered protection rather than the first step to the gallows. She had disliked the frosty way they'd been received at the colliery by a haughty Mrs Wall but, despite her most recent argument that she had as strong a motive to kill Morris as any of the others, she didn't think the woman being restrained on the chair looked anything like a cold-blooded predator.

'Stand back, men,' Burnley commanded. 'There's no room to swing a cat in here.' He nodded to Kember. 'Let's go to the canteen.'

Kember shook his head. 'It's not a good idea to have your men in the same room during questioning,' he said, as the men began to voice their disapproval.

'Nonsense,' Burnley replied, with a dismissive wave of his hand. 'We've all been suspected of murder so we'd like to know the truth. Finally. And if Miss Hayes is staying . . .'

'Officer Hayes is on secondment to the police for the purposes of this investigation and is entitled to stay. However, should there be a trial, none of what is said here will be permitted in court if your men stay. To satisfy legal procedure and get to the truth, I must insist they leave this room.'

Burnley considered this.

'All right, men,' he said, in a commanding voice. 'It's late and there is nothing you can do here tonight. Return to your dormitory and I will speak to you in the morning.'

The men complained and grumbled as they turned away and Burnley ushered the reluctant Thatcher before him, clearing the room of miners. Lizzie stepped back out of their way and trod on something hard that almost turned her ankle. She swore under her breath at the sharp pain and looked down at the offending article. A wedge of wood lay on its side where she'd kicked it.

'Mr Burnley?' Kember said, his eyebrows raised as Burnley also went to leave. 'You should stay.'

'Me?' Burnley said in surprise. 'Whatever for?'

Kember took a deep breath and Lizzie could sense the effort it took for him to hold his tongue. They were still snowbound in the middle of nowhere, at least until the morning, and Watson was in no fit state to offer assistance.

'I would have thought that was obvious.' Kember took a chair and invited Burnley to do the same. 'You are both still suspects.'

'Why me?' Burnley said, his face a mask of incredulity.

Lizzie picked up the wooden wedge, pocketed it and drew up the last chair, instinctively going to sit next to Kember as she was used to doing in the police station back at Scotney village. Burnley tried to wave her away but she sat down anyway and looked at him in a way that suggested flapping his arms like a penguin would get him nowhere. He glowered at her and sat on another chair.

'Before I begin,' Kember spoke through the tension, 'let me make one thing clear. If there are any interruptions from either of you, I shall arrest you here and now, and lock you in until Inspector Watson's men arrive to take you to Canterbury for questioning.' His cold gaze remained steady on Burnley's face.

Only the walrus moustache set Burnley's grey face and rigid expression apart from a bust that Lizzie had once seen in the British Museum, trying to look majestic and important but, in reality, standing dusty and forgotten in a distant corner. Despite his glare, he gave a curt nod of acquiescence before he sat.

All the mine workers seemed content they had caught the murderer, and pleased the police suggestion that it was one of their own had been proved wrong, but Lizzie began to doubt herself. Something niggled at the back of her mind. She'd considered Mrs Wall a prime suspect for being the murderer but could the small woman who sat behind a desk all day, every day, have the strength to go out hunting detectives? Any accusation that Mrs Wall was a mastermind, or at least involved in some kind of conspiracy, wouldn't have surprised Lizzie in the slightest. But bludgeoning victims to the ground? She shook her head to dismiss her previous conclusions and clear her mind. She needed to look at this differently.

Kember took out his notebook and pen. 'Mr Burnley, Mrs Wall, you are not under arrest at the present time but I do need to ask you a few questions.'

Burnley drew a sharp intake of breath at Kember's statement and Lizzie noticed Mrs Wall's hands in her lap, the fingers interlocked as if in silent prayer or an effort to stop them from shaking.

'This has been a difficult time for everyone but you must tell me why you came here tonight to kill me, Mrs Wall.'

Mrs Wall looked up, eyes wide with shock, and Lizzie could see the glistening of unshed tears.

'Kill? No!' Her voice cracked and wavered. A sob escaped and she put her hands to her chest. 'I wanted to see Mr Burnley,' she said, in a voice so quiet that Lizzie could hardly hear. 'I knew he hadn't gone to his overnight room because I saw him head towards his office. When yourself and Miss Hayes didn't return, I went to find him.'

'Why did you want to see Mr Burnley?' Kember asked.

'I thought he might need something before he retired for the night.'

Lizzie saw Mrs Wall's gaze dip to the left. A lie. Kember sat back in his chair, appearing to treat the interview like no more than a friendly chat. A good ploy, she thought.

'How did you know to find us here?' Kember said.

'This was where Mr Burnley had said you were.' Mrs Wall tightened the knot of the headscarf she still wore. 'He was going to speak to you, so I put two and two together.'

'Did you not wonder why we hadn't returned?'

'I was curious, of course . . .'

'After the fires, did you not think it dangerous to be outside in the dark?'

'No, I—'

Mrs Wall stopped and looked away.

Lizzie frowned. If Mrs Wall knew where they were but wasn't frightened of being attacked, did that mean she *was* the murderer, or that she knew who was?

'Mrs Wall,' Lizzie said, ignoring the heavy frown from Burnley. 'I know you like to keep the office clean and tidy and you have plenty of dusters in your desk drawer, but why do you need so many?'

'How do you . . . ?'

'We spilt Ribena and needed a cloth. The inspector had seen you put your polish and duster away.' Lizzie paused for a second. 'The colliery fire brigade found dusters blocking some of the air bricks in Hut Six. Do you know why your dusters would be used for such a purpose?' It was Kember's turn to throw her a look that she ignored.

'No,' Mrs Wall said, flatly.

Lizzie almost missed the gesture but a tiny nod contradicted the woman's words.

'Did Mr Burnley ask you to help him?'

Burnley went to speak, his face turning red, but he deflated when Kember turned a stony stare on him.

'Do you know what whitedamp is?' Kember said.

'Of course,' Mrs Wall said, her voice back to barely audible again. 'It's the mining term for carbon monoxide gas in the pit tunnels.'

'So, you know that blocking the airflow through a building where a coal fire is burning could cause a build-up of carbon monoxide?'

'Yes.'

'Is that why you blocked the air bricks with your dusters?'

'I didn't.' She looked imploringly at Burnley, then at Lizzie.

Interesting, Lizzie thought. She looked to her boss first and only then to her as another woman.

'I think you are a very resourceful woman, Mrs Wall,' Kember said. 'You run Mr Burnley's office like clockwork, work late to ensure everything runs smoothly for him, and you even drove an ambulance in the last war, I believe.'

'I did, yes.' Another glance at Burnley.

'So, you would be able to drive one of the colliery lorries?'

'Yes, if asked.' Mrs Wall looked at Kember suspiciously. 'But why would I be, when we have enough drivers?'

The question in the response appeared automatic to Lizzie, as though Mrs Wall genuinely considered the suggestion that she would drive a colliery lorry quite absurd.

'Officer Hayes and I saw you and Mr Burnley beside the lorry that had been hidden under a tarpaulin,' Kember said, writing something in his book. 'There's no use denying it because we followed you and ended up in the canteen, where you'd just grabbed a hot cup of tea.'

Another glance from Mrs Wall to Burnley reinforced the belief Lizzie still held in her mind.

'We were a lorry short and one of the men said they'd seen one parked next to a building,' Mrs Wall said. 'Mr Burnley and I found the lorry with its number plate covered. We were worried because you had said a lorry had run you off the road.'

'You didn't think it would reflect badly on you if you didn't mention it to me?' Kember said, his eyebrows raised in question.

'Mr Burnley thought it would reflect badly on the colliery if we did.' This time she avoided Burnley's gaze.

Burnley leant forward, his face still flushed. 'I think what Mrs Wall is trying to say, Inspector, is that we didn't want to jump to conclusions. After all, you yourself said it was a farm lorry.'

Although Kember must have heard the interruption, he gave no indication and his eyes remained focused on Mrs Wall.

'We know that DI Watson arrived back at the colliery this evening and ordered the pit reopened to rescue me and Officer Hayes from certain death,' Kember said. 'After our bodies weren't found at the bottom of the pit shaft, he started searching the site for us and found the lorry. Was it you who knocked him unconscious?'

'No!' Mrs Wall's eyes were open wide again.

'Do you know who did?' Kember glanced at Burnley.

'No,' she said, quieter.

'Did you follow me and Officer Hayes?'

'No.'

'When Officer Hayes and I became separated, did you attack her as you had DI Watson?'

'No! I didn't attack anybody.'

'Did Mr Burnley?'

'What? No!'

The anguish on Mrs Wall's face and the way she wrung her hands suggested that was the truth, but Lizzie remained unconvinced about her total innocence. The woman knew more than she was letting on, and probably who had attacked them.

'Do you know who did, Mrs Wall?' Lizzie encouraged softly, noticing the slightest of head shakes by Mrs Wall. 'We found footprints outside the fan house where the airlock door had been wedged shut. We found others at the scene of both attacks, more leading towards Hut Two after the fire was started with Inspector Kember inside, and another in the ARP wardens' office. They were all very small, like those of a woman's winter boot.' Lizzie glanced down at Mrs Wall's boots. 'Were those your footprints?'

'I'm not the only person with small feet in the colliery,' Mrs Wall protested. 'There are other women here and not all the men are size twe—'

Lizzie saw Burnley nod and Kember write something in his book, and she looked again at the pointed toes of Mrs Wall's boots.

'When Officer Hayes and I went to Hut Six, we found the door unlocked and a key in the hole,' Kember said. 'According to Mr Burnley, he checked the door after Inspector Watson herded him inside with his men and confirmed it had been locked. Do you know who unlocked it after Inspector Watson left?'

Mrs Wall looked to Burnley again but the mine owner appeared lost in his own thoughts.

'When we went to look for Inspector Watson, I locked the door,' Kember continued. 'After we found the injured inspector and took him to Hut Six, we found it unlocked again and with another key in the hole. Where did you get the second key?'

Mrs Wall hesitated, as though caught in two minds, and sighed. 'From the cupboard in the office,' she said at last, with a guilty glance at Burnley. 'We keep all the spare keys for the colliery in there.'

'Does that mean you have access to all the dormitory huts?' Kember said, with a slight tilt of his head.

'I suppose so. Everywhere. Why?'

'Why didn't you tell the men you'd unlocked the door?'

'Because I ran away before I could say anything. I thought I saw someone and was frightened. I left the key behind by accident.'

Kember paused to consult his notebook. 'Why unlock the door at all?'

Mrs Wall looked away. 'Because I thought it was unfair to lock up Mr Burnley when he's innocent.'

The notion that Burnley had done nothing wrong intrigued Lizzie and she leant forward in her chair. 'How do you know he is?'

'Now look here, Inspector,' Burnley interrupted. 'Investigation or not, Miss Hayes can't go around casting unfounded aspersions.'

'I do apologise, Mr Burnley,' Lizzie said, hoping Kember wouldn't eject her from the room. 'I merely sought to establish the basis of Mrs Wall's assertion. Perhaps I could have phrased it a little better.'

'Perhaps you could have,' Burnley snapped.

Mrs Wall's mouth began to move but then her lips clamped shut, as though the urge to speak had been overruled. Lizzie could see a pattern building. Even when Mrs Wall did say something, her words came across as guarded, as though the whole truth was too unpalatable to give voice to.

'Where were you when the fire alarm sounded?' Kember asked.

Mrs Wall looked at him for a few seconds, which Lizzie found intriguing. Even the innocent pause, hesitate, stutter and falter, whether under pressure or not, but the twitch of her head, the smallest of shakes, was the body's way of revealing that what was to come was an untruth.

'I was in my office,' Mrs Wall replied. 'I heard the alarm bell and went outside to see where the fire was and I saw the glow from the flames as the fire brigade rushed past with the water bowser. I was worried that Hut Six was on fire with Mr Burnley trapped inside so I followed for a moment. When I saw Mr Burnley following the bowser and realised the fire was in Hut Two, I went back to the office.'

Lizzie thought most of that had a ring of truth, not least because Mrs Wall had used hand gestures to illustrate her points. That was a natural and unconscious thing to do when describing true events. So which bit had been the lie, leaving the office, going back to it, or being there at all?

'What were you doing in your office at that time of night?' Kember said. 'Your day's work must have finished hours before.'

'As you are aware, Inspector, the roads are impassable at the moment and there was no chance that I would be able to get home. I keep a change of clothes in the office, along with a folding camp bed, for emergencies. I have done since the start of the Battle of Britain and have continued to do so throughout the Blitz. There is a lot of colliery paperwork to catch up on so I'd agreed to help Mr Burnley by staying a little later each day. That's why I got trapped by the snowstorm.'

'Did you not hear the air raid warning?' Lizzie asked, thinking that most people would have headed for the nearest shelter.

Mrs Wall looked at Lizzie. 'I heard the siren and peeked outside. The lights were off but the weather was still bad and the clouds were thick. We've never been bombed here during a rain storm, never mind a snowstorm, so I thought it would be a false alarm.'

'Talking of which . . .' Kember tapped his pen against the end of his nose. 'As you have access to the spare keys, did you unlock the air raid siren box and start the alarm?'

'Why on earth would I do that?' Mrs Wall said, with a frown.

'To allow you to move around and carry out your murderous work.'

'Don't be ridiculous.' Mrs Wall threw a horrified glance at Burnley. 'I'm not Jack the Ripper, I'm a secretary who happens to be devoted to her employer.' Her hands had stopped their wringing and her feet were still, as though her words had stopped time.

'Is that why you killed Christopher Morris?' Lizzie said. 'Because Mr Burnley said he wanted rid of Morris because he was a communist agitator?'

'Are you suggest—' Burnley stopped short when Kember held up his hand.

Mrs Wall batted away the tears running down her cheeks. 'Morris needed teaching a lesson, but I didn't kill anyone and Mr Burnley didn't ask me anything.'

Lizzie heard the slight emphasis on Burnley's name and saw Mrs Wall flash Kember a look of terror, as though she thought she'd said too much and the cat was almost out of the bag. Lizzie and Kember watched as she almost physically deflated before their eyes, and sensed something important, something serious lying just below the surface, needing to be said. Burnley was silent, his lips slightly parted as though he wanted to say something too but couldn't find the words. Very unlike him.

'Why?' Lizzie urged.

Mrs Wall bowed her head.

'Why did Christopher Morris need to be taught a lesson?'

Mrs Wall drew a sobbing breath but remained silent.

'Mrs Wall,' Kember said. 'Why did you come here this evening?'

Lizzie saw some of the tension creep back across her tear-streaked face.

'I've already said; I wanted to make sure Mr Burnley had everything he needed.' Mrs Wall's fingers started to fidget again.

'I don't believe you,' Kember said, bluntly.

'Why ever not?' Mrs Wall said, startled.

'Because I find it difficult to believe that a woman would blunder about in the pitch dark attending to her boss's needs when there's a murderer to be apprehended.'

'Hardly blundering, Inspector,' Burnley said. 'Mrs Wall's worked here for years and knows the place like the back of her hand. I'm sure she's not afraid of the dark.'

'And yet,' Kember said, directing his words to Mrs Wall. 'When we saw you outside earlier, you said you'd been frightened by the possibility that someone was following you, but then you ended up here brandishing a paperknife. If not to kill me, who were you expecting?'

Mrs Wall tightened the knot of the headscarf that remained fixed over her hair.

Exactly, Lizzie thought. *Who?* On the one hand, Mrs Wall might be implicated in the murder of Christopher Morris. On the other hand, she could be mixed up in the conspiracy Lizzie was sure was being concealed. Even if she was guilty of both, Mrs Wall was still another victim. She put her hand in her pocket and made a decision.

Kember leant forward. 'Did you—'

'I think we should retire and continue in the morning.' Lizzie cut across him and stood up. 'As Mr Burnley said, it's late and we've all had a long day.' She ignored Kember's glare and opened the office door. She'd felt the questioning veering on to the wrong path and needed time to think. For all Mrs Wall's candour, Lizzie could sense her reluctance to reveal any more. Continuing to question her tonight might make her retreat into herself, and the further revelations that Lizzie was certain she had kept back would remain undisclosed.

The men seemed loath to move but Burnley eventually put his hands on his knees and pushed himself up from his chair.

'The camp beds are still in the bar and office of the social club,' he said. 'I suggest you make good use of them and we'll reconvene in the morning.'

Lizzie almost laughed at the gall of the man. Burnley had announced this to Kember as though she were not in the room but it wasn't a matter to start a confrontation over, this time.

Kember, still glowering, stood and waited for Mrs Wall to do the same. They filed into the corridor, where Burnley waited until the others reached the outer door before switching off the light. He opened the pithead door and stepped out, an arctic blast making its presence known to them all, but at least the snow hadn't returned. Lizzie walked next to Mrs Wall as they crunched along the icy path behind Burnley. Kember brought up the rear.

When they reached the clubhouse, shivering despite the short walk, Mrs Wall stepped forward and produced a key. She unlocked the outer doors and they followed Burnley past the blackout curtains and through the inner doors. Light from a lamp left on in the office seeped into the eerie deserted bar, where someone had moved a few tables and erected two camp beds in the clearing.

'I'll sleep in the office,' Kember said, switching on one of the overhead lights. 'Officer Hayes and Mrs Wall can take the camp beds.'

'That won't be necessary,' Mrs Wall protested. 'I have my own bed in the colliery office.'

Kember stepped in front of her to prevent her from passing. 'I must insist on you staying here, for your own protection if nothing else. I'll keep watch alternately with Officer Hayes.'

Mrs Wall, wide-eyed with anger and surprise, looked to Burnley but his face was impassive. Lizzie felt suddenly vulnerable. She had changed her mind about those two so many times in the last few hours that sharing a room with Mrs Wall in beds a few feet apart held little appeal. What if she was wrong and the spiky secretary turned out to be the kind of woman who really would strangle you in your bed? What if Burnley came for Mrs Wall and killed her instead?

'I'll leave you to thrash out your arrangements,' Burnley said, avoiding an imploring look from Mrs Wall. 'The club won't open until midday tomorrow but I'll return at eight. It should be getting light by then and the men will want news.'

Left on their own in the bar room, Kember disappeared into the office to check his sleeping arrangements and Lizzie shook her head to clear it of negative thoughts. She hoped Mrs Wall was a heavy sleeper. The events of the day had already begun to replay in her head and she needed time and quiet to allow her conscious and subconscious mind to combine and do its work. The clock on the wall behind the bar showed well after midnight and she knew sleep would be difficult to come by once her train of thought had been set in motion. It promised to be a long night.

CHAPTER TWENTY

Kember endured an uncomfortable night in the clubhouse office as the temperature dropped. Taking first watch, he rummaged through the paperwork on the desk for no better reason than to occupy and distract his mind. It didn't work. At gone two o'clock, the office became so cold that he sat in the chair with two blankets pulled tightly around him. His back started aching about an hour in and no end of fidgeting and adjustment alleviated it. To compound matters, he could hear snoring from beyond the office door which stood ajar. Around three 0'clock, he got up to stretch his back muscles and peeked through the gap in the door. Mrs Wall was asleep, and so obviously the one guilty of snoring. He could see Lizzie sitting at one of the tables, her back to him. A column of smoke drifted up and spread across the ceiling, although he couldn't see the cigarette she was smoking.

He thought about going to sit with her or inviting her to the office but she seemed deep in thought and he knew what that meant. She'd grabbed him by the throat on one occasion when he'd disturbed her. She'd been thinking like the murderer they were trying to find and had turned on him with the look of a killer. She'd snapped out of it quick enough but he now knew better than to interrupt her thinking. Instead, he sat at the office desk for a while, mulling over the events of the last two days. He knew Burnley,

Mrs Wall and all the men in Hut Six were guilty to a greater or lesser degree but how could he prove any of it? Administering a noxious substance, intimidation, conspiracy to murder, assaults of almost every kind including on a police officer, attempted murder, actual murder. He sighed. It was as though a psychopath had been through the copy of *Sir Howard Vincent's Police Code* sitting in his desk drawer in Tonbridge Police HQ and drawn up a personal wish list.

Handing over to Lizzie at four o'clock, he climbed into the creaky camp bed fully clothed and wrapped himself in the blankets once again, but the warmth and comfort he enjoyed in his bed at the Castle pub in Scotney eluded him. Exhaustion overcame him eventually and he slept for an hour, awaking to the sound of something being moved in the bar room. He hauled himself off the bed and stretched. Despite a lukewarm pipe running along the bottom of one wall, the air was chilled and his breath just visible when he exhaled. He moved the blackout curtain aside and saw the glimmer of first light through the translucent lens of ice on the inside of the window. The snow had not returned, bringing hope that the roads could be cleared quite soon. His stomach reminded him that he hadn't eaten since early yesterday evening and he wondered whether they had any prospect of breakfast. He shivered and went out to the bar.

The sound he'd heard was the stacking of one camp bed on the other. He saw Lizzie standing at the window, peering beyond the curtain and ice as he had just done, and Mrs Wall sitting at one of the tables, a glass of water in front of her. Lizzie turned at the sound of him clearing his throat.

'How did you sleep?' she asked.

'In fits and starts,' he replied. 'You?'

'Same.'

'I slept like a log,' Mrs Wall said, and took a swig from her glass. 'That camp bed is better than the one I have in the colliery office.'

Kember marvelled at how bad her other camp bed must be, considering his own broken night's sleep. He indicated the curtains.

'I suppose we can take the blackout screens down,' he said, and joined Lizzie.

Mrs Wall stood and moved away from them. 'If you don't mind, I need to powder my nose,' she said, and disappeared through a door to the lavatory.

As they began opening the thin drapes and removing the additional screens, Kember spoke in a low voice. 'I've been thinking all night. Mrs Wall is the only one who could have killed Morris and Collins, and I'm sure how close she is to Burnley had something to do with it.'

Lizzie shook her head. 'I think you're wrong.'

Such an unexpected rebuttal rendered Kember momentarily speechless and they continued to remove screens, letting light into the clubhouse.

'She is the only one with access to all the keys,' he said. 'She has the dusters in her drawer. She has Burnley's authority behind her and is so well known by the men, many of whom ignore her and the other women because they dislike the idea of them in a man's workplace, that she can go anywhere on the colliery almost invisibly. She had the means and motive, and the kind of opportunities that Burnley himself and the men of Hut Six, even collectively, did not have. There must be more between her and Burnley than meets the eye. It has to be . . . her.'

The cold blue steel of Lizzie's eyes made him falter.

'Even allowing for the fact that Morris was a thoroughly bad man with many enemies who might want him dead,' she said. 'That doesn't mean she's the guilty party.'

He frowned. 'What do you mean? I thought—'

'There are other possibilities. We know from our own experience that she is not always at her desk and the office isn't locked. Anyway, I spoke to her last night and I sensed something dreadful had happened to her. I think—'

Lizzie stopped as Mrs Wall emerged from the lavatory.

'Been talking about me and Mr Burnley, have you?' Mrs Wall said. 'I've suffered that a lot.'

Kember felt a sudden flush of embarrassment. Men rarely wasted time judging other men unless it served a particular purpose. Yes, men competed with men, a far more exciting pastime with the potential for profit, but they judged women. Women competed with women *and* judged each other, destructive in so many ways. Women also judged themselves, often more harshly than any other person would. Certain behaviour, when by a man, was applauded, largely by men. The same behaviour by a woman was often roundly condemned by men and women alike. The double standard was visible and known to all throughout every class of society and Kember wondered whether he could ever escape a doctrine so ingrained in the mind that thoughts and reactions were almost innate.

'We are discussing the investigation, Mrs Wall,' Lizzie said. 'Have you remembered anything you'd like to tell us?'

Mrs Wall shook her head. 'Nothing that would do anyone any good.'

Kember was about to ask her what she meant by that when Burnley arrived with a squeak of the door and a blast of cold air from outside. Thatcher and the men of Hut Six followed and Kember saw Mrs Wall tense at the sudden invasion. Burnley's inflamed cheek, the result of the scuffle in the office, looked red and puffy against the dark blue and purple patch of his black eye, but he seemed oblivious.

'Has communication been restored to the outside world?' Kember asked.

'I'm afraid not,' Burnley replied. 'I've heard the tractors with their snow blades have been out and I've had my men clearing the lane for the last half an hour so it shouldn't be long. I've got coal to shift and God knows when the GPO will have the telephone lines back up.'

'I didn't expect all of you quite so early.' Kember looked at the men of Hut Six who had fanned out and sat at various tables. They looked as dishevelled as they had in the pithead office a few hours ago, suggesting sleep had eluded them also.

'I promised the men last night that we'd give them an explanation this morning. By that, I mean you, of course.' The men nodded, muttered to each other, shook their heads and looked on. 'They came to find me in my office and no amount of appeasement would deflect them.'

I bet you didn't try that hard, Kember thought as he walked across to where Mrs Wall sat frozen to her chair. Lizzie remained standing by the bar counter. He took a breath but had no time to say a word.

The door squeaked and Detective Inspector Watson walked into the bar room.

'Have you missed me?' he said.

◆ ◆ ◆

Surprise hit the gathering like a tidal wave and the men cursed under their breaths, glancing at each other with frowns or raised eyebrows, chattering like a troupe of monkeys disturbed in their zoo cage. Lizzie stepped forward to take Watson's arm. She thought he looked ashen, as though not all the blood he'd lost had been replenished. A dressing more in keeping with modern medicine and kept in place by a white bandage, wrapped around his head and fixed with a safety pin, had replaced the temporary one administered by her in the dormitory.

'Should you be up and about in your condition?' Kember said.

'I'm not pregnant,' Watson replied, with a smile.

'You look rough though.'

'Hmm. I feel like warm shit on a cold shovel, but I'll live. You don't look that chipper yourself.' He beckoned them towards the clubhouse office.

'Do you know who hit you?' Lizzie asked.

'No,' Watson said. 'He came at me from behind and I went out like a light before I hit the ground. It seems I have both of you to thank for saving my life.'

'Lizzie played Florence Nightingale and patched you up,' Kember said. 'That was after she'd been attacked herself.'

'Jesus Christ,' Watson said. 'Are you all right?'

'I was wearing a miner's helmet at the time,' Lizzie said. She looked hard at Kember, not appreciating being lumped in with nurses again.

Watson glanced at the bar. 'I could do with a drink. Medicinal, mind.'

'I'm not sure Burnley would allow you to drink his profits,' Kember said. 'He told us you arrived and went looking for us. I appreciate that.'

'Don't thank me. You'd done a bunk by the time his men got to the shaft bottom and all I got was a clout on the head blundering around this bloody place in the snow.'

'Still, getting the fan back on could have saved our lives.'

'Could have?' Watson looked up at Kember.

'Long story,' Kember said. 'We'd made our way up an escape tunnel when the fan came on. Bloody cold it was.'

Watson smiled. 'Now there's gratitude.' His face became suddenly serious. 'Did you find who did it? The attacks? The murder?'

'It's two murders now,' Kember said. 'They killed one of the fan house managers who also doubled as an ARP warden.'

Watson sighed. 'What a mess.'

They returned to the bar and Watson lowered himself on to a chair. That was when Lizzie saw the small round-toed boot print among the other muddy prints on the floor, and knew.

'Looks like tea is needed all round,' Burnley said, as he took a chair near his men. He nodded at Lizzie. 'Be a dear. You can get to the canteen through the room behind the bar.'

Lizzie clenched her jaw and glared back at him but he was ignoring her. *No*, she thought, *he's not ignoring me. It's as if I don't exist as an equal and the provision of tea, even by someone not employed by him, is his right. I am a woman; therefore, I make the tea.* Both Watson and Mrs Wall, not the burly mine owner, looked like they could do with a hot restorative. She looked to Kember, for whom cups of tea made by Sergeant Wright back at Scotney village were a common sight, but he pressed his lips together as his eyebrows flickered upwards, and gave her a miniscule nod. She knew he was right; they needed to pick their moment with care.

Lizzie walked behind the bar and into a square room, which had another door on the far side. This opened into a short hallway that led to the servery, where the women she'd seen there the previous day gave her dirty looks as they prepared for the breakfast onslaught before the start of the fore shift. In answer to her query about tea, mentioning that it had been requested by Mr Burnley, one of the women nodded to an urn on a table at the back. Lizzie almost laughed. It was one thing to be relegated to serving girl by the mine owner, quite another to be dismissed as such by the canteen women as well, but it wasn't a battle worth fighting. The dull sound when Lizzie gingerly tapped it confirmed it had been filled but the warm metal told her it had not been on for quite long enough. She pushed through a swing door and entered the kitchen. For the size of the colliery and the number of workers it catered for, the kitchen seemed remarkably small. *Another of Burnley's economies*, she thought.

Having been directed to a kettle, teapot, tea caddy, tea strainer, mug and milk, but no sugar, Lizzie made two hot drinks and returned to the dining room, where she took particular joy in Burnley's expression when she placed one mug of tea in front of Mrs Wall and gave the other to Watson. Lizzie acknowledged the gesture as petty but it brought her a disproportionate level of satisfaction. Sometimes you had to find pleasure where you could.

The men had rearranged their chairs since she'd left the room, but only so they could all have a better view of Kember and Mrs Wall. Burnley had promised them an explanation and they were waiting to collect. Armstrong's mouth drooped at the corners as if saddened by the whole affair. Ramsey picked the skin around his thumbnails, displaying a nervousness Lizzie would have expected from the accused rather than a suspected accomplice. Thatcher had taken a seat near the door with a good view of Kember and Burnley, but he watched Mrs Wall unwaveringly. Quayle and Pine were murmuring to each other, the former rubbing and wringing his hands as though he had something to tell and keep in at the same time. Pine himself looked equally as uncomfortable. Young's relaxed position, leaning against the back of his chair, did not disguise the crossed arms and legs that formed a double barrier against whatever was about to unfold in front of him.

At first, they reminded Lizzie of an audience waiting for a performance to begin, although the overhead lighting and thin beige curtains were a far cry from the spotlights and red velvet drapes of a theatre. On the way over last night, Lizzie had wondered whether only she and Kember stood for due process rather than a lynching, and the more she looked at the assembled men the more they looked like a gathering of co-conspirators. Even though the men made no attempt to approach Mrs Wall or speak to her, Lizzie feared a kangaroo court might be about to sit in session. If that was so, she had a surprise for them.

The tension in the room was almost palpable as Kember stepped forward and cleared his throat to speak. Lizzie knew he had no doubt that these men were guilty of using naturally occurring mine gas to force Morris from the colliery. She knew he had no doubt that Mrs Wall had administered the final fatal dose by blocking the air bricks. Knowing or thinking you knew how, when and why a crime had been committed was not the same as being able to prove who did it, and he had no conclusive proof. Here he was, about to show his full hand to the men and woman he thought were guilty but was loath to arrest any of them with the little he had. Alongside the dusters, the adjustable spanner used as a cudgel had constituted the totality of the scant physical evidence. Whatever highs and lows he'd had in his career as a police officer, she sensed his enveloping frustration at the lack of conclusive proof, and she prayed that any fingerprints and forensic traces on the spanner hadn't been contaminated and completely lost, for his sake.

'Gentlemen,' Kember began. 'I was brought in to establish whether the initial investigation into the death of Christopher Morris had missed anything of importance. There appeared to be a discrepancy between the idea that a tragic accident had occurred and the evidence discovered by Detective Inspector Watson's men.'

'You're saying that you were sent here to see if he mucked up, don't you mean?' Burnley interrupted.

Lizzie saw Watson raise one eyebrow, looking mildly amused at Burnley's suggestion, but he and the other men remained silent.

Kember looked at each man in turn as he continued.

'Detective Inspector Watson came up against a good measure of resistance during his initial investigation. When I first arrived, I experienced a lot more cooperation but still a little hostility. I can understand Mr Burnley's reluctance to compromise the running of his business, and to some extent, I can understand your suspicion towards yet another policeman invading your close-knit domain. But a man had died. Oh, I know you all answered my questions but I'm afraid I'm not one to take things at face value. I found your answers guarded, deflective and unsatisfactory, which gave rise to even more questions at the end of my first day on this case. My suspicions were not allayed after Inspector Watson and I left here the day before yesterday, when what I assumed to be a farm lorry tried to run the inspector's car off the road. It failed, we survived and Officer Hayes and I found the lorry the following day, hidden in this colliery under a tarpaulin.'

Kember reached inside his jacket and retrieved two folded sheets of paper; the typed copy of the original post-mortem summary and a handwritten copy of Dr Headley's notes from the second post-mortem.

'The colliery physician, Dr Paine, initially recorded the cause of Mr Morris's death as' – he unfolded the sheets and made a show of consulting their contents – '"a heart attack brought on by exhaustion and physical stress". Dr Gunstone, a local pathologist from Canterbury, performed a post-mortem and agreed. Despite this, Inspector Watson believed he had cause to doubt the medical conclusions and went out on a limb to convince his senior officer to not close the investigation. As a compromise, I was called upon to review the investigation. While I completed my initial inquiries here, Dr Headley, a renowned Home Office pathologist whom I brought with me from Tonbridge, performed a second post-mortem on Mr Morris back in Canterbury. He discovered certain specific peculiarities not recorded in Dr Gunstone's report that shed a different light on the cause of death. His assessment concluded that Mr Morris had died of carbon monoxide poisoning, something you call whitedamp. Now, whether that additional information had been missed, overlooked or discounted by Drs Paine and Gunstone is a matter of speculation.'

Lizzie noted Kember's look of satisfaction when he glanced at Burnley after his inference of possible bribery and saw the mine owner avert his eyes, a look of discomfort on his face. It may have been the fixed expressions of the men from Hut Six, the way Thatcher leant forward as if to hear Kember's words clearer, or the haunted look in Mrs Wall's eyes, but Lizzie almost felt able to touch the tension in the room.

'If that had been all,' Kember continued, 'my review may not have progressed much further but whoever initiated the incident with the lorry miscalculated the effect it would have. It merely served to confirm that there was more to the death of Mr Morris than met the eye. His asphyxiation by whitedamp was unusual because he was an experienced miner, an overman, one of the safety team tasked with making sure the mine was safe and fit to be worked. This is where it became complicated. How could Mr Morris have died of whitedamp when the other men he worked with did not? A further complexity stemmed from the fact that he died in the early hours of the morning, surrounded by other men sleeping in the dormitory of Hut Six.'

This time, Lizzie noticed the expressions on the faces of Armstrong and Young remained impassive while Ramsey, Quayle and Pine shifted uneasily on their chairs. Thatcher continued to lean forward, seemingly less affected but more interested in what he had to say.

'Officer Hayes, who helped previous police investigations with her particular qualifications regarding the assessment of criminal behaviour, arrived early yesterday morning to assist me. To say the chain of events that it set in motion has been traumatic would be an understatement. Our lives have been at risk from the moment we began a new round of interviews, culminating in the apprehension of Mrs Wall as we lay in wait for the murderer to take the bait and spring our trap.'

It was Mrs Wall's turn to avert her eyes but Kember stared at the men again.

'Long before then, Officer Hayes and I had established that Mr Burnley and the men of Hut Six had very good motives for wanting Mr Morris to leave the colliery. Paul Ramsey, a fireman on the same shift, was bullied by Morris to such a degree that his life was made a misery. Edward Pine, the onsetter on that shift, had been cheated out of hundreds of pounds playing cards with Morris. It was common knowledge that Morris had an affair with the wife of Terrance Armstrong, the winding engineman. The brother of Victor Young, the fan house foreman who ensured the mine was well ventilated, had been injured in a mining accident in a pit up north. Everyone deemed a man called Roy Jackson responsible because of his habitual negligence but the incident was never properly investigated because he lost his job after being prosecuted as a strike leader. Blacklisted and out of work, he came south, as many others did after the strike and during the depression, and Roy Jackson became Christopher Morris.'

Studying each of the men as Kember spoke, Lizzie could see that none of this had come as a revelation to them, which made her belief about their complicity even stronger. Kember nodded towards Thatcher as he continued.

'Alastair Thatcher also lost his job in the depression and came south to find work years later, finally turning up here. Mr Burnley discovered Morris had an unsavoury past and became fearful that his mine would be run into the ground by what he saw as a communist agitator. If there's one thing Mr Burnley knows about, it is the value of money and power, and he offered Morris a promotion to the overman's job to keep him on side, snubbing a far better and more deserving candidate in the other fore shift fireman, Harold Quayle.'

Lizzie could see the muscles of Quayle's jaw moving as he clenched and unclenched his teeth.

'Morris was a deeply unpleasant, unethical, crooked man, and as Mrs Wall admitted to us not long ago, he needed to be taught a lesson.'

Mrs Wall closed her eyes as though not seeing would make all this go away. Lizzie knew that didn't work; she'd tried that strategy before. The men were uneasy, as if a closely guarded secret was being exposed like the ripping of a dressing off a gaping wound.

'Here is where I founder,' Kember said. 'You all had a reason to want Morris dead but you are all hard-working men whose mothers, I'm sure, would insist wouldn't hurt a fly in ordinary circumstances. Mr Burnley's pride in himself and his mine would never allow for unpleasantness that could harm his reputation. Yet, something had to be done and I believe all of you conspired to drive Morris from the colliery by poisoning him with whitedamp.'

The men muttered their dissent but fidgeted even more and threw each other worried glances. This gave Lizzie a pleasant tingle in her chest. Their reaction confirmed that Kember was on the right track.

'An overman would know about the effects of whitedamp so Morris must have been puzzled when he became ill but others did not. He may have begun to think he'd become susceptible to the gas through exposure, age or infirmity. He may have started to consider the mine itself a danger, rather than there being anything wrong with himself. He may have been on the verge of death or of walking away from the mine. We'll never know because I believe one of you considered that merely driving him away was insufficient recompense for his crimes and decided to take things one step further.'

Burnley shot to his feet. 'I thought we were here for a rational explanation, Inspector, not accusations.' His walrus moustache quivered and his eyes blazed but it seemed no more than bluster.

'Sit down, please, Mr Burnley,' Kember said.

Watson seemed content with the proceedings, his empty mug on the table in front of him, but it was the lingering look Kember gave Mrs Wall that troubled Lizzie. The secretary seemed less than enamoured with what Kember had said so far, her half-full mug abandoned on the table near Watson's. The ball of anxiety building in the pit of Lizzie's stomach warned her that Kember might be about to talk himself in the wrong direction so she fixed him with a stare that she hoped he'd recognise as a signal to proceed with caution. She'd had the whole night to bring her skills to bear on her experiences over the last twenty-four hours and her conclusion had surprised even her.

'You men are experts in coal mine gases and know all about timings, saturation, build-up and effects,' Kember said. 'It's my belief that the fore shift safety team arranged for Young to disengage the ventilation fan in the lead up to and during the morning inspection, resulting in a build-up of gas in the tunnels. This should have been detected but Ramsey fooled Morris by keeping the Davy lamp out of his way and by using the oxygen in the Haldane cage to keep the canary singing. Officer Hayes and I discovered oxygen tanks stored underground for emergencies were depleted and I suspect Ramsey and Quayle used them on themselves in a similar way. Morris was probably too full of himself and his bullying ways to notice and Quayle feigned a sprained ankle to get more relief and respite from the constant and steady doses of carbon monoxide—'

'Ridiculous,' Burnley interrupted again. 'The whole of the fore shift would have known.'

'Not necessarily,' Kember said. 'We suspect the fan was engaged long enough before the full fore shift went down the pit, to clear as much gas as possible. But the ploy to force Morris out was failing, Ramsey was getting sicker by the day and the men possibly thought about giving up.' He looked directly at the men. 'You are miners, honourable men in an honourable profession, not cold-blooded killers. Doctors take an oath to save lives and we believe you have a similar code of honour. Mr Burnley calling out the fire brigade to save me from the fire in Hut Two, you ensuring Officer Hayes and Inspector Watson were rescued from the burning Hut Six, and warning Mr Burnley that we were trapped underground, when Inspector Watson arrived, are examples of basic humanity but also of that code. Fire, poisonous gas and explosion; they are to be defended against at all cost. If you'd really wanted us dead, surely those would have been the times to make it happen, but you stepped back from the edge. You wanted Morris out but no one needed to die.'

Kember glanced at Mrs Wall, who looked up at him defiantly, and another ripple of anxiety passed through Lizzie. The way this was going, she worried that she might have to jump in at any moment. The thought of interrupting Kember, a Scotland Yard detective, in front of all these men made her throat constrict and she drew a deep faltering breath to assure herself she could still breathe. She knew her skills and experience mattered but still the self-doubt pecked at her.

'The killer, or killers, couldn't let that happen,' Kember continued. 'Knowing all about the dangers of carbon monoxide, they took matters into their own hands, using the cleaning dusters Mrs Wall kept in her desk drawer in a way for which they were not intended. Performing their checks after the fire, the colliery fire brigade found a few dusters stuffed into the air bricks and a stepladder hidden behind the hut, left behind in the killer's haste to clean up. The ladder suggests he or she must have known that blocking the air bricks alone wouldn't restrict the airflow enough to trap sufficient carbon monoxide. Partially blocking the flue as well would cause a build-up in the dormitory without filling the hut with too much smoke and ensure one final dose from the coal fire in the stove would be enough to prove fatal to Morris. Ramsey might get ill again but he would recover and that was a small price to pay to get rid of Morris. The other men in the hut probably wouldn't realise they'd inhaled carbon monoxide, even if they awoke with headaches.'

Watching the men, Lizzie was intrigued by their array of clasped wrists, folded arms, furtive glances and set jaws, all indicative of hidden truths and unconscious defensive measures.

'It wouldn't have taken long to take effect,' Kember went on. 'Dr Headley said that carbon monoxide is created when there's not enough oxygen for the coal to burn properly. With little fresh air coming in through the bricks, the poison gas would have built up rapidly. Once sufficient time had passed to ensure a fatal dose, the flue and bricks could have been unblocked and the through draught would have helped clear the room of what little smoke may have seeped through. Inspector Watson's investigation never spotted the dusters in the air bricks but that wasn't surprising because the stated cause of death gave him no reason to look.'

Lizzie noticed Kember give Watson an apologetic shrug, it being the kind of obscure detail anyone could have missed, especially since Drs Paine and Gunstone may have been bribed to give a false cause of death, but Watson's jaw clenched and his lips pressed into a thin line.

'When Officer Hayes and I decided to go against Mr Burnley's wishes and inspect the pit last night, we unwittingly provided the killer with an opportunity to implicate Mr Burnley and get rid of our interference.'

Lizzie watched as Burnley's head slowly turned away from Kember and towards Mrs Wall, his face carrying pinched lines of hurt. Mrs Wall flicked a glance at him, then away, before her head dropped a little lower. Lizzie knew the time to intervene was nearing and the mere thought made taking the next breath a struggle, but not wanting to interrupt Kember just yet stopped her from using the rubber band. Instead, she pinched the flesh on the back of her wrist to give her brain the jolt it needed.

'Burnley said that you men became worried and told him we were down there,' Kember said. 'Maybe Inspector Watson turning up was our saviour. Either way, we could have been rescued too late to escape a single fatal dose of carbon monoxide but we found our own way out through the escape route up the fan drift. The airlock had been jammed shut but emergency equipment is stored inside so it was easy enough to break out. It had been done deliberately because we found a shattered wedge of wood and a small footprint outside the door, so we know the killer believed they'd thought of everything to keep us down there. Realising we'd escaped certain death when the men went down the pit and found us gone, and suspecting the jammed airlock wouldn't be sufficient to stop us, the killer had to take things further. Inspector Watson found the lorry, as we did, but he was followed in the snowstorm and got a smack on the head for his trouble. The killer even set off the air raid siren to douse the lights so they could work in the dark, knowing the place like the back of their hand. Officer Hayes also received a blow to the head but her helmet saved her from having her skull cracked open.'

Lizzie had to force herself to breathe, hearing the attack recounted. She looked around the gathering but no one seemed to be aware of her struggle, concentrating as they were on Kember's every word.

'We continued our search and found Inspector Watson lying unconscious on the ground near the lorry,' Kember said. 'Hut Six had been locked by him because he considered you all to be suspects. Why then did we find the key in the door of the unlocked hut that first time? Why, having locked it again with that key when we left to look for Inspector Watson, did we find it unlocked and another key in the door when we returned?'

'What do you mean, unlocked that first time?' Armstrong said, shocked.

Lizzie could almost feel the anger surging from the men, but it was tempered with an underlying tension that told a different story.

'You never told us that,' Quayle said, pointing at Burnley.

'I didn't know at the time,' Burnley shot back.

'We could have got out,' Young complained.

'And gone where, in a snowstorm?' Burnley said, eyebrows raised.

'Gentlemen,' Kember said, his voice moderate but firm.

Lizzie suspected that directing their anger towards Burnley was more to disguise their disquiet about being suspects in two murders rather than ire at not being told they had been freed from their hut. The men grumbled and shifted in their seats but slowly quietened.

'Thank you,' Kember said. 'When Officer Hayes and I rested in Hut Two, before we went down the pit, I spotted signs that someone had been in there before us and I wanted to investigate it further. Mr Burnley went to check why the all-clear hadn't sounded and found the body of Gordon Collins, the duty ARP warden. We suspect the killer wanted the lights to remain off and, becoming increasingly desperate, had to kill Collins to prevent him sounding the all-clear. While Mr Burnley was at the pithead, I went to Hut Two and found an adjustable spanner hidden in the rafters.'

Kember took the spanner from his pocket and held it up for the men to see.

'The curious thing is, I saw the clue to its hiding place before it had been used to attack Officer Hayes, Inspector Watson and Gordon Collins. I think someone planned to use it on Morris as a last resort and hid it in the unused hut a while ago, but events took a different turn and it was left deliberately in a manner for me to find it. For a while I thought that someone was Mr Burnley, aided by Mrs Wall.'

Mr Burnley stood abruptly but Kember's sharp look forestalled any retort and he sat heavily on his chair, eyes blazing.

'Another curious thing,' Kember said. 'This spanner is solid and heavy enough to kill with one blow, which brings me back to someone only wanting to kill Morris. Everything else has been about diverting attention away from whoever the killer is, to the extent that they tried to frame Mr Burnley, who isn't popular with the workers.'

Burnley's eyebrows shot up with surprise, and in any other situation Lizzie might have laughed.

'I believe someone unlocked the door prior to the attack on the inspector to remove the alibi of the men being locked in,' Kember said. 'Mrs Wall admitted unlocking the door the second time because she said she couldn't bear the injustice of innocent men being locked up. I was certain Mr Burnley was at the heart of it all but after Hut Two was set ablaze with me inside, Mr Burnley called the fire brigade and helped with the evacuation of Hut Two, not the actions of a murderer.'

Burnley nodded in affirmation.

'I saw more small footprints in the snow leading to Hut Two,' Kember continued. 'We also found the muddy print of a small boot in the pithead office where Collins was killed.'

'How small?' Ramsey said. 'Are we talking about a nipper?'

Kember ignored the question. 'With Hut Two destroyed, Officer Hayes and I were supposed to spend the night in the social club, the only place available at short notice, but I decided to set a trap for the killer. By pretending that Officer Hayes had gone to the social club but I had stayed alone at the pithead, I hoped to draw the killer into attacking me. Officer Hayes, Mr Burnley and Alastair Thatcher would hide and jump out when the trap was sprung. It worked, although there was quite a scuffle and Mr Burnley got a nasty blow to his face.'

Burnley's hand went automatically to his face and his fingers touched his bruised cheek.

Kember took a breath and said, 'The final actions of one person in this room led to the death of Morris and brought the police to your door, confounding all your efforts that had gone before which may never have been discovered. It brought Inspector Watson back here again, with Officer Hayes and myself, the result of which has been the attempt on all our lives and the tragic death of Collins. As you know, we caught Mrs Wall last night and—'

'So, she's as guilty as sin?' Pine said.

The room erupted in a cacophony of shouted questions and comments. Burnley leapt to his feet again, as did Victor Young and Harold Quayle. Lizzie felt as though her mind and body would explode if she didn't say something soon as she watched Kember use quietening gestures with his hands to get the men to calm down and sit. The whole thing was becoming like a fatuous drunken debate in a pub that threatened to get out of hand and end in a brawl. Only, there was no beer and this was serious.

'If I may,' Lizzie said loudly, stepping forward suddenly so all the men could see her. They all stopped as if caught squabbling by a headmistress.

Kember frowned and put a hand on her elbow. 'This isn't the time,' he hissed.

Lizzie pulled away. 'It's the perfect time.'

She stood at the centre of the gathering, acutely aware of the exposed position she had put herself in. The killer could attack her at any moment, although that was unlikely in present company, but it was the possibility of her own mind attacking her that worried her the most. Pinching herself had not proved sufficient to subdue a flare of anxiety as she stood in front of the men, and using her mislaid little blue jar was out of the question, as were all but one of her countermeasures. She could feel the constriction in her chest and throat beginning already but couldn't sit back down and let Kember blunder into making a mistake. The men were looking at her with expressions that ranged from amusement, through annoyance and anger to disgust. Reminding herself that she had stood up to better men than these, the AIB being a case in point, she took a deep breath and cleared her throat to disguise the sharp snap of the rubber band on her right wrist.

◆ ◆ ◆

Kember saw the familiar struggle in Lizzie's face and the way she opened her mouth to draw in more air. He heard the rubber band slap her wrist and felt an unexpected wave of protectiveness towards her. It wasn't that he felt she was in any physical danger, now they had Mrs Wall in their custody, but he knew how hard her anxiety hit from time to time and didn't want her ripped apart like a deer in the midst of wolves. He looked into her eyes, expecting vulnerability, but they exuded a depth of determination he'd also seen before. He nodded and moved aside to allow her to speak.

'Inspector Kember is correct in everything he has said so far,' Lizzie began. 'But he is a man of hard facts and evidence and these do not always add up to the full picture. As he said, I have certain skills and experience that allow me to see things from a different perspective. I can often tell when someone is lying by the way they sit, the gestures they make and the things they do or do not say. You have all lied to us in one way or another and that is perfectly understandable.'

A chorus of disapproval went up from the miners. Kember had pretty much called them liars too but hearing it in such stark terms from a woman unsettled them. *We're certainly hitting some nerves this morning*, Kember thought. The furore soon died down but the fidgeting continued.

'If you've committed a crime of any kind, why would you want to tell us the truth?' Lizzie said. 'Especially in front of the police and Mr Burnley. In my experience, the best lies are based on truth and you have all been quite adept. The problem is, you have to remember all the time what has been said, by whom, when and to whom, even more so if there is a group of you. Inspector Kember believes our work has uncovered the truth. I do too, but not with quite the same result.'

Kember had been about to interject but he deflated as Lizzie's statement took the wind out of his sails. Her support for his assertion that they'd attained the truth pleased him in a way that took him by surprise, but his eyebrows knitted in a frown of confusion at the suggestion that there might be more than one truth.

'To commit murder, you need the means, motive and opportunity,' Lizzie said. 'Inspector Kember stated your motives and the means employed to poison Morris with whitedamp, but did any of you have the opportunity to kill him and attack us? Were you one or many?'

'Or none of us,' Burnley spat.

Lizzie shrugged, took another deep breath, and let it out in a slow sigh. To Kember, she seemed disappointed with those present as if they still could not see what she could. She looked around the room as though willing the real killer to make a mistake and reveal themselves. Kember felt a tingle of trepidation.

'It is true, Mrs Wall came to the pithead office last night and was taken into custody by Inspector Kember. It is also true that her secretarial work and close proximity to Mr Burnley afforded her many opportunities for eavesdropping that put her in a unique position to know what was going on in the colliery.' Lizzie nodded at Mrs Wall who looked back with a slight tilt of her head, as though not quite sure where this was going. 'Watching our repeat questioning and probing must have scared Mrs Wall from the outset. Inspector Watson and his men had left the colliery apparently satisfied so the return of the police would have worried any guilty party. Was the lorry that tried to warn us away by running the two inspectors off the road really driven by Mrs Wall?' Lizzie ignored the smirks of the men and the frown from Mrs Wall. 'It's possible. After all, she had been an ambulance driver in the Great War. What about the bundle of stores that dropped from a height but missed us? Using the pulley system wouldn't have required much strength. Did she arrange for that so-called accident to occur?'

'Mrs Wall is my *secretary*,' Burnley said, shaking his head. 'She wouldn't do all this. She's a *woman*.'

'So am I, Mr Burnley, and I fly warplanes.' Lizzie fixed him with a cold stare until he averted his eyes.

Kember wanted to jump in and stop her, but he merely raised his eyebrows as she turned to him. A look passed between them that he hoped would convey that he was allowing her as much leeway as he dared to explain herself, and that her reputation and credibility were at stake. If she got this wrong, he could never let her work with him again.

'Our decision to inspect the mine was a turning point,' she said.

Lizzie pointed to the floor and Kember realised this had become a performance where she had to hold the attention of the audience, even if they were all as guilty as each other. That so many men, so close in the bar room, were looking at her and waiting for her to falter could cause her anxiety to bubble through again. He recognised her need to use the momentum of her analysis to carry her through as she jabbed her finger towards the floor once again.

'We knew that going underground yesterday evening, against Mr Burnley's wishes, might uncover evidence to prove our theory so we lied to the men and fooled them into taking us down.' She ignored the murmurs of anger. 'Did Mrs Wall see an opportunity to get rid of us by trapping us underground and letting the gas do its work, as the inspector suggested? After all, it would have been deemed an accident and our own fault for insisting on going down early. Mrs Wall has admitted that she is devoted to Mr Burnley—'

Burnley shot to his feet, his mouth flapping without sound. Ramsey and Quayle also stood, and all the miners shouted questions at Burnley, Mrs Wall, Kember and Watson. Kember was intrigued that Lizzie wasn't a target in the verbal melee, and relieved that she seemed to be holding her anxieties in check. When the room had calmed, Lizzie continued.

'Mrs Wall hated Christopher Morris, but whatever game was in play to drive him from the colliery, avoiding implicating Mr Burnley and keeping him from harm would always have been foremost in her thoughts. She had access to all the spare keys for the entire colliery so it would have been easy for her to slip out and open the hut that Inspector Watson had locked. I did wonder whether the arrival of Inspector Kember and myself with the unconscious Inspector Watson had interrupted the release of the men, but then a thought struck me and niggled at the back of my mind. Would I have bothered to let the men out against the orders of a police detective when the colliery was snowbound and there was nowhere to go?'

Kember watched Lizzie nod slowly, her eyes focused somewhere in the distance beyond the walls, and he worried about her.

If she began to do what he regarded as 'her thing', here in front of the men, none of them would take her seriously, least of all Watson. He prepared to step in.

'I might have done, if I *knew* they had been wrongfully locked up,' Lizzie said, as her eyes refocused on the gathered men.

Her flicked glance Kember's way stopped him from making a move, but the gesture did not match the steel in her eyes nor her stony expression.

'But was there another reason?' Lizzie said. 'Did Mrs Wall want to tell Mr Burnley something right away? Was he and the other men in danger?' She shrugged again. 'She never got the chance to speak to him because we turned up.' She waved a hand at the detectives.

'All very interesting,' Burnley said, 'but what's the point of this?'

'Your good fortune was my misfortune,' Lizzie rounded on Burnley. 'And that of your men. Inspector Kember asked you to check the air raid siren over at the pithead offices, but he locked the rest of us in Hut Six, hoping to keep us safe from the actual murderer. While I was talking to you all, learning through your spoken words and body language how guilty you all might have been, someone was watching the inspector, hunting him, knowing we were going nowhere. Could that someone have wanted Mr Burnley as far away as possible from what was coming next, or was that happenstance? Who is the arsonist who wanted to get rid of me, the inspectors and everyone else in Hut Six? The person who was closest to Mr Burnley, perhaps?'

The men leapt to their feet again, anger and vitriol in their voices as they demanded justice for having been attacked by their co-conspirator. Kember stepped in this time and placated the men with assurances that the guilty would be punished. In any other circumstance, he would have been amused that they were satisfied by this despite their own obvious guilt at having wanted Christopher

Morris gone. He caught movement out of the corner of his eye and saw Thatcher staring at Mrs Wall with a face as red as if he'd just come in from the freezing cold.

With calm restored, Kember intended to take over but Lizzie urged him to one side again. He guessed she was nearing her conclusion and a wave of apprehension made him tense. He tried to dismiss it as caused by lack of sleep but the feeling ran deeper than mere fatigue, and her safety sprang to the forefront of his mind. The tension was making his calf and thigh muscles ache but he kept his eyes on the men as Lizzie continued.

'It's true that Mrs Wall has lied to us throughout this investigation but I thought it was to protect Mr Burnley. When she admitted her urge to protect him and do all she could for him it reinforced that belief, but I've spoken to many criminals and victims before and I got the sense that something else lay behind the barrier she had put between us.'

Kember saw Lizzie's eyes flash him a warning as she turned to crouch in front of Mrs Wall. It was a look she had never given him before, and the sense of foreboding it conveyed weighed unexpectedly heavy on his heart. He realised that she was descending to the woman's physical level to make herself less imposing and intimidating, as he would to a frightened child. Whatever Lizzie was trying to coax from Mrs Wall, he knew it couldn't be anything good.

'I believe something dreadful happened,' Lizzie said.

Mrs Wall shook her head but her eyes said different.

'These men don't understand,' Lizzie said. 'They'll never understand and will remain ignorant of these things unless you explain to them.'

'I don't want to say the words,' Mrs Wall said.

Lizzie spoke tenderly as though comforting a child. 'No one here will think any less of you, Rosemary.'

The secretary looked up at the mention of her first name, her eyes imploring. A silence so thick with tension had descended that Kember thought the roaring in his ears must be heard by all around him. He could see Mrs Wall's hands trembling, like a small injured bird nestling in her lap. Wounded. Defeated. Vulnerable.

'Because . . .' Mrs Wall whispered.

The air remained silent and still, the calm before the storm. Lizzie nodded slowly, encouragingly. Kember felt he could almost touch the raw emotion arcing between the two women, a lump in his throat, realising what was coming.

'It's all right, Rosemary,' Lizzie urged, seemingly on the verge of crying herself. 'Take your time.'

'Because . . . Morris raped me.'

Kember felt his heart sink and an ache settle in his stomach as his fears were realised. The men's faces froze; Burnley's turned to marble. Tears flowed down the cheeks of Mrs Wall.

'I'm so sorry,' Kember said, his voice croaky, writing in his book again as if occupying his hands was the best thing to do. 'That must have been horrendous and frightening.'

'I said, *no*.' A sob escaped. 'I tried to push him off . . .'

'Did you tell anyone?' Lizzie asked.

Mrs Wall shook her head. 'Not at first,' she whispered.

'Can you tell me – us – what happened? Take your time.'

Mrs Wall sniffed and wiped her cheeks. 'I stayed late one night to finish some paperwork, trying to please Mr Burnley so he'd notice me.' Burnley squeezed his eyes shut. 'Morris came to the office; said he'd seen the light on. Mr Burnley hadn't gone home but he had retired to his overnight room. Morris had seen him go and thought he'd take his chances. He . . . He . . .'

'I get the picture, Mrs Wall,' Kember said, and gave her an encouraging nod. 'No need to spell it out here.'

'I didn't kill him.' Mrs Wall shook her head. 'Honest, I didn't.'

Kember nodded again. 'Do you know who did?'

Mrs Wall took a handkerchief from her pocket and wiped her nose.

'Do the men of Hut Six know you were attacked?' Lizzie asked.

Mrs Wall sniffed. 'They do, but they didn't at the time. Not for a while.'

'Does Thatcher?'

'Yes,' she said, her voice a whisper.

'Anyone else?'

'No.'

'How did Thatcher find out, when he lives in a different hut?' Kember asked, watching the banksman out of the corner of his eye.

'Because . . .' Mrs Wall wiped her nose. 'Because I told him. He told the others.'

Silence descended on the room again.

Tears continued to course down her cheeks, but although guilt still etched her face, she looked as though a weight had been lifted. After his initial shock, Burnley looked mildly confused, as though talking to a stranger like Lizzie in a room full of miners rather than the police was something he could not comprehend.

Lizzie sat on a chair, holding Mrs Wall's hand, comforting.

Kember thought he understood. Telling a man what another man had done, even if she was believed, would elicit a man's response; sympathetic, at best, not empathetic. In his experience, you would only reveal the horror of such an intimate violation to your closest confidante, if you told anyone at all. But now, at a time like this, one woman needed another to listen to her account of a violation so traumatic that their shared fears would push aside any preconceptions, prejudices or judgements.

Even before the war, most women kept quiet, knowing they would never be believed or, if they could find someone to believe them, there would be no evidence to get a conviction. It was your word against theirs. How often had women let it happen because they were threatened, physically overpowered or too frightened to resist? How many women had been told that by flirting they'd asked for it? How many times had a woman been blamed for dressing in a less than demure fashion, or for being in the wrong place at the wrong time, as though their actions had been the catalyst? It was never the rapist's fault, always the woman's for enticing the man. And with the blackout, the incidence of rape had shot up. If that much was acknowledged, how much was not? *Perhaps the full horror will remain unreported and unrecorded*, he thought, *never to be fully known.*

Lizzie stood to continue her account and the men fidgeted as though embarrassed.

'Each of you had a reason to hate Morris but none of you had been directly physically attacked and violated in the way Mrs Wall had endured. Make no mistake, the rape of a woman is as bad as murder because it can kill who you are inside and leave you in a living hell.'

The men couldn't meet her gaze and Kember wondered if they were ashamed that one of their own could stoop to that level. Perhaps one or more were guilty of not taking no for an answer, if they had a drink inside them. He'd seen it many times in London where the numerous pubs, clubs, bars and dancehalls afforded constant opportunities for getting a woman tipsy. If the result was the same, was it any different from attacking someone in a dark alley?

'Hold on,' Ramsey said, his voice deep and questioning. 'If you accept she had the biggest reason to want Morris dead, why is she not as guilty as you've been painting her?'

She was, as far as Kember was concerned, and he wasn't surprised at the furore that erupted. Lizzie merely waited for the men to calm down before she continued.

'We saw Mrs Wall outside in the dark several times and she seemed nervous but not afraid. She drove ambulances in the Great War. She had dusters in her office and access to all the keys. She knew about whitedamp. She was devoted to Mr Burnley, who disliked Morris from the outset. She knew all the goings-on in the colliery. We found small boot prints at every scene and she has small feet. Guilty, you'd think, and so did we.'

Kember gave her a look he hoped conveyed that he still did.

'But we spoke to someone else who drove lorries for a living before coming here to work,' Lizzie said. 'Someone who also had access to the dusters and keys, and knew about whitedamp. Someone who wears small boots that are round-toed, not pointed like Mrs Wall's, and who has an equally compelling motive for murder. They had become desperate as our investigation progressed. The situation was getting out of control and slipping away from them so they'd had to resort to increasingly violent solutions. They dropped the stores on us and forced Mrs Wall to tell Mr Burnley the pit was still open, knowing he would close it down, trapping us underground. They attacked me and Inspector Watson. I believe Mrs Wall wasn't afraid when we met her outside last night because she knew who the killer was and thought she was safe. But murderers under pressure often become paranoid and resort to the most drastic measures. I believe Mrs Wall had become terrified that they were considering something so awful that her conscience had forced her to unlock the door. She told us that she was in the colliery office when the fires started but I think she was outside, trying to stop the killer from murdering us all.'

Kember could see uncertainty in the expressions of the assembled men and he too was beginning to share their confusion. *Where are you going with this, Lizzie?* he thought.

'You may think that's an outlandish claim but in the back of my mind I knew something wasn't quite right,' she continued. 'I'd seen something in Mrs Wall's office, a photograph on her desk. All through our questioning I thought she had been lying to protect someone, perhaps Mr Burnley, and then it all clicked into place.' She took the piece of shaped wood from her pocket and held it so all could see it.

'It's a door wedge,' Quayle said.

'Yes, from the pithead office,' Lizzie confirmed.

'She didn't kill Morris with that, surely?'

Watson sat forward on his chair, pain etched on his face but curiosity in his eyes, as Kember took a step towards Lizzie. The atmosphere in the room had become colder, more tense than before, as though something lurking in the shadows was about to strike. Kember wondered if his own instincts as a copper had flashed him a warning or whether he had become more attuned to Lizzie's. That's when he thought he heard a bell. It sounded too tinkly to be coming from a church; it had to be a police car. Glances of unease between the men showed they had heard it too.

'She didn't kill anyone,' Lizzie said. 'She came to the pithead office last night armed with a paperknife to warn and defend us against the man she believed had gone too far. I hid behind the open door of the office, ready to close it when the killer entered, trapping them inside. That didn't happen because I couldn't move the door. After the scuffle, I was let free and found this on the floor. It seemed too much of a coincidence for it to have been kicked under the door by accident in such a way as to wedge it open. I realised that I had been the one deliberately trapped so I couldn't intervene.'

'But you told us Mrs Wall walked in,' Young said. 'Couldn't she have put it there while you were all hiding in wait?'

'Mrs Wall walked straight in without hesitation. It couldn't have been her who placed the wedge and there were only three other people in that room, besides me. As much as she was glad that

Morris was dead, I believe she'd had enough of the lies and killing. The spanner used on Mr Burnley hadn't been brought in by her because Inspector Kember had it in his pocket. I believe the person who took it was desperate to warn Mrs Wall against her talking and to deflect attention from themselves back to Mr Burnley by making it appear that he was attacking them. Unfortunately for the killer, in the dim light and amid the scuffle, Mr Burnley received the blow intended for Kember.'

Kember held up his hand to stop the angry babbling that ensued.

'So, what's a picture on a desk got to do with anything?' Armstrong said.

Kember remembered being shown the photograph and had been wondering the same thing. He wished he'd taken more notice at the time, but as far as he could recall, it was just another family portrait on a clerical worker's desk.

'People display photographs of those they love,' Lizzie said. 'Mrs Wall's mother and father are in that family group, with her standing at their side and a small boy sitting on her mother's lap. Her father was a small man, shorter than his wife. All were wearing spectacles except the boy, who I suspect was too young to need them at the time the photograph was taken. All had curly hair.'

Everyone looked at Mrs Wall as if to remind themselves of her hairstyle. Even Lizzie turned to her and Kember felt the tension of the torturer's rack turn up another notch.

'Your married name is Wall,' Lizzie said, 'but I believe your maiden name is the same as the small boy in the photograph who grew up to be a short man with small feet, curly hair and spectacles. Someone who would do anything to avenge the rape you endured.'

Mrs Wall nodded. 'Alastair's my brother,' she said, and bowed her head.

Kember leapt to his feet and flung up an arm to deflect a chair thrown by Thatcher. Pain lanced through his elbow but he joined the miners in their rush to the door, knocking over furniture in their haste and anger.

Thatcher had already escaped into the bright but freezing morning.

CHAPTER TWENTY-ONE

Kember slithered on the icy concrete slabs, unable to keep up with the chasing miners as they passed the busy canteen next door, open and in full swing, donkey-jacketed men filing in through the doors for their breakfast like a line of ants through a kitchen. Many turned in curiosity as the miners hurried past, followed by Kember in his overcoat, but their empty bellies kept them shuffling towards the smell of food.

A cry came from Ramsey up ahead as the rest of them entered the pit yard.

'Where's the bastard?' he spat.

'Must be around here somewhere,' Pine said. 'He's only a scrawny little short-house.'

They all swivelled their heads left and right, undecided which way to look first, their collective exhalations like the gasps of over-exercised horses. Kember arrived, adding his own rasping breaths to theirs, the freezing air searing his lungs.

'I don't want him hurt,' he demanded, not expecting to be obeyed. 'You've got enough on your plates already.'

The chorus of dissent left him worried that Thatcher wouldn't make it out alive. Mob rule was never the answer and he wanted the due process of the law to be worked through, even though that would see Thatcher hanged. He kept an eye out for their quarry as the men split up and began searching in doorways, between piles of boxes and behind a parked tractor.

'There he is!' Armstrong's call rent the air and all heads turned towards his shout.

Thatcher had broken cover and was running behind a bull-dozer, his feet dragging through a snowdrift. The miners had easier progress through the track he left but he moved swiftly for a small man, nimbly skirting other bits of machinery. He veered to his right and almost disappeared from view around a corner of the building towards the colliery office but bounced back into sight, staggering but not falling. Kember's mouth almost dropped open in surprise when the burly form of Sergeant Dennis Wright strode into view, his six-foot frame towering over Thatcher.

Thatcher turned to run the other way and managed a few strides before the men of Hut Six fell on him like wolves, landing a flurry of blows. By the time Kember reached them seconds later, they had already exacted a measure of revenge for being accused of the murders he'd committed. Young and Quayle had an arm apiece, Thatcher slumped in defeat between them, his front covered in snow, his glasses askew. Armstrong and Pine were rubbing their knuckles.

'The little bastard got my nose,' Ramsey said dabbing a trickle of blood with a piece of grubby cloth.

Thatcher raised his head and Kember saw the red around his cheeks and jaw where punches had landed. His nose was bleeding, dripping red down his chin and the front of his work shirt, and his lip was already swelling. Four uniformed constables joined Wright in the pit yard, one of whom arrested Thatcher and handcuffed him at Kember's direction. He didn't want him hurt any more than he had been already and instructed the other officers to keep the miners at bay.

Sergeant Wright came across to Kember and saluted.

'Been having a busy time, sir?'

'You could say that,' Kember replied. 'What the devil are you doing here? I thought all the roads were blocked.' Even as he spoke, he heard the sound of powerful engines and suspected the two bulldozers he'd seen two days ago near the entrance were shoving piles of snow to either side of the track, clearing a wider way through.

'Compared to this, we've had no more than a heavy dusting in west Kent and around Scotney. It got thicker the further east I came and the telephone lines are down all around here and Canterbury. The farmers have been out in force with snow blades on their tractors, thank God. I—'

They turned at the sound of wailing and Kember saw Mrs Wall, light glistening on her cheeks slick with tears, being held up by Burnley, his face still a mask of shock, and Watson struggling along behind with Lizzie at his side. As they approached, he held out an arm to prevent them passing.

'Put that man in the car,' Kember ordered. He looked at Wright. 'I take it you do have a car?'

'Two, sir,' Wright said. 'I brought the Wolseley to Canterbury Police headquarters, where I thought you'd be. When they said you were here with Inspector Watson but they'd not heard from you, I suggested we might take a look, to see if you needed any help.'

'I appreciate that, Sergeant,' Kember said.

The six of them followed a few steps behind Thatcher and his escort while the other three constables brought up the rear and ensured the miners kept their distance. They soon reached Burnley's office where two Wolseley police cars were parked near the steps, one belonging to Wright. Watson's snow-covered Austin could be seen beyond, next to Lizzie's Norton motorbike.

'I need to speak to my brother,' Mrs Wall said through sobs, as the constable put Thatcher in the back seat and got in with him. 'Why couldn't you just let things be?' she shouted across. 'I only wanted Morris taught a lesson.'

'He raped you,' Thatcher spat back. 'He deserved it. If I'd had my way, I'd have done it simpler and sooner.'

The men of Hut Six surged forward, shouting obscenities, but the three constables stood their ground.

'We wanted him driven away, not killed,' Mrs Wall said, a plaintive squeak to her voice. 'All of us. What good is he dead? I wanted him to suffer.' She almost screamed the last words at her brother as the constable slammed the car door shut. 'And Gordon Collins did nothing to me!' she shouted.

'I'm afraid you'll have to go too,' Kember said, in a voice he hoped exuded calm.

It had no effect on Mrs Wall.

'Why?' she snapped. 'I didn't kill anyone.'

'You conspired against Morris,' Lizzie said, putting her arm around Mrs Wall. 'You've broken all sorts of laws I'm sure you'll be told about soon enough.'

'Enough to be hanged?' Mrs Wall face was taut with bitterness. 'After what I've been through?'

Kember could see Lizzie's internal conflict playing out on her face. Having been attacked herself, she had empathy and sympathy in abundance but Mrs Wall had endured the kind of violation at the hands of a man, the effects of which few men could even begin to understand. With so many men around her who had the same objective, to get rid of Morris and exorcise their demons, Mrs Wall had joined with them and sought the only kind of retribution within her control. Her brother had taken that away from her and made the suffering all about him. Yes, Lizzie could understand it all but was as law-abiding as they came. Justice must not only be done, but must also be seen to be done.

Mrs Wall swept her arm around, indicating the miners. 'What about them? They conspired too.'

'Maybe,' Kember said.

Tears sprang to her eyes again.

'But you said back there . . .'

'I have nothing but suspicion, conjecture and your word against theirs,' Kember said apologetically. 'We'll take statements, of course, do what we can, but they were asleep in the same room as Morris when your brother administered the final dose that killed him by blocking the air bricks and flue. He killed Collins, attacked Officer Hayes and Inspector Watson. The evidence is on the spanner and I'm sure we'll find more now we know who and what to look into.'

The miners had quietened so Watson beckoned to his men. 'Take Mrs Wall in mine,' he said, handing his keys to a constable. 'Put her in the back.' He nodded at the second man. 'You can drive Thatcher.' To the last, he said, 'You're with me.'

'What about me?' Burnley said. His voice sounded small. 'I should go with Mrs Wall.'

'I need you to stay with your men, please, sir,' Watson said. 'We need to question you all again, and I need the truth this time.'

As the beaten figure of Mrs Wall was led away, Burnley looked around meekly and wandered back to where his men stood talking.

Watson nodded once to Kember and held out his hand. Kember shook it with a firm grip and nodded back. Lizzie offered her hand and Watson took it in his immediately. 'Officer Hayes. You are a credit to your uniform and an invaluable asset to this man. You may not be a policewoman but if it was up to me, I would happily have you on my team of detectives. Unfortunately—'

'It's not up to you,' Lizzie said with a smile.

'No.' Watson gave her a wry smile. 'I'll take new statements from Burnley and his men but I don't expect much by way of cooperation.'

'Oh, I don't know,' Lizzie said. 'Putting themselves and others at risk was wrong but Thatcher was the one with murderous intent. They'll want to implicate him as much as possible and distance themselves from any suggestion that they were in any way part of his plans. You may get more information than you bargained for.'

Watson shrugged. 'Too much, too little, never the right kind.' He looked at Kember. 'I won't delay you by asking you to come to Canterbury. I'm sure you're heartily sick of us. You can submit your report to Chief Inspector Hartson and he'll forward it on.'

'Thank y—'

'Inspector Kember?' Wright said.

Kember frowned. Wright wasn't usually one to interrupt. 'Yes, what is it?'

'I'll leave you to it,' Watson said, with a reassuring nod and wink before he turned away.

'I heard you mention Chief Inspector Hartson, sir,' Wright said. 'I didn't want to interrupt cos I was waiting for the right moment but he tried to telephone Chief Inspector Brignull yesterday to pass on an urgent message. Not being able to get through and having no spare men, he turned to me because I worked for you recently. Told me to get down here straight away. It's the reason we struggled to get through to the colliery so early, that and not hearing from DI Watson.'

'Well, what is it?' Kember felt a knot in the pit of his stomach and feared the worst. An urgent message from Hartson could not contain good news.

'I'm sorry, sir, but it's your son. His Spitfire was shot down two days ago over Ramsgate. He's alive but he's been taken to the Queen Victoria Cottage Hospital near East Grinstead.'

Kember felt the ground tilt beneath his feet and he took a step sideways to steady himself. Lizzie was at his side, hand on his elbow, worried, supportive. He blinked to clear his vision and took a breath.

'Why East Grinstead?' Kember asked, afraid of the answer.

Wright's face was solemn. 'They treat burns.'

CHAPTER
TWENTY-TWO

The first time Lizzie had worked with Kember she had watched him being whisked away at the end of the case, not knowing how he felt or whether she would ever see him again. Standing here, now, in the dirty snow and slush, her feelings of worry, loss and helplessness from that day came flooding back and she fought a wave of nausea. She looked at him and recognised similar anguish on his face. He seemed shaken, shell-shocked, and her ability to comfort him drained away the longer they stood there.

'Do you need some water, sir?' Wright asked.

'Something stronger, I think,' Kember said, 'but I've no time. I need to see my son.'

'Of course. Chief Inspector Hartson has authorised forty-eight hours' compassionate leave for you, sir, from the time of delivery of the message. Your suitcase is in the car.'

Kember nodded. 'Does my daughter know?'

'He thought it best if you informed her, sir.' Wright held out a slip of paper. 'The address of the hospital.'

Lizzie watched Kember take it as though handling the most delicate artefact in the world, his eyes searching the paper as though seeking an error that would make everything all right again. She knew he had to leave straight away, and couldn't blame him. If it had been . . . She resolved to call her brother as soon as she arrived back in Scotney.

Kember turned his head to look at her and she tried to speak but her throat was parched and her lips couldn't form the right words. 'Go', was all she managed to say. Their ordeal in the depths of the pit had brought them closer, but once again, events conspired to take them away from each other again. Once he submitted his report and her part in the case was known by Chief Inspector Hartson, Flight Captain Ellenden-Pitt and Group Captain Dallington, both their careers could be over. He had been warned before about letting her help with an investigation. She still had to endure the humiliating possibility of being permanently grounded by the stuffed shirts of the Accidents Investigation Branch. *What a way to live a life*, she thought.

Lizzie almost stepped back in surprise when Kember dipped his head and gave her a brief kiss on the lips. After what he'd said yesterday, it was a risky thing to do. She glanced around, fearful of who had seen, but Wright had left them to start his police Wolseley and the men of Hut Six had been shepherded with Burnley into his office ready for questioning by Watson and his constable. Still, even with no one watching it was the first time either of them had shown the other any affection in public.

'I have to go,' he said.

Her stomach churned. 'Of course, you must,' she said.

She walked with him to where Wright had the Wolseley running and watched him slip into the passenger seat. The two cars from Canterbury with Thatcher and Mrs Wall on board were first to pull away from the front of the office and Lizzie managed a thin smile and a nod in response to Kember's sorrowful wave as Wright's car followed, slicing through the muddy snow of the track on their way to the lane.

Wright would take him straight to the hospital and she ought to get back to Scotney to see if there was any news from the AIB. She retrieved her gauntlets from the office, used them to brush snow from the saddle and handlebars of her black Norton motorbike and sighed, a cloud of white breath hanging hesitant for a moment as though it too was troubled by uncertainty.

Then it drifted away and she was left alone.

AUTHOR'S NOTE

While searching for an excuse to take Lizzie Hayes to Bekesbourne to meet Kember, I remembered a chapter in *Spitfire Girl* (Head of Zeus, 2014), the autobiography of Air Transport Auxiliary pilot Jackie Moggridge (née Sorour). In it, she recounts the events of January 1941, when she took off from South Wales and Amy Johnson took off from Blackpool. Both were bound for Kidlington but neither made it, and only Jackie got down safely. They both flew above the clouds in bad weather but Amy's Airspeed Oxford drifted off course and ended up over the Thames estuary. She baled out and her parachute was seen by the patrolling *HMS Haslemere*. Its captain, Lieutenant Commander Walter Fletcher, dived in the icy water but Amy disappeared and her body was never found. Walter later died of exposure and shock and is buried in Woodlands Cemetery, Gillingham, Kent. He was posthumously awarded the Albert Medal. Amy Johnson CBE is commemorated at the Air Forces Memorial at Runnymede, Surrey and a statue of her stands on the seafront at Herne Bay, Kent.

As part of my research, I spent an interesting couple of days at the National Coal Mining Museum near Wakefield, exploring the Hope and Caphouse collieries, learning about access to the pits, the tally system used to keep track of who was underground, ventilation, fan drifts and the effects of poisonous gases. As I recount in my story, many hard-line union men travelled south from northern pits to the Kent coalfield after being blacklisted in the 1926 general strike, the result of which Betteshanger Colliery became the most militant in Kent. After striking in 1938, Betteshanger went on to become the only pit to strike in World War Two (1942) and the last to return to work following the 1984–85 miners' strike. Today, little remains of the Kent mining industry beyond a short section of the East Kent Heritage Railway, Betteshanger Park and Coal Mine Museum, a neglected 'Miners Trail', and some scattered buildings, statues and plaques.

A few villages built to house the influx of miners to the area do hold some visual clues to their coal mining heritage. For example, Hersden near Canterbury, built to serve the Chislet Colliery, has a social club that is still called the Chislet Colliery Welfare Club, and the village of Aylesham, built for the Snowdown Colliery and still hosting a rugby club called Snowdown Colliery RFC, has retained its original road layout designed to look like the shape of pithead winding gear when seen from the air. I'm sure there are many other examples if you take time to look.

As with my previous books, food plays a small part in the texture of my story. I was born in 1959 and grew up with such delicacies as Spam sandwiches, bubble and squeak, corned beef fritters, bread and dripping, bags of broken biscuits, dried fruit scones, bread pudding, etc. There is a simple joy in holding a slice of bread on a toasting fork over an open fire and slathering butter on the resulting hot toast that sticking two slices in a toaster cannot replicate. These cheap and cheerful foods eaten with frugal necessity during wartime, and after, by my grandparents and parents, may seem odd and old-fashioned these days but the prosperity and culinary diversity Britain was set to enjoy was still to come.

When I was a young boy in primary school in the 1960s, my mother worked in the Paynes chocolate factory in Croydon (where

Poppets were made) and I would go with her and my father to the annual family sports day held on the factory's adjacent sports field. I remember my mother competing barefoot one year and winning the egg and spoon race!

My parents also took me to see the Victorian dinosaur models in Crystal Palace Park. I photographed them a few years later for a secondary school project and I saw them many times after during visits to the park and nearby swimming pool. When I met my wife, it was a surprise to learn that her grandfather, Stanley Paterson, once had the job of painting the dinosaurs for several years, so I thought it would be fun to mention them.

It's strange how many of one's memories surface while writing fiction.

ACKNOWLEDGEMENTS

A big thank you to my wife, Jane, our daughters, Laura and Holly, and G'ma Mavis for once again listening to my incoherent ramblings about plot points, murder methods, timelines, etc. Thanks also to my brother Steven, whose personal insights are always a great help when writing the character of Lizzie Hayes. I suspect more airshows and history experiences await us.

Thanks also to the myriad authors who continue to offer encouragement, including Martin Edwards, William Shaw, Lisa Cutts, T.E. (Tim) Kinsey, Vaseem Khan, Maggie Gee and many others, and to my Curtis Brown Creative stablemates who are a constant source of inspiration, especially Lizzie Mary Cullen, whose sensitivity reading was particularly valuable this time.

A special mention goes to Glenn 'Big Bird' Bryan of the National Coal Mining Museum near Wakefield. His knowledge of the Caphouse Colliery and mining in general, all the banter and anecdotes, and the snippets of information he fed us to keep us interested and entertained during the underground pit tour were superb. Clearly, he is a man who loved his job as a miner, and now enjoys being a guide, but I'm sure he's never had to field so many unusual questions from one person about how long it might take for the mine to fill with whitedamp if the fans were turned off, how long someone could survive, and so on. I think he was relieved when I said I was a writer!

For me, the holy trinity of being an author is to achieve publication, see your book on the shelf of a bookshop and appear on an author panel at a literary festival. So, for bringing my Kember and Hayes series to life and making my publication dream come true: thank you to my agent, Nelle Andrew, and everyone at Rachel Mills Literary; Victoria Haslam, Leodora Darlington, Nicole Wagner, Rebecca Hills, Bill Massey, Sadie Mayne, Swati Gamble, Victoria Oundjian, everyone at Thomas & Mercer and Amazon Publishing; and audiobook narrator Sarah Zimmerman. Thanks also to: Adrian Muller and Donna Moore of Bristol CrimeFest for allowing me to appear on a panel for the first time and babble on about my books alongside some fantastic authors; Kirsty Eastham for offering encouragement and thus helping calm my jangling nerves before that panel; Barbara Norrey who introduced me to the readers of the UK Crime Book Club; and Edouard Gallais for completing the trinity by making Waterstones Bristol the first UK bookshop to display my novels.

Thank you all.

ABOUT THE AUTHOR

Born in Croydon, Surrey, in 1959, Neil Daws has been a decent waiter, an average baker and a pretty good printer, but most notably a diligent civil servant, retiring in 2015 after thirty years, twenty spent in security and counter-terrorism. Enthralled by tales of adventure and exploration, he became a hiker, skier, lover of travel, history and maps, and is a long-standing Fellow of the Royal Geographical Society. Following the death of his father and uncle from heart disease, he became a volunteer fundraiser and was awarded an MBE for charitable services in 2006. An alumnus of the Curtis Brown Creative writing school, he achieved Highly Commended in the Blue Pencil Agency's First Novel Award 2019, where he met his agent, Nelle Andrew of Rachel Mills Literary. He is finally making use of his Open University psychology degree and interest in history, especially World War Two, to write historical crime fiction. Most importantly, he has a wife and two daughters and lives in his adopted county of Kent.

Follow the Author on Amazon

If you enjoyed this book, follow N. R. Daws on Amazon to be notified when the author releases a new book!
To do this, please follow these instructions:

Desktop:

1) Search for the author's name on Amazon or in the Amazon App.
2) Click on the author's name to arrive on their Amazon page.
3) Click the 'Follow' button.

Mobile and Tablet:

1) Search for the author's name on Amazon or in the Amazon App.
2) Click on one of the author's books.
3) Click on the author's name to arrive on their Amazon page.
4) Click the 'Follow' button.

Kindle eReader and Kindle App:

If you enjoyed this book on a Kindle eReader or in the Kindle App, you will find the author 'Follow' button after the last page.